NEVER
SIGNED
an
NDA

I NEVER SIGNED an NDA

PENNY LOVELL

Whitley Heights Imprint
Los Angeles

Cover design by Penny Lovell, Kimball Hastings and Adam Lovell.
Copy editing by Chris Bird and Megan McLaughlin.
Star illustration by artist Ryan Cronin.
Interior book design by Laura Lis Scott.

Library of Congress Control Number: 2024902865

ISBN 979-8-9900049-3-1 [paperback]
ISBN 979-8-9900049-9-3 [hardcover]
ISBN 979-8-9900049-7-9 [ebook]

For Imogen, Mole and Ruth

CONTENTS

NDA

noun

1. A nondisclosure agreement. "I never signed an NDA"

A nondisclosure agreement (NDA), also known as a confidentiality agreement, is a legally binding contract in which one party agrees to give a second party confidential information about its business or products and the second party agrees not to share this information with anyone for a specified period.

Cast of Characters

Ed Barker	Husband of Chloe barker/country singer superstar
Eduardo Quiroz	Playboy/current boyfriend of Juliet Hunt
Elliot White	Husband of Lara White
Erin	Junior publicist at Marco's PR firm
Eve Wright	Publicist for Janie Jones at Unentitled PR
Evie Astley	Daughter of Alma Astley and Jamie Delancy
George Bois	Partner/Manager of Fred's Restaurant Beverly Hills
Gerald	Representative for Dazzle Diamonds
Iggy Evans	Jonny and Tabitha's puppy
Ines	French PR for Henri LeRoque
Jacob	Freelance makeup artist
Jackie	Longtime bodyguard/self-appointed mother to Ava-Lily Manderson
Jamie Delancy	Younger ex-model husband of Alma Astley
Janet	Head of PR for Daisy Dupont
Jerome	Creative Director, French house of Bebe Klein
Jemima Astley	Daughter of Alma Astley and Jamie Delancy
Joseph	Bodyguard of Lara White
Juliet Hunt	World famous actress/producer
June Taylor	Van Nuys Bowling Alley manager
Kara	Long-suffering assistant to Juliet Hunt
Kelly	Long-suffering assistant to Lara White
Lucia Rosa	Creative Director, French House of Cedric Tatou
Luke	VP of VIP at French house Henri LeRoque
Marilyn	OG celebrity makeup artist
Marco	Power publicist, clients include Juliet Hunt and Jason Bird
Nigel Jolly	Jeweler to the stars
Orlando	Celebrity style contriver
Paola	Babysitter for Belinda Grant's daughter Rose
Pat	Publicist for Ava-Lily Manderson
Peter Porter-Jones	Producer/husband of Caroline Porter-Jones

Richard	OG celebrity hairstylist
Rose Grant	Daughter of Belinda
Savannah Bass	Third assistant to Alma Astley
Sophia Porter	Iconic actress/mother of Caroline Porter-Jones
Toto White	Untrained dog of Lara White
Ulysses	Beloved cat of Ava-Lily Manderson
Yelena	Veteran Hollywood seamstress

SATURDAY 24TH FEBRUARY 2018

"Hollywood is a strange place if you
are in trouble. Everybody thinks
it's contagious."
—Judy Garland

Dead

"DING DONG! THE WITCH IS DEAD" was the original working title of Breaking Hollywood's latest online cover story. It took thirteen minutes for the staff writer covering the graveyard shift to massage it to the rather less accurate:

Alma Astley, revered feminist mega agent, Head of AARDA (Alma Astley Roger Dunn Associates) and #AlsoMe Chairwoman, dies unexpectedly at 56.

By Randy Smith. Posted 8:13 am

The news of Alma Astley's death has rocked Hollywood today, just over a week before the Oscars. The unparalleled agent ruled the entertainment business with a couture-clad fist for two decades, clambering in her five-inch heels from the lowly basement to the heights of representing Hollywood's brightest stars. Notable female clients included Lara White, Chloe Barker, Ava-Lily Manderson, Emily de Vries, Janie Jones, and Juliet Hunt, while males included Jason Bird, Brandon Loopner, Raphael Lopez, and Henry Wicker.

For the last 22 years, Ms. Astley has left every ceremony with a winner. Between them, her clients have racked up 46 Oscars, and in this infamously fickle world, it's significant that they rarely, if ever, chose to leave her. However, many were dismissed by the 'Witch of Hollywood'— affectionately nicknamed for her star-making magic.

According to multiple sources, Astley died in her Beverly Hills penthouse office on Friday between 6 and 10pm. Her body was discovered at 5:30am Saturday by her third assistant. Anonymous sources tell us that in recent weeks, it was not unusual for Ms. Astley to sleep at the Beverly Hills Hotel, where she retained a suite.

She leaves behind her husband, Jamie Delancy, 38, their twins Evie and Jemima, 14, and a son from a previous marriage, Albert, 32. The rest of her family reside in Northern England and are rumored to be estranged.

No word yet on the cause of death, and at the time of posting, no statement has been issued by the police department. However, the building is sealed off and security is tight. It's thought that the last person to see her alive was power celebrity stylist Belinda Grant, who works with several stars on Ms. Astley's roster. Ms. Grant, who had a 6pm meeting with Astley in her office, has thus far not responded to our request for comment but is believed to be cooperating fully with the police investigation.

This story will be updated as more information becomes available.

*****Story edited at 11:44am to include tweets below*****

Tweet from LARA! @theLaraWhite
I awoke this morning to hear the devastating news that my beloved agent of so many years is gone. In the words of the original blockbuster screenwriter, Mr. William Shakespeare, "Death lies on her like an untimely frost." She was my second mama, and my bursting heart is shattered #ripAlma ♥

Tweet from Oscar winner @Jasonbird
As my dear friend and frequent director Woody famously said, 'If God exists, I hope he has a good excuse' #ripalmaastley

Tweet from Janielovesyou @therealJaniejones
She stood by me through all the tabloid terrors and never blinked. What to do when your rock is now sand? I am so very sad today. My broken heart beats for her family, friends and other clients

Tweet from Emilydevries @emilydevries
I am so shocked and saddened by the terrible news this morning. Alma was unwavering in her commitment to her clients and instrumental in my success. My heart goes out to her family. Until we meet again, Alma, rest in peace. To quote Irving Berlin, 'The song is ended, but the melody lingers on.' Hollywood will never be the same ♥

EARLIER THAT MORNING

"You can take all the sincerity in Hollywood, place it in the navel of a fruit fly, and still have room enough for three caraway seeds and a producer's heart."
—Fred Allen

Rookie Dressing

RIDING IN CARS WITH DETECTIVES
Beverly Hills. 6:20 am

THE BLACK DODGE CHARGER SPED AGGRESSIVELY down the main artery of Beverly Hills. Cheryl, riding shotgun and as yet unfamiliar with LA traffic patterns, was unaware that this rapid progress was only possible because this day, at this hour, was one of the rare and precious moments when the town was low-pressure and sleepy. She sat in what passed for morning silence—interrupted only by the hum of a few engines—mesmerized by the glowing violet and coral-streaked sunrise bouncing off clouds and reflecting theatrically in towering, glass-fronted buildings. Conversely, her new partner, Ortiz, was irritated by the early start and hiding behind black Ray Bans. She was oblivious to the familiar joys of LA nature but enjoying the open road as she weaved sharply across two lanes to pull up at their Wilshire Boulevard destination. She slammed the car into park and immediately flipped a switch to open the passenger window, letting in a gust of biting air that jolted them both. Cheryl flashed her badge to the approaching junior cop posted outside the AARDA building.

"Detectives Hall and Ortiz."

"Yes, ma'am, you need to go to the penthouse floor."

Exhilarated by the beat of a new case in a new town, Cheryl grabbed her coffee and climbed out of the car, responding to the waiting cop as she hooked her badge back onto her belt, opposite her worn semi-concealed holster. "What's your name? And fill us in on who's here already."

She shivered in her lightweight brown suit and buttoned up the blazer as he replied, "I'm Bennett, ma'am, and my partner Loughlin is stationed upstairs. We got here 10 minutes ago and sealed the scene. You guys are the first after us."

"Thanks." Cheryl turned to Ortiz. "Man, it's cold."

"Yup," Ortiz replied, tossing the car keys to the rookie. "Layers. Gotta get with layers in LA. I'm sure you'll get the hang of it. Unlike the people—I doubt you'll get used to those fuckers. I can't believe that this, of all cases, is your first West Coaster. Man, it's gonna be fun to watch you acclimatize in *all* the ways, weather and otherwise."

Cheryl drained her coffee and scrutinized Ortiz thoroughly for the first time that morning. Her thick black hair was pulled back in a stubby ponytail. Aside from a thin grey scarf in pilled viscose fabric, she was entirely clad in black: slim, well-fitted puffer over a cotton button-down, black jeans stretched over short, sturdy legs, and, lastly, worn but polished Cuban boots that elevated her to a little over 5′4″. *Compact*, she thought, shivering again.

Ortiz shook her head, sighing as she untied her scarf and tossed it to Cheryl. "Here, put this on. I don't think it matches good—not sure grey and brown is a thing—but it'll do for now. We'll pick you up a coat later. Just remember, it's *cold* here when the winter sun ain't on ya, and you've yet to meet the icy, climate-busting AC."

Cheryl nodded gratefully and wrapped the scarf around her neck as they pushed open the heavy, gold-framed glass double doors and entered a pristine, polished white marble lobby. Walking side by side, they headed towards the only structure in the immense room, a gigantic, C-shaped reception desk manned by a large, sharply-suited security guard. Unusually self-conscious, Cheryl toyed with the borrowed scarf and looked down at her Long Tall Sally suit, feeling drab and shabby.

Ortiz a wide smile lighting up her normally sardonic face, blurted out, "I never thought I'd be giving no one clothes advice. Something new every day in this job."

Grinning back, Cheryl replied, "Everyone's so fancy here. Not to mention, it *always* looks warm; you'd never know it gets cold from TV. The visuals on LA weather are real misleading."

"Yeah, well, that's the thing." Ortiz paused to look up at the louvers of gold-coated aluminum undulating like rippling waves across the ceiling. "From a distance, this place looks like a lot of glowing, magical things that it most definitely ain't . . ."

"Fathers may do as they please.
Mothers must please the world."

Single Mum Style

BELINDA CREPT INTO ROSE'S COOL BEDROOM, dark but for the light-tinged edges of the blackout blinds and faintly glowing neon decals on the customized bunk bed. Adjusting to the darkness, she sighed at the sight of her sleeping child, head and torso wrapped in a shimmering unicorn blanket, long limbs tumbling off the mattress edge. She crouched down, knees cracking, and inhaled the faint scent of old Pantene in tangled, dirty-blonde curls.

Maybe just two minutes, she thought, looking at her vintage Rolex before lying down, gently tugging at the violet linen duvet cover as she nuzzled up to her daughter.

"Hi, Mommy," Rose mumbled sleepily as she reflexively curved her body into Belinda's. "You smell good"—she paused—"like Daddy."

"Aw, thanks, Buttercup," Belinda whispered, "I used his aftershave by mistake." She flushed in the dark, ashamed of the lie. The smell of a man—even him—somehow made her feel less fearful at night. "Don't wake up; it's horribly early. I just wanted to cuddle you before I go to work."

"You're always at work." Rose twisted her head, sharing morning breath, a new aroma—no longer baby, not quite teen. "And my unicorn name is Moonheart since, like, Christmas! Paola always remembers."

"Oh yes, sorry, Moonheart. I promise it will get much better soon once the Oscars are over next week."

"Oscars, Oscars, Oscars. It's been forever, it's not fair." Then she added more hopefully, "Can I come with you today, pleeease? It's Saturday."

"No, I'm sorry, darling. Not this week. Oh, please don't cry, my love." Distraught at Rose's brimming hazel eyes, Belinda kissed her face and lightly massaged her shoulder. "Please remember I do this for us so we can afford to live in this lovely little house and buy fun things." *Like food*, she deadpanned mentally. "I'll be back for an hour after my fitting with Chloe this morning, okay? We can have lunch before I go to the photo shoot."

"Whatever, Mom," Rose answered, dejected but dutiful, and turned to face the wall, pulling a cluster of Beeny Boos into her arms, each of the stuffed characters a marker for one of her mom's work trips. Belinda sighed guiltily at the sprawling, flammable army that covered too much of the bed's surface.

"Can we have pizza for lunch, Mom? Pretend we're in Italy with Daddy?"

"Yes, darling, but I think he's in Greece now, so maybe we should have hummus? Anyway, sssh, let's be quiet."

"Okay, Mama. Love you. But hummus is *gross*."

"Just try it again! I'm sure you'll like it one day. And I love you more." They argued briefly about the merits of mushed chickpeas and who loved who more, then, succumbing to weariness, closed their eyes, hugging tightly in melancholy silence.

A few minutes later, Belinda, teetering blissfully between slumber and sleep, was roused by a quiet knock on the door, Jasper's melodious voice waking her entirely as he quietly announced, *"It's time to go, boss."* Extricating herself, she gently stroked Rose's unicorn-covered head and stood, drinking in her child momentarily before tiptoeing out of the room on her bare, pedicured feet.

Jasper, yawning, stood waiting halfway down the narrow, picture-covered hallway. Wet dark curls brushed the shoulders of his Gucci knock-off sequined bomber, and the familiar and comforting smell of Le Labo Santal filled the air. Belinda inhaled his scent and, as always, immediately brightened.

"Brave of you to want to look at his mug every day," he whispered, his handsome face grimacing as he pointed to a small, framed picture of Belinda's shirtless ex-husband strumming a vintage guitar.

"It's for Rose. Why do you think it's down there at her eye level?"

"I'd be throwing eggs at it myself, but single parent medals for you. Rose looks like you made her all by yourself, by the way. Not one hint of him. Those dreamy hazel eyes and lush lips. Good job, really, because he's kinda douchey to look at. No offense. You couldn't find a framer pic with some clothes? Did he wax? That's some smooth, tanned skin right there."

"Rose has his curls, and anyway fuck off, Jasper. I'm trying to remind her she does, in fact, have a father—even though his only real involvement was in her conception," replied Belinda tersely as they walked stealthily out of the hallway. Silently closing the door, she rubbed her eyes and asked, "Is Paola here?"

"Yep. In the kitchen, looking knackered, just like us. Doing laundry *already*! You don't deserve that woman. I mean, it's basically the middle of the night."

"Oh, don't I know it," Belinda agreed, engulfed by panic about the mounting cost of Paola's hours. She took a deep breath, feeling guilty for snapping, and, switching gears, pointed to his platform Doc Martins.

"You, with your fabulous Cuban genes, never look knackered—and I'm *loving* the new footwear; you're so *elevated* this morning, Jas!"

"No shame here, boo. I am a proud 5'11" hunk in these 4-inch freebies, reveling in how the height-blessed feel daily. *But* I can see from the view up here that *you* need to brush your hair. It's giving me dirty sex vibes." He reached over and affectionately smoothed her tangled bleached mop as she, in the poshest version of her British accent, shrieked, "As *IF!*" She mimicked retching. "No sex until I've reached step 1200 of my narcissism recovery program. On the bright side, I finally have an effective skill with men—avoiding them."

"HA, avoiding narcissists, that's FUNNY! Maybe you can figure out a way to not fuck one, but we both know you'd have to quit your job if you developed a full-blown aversion."

Sighing, Belinda perched on the arm of her grey tweed couch, inhaling the charred aroma of last night's fire. Slipping into the sneakers she'd kicked off on getting home, she did her best to ignore the untidiness of her cozy, mid-century lounge-cum-overspill office. With her anxiety fully triggered, she could barely cope with her racing thoughts. *Will Lara need more shoe choices for the Oscars lunch on Monday? Duh* . . . She shook her head. *Of course, she will; there aren't enough shoes in the world.* Her face flashed angst as she wondered what country Rose's dad was shagging his way through now. *Still Greece?* She mentally congratulated herself for finally thinking of him as Rose's dad, not her ex. It was a method she was working on in therapy, one of the attempts to keep her blood pressure low. *Fuck, the pressure of the Oscars is probably gonna send that number right back up*, making a mental note to find her home blood pressure monitor. *The way everyone's behaving, I should probably buy one for all my clients* . . . *Speaking of* . . . *did Calvin FedEx the peach gown Jasper found for Janie? Maybe it arrived in the middle of all the Elle shoot samples? Shit, were there enough boxes? Did all the couture looks from Paris get through customs? Jasper must have double-checked? Who would blame him if he hadn't, though? There's only one of him. He deserves some sleep and a big raise, but how, with this ridiculous mortgage? Maybe Rose's dad will send money this month? Pay his credit card debt, for once. STUPID, you are stupid; of course he won't, he never does. Why did I pick him? Fucking musicians. Will Chloe blame me for the Bebe Klein dress she's contracted to wear to the premiere? She's not a kid—she knows I don't have that power. Oh god, is Rose okay? Is she going to end up notorious on a teen reality show because of my work?*

Oh god, STOP! Belinda wailed inwardly as she finished tying the laces of her second silver Air Jordan sneaker. Standing up, she stumbled over a discarded Jimmy Choo pump. "Enough!" she whispered, clenching and unclenching her fists. *Pick one worry, Belinda, you crazy bitch. Just one.* After considering for a few seconds, she bent over and picked up the pump. "Hey Jas, do we have enough shoe options for Lara?"

"As I said yesterday morning, and on the hour for the whole day, we could stock the Saks shoe department and then some." Intuiting the return of her edgy energy, he changed tack. "Annnnd, moving swiftly on. I've loaded the car with all the garment bags for Chloe's fitting. I'll switch them out with the Elle photo shoot samples when we come back. All the samples you prioritized are present and correct. So many we'd need a tank to transport them all at the same time. Our new intern is on a yacht in Palm Beach with her family this weekend; it's the dog's birthday or some shit. She's back on Monday. And I've got your purse because you left it in the car last night, not because I've been rifling through your house. Assuming the Celine is this hour's purse of choice?"

"Very funny, Jas. Actually, the Lanvin one they gave me last week would be better with my outfit, don't you think?" She looked over, seeking his approval. "That Celine tote is massive; I used it yesterday to try and look businessy—not that it helped." She shook her head, shuddering, recalling the feel of the frozen office and the matching demeanor of Alma Astley.

"Gurl, you are so cranky this morning. Did you have coffee yet?"

"No time—I'll grab the Lanvin and a banana and meet you in the car."

"Hrmph, please don't diminish our fabulous moving office with such a basic label, Belinda. *Coco* has feelings!"

"Most of the successful people in Hollywood are failures as human beings."
—Marlon Brando

A Birkin & a Body

POLICE WITNESS INTERVIEW: SAVANNAH BASS
Third assistant to Alma Astley. 6:52 am

"YES, WE'RE READY. THANK YOU, SERGEANT." Detective Ortiz put her iPhone down on the enormous polished-metal table and walked—coffee in hand—to the door, flicking up the switch that instantly turned the spotless glass walls cloudy and opaque, lending privacy to the chic, starkly furnished white boardroom. "Now, if only I could find the thermostat," she muttered, pinching blood back into the tip of her freckled nose and turning to Cheryl. "Someone's bringing Savannah Bass down now—she was still in the restroom. Also, the M.E. and C.S.I. teams just arrived."

Cheryl nodded, staring out the window, chewing on an energy bar she'd found in her jacket pocket and ignoring the panoramic view west from Beverly Hills, which ended majestically wherae the ocean merged into the sky. Instead, she thought carefully about Alma Astley's dead body, meticulously running over each detail of the scene upstairs.

"Are you sure you wanna take the lead on this? No disrespect, boss, but you just got here and this town, *especially* Beverly Hills, is a whole ball of crazy."

"I'm good. I prefer just to dive in"—she yawned, screwing up the bar wrapper and shoving it in her pocket—"but thanks, Ortiz, and for chris-sakes, do you have a first name?"

"Look, boss, think of it as my first and last name, like Prince or Shakira. Might tell you one day, if you actually stick it out here in—as the tourists call it—'*the City of Angels*,'" she snorted and added disparagingly, "Like an angel would live *here*. Those pretty wings would just fly on by and fly away cos they already know—like you will one day—that it might look like heaven, but it's the demons who flock here."

Cheryl shook her head. "You got no faith, Ortiz, and what's with all this tryin' to get me to hate on LA? You tryna get my job or something?"

"Well, yeah, obviously." Ortiz rolled her eyes. "But it ain't my faith that's the problem. I've seen it before—you East Coasters don't do well here; it's a rollercoaster of love and hate. Mostly hate for the first couple years. I'm jus' tryna help! Jesus, I was born here, and I haven't fully decided how the ride's gonna end."

Cheryl smiled wryly and flipped her off. She liked her new partner. Ortiz's nihilistic assessments of LA had the opposite effect, rapidly endearing Cheryl to the town. Eager to get started, she was pleased to see a tall, willowy blonde in a sharp cream—probably cashmere—coat stroll into the room. Could she be any more vanilla? Cheryl thought, looking down at her own dry, brown hands. Only the rich and confident can pull off that level of stain risk. "Good morning, Ms. Bass," said Cheryl before introducing herself and Ortiz. "How are you feeling? Must have been quite a shock." She spoke gently, gesturing for her to sit and putting her muted black iPhone in clear view on the silver table. "I'm just gonna record this, okay?" She sat down in the chair opposite her, smiling sympathetically.

"Yaaaa, sure. You can call me Savannah, and shock is, like, an under-statement. I've literally never seen a dead body before." She paused, still standing, and shuddered. "My mom maybe, questionable whether that woman has a pulse." Her voice, a slow vocal fry, was almost expressionless.

"Of course," Cheryl replied, suppressing a smile. Savannah was unin-tentionally comical. She ran through her other first impressions: strong top notes of an expensive scent with base notes of vomit and peppermint. Her body language was privileged and blasé, yet her beautiful, smooth face twitched periodically. Her eyes were intermittently alert, but mostly, her expression seemed indifferent.

Savannah unhurriedly sat down, heavy gold bangles jangling on both wrists. The expensive-looking camel purse she tossed onto the adjacent chair looked familiar to Cheryl. She tentatively identified it as a Birkin, helped by the marathons of KUWTK her sister had had playing in the background of their Boston apartment.

"You like it?" Savannah asked, following her gaze. "My mom gave it to me to carry to work. Yawn fest. A Birkin—What am I, like 30?" She pulled out her camel-cased phone and, using the reverse camera as a mirror, wiped a touch of smudged mascara from under one blue eye. Those eyes are the only colorful thing about her, Cheryl observed. "Oh god! LOOK at my face. Can I fix my makeup while we talk?"

"Well . . . sure." Cheryl looked at Ortiz, who merely raised an eyebrow.

"Thanks. I look *awful*." Savannah pulled out a small black bag with 'Makeup' helpfully stitched on it in white and arranged a line of glossy products in front of her on the table. Taking a slim gold pin, she secured her sleek, white-blonde hair into a low bun and, selecting a Tom Ford tube, squeezed a dab of beige onto the back of her hand and started dabbing her face expertly, using a sponge egg. "What do you need to know?"

"Firstly, Savannah, you arrived at work at 5:30 this morning. Why so early on a weekend?"

"Oh. Alma sometimes comes in on Saturdays, especially since she's been staying at the Bev Hills."

"The Bev Hills?"

Surprised, Savannah looked up from contouring her right cheek: "Yaaaa, the Beverly Hills Hotel. She's had a permanent suite there for about two months. I don't hear that much, what with my desk being downstairs in the dungeons, but, like, people have been whispering about trouble with the hot hubster." She shrugged and started contouring her left cheek. "Ask Dustin—her first assistant—you know who he is?" Cheryl nodded, then glanced at Ortiz, who was clearly just as fascinated as she was by Savannah's elaborate makeup routine. "Anyway, he literally knows all the personal stuff. Simp. Like he's—*he was*—her total kiss-ass lapdog—"

"And why did she want you here so early?"

"Oh my god, it's literally so dumb. Like some Boomer or Gen X—whatever, just *old*—power ritual." She looked up briefly from her mirror to roll her eyes. "They like to believe it's to make you tough and a problem solver, but like, it's pretty obvious, well, to anyone with, like, a brain, it's just bored tragics disrespecting to get their geriatric kicks. Like, don't they know they're supposed to leave the ladder down, not literally kick everyone coming up in the head? I don't think they can even spell woke." Cheryl nodded solicitously, encouraging her to continue.

"Like, the rule is that I, the lowest assistant, *always* have to be at work before Alma. It would basically be fine if I ever knew *what time* she was coming in—it could be 5 am, it could be 10 am. She doesn't share that info." She rolled her tongue inside her lips and moved on to painting her professionally sculpted nose. "I also have to make sure her favorite gold cup is on her desk containing a *boiling* hot double shot of Black Ivory Coffee, you know, the one that's literally made from elephant poop?"

"But, whaa—How?" said Cheryl, floundering, before quickly regaining her train of thought. "How do you figure out what time to arrive and when to make the coffee?"

"It's crazy delicious, actually, all the best Michelin-starred restaurants have it. I tried it. Who wouldn't?"

Me, thought Ortiz, suppressing a retch.

"And getting it hot is easy. As soon as I arrive, I like, make the espresso in the hospitality kitchen. When security—posted outside waiting—see her car turn into the parking lot, they text me, and I blast it in Dustin's hidden microwave. Alma thinks it's a filing cabinet. She would—would've—fired me on the spot if she found out I did that to her precious coffee. I don't know how Dustin got the microwave past her, but he probably worked it because he literally lives off two-minute noodles. Tragic."

Spot the emotion. Tough one this, Cheryl thought, watching her closely. "Anyways, every morning, I wait up on the penthouse floor until it's time to position her drink, then I go downstairs as it's super important that I'm gone before she gets up to the floor. Like, having to set eyes on a lowly assistant would turn her to dust. Oh, my bad, that's like tasteless. Then, I just answer the phones and await orders. I might only have seen her three times since I started here, and one of those times, she was dead.

What?" She paused as she observed Cheryl's speculative expression. "It's not like what she has me do is *hard*. I graduated cum laude from Duke." She yawned. "And, honestly, I get all my best social media likes while I'm waiting for her. Because I post stuff so early, it's giving that I live in New York. Which is iconic, obvs."

Cheryl, absorbing this, paused for a few seconds to watch Savannah thickly penciling in one eyebrow, then continued, "So, if you don't know what time she's coming in, you have to get here—"

"Yaaaa, that's right," Savannah moved to her other eyebrow. "I have to get here, like, really ridiculously early. Occasionally, I, like, risk it, sleep in, and arrive at 7:30. It's like '*might get fired*' roulette. Sometimes, when I'm super bored, even *I* think it's entertaining. My besties love it, but then that's because they find my having a job soooo hilarious. I mean, those guys could never—"

"I see," interrupted Cheryl, "and you choose to work here because?"

"It's how I get my allowance, and Mommy dearest won't release the first lump sum of my trust fund next year if I don't. I'm gonna create my vegan beauty line with it. I'm really focusing on organic foundation for *all* skin tones. There isn't nearly enough out there for women of color. I'll send you guys some samples if you like, or is that, like, bribery? Your skin color really is gorgeous, Detective Cheryl, and your weave is excellent, too, love a shoulder-length bob. You are totally hot for a cop. You might wanna reconsider brown as your color, though—too matchy. Do you photograph well? I'm thinking of using normal girls and gays for my line to keep it, like, totally real." She pouted, lining her lips with a nude pencil. "Basically, my mom pays me to work here. Alma hired me, like, as a favor. I actually don't know how much AARDA pays me—our family business manager deals, obvs—but I think it's a pittance. I Uber-Eats Alma's other assistants' lunch most days, not that they ever thank me, because poor things (and I mean *poor*, like literally broke)—they do this *voluntarily*. Why on earth anyone would put up with this shit and not get 25k a month is, like, beyond me." She shrugged, sharpened her lip pencil, and returned it to the bag.

Ortiz, blowing her cold fingers warm and seeing Cheryl stunned into silence as she did the math, took over. "So that's how you came to find the deceased at approximately 5:40 am?"

"Yaaaa." Savannah filled in her lips using a lip brush and NARS neutrals lip palette. "On Saturdays, I'm supposed to check her office when I arrive since we leave before her on Fridays. Not that there is ever anything on her desk—like, it's always empty. Super strange. No paper or photos. Not even a pen. It's more like a museum than an office and always *freezing*. Anyway. I went in, and I, well—There she was." She stopped applying her makeup for the first time and gagged slightly. "It's so weird. I, like, never vomit, not even when I once, like, accidentally ate a real hot dog. Do you know they're made with blitzed bones and fat? *GROSS*."

"Anyway, back to the deceased," said Ortiz gruffly, sprinting past this unwelcome insight into her favorite food.

"But please, take your time," Cheryl added. "Would you like some water?"

"No, I'm totally hydrated." Savannah put down her lip palette. "It was so surreal, she was kinda hanging—well, you saw her—over the stair railing, blood on her head, with her leg sticking out at a really weird angle. She was in pink, right? Like, I didn't dream that? She was wearing a pink top and pink socks? Like I said, *weird*. No *way* she'd wear pink. Are you sure it's really her?"

"We believe it is her, yes. And after you discovered her, what did you do?"

"Well, I ran out of there so fucking fast. I didn't get close. I didn't wanna see anything up close. I called you guys, like, immediately, and then I called down to security from Dustin's desk. But I guarded the door until your colleagues arrived. I figured I should do that. I literally heart crime shows. I think I'd be an awesome cop. Then I went to the restroom and threw up. I'm sure it's all on the camera; they are so uptight about security here. I know it's good because it's the same as our system at home."

"Yes, we are reviewing security. Did you see anyone else? To your knowledge, was there anyone on her floor beside you?"

"That early? Literally, no. Apart from the night guard from the desk downstairs, no one was here, and he would have been outside, freezing his hot butt off, waiting for Alma."

"Yes, our team has spoken to him already."

　　　　　　　　　　　　　　　　　　　　　Penny Lovell

Savannah's phone pinged loudly. She swiped her lips with gloss and, glancing down at the message, asked, "Sorry, but like, how much longer do you think this will take?" Scooping the remaining makeup back into the bad, she released her blonde, salon-kissed hair, shaking it down her back. "My mom is downstairs, and we're gonna sweat off this horror at our Sacred Spin class."

FIRE THE STYLIST

Dishing Daily Doses of Fashion Justice

RIP (ALMOST FAMOUS) ALMA ASTLEY.

Posted on February 24, 2018

BREAKING NEWS, Firers! It's a blue (dare we say <u>cerulean</u>?) day for Hollywood. <u>Alma Astley</u>, 56, may not be a household name to the uninitiated. Still, the infamous agent's death within the LAST COUPLE OF HOURS is reverberating in every corner of Tinsel Town. The magnificent British <u>former supermodel</u> rose to unprecedented heights in her second career, and she and her svelte figure did it <u>dressed to kill</u>. Relationships with numerous <u>elite designers</u> started in her youth and continued, despite her age, until her abrupt death yesterday. She'll undoubtedly be the chicest of ghosts.

In life, Alma was frequently seen on the red carpet in couture outfits from giants such as <u>Louis Vuitton</u>, <u>Chanel</u>, <u>Dior</u>, <u>Henri LeRoque</u>, and <u>Bebe Klein</u>. It says something about her formidable nature that she regularly killed <u>her clients</u> in the fashion stakes—indeed, it was positively expected of her.

The last person to see Alma alive was reportedly power stylist <u>Belinda Grant.</u> Let's hope that in their final meeting, they addressed the atrocious street looks worn recently by their joint client and #FireTheStylist regular, Lara White.

That aside, today we mourn the crushing loss of a <u>BEHIND THE SCENES ICON</u> with a slide show of her most <u>memorable moments</u>.

Comment below to let us know your favorite look!

(To review our community guidelines, please click here)

> **@jancandoit** No idea who she is but why so much black? Borrring. I like number 3 because it's red #RIP

> **@fashionismyreligionnnn** Omg. I wish I had followed her when she was alive, her style is ON POINT. RIP (I ♥)

> **@mylovingheart22** Are you serious with this post? How ghoulish are you guys? A woman has DIED. Who gives a rat's ass what she wore. Unfollow

> **@gaytodayandalways** Rest in couture, QUEEN. Taken too soon. EVERY SINGLE THING SHE WORE WAS DIVINE!

"The only free cheese is in the mouse trap."
—Russian proverb

Fried with Freebies

RIDING IN CARS WITH STYLISTS
Villa Carlotta, Hollywood. 7:30 am

BELINDA AND JASPER PULLED UP OUTSIDE the elegant cream 1920s Spanish Colonial building, which covered a whole block of an untypically quiet Franklin Village. The early morning sun illuminated the empty sidewalks and adjacent shuttered restaurants, swept clean of litter but ingrained with dirt and a lingering whiff of discarded food. Only one human cut the solitude, a child-sized young woman in sunglasses bigger than her face, who stood outside the regal navy entrance smoking lethargically as she waited for her mini bulldog to shit.

"How sad is it that I can name the label of every item that girl is wearing?" Belinda asked before rattling off: "JW Anderson peach fleece PJs, Moncler striped beanie, gloves and scarf, Givenchy platform biker boots, Dior Glasses—I'm not 100% sure who made the dog's sweater, though. Gucci?"

"Who else?" Eying the girl's muscular, spray-tanned stomach, Jasper added, "Why is her midriff the only body part that doesn't feel the cold?"

"Dude, if I had a six-pack like that, I'd cut all my thousand-dollar ski pajamas up, too," said Belinda, staring out the window. "Ugh, the fucking coffee shop is closed! 'The Bourgeois Pig' is the perfect name for a business that hates capitalism, as evidenced by not being open *in the morning*. Jesus, I love Chloe, but why couldn't this fitting be later?"

"All about their lives, boo, you know that. And 10/10, everyone on this block is hungover on this fine Saturday morning—no organic oak milk matcha needed before ten. What a gorgeous building, but no fucking street parking, OF COURSE. Is it a hotel?"

"Nah, it's short-term apartments. A sort of boutique hotel meets Parisian apartment for celebs/the art world mostly. I came here to meet with Clara Brightley when she was in town. It looks kinda like the Chateau Marmont inside, but fresher and with no room service, sex stains, or Hollywood royalty infamy."

"Or valet? Fuck. AND YOU CAN FUCK OFF AND DRIVE ROUND ME, ASSHOLE! Why is Mr. Pretentious Saab in such hurry on a Saturday morning anyway? Drive of shame?"

They both laughed as Jasper swung around the corner and pulled over again. "You get out and go up, Boss. I'll find parking and get back with the stuff as soon as . . ."

"But what if you can only find a spot that's miles away?" Belinda protested weakly, then immediately capitulated. "Well, we'd best not both be late. At least give me a couple of bags to carry."

"Take the gifting stuff behind your seat—there's another Bebe Klein handbag for her and one for you—because how will the two of you *survive* without a new bag? I don't know which is which, so take both up. Also, Shrunx sent her an essentials kit, probably because of all the tabloid shit about her baby weight. Subtle they are NOT. There are Gucci white monogrammed cashmere sweaters for the kids. I think they must have been sent before she signed the Bebe Klein contract. Oh, and Shoop messengered over a gift-wrapped god knows what, but it's heavy—I'm praying it's a crystal-scented cast of Tilly's vadge. I would DIE! It's probably a vibrator, though—vibrators have taken over from candles as the celeb gift du jour. It better be neon."

FIRE THE STYLIST

Dishing Daily Doses of Fashion Justice

CHLOE BARKER at the Photo Call
for "The Go-Between.

Posted February 20, 2018

Chloe Barker (33), seen here at the Four Seasons, Beverly Hills, in yet another head-to-toe Bebe Klein. SNOOZE.

She may now be excessively wealthy due to the rumored $6 MILLION contract this newly minted Bebe Klein ambassador signed last month, but it sure has dimmed her red-carpet light. It's a good job that the modern reimagining of The Go-Between, set in Detroit and replacing the outmoded letter with texts, is set to be a smash.

We were going to leave it there, but since it's a slow red-carpet day, and as we were feeling charitable, we took a second look for some positive aspects:

- The peach button-down is pretty

- The silver leather gaucho pants are fitted perfectly

- Matching silver ankle boots are so next season!

- Her body is banging again (finally!)

Firers may remember Chloe had a HUGE weight gain for her second pregnancy (many assumed she was expecting twins!), plus she took a few weeks to lose those extra pounds.

BRAVO to Chloe for ignoring the body shamers and taking her time!

I suppose we can let her stylist, Belinda Grant, off the hook on this one since we can't imagine Jerome, the wunderkind designer at Bebe Klein (yes, they do only go by one name), letting her make any decisions.

What do you think, guys? Did Chloe sell out?

As always, leave comments below!

(To review our community guidelines, please click here)

> **@meeeeeee.** Jerome is indeed a freakin' wunderkind. They single-handedly saved that stuffy old brand and its ubiquitous tacky

handbags. They are a f*cking genius; she is lucky to breathe their air. FaSHUN is changing people, get over it and get on with the future. #jerome #bebeklein #nonbinary

@anon69 - Love her! Her body is amazing! She looks good in anything. This is just as well because this overpriced exclusive brand looks good on no one else

@momof5boys - What a stupid outfit, is she going to outer space? Fashion is so weird these days. She should fire her stylist for sure

@cupcakelife - Does she eat? Why does that hunk of a husband want a stick woman? I'd really like to cake his cup

@tellitlikeitis - She's got enormous ears.

@lifesucksass - Are there sweat rings under her arms? EW!

"Life in the movie business is like the beginning of a new love affair: it's full of surprise and you're constantly getting fucked."
—David Mamet

Dying in Pink

POLICE WITNESS INTERVIEW: DUSTIN JOHNSON
First (executive) assistant to Alma Astley. 7:45 am

"HELLO, DUSTIN," SAID CHERYL, standing to greet him. "Thank you for coming in so quickly. We spoke on the phone. I'm Detective Hall, and this is my partner, Detective Ortiz. Once again, I'm sorry for your loss." She tried to gauge the level of his grief but found him as yet unreadable. "Please take a seat."

Cheryl imperceptibly recoiled at the sweet, cloying smell of alcohol oozing from Dustin's pores and wafting across the room. She couldn't see his eyes, as they were covered by mirrored Versace glasses, but he was obviously hungover and suffering, carrying in one hand a giant coffee with a coconut water balanced on top, while simultaneously reaching to pull out a Red Bull from the sleek black drinks fridge with the other. He kicked the door shut and carefully made his way to the seat recently vacated by Savannah.

Ortiz, inscrutable as ever, stood by the window casually crunching on some powerful British mints she'd found in a tiny silver bowl in the shape of a teardrop, silently watching as he placed the three drinks on the table, pulled down the sleeves of his tight, fluffy zebra print sweater, and crossed his arms tightly. Walking over to them, she sat and observed, "This room sure is uncomfortable, and it's freaking COLD."

"Oh yes, it's climate-controlled to be that way," Dustin, pale beneath his tan, took off his glasses and fixed his pale blue gaze at Ortiz, massaging his temples. "Officially, it's to encourage efficiency, but in reality, it's to torture the lesser people relegated to this room. There's a fabulous and much warmer boardroom next door for VIP meetings—would you like to go in there instead? I haven't had a chance to eat yet, and there are snacks."

"Yes!" replied Ortiz, enthusiastically. "Let's do that before my ass actually gets frozen to this metal chair. Is it made from dry-cleaning hangers?" she asked, running her finger along the white, powder-coated latticework.

"HA! Very funny, detective. These are Tom Dixon Pylon chairs," Dustin sniffed. "Original ones. Each cost more than my car . . . yours too, probably. But yes, I guess they are more for looking *at* than sitting *on*."

"That cool if we move rooms, boss?"

"Sure," Cheryl nodded and Dustin sashayed out into the corridor. They followed him to a discreet door, which unless you looked closely appeared to be part of the sleek white paneling. Handing two of his three drinks to Ortiz, he entered the code. As they followed him in, Ortiz observed his shredded jeans and murmured to Cheryl, "His pert, bronzed ass must be freezing. Ya thinks he's free ballin'?"

Ignoring her, Cheryl observed the sumptuous room before sitting on one of the two emerald-green velvet couches, placing her phone next to a gilded vase of dahlias on the teak coffee table. Ortiz sank enthusiastically into a plump, tobacco-colored leather armchair with a view of the ocean, then subtly shifted forward as she realized her feet no longer touched the ground. Sweat beading on her forehead, she removed her puffer jacket and pointed at a wall. "Is that a Rothko?"

Cheryl shrugged. "I know nothin' about paintings."

"Pretty sure it is. There's, like, a bajillion dollars of art on these walls. And it feels kinda disrespectful to walk on this freaking fur rug. You reckon we should take off our cheap shoes?"

"It's the gold falcons on the wallpaper for me," said Cheryl, finally engaging in the interior design talk. "Speaks volumes."

Accustomed to the opulence, Dustin walked straight into the custom mint-green Miele kitchen, located discreetly around a corner, and took a bag of maple bacon popcorn out of a walk-in pantry. Returning, he sat neatly on the couch opposite Cheryl, propping up his back with a mink cushion.

"You want anything?" he asked as an afterthought, glancing at them both.

"Sure." Ortiz, always hungry, chimed in, "What ya got?"

"More like what don't we got," he replied, sighing as he stood again and beckoned her to accompany him. Not wanting to struggle out of the chair, she replied, "Oh, anything will do, you pick."

"Vegan Paleo Puffs, detective? Would those suit your palate?" he asked dryly on his way to the kitchen.

"Oh, I love 'em," she deadpanned, not missing a beat.

"Nothing for me," Cheryl said, looking hard at Ortiz as she awaited his return. "Now, Dustin, how long have you worked for Alma?"

"Four years and three weeks." He tossed Ortiz the chips and sat, a wave of hangover visibly hitting him.

"And would you say you are close?"

"Well, if anyone were close to her, it would be me," Dustin replied with pride. "I've lasted the longest by YEARS of anyone who's worked with her. I'm very efficient. In fact, I'm totally ready to be an agent; even Alma agrees, but it's so hard to replace me. There really is no AARDA without Alma and no Alma without someone like me." He caught himself. "Well . . . I guess there is no Alma now. Shit."

"Let's go back to yesterday, Dustin. We've already interviewed security and looked at the security footage. Belinda Grant entered Alma's office at 5:45, left at 5:53, stood outside on her phone, and re-entered at 5:58, leaving again 10 seconds later carrying an envelope addressed to her."

"Yes, that was her contract with Janie Jones. Jasper, her *gorgeous* assistant—well, he's a bit of a short ass, but still. Anyway, he texted me that she had left it behind, and as Alma was already upstairs in her private mezzanine area, I told him to tell her to run back in and get it." Choking on his popcorn, he took a long gulp of Red Bull.

"I had a hot date last night, and I really didn't want to have to come in this morning to grab it for them. You see, besides morning elephant coffee, Alma doesn't let any assistant except me near her desk. She also won't let anyone email contracts. She's so old school—was so . . ." He shook his head, with its blonde-tipped bed hair, and wiped the moisture from just visible crow's feet.

Emotional tears or tired, leaky eyes? Cheryl couldn't decide.

"I left about 4:45 and double-confirmed in person with security to let Belinda up to Alma's floor. Obviously, I'd emailed them earlier, but you can't be too careful. The staff turnover is ridiculous—people just don't wanna work these days. Then I went to work out and get ready for my date. You can check with my gym."

"Okay, great. Which gym?"

"Barry's in Weho."

"West Hollywood," Ortiz clarified for Cheryl, "LA-speak. You'll get used to it. And before you left? Alma was out?"

"Yeah, she was with her kids at the dentist on Brighton Way. The details are on her schedule," he said, pulling out his phone. "Should I email it to you?" Cheryl nodded, handing him her card. "She walked there and took a detour to the bank on the way back—City National, if you need to know."

"Wait," Ortiz interrupted, "she *walked* there?"

"What, like on her *legs*?" Cheryl rolled her eyes sarcastically.

"Oh honey," said Dustin, glancing at Ortiz before they regarded Cheryl condescendingly.

"She's new to town, Dustin," said Ortiz, then clarified to Cheryl, "NO one walks anywhere in LA."

"Like *never*," Dustin chimed in.

Cheryl, unimpressed after a lifetime spent on the T in Boston, pressed on. "Alma's other assistant"—she checked her notes—"Alison Kennedy? Tell me about her. We've already talked to Savannah."

"Ah yes, Savannah! That's what she's called!" said Dustin, adding defensively, "I don't see her much, and the thirds don't usually last. For god's sake, they don't even get a name; the email address is 'Astley 3rd assistant.' Anyway, I feel terrible for her. Is she okay?"

"She's doing as you might expect." Ortiz left this open for interpretation.

"Oh, good. Glad to hear that. And yes, Alison is the second. She's been on vacation this week. Brave of her to take it—junior assistants don't usually dare—but I suppose she does have endometriosis. Alma always had us leave by six on Fridays, but she changed that to 5:30 yesterday. She did request a photocopier to be left in her office, which was strange. She can't even charge her phone."

★ ★ ★

FLASHBACK
Beverly Hills
Friday 23rd February. 4:30 pm

Alma, 6' 3" in Louboutin heels, marched her endless fishnet-clad legs down Rodeo Drive towards Wilshire Boulevard, blithely unaware of anyone in her path or the stares she drew. Famously, an ex-supermodel—a 10ft Helmut Newton portrait (naked save for thigh-high patent boots and a riding crop) hung in her office, positioned on the wall behind her desk so that her magnificent breasts were directly in the eye-line of visitors, and, when seated, they appeared to be resting on Alma's head.

As always, her fine red hair was scraped back into the nape of her neck with wet-look wax. The luminous white skin of her chiseled, botoxed face was crowned by legendary glacial blue eyes, though today, as on most days, they were covered by black oversized Tom Fords.

Alma pulled out her phone and jabbed her speed dial, sighing impatiently as she waited.

"Get me Dustin—Dustin, it took that rich Hollywood inbred three INTERMINABLE rings to answer. Good, see that you do. I'm taking a slight detour to City National. Have them ready for me, please. I'll be there in four minutes and need my number four safety deposit box. Also, have a photocopier brought to my office before I return"—she glanced at her diamond-encrusted Jaeger Le Coutre watch—"in 23 minutes and ensure it is positioned attractively. Clear the office once it's delivered and leave Janie's stylist's contract on my desk. No, I won't need you. OF COURSE, I know how to use one. Please don't insult my intelligence, Dustin. Now run what's left of my schedule this afternoon." She listened before briefly answering, "Push the stylist to 6; she gets 10 minutes max." *Click.*

⋆ ⋆ ⋆

"Did she say what she wanted the photocopier for?" Cheryl, sweating, slid off her jacket, then clamped her arms down to hide the sweat patches on her white shirt.

"No. But then Alma doesn't ever explain herself, so I've honestly stopped wondering. She might have just wanted to fuck with me. She likes creating hurdles for people and thinks it, to quote her, '*separates the wheat from the chaff.*' I think that's some British saying. My guess is she probably didn't even use it—the photocopier, that is."

"I'm sure C.S.I. is on it, but make sure they check the photocopy memory," said Cheryl, looking at Ortiz, who nodded, picked up her phone, and started typing.

"How did you get the photocopier so fast?"

"Have you not been listening, detective? I'm a boy wizard in a sea of muggles."

"We heard she was having marital problems. Was that something you knew about?"

"I know *the most* for sure, but I don't know *everything*, and yeah, she had a suite at The Bev Hills."

"The hotel. Yes, we know that." Cheryl smiled smugly at Ortiz.

"She didn't stay there all the time. Just when they were fighting, I guess. You wouldn't know she had a husband at the office, to be honest. She didn't mention him, and he didn't come in. Mostly, I knew when shit wasn't good because she had me buying clothes for him *non-stop*. That's what Alma did when she was having problems: shop. Well, have me shop."

"So, you've seen nothing concrete? Just a hotel suite she didn't always use and excessive shopping?"

"Well, when you put it like that—she was off though." He paused, huffily adding, "I've worked for her for four years, so I know *that*."

"Can you define off?"

"Well, she was tetchy lately, even for her. Lara White was stalking her about #AlsoMe, and extra contact with Lara is never a good thing; she's the devil incarnate. Jason Bird was up to his usual kinky, rapey shit, losing roles left and right, and Alma *was* making him go to rehab. Janie

Penny Lovell

Jones has been trying to get out of shooting Combat Queen 6—like that isn't the only reason the world knows who she is." He looked pointedly at Cheryl. "You know who she is, right?" Cheryl nodded, thinking how very surreal this conversation was. The dismissive, wearied way the man opposite her talked about these legendary characters, as if describing tiresome adolescents.

Dustin nodded back, relieved. "Well, it would be a big loss of commission for AARDA, not to mention the breaking contract nightmare. Alma does not like mess. But dear Janie ignores minor irritating things like the law, naturally. Lastly, Caroline Porter-Jones has been *begging* to return to Alma, which she should have known was never gonna happen. You don't leave Alma, period. And to want to come back?" He snorted loudly and choked on his tequila-tinged saliva. "It's rumored Caroline was saying some nasty things after talking with Alma at HFCL last week. But girl-friend's such a wimp, just a basic housewife from Brentwood these days; she probably made some bitchy comment about Alma's dress being five minutes old. Which would have been a lie, duh."

Ortiz, finishing up the 'Fiery Hot' Paleo Puffs, started to choke. "Okay, this is useful," said Cheryl, tossing Ortiz a mini-Voss water from the coffee table. "We're gonna need contact information for them all. What's HFCL?"

"Hollywood For Children's Literacy."

"Could anyone be *against that*?" Cheryl asked neutrally. "Anyway, moving on. Would you say she was a difficult boss?"

Dustin snorted again. Dustin was very much a snorter, Ortiz thought drily. "Well, let me put it this way: do you know who Jesse Livermore is? Probably not, since you guys aren't ancient wanker bankers, and you don't work *here*. He caused the stock market crash of 1929, like centuries ago. Jesse had a chauffeur who bribed all the traffic light operators—yeah, like, they did it manually then, can you fucking—oops, freaking—believe it? Dude made sure the Rolls never had to stop; every light on Mr. Livermore's early morning drive was green." He paused. "Amazing, right? What a pathetic job, standing there all day turning a light three colors." He paused. "Anyway, I've lost count of how many times she coldly recounted that story to me in the beginning. It got narrowed down eventually. These days,

I can judge my performance by the number of times she has (or hasn't) snapped 'GREEN LIGHT, Dustin.' He mimicked a British accent and suddenly slumped forward, a wave of grief contorting his handsome, lightly botoxed face.

"Anyway, she had so many stories like that one. Alma's a total nerd on the quiet. She also loves—I mean loved—quotes. She collects them. We send 'Alma's quote' to the clients every week. *Shit*, that reminds me, I should take them off auto-send—we cue them up monthly. Jesus, imagine getting inspirational quotes from the other side." He picked up his phone and tapped intently for a few moments. "There, sorted. Alma's weekly quote, like her, is no more." He wiped his eyes and shoved a handful of popcorn into his mouth.

"Okay, moving on, can we discuss her outfit?" Cheryl asked softly.

"Oh, sure!" Dustin pepped up. "I think she was in the Fall 2019 black Balenciaga mini tunic. Yes! That was it. The one I had them send from Paris, with thigh-high Loubs—that's Louboutins—as in Christian," he explained to Cheryl. "Her bag was—hold on—I know this . . . YES! The limited-edition Croc YSL uptown tote. And two bike-chain cognac pavé bracelets from Pomellato. So CHIC." He nodded, a self-congratulatory smile forming in celebration of his excellent memory.

"Actually"—Cheryl, oblivious to the designer names, continued—"I bring this up because Savannah—your third assistant—was shocked to find Alma wearing a pale pink bowling shirt, and pink socks. The shirt had 'Anna' stitched on the front and 'Van Nuys Bowl' on the back."

"WHAT? *NO! That's impossible.*"

"Yes, Dustin. Yes."

"*SHUT UP!* I'd *never* buy her such things. Can you say that again?" He shook his head vigorously. "NO, she would never. It can't be true. In all the years I've been with her, I have literally never seen her in anything Cruella wouldn't wear. Trust me, I know about her style. And I ordered everything. Baby pink? Bowling? No way, Jose. It must be someone else. Someone else died in there. ANNA? Who the fuck is Anna? It literally *CAN'T* have been her," he concluded, looking hopeful.

"I'm afraid we believe the deceased was Alma, Dustin," Cheryl stated firmly but gently.

Penny Lovell

"I . . . wow . . . I . . . *jeesus.* I don't know if I'm more shocked she's dead or that she was wearing polyester. And pink? She'd literally *die* if she knew she'd *died in pink.*"

"Yes, well, we're still looking into that. Now, let's return to her office. There are multiple cameras in the corridor leading to her office from the elevator, but no cameras in her office, on the mezzanine level suite, or in the private elevator. Is that correct?"

"Yes, she's totally private. Very few people used that elevator, only the very famous and even then, only when absolutely necessary."

"So, theoretically, someone could have come up in her elevator without being seen?"

"Yeah, but she'd have to give them the code in advance, which she rarely does as once a client is introduced to the private elevator, they never want to come in the regular way again. *Egomaniacs.* Needless to say, she offered it to only a select few and reset the code immediately after they left."

"And the select few who've used the elevator recently are?"

"Last week only Jason Bird. She was planning meetings with Lara White and Janie Jones on Monday and possibly another with Jason, but I'm unsure about that as he was leaving for rehab. I initially put them on the calendar, but she took over the details."

"And they would be given the code?"

"Usually, yep, but I'm pretty sure she would've given it to them on Monday just before they arrived."

"Does anyone else have the code, or is there a master override?"

"No idea. Honestly, I've never thought about it. When they serviced it, she would just give me the info for them and change it afterward. Now that I think about it, how on earth did she remember all these different codes? Fuck, I can't believe she was in pink."

"Other than the code, was it unusual for her to organize details herself, Dustin? For example, the meeting on Monday? She does have three assistants."

"It's hard to say. I used to think I knew literally everything—since I did—literally everything. I mean, I even buy her hemorrhoid cream and liaise with her plastic surgeon, but I guess we're learning just how much I *don't* know."

"Can you confirm there are no cameras in her private parking garage?"

"Yup, I can. She had them taken down too, for the stalked to avoid their hunters—or, as you'd call them, the paps."

"Paparazzi," Ortiz mouthed to Cheryl.

"I know *that.*"

Dustin continued, "And she was . . . just very paranoid about privacy all around. Mind you, with the amount of fires we put out here, it's good to have a secure base camp, if you know what I mean. If she deigns to help you, you can get in and out of here without the world being any the wiser." He continued proudly, "One person, who shall remain nameless, lived through a very intense 10-day scandal in her suite upstairs while the world's press searched for them in Paris."

Cheryl's brow furrowed. "But, in general, this doesn't seem very safe?"

"Oh, Alma thought she was invincible. Everyone thought Alma was invincible. She was much more concerned about a security guard selling footage of a client, à la Beyoncé Met Gala debacle."

"Right, got it." Cheryl replied, clearly not getting it.

"Oh, detective, what planet do you live on?" Dustin rolled his eyes at Ortiz before expanding: "Beyoncé standing in an elevator smoothing her dress while Solange had family fisticuffs with her brother-in-law—that's Jay Z, in case you didn't know. Anyway, it woulda just been a *private* Met Ball after-party meets New Jersey Thanksgiving moment had somebody from the hotel not sold the elevator footage to the world press. It's a vintage tabloid moment, but still totally unforgettable."

"Ah, I see. Okay,' Cheryl tried to hide how unusually discombobulated she was in this strange new world. "Moving on. Aside from the actors mentioned before, do you know of any enemies she might have had?"

"Well, I can't think of anyone who didn't loathe her, apart from me, George (the manager of Fred's), Jamie, and 50/50 on her kids. Professionally they all loved her, of course, selfish bastards, but like her? Nope. I listen in on most of her calls, so I know almost everything that's going on, and aside from what I already told you, I don't think there's anything else."

"You listen in on her phone calls?"

"Duh." Dustin shrugged.

"This is standard? She wants, I mean, she wanted you to?" said Cheryl, visibly perplexed.

"Of course! What if she forgets something when she's on the line or needs something done immediately, like in real-time?" He looked at Cheryl like she was an alien. "And she wants notes so she can remember all the things she's said. Like, it's no biggie, I signed a fucking crazy NDA. *SHIT!*" His face registered fear. "Can they sue me for telling you this stuff?"

Ortiz answered, "So far, you haven't told us anything that isn't hearsay and speculation. And if a crime has been committed and her death is not accidental, your nondisclosure agreement would be null and void."

"Oh, thank god. I'm sorry, I really need to book an appointment with my therapist. This is gonna blow his mind. Can I go now?" He sniffed his armpit. "I need a shower. Also, I've got a lot of clients to cajole into staying with me. Let's be honest, I did most of the work anyway, and surely they know that?"

Ruthless, thought Cheryl, but out loud said, "Yes, I think we're good for now, Dustin. Please send us the details for"—checking her notes—"Lara White, Jason Bird, Janie Jones, and Caroline Porter-Jones. We'll be in touch with any follow-up questions."

Dustin, lagging now, pulled out his phone and air-dropped the contacts to Cheryl before standing up and walking hesitantly to the door. Turning back, he asked, "Is she still up there? Does Jamie know yet? And, ugh, *the kids*. Oh, well, onwards . . ." He turned, not waiting for an answer, and left the room, draining his coconut water.

As the brushed gold elevator door closed, Cheryl turned to Ortiz, mouth open.

"Whaaat, girl? I told you to let me lead. This is a whole other world, a whole other species. You just wait. You ain't seen nuthin."

"Does he love her or hate her? I can't tell."

"It's like that kidnapper syndrome, wassit called again?"

"Stockholm Syndrome."

"Yeah, Cheryl, there's a lotta that here. You'll see."

"But 'friend' in Hollywood, is a malleable
term, one that has its own definition not
to be found in a dictionary."
—Stephen Galloway

Couture Conniptions

FITTING WITH CHLOE BARKER
Apartment 35, Villa Carlotta, Hollywood. 7:30 am

"MORNING, BELS," CHLOE UTTERED SWEETLY, her pixie features registering surprise as she almost toppled backward, trying to pull open the heavy hunter-green vintage door. Her olive-doe eyes looked timidly past Belinda into the Art Deco hallway, and she adjusted her floral robe to cover a tiny escaping breast. "Is Jasper coming?"

"Yes! Sometime this century, I hope. Sorry, parking was a bitch."

"Oh no, Bels, I'm sorry, my driver says that every day. And sorry it had to be so early; you must be flat out with the Oscars."

"No worries. Are you working later today? Is that why so early?"

"Umm . . . no," Chloe mumbled, distracted by her phone as she perched delicately on the edge of a gold-fringed damask poof. Belinda, still standing, looked down at her greasy roots and top knot, getting a subtle waft of BO as Chloe's silky robe slipped off one shoulder. "I just wanted to spend time with my girls today. I've been shooting so much recently, and they hate being stuck in the trailer." Chloe slid her phone into her robe pocket and began her usual succession of attention-deflecting questions. "Speaking of which, how's Rose, Bels? She looks so big on your Instagram. Is she impressed by her glamorous, busy mama? Has her dad resurfaced at all?"

"No, he's still busy not finding himself somewhere in the world. Greece, I think, and Rose is so-so." Belinda looked pained. "Can you believe it's been two years since he left the country permanently? She's mostly used to it now. He FaceTimes from random hotels once in a while, which both thrills and devastates her. As for me, well, I haven't been able to spend as much time with her recently..." Belinda looked sadly at her screensaver for a few seconds, silently reprimanding herself for getting emotional at work. She showed Chloe the phone image. "She looks and smells fantastic in her sleep, which is the only time I really see her at the moment, and my nanny Paola tells me she hasn't started smoking yet, so ... a good sign, I think?"

Chloe let out a silvery, self-conscious laugh. "No way, not with you around! You should have brought her with you! I wouldn't mind, and the girls would love a big girl to admire!"

Belinda smiled with her mouth, thinking if she ever did this, it would only be a few short hours before someone on Chloe's team twisted it into a problem: *To succeed, a mother must seem childless at work and workless at home.* But out loud she answered, "Another time, maybe. Look, I bring gifts!"

"Oh, another bag from Jerome?" Chloe asked, glancing at the luxe maroon shopping bags without enthusiasm.

"Yes, I think so. One is for me, but I'm not sure which one as the tags fell off. There'll be a note inside, though." Chloe opened both shopping bags and read the labels before passing the correct one to Belinda, and in tandem, they pulled the purses out of protective dust bags.

"Oh, yours is *gorge*," Chloe exclaimed, wrinkling her delicate nose dismissively at the one she held. "I love geometric print, and that miniature size is so freaking cute."

Belinda glanced at Chloe's wait-listed and hungered-after hand-graffitied box bag. "You don't like it?"

"It's okay, but it's not really *me*. I'll give it to my sister-in-law or housekeeper." Chloe's eyes lingered a few more seconds on Belinda's bag.

"Do you want to swap?"

"*Really*? Oh, amazing." Chloe cheered up. "Are you sure? Do you even like mine?"

No, Belinda screamed inside while smiling and nodding yes.

"It doesn't seem very you, but if you really do like it! Thanks, Bel! And you can borrow it back anytime!" She threw Belinda's mini bag on the emerald velvet couch and skipped lightly to the door to answer a tentative knock.

"Well, hello, ladies! Sorry for the delay. The car is parked on Mars," Jasper gasped, wheeling in a porter's cart stuffed with garment bags and two large, battered suitcases, his handsome face cerise and sweaty.

"Wow, all of this for two Bebe Klein looks?" Chloe glanced quizzically at Belinda, tucking her other boob back under the robe.

"No, Chloe, it's just one from Bebe. I sent you the image of the dress Jerome approved for the premiere. It's pretty cool. I managed to negotiate us out of the milkmaid mini they previously favored. But you can wear another designer for the junkets and The Late Show."

"I'm doing Colbert? Oh, I don't think I knew that. I should read my emails sometimes. But what about the contract? The two pages of forbidden labels? Alma grudgingly said she would try to get it reduced and then just responded '*$6 MILLION*' any time I brought it up, so I concluded she hadn't succeeded and gave up. Sorry guys," she added guiltily, "I tried to read the contract but got bored. I'm terrible at that stuff. You looked, though?"

"Oh yes, it was my bedtime reading last week," said Jasper. "You'll be happy to know that a mere 67 brands aren't allowed on your person."

Seeing Chloe's face fall, Belinda interjected, "But all is not lost; there's still a few good ones! We have Dries Van Noten, Rosie Assoulin, Off-White, Alliette, Simone Rocha, Molly Goddard . . ." She trailed off as Chloe, indifferent, floated towards the kitchen.

Jasper pulled the suitcases of shoes off the cart, wondering how much griping about a six-million-dollar payday was too much, but out loud asking, "Where should I set up?"

"Oh, right where you are."

Jasper surveyed the minimalist, Parisian-inspired lounge: stark white walls and original rickety wooden flooring covered by a faded pink Turkish rug. An uncomfortable mid-century velvet couch with mismatched cushions and a faux art-deco bronzed glass coffee table covered in annotated scripts.

"There's enough room, right? Ed's sleeping in the bedroom."

"Oh god, Chloe, I didn't realize he was here. Sorry, are we being too loud?" asked Belinda, concerned about Chloe's country singer/songwriter husband.

"Oh no! He sleeps like a rock. Lucky bastard. He's only here from Nashville for a few days—recording at night. The babies that never sleep are in the apartment next door with my mom and are probably on their second breakfast already. I haven't seen them yet. Can I get you guys coffee? There's a machine in this très chic kitchen."

"*YESSSS!* Oh, yes, please," yelped Belinda excitedly. "Thank *you*."

"Bels, come and chat while Jasper sets up." Belinda followed her into the compact, black-and-white Art Deco kitchen. She sat down at a small round marble table, watching Chloe wrestle comedically with a basic Nespresso machine, both boobs now fully exposed.

"How are you feeling about the Bebe Klein contract now? Better?"

"Oh, it's alright. I don't love the clothes, but the money was too much to turn down, and I know people will make it work. The campaign pictures came back okay. Better than expected. It was weird not having my stylist or publicity team there though. I probably should have asked to include for both of you to be in the contract, but you know how bad I am at making waves." She quickly moved on from the uncomfortable thought. "Now, Bels, tell me, are you okay? How is the dreadful Lara White? I heard she's presenting at the Oscars. Did you see Alma about your Janie Jones contract? Sorry, I didn't have time to text back any advice."

"Oh, it's okay. I probably shouldn't have asked you—I was in a panic. Honestly, it was a shocking meeting, the long and short of which is that I'm not sure I can afford to stay with Janie. Losing money is not really the point of working."

"Oh, I'm sorry. Alma is a terror. I almost left her years ago, but thankfully, I got some strict advice from an A-lister friend, who told me I could never leave, or she would destroy my career, Mafia-style, as she did with Chris Jackson. Once in, there is no out."

"Oh my god. Really? I've lost count of the number of articles I've seen about Chris Jackson and his spectacular downfall, but I don't think I once heard a mention of Alma?" They both shook their heads nervously, thinking of her.

"Why do you think I'm still at AARDA? Thankfully, I don't see her very much. It feels like Dustin is my agent at this point. I like the quotes he pretends she sends me. Listen to this one from yesterday." She pulled out her phone, scrolled down her emails, and pronounced dramatically: "*If life were predictable, it would cease to be life and be without flavor – Eleanor Roosevelt.*" She turned back to the coffee machine. "Oh shit, Belinda, I don't know how to use this thing. I only drink matcha. Can Jasper make the coffee?"

🔒 firethestylist.com

NEWSLETTER   *ABOUT*   *PRESS*   *CONTACT*

FIRE THE STYLIST

Dishing Daily Doses of Fashion Justice

JULIET HUNT leaving KOI
Restaurant, West Hollywood.

Posted February 23, 2018

Pretty Woman. Minus Richard Gere,' Nuff Said.

Side note—is Juliet Hunt ILL? 37-year-old #JHUNT is so WHITE. Where is her fabulous golden hue? Maybe she should borrow yet another private jet and take herself off to the now infamous yacht in Croatia, get a tan, and also tan the hide off her naughty, lady-loving BF?

What do you guys think? Should she HIRE a stylist?

As always, leave a comment below!

(To review our community guidelines, please click here)

> **@jonesisfire** She's amazing. You guys are just jealous bitches.

> **@mama2boyz** This Woman's Rainbow Foundation does so much for charity. Who cares what she wears? Get a real job

> **@loveislove69** It took me a few mins—had to look up Pretty Woman AND Richard Gere. LOL. Cool ref to an ancient classic movie! YOU NAILED IT!

> **@nonamerequired** what's wrong with simple form-fitting style? And how old are you guys? For that matter, who are you? How well would you hold up to your scrutiny? Interesting that you snark and snipe others but hide from judgment ☺ #hypocrites

> **@delilahdoesthings** THIRSTY and EXTRA

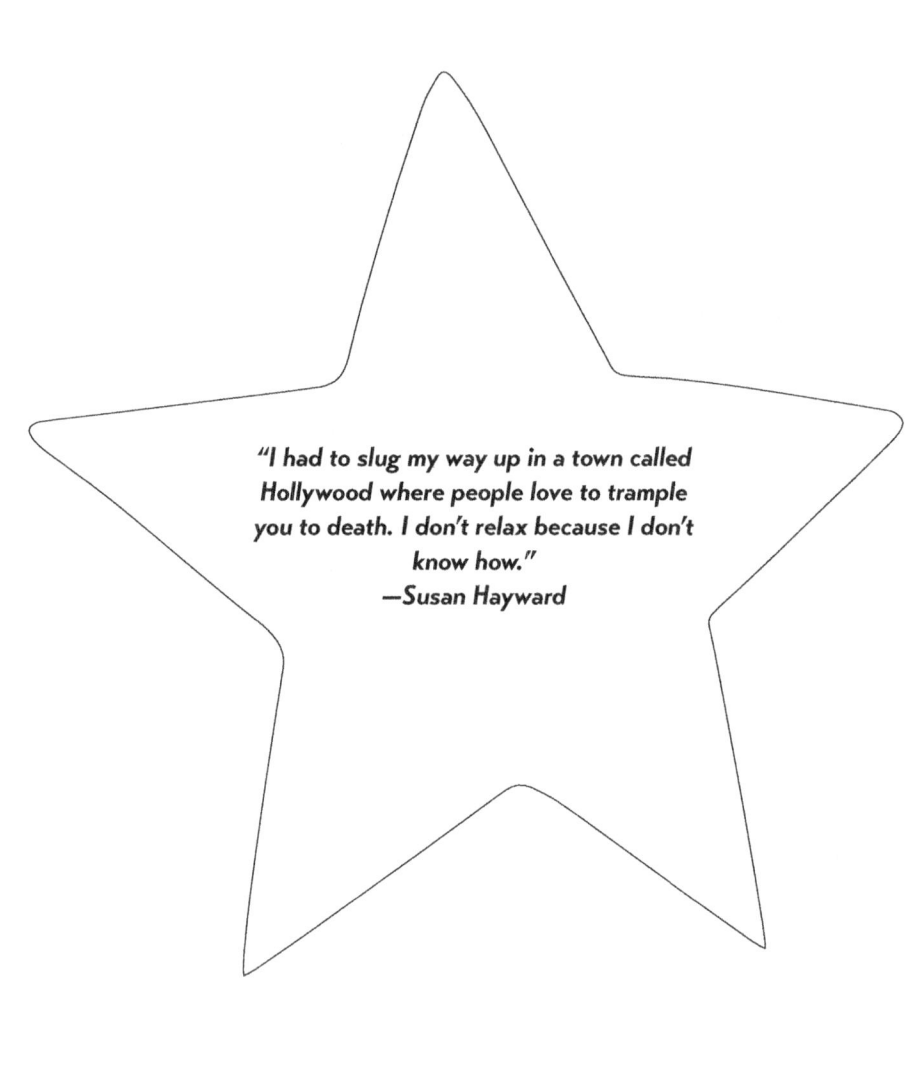

"I had to slug my way up in a town called Hollywood where people love to trample you to death. I don't relax because I don't know how."
—Susan Hayward

Tits & Terms

BELINDA, ASHEN-FACED, MARCHED ANXIOUSLY up and down her lounge—iPhone at her ear—praying out loud, "Pick up Jasper. *Please pick up.*"

"*My god*, lady. Do you realize you have called me three times in a row? Is your phone malfunctioning? I just dropped you off like ten minutes ago—can't a gay get a second to himself—"

"Alma's dead, Jas." Belinda cut him off. "Did you hear?"

"*WHAT THE FUCK*? Oh my god. Like dead dead? Not shocked in a good way, dead?"

"*Dead*, dead. Apparently, it happened last night."

"And how would I have heard?"

"Oh, come on, you hear everything."

"Well, this doesn't technically come under the usual celeb/fashion gossip umbrella, now does it? Hang on. You didn't kill her, did you? I know she wasn't your favorite, but that's a tad extreme."

"Jasper. *STOP*. I'm freaking out here."

"Sorry, too soon. I'll get a grip. How did *you* find out?"

"I just got off the phone with the cops. They left me a bunch of messages when we were with Chloe, which I ignored because I didn't recognize the number. They are coming over in a bit."

"Shit, gurl. Do you want me to come back? Moral support?"

Belinda sighed, sitting down on the couch. "I asked if they needed to talk to you, but no. Go have your breakfast break. I'll be okay. I mean, I didn't do anything wrong."

"How did she die?"

"They didn't say. Just that they believe I was the last person to see her."

"Well, the cost of some bras and a few hundy a month raise can't be considered a motive now, can it."

"Jasper! Fuck off and eat. I'm going to tell Rose the cops are coming. Man, she'll be pissed if they interrupt our lunch."

"Can't win no matter who you kill! Byeeeee."

Belinda laughed despite herself and, dropping the phone beside her, called out for her daughter.

★ ★ ★

An hour later Rose, not missing a beat of her TikTok dance, yelled, "*Mom, the door!*"

"Thanks, baby. Can you take the iPad and go to your room?"

"This lady who died, did you say she's the one who works with Lara? Will Lara still be in movies without her?"

"Yes, my darling."

"Oh YAY! *Thank god!* I love Lara!" Visibly relieved, Rose twirled around in her tie-dye tracksuit, adding, "But I don't like her poopy, biting dog; it ruined my life. Did you tell her never ever to bring it here again?" Not waiting for an answer, she slid her indignant 10-year-old body down the hallway into her room, only pausing to blow a kiss at her framed dad.

"Hi, detective," said Belinda, opening the door nervously, "please come in. C-can I get you coffee? Juice? Water?"

"Good morning, Ms. Grant, I'm Detective Hall, call me Cheryl, and that's my partner Detective Ortiz." She pointed at the figure pacing the cul-de-sac, yelling into her phone, "*The fuck you will, Pedro!*"

"Hmm, she might be a while. Let's just start. I don't need a drink, thank you. But where should we sit?"

"The couch is good?" asked Belinda, looking across the open-plan room at the worn teak dining room table entirely covered by a rainbow of clutches in every proportion and style. "Sorry about the mess, it's overspill from my office. Things are crazy this week."

"Yes, I gathered it's Oscar week. Which is kinda like Christmas week elsewhere? Is everything that happens this week blamed on Oscar week? So far, I've heard traffic, street closures, people's availability, and sanity. I'm just here from Boston, so it's all new. Anyways, let's sit. The couch is great."

"Ah, yes. We have our own unique calendar, detective. Oscar week, awards season, SAG awards, Critics Choice awards, pilot season, TCAs—Television Critics' Awards," Belinda added helpfully as they sat. "A new language for you to learn, like I once did," Belinda shook her head ruefully. "It was all terrifying and thrilling at first."

"Yes, it does feel a bit like I've landed on a different planet," agreed Cheryl. "Hopefully, these events won't be rife with crime, which brings me back to the case. Can you tell me everything you recall about your meeting with Alma Astley on Friday?"

★ ★ ★

FLASHBACK
Alma's office
Friday 23rd February. 5:40 pm

"Belinda. You are early! I said 6 pm!" Alma, standing by the corner of her desk sealing a large embossed Smythson envelope, was irritated. "Did you not get the message? Can you or your people not read emails?"

Belinda wavered in the doorway, smiling nervously. "Oh no, I-I-I didn't. I'm so terribly sorry, Alma. Oscar week is nuts, as you—well—obviously know. I will talk to my agent, Devon. Can I come back? S-s-should I wait outside?"

"No!" Alma set the envelope on the empty desk, walked around to her oversized white egg chair, and sat down. "You are here now. Just sit while

I check my email." Crossing her gazelle-like legs, Alma spun around out of sight.

Belinda, frozen by the arctic air conditioning, perched awkwardly on a metal art piece that doubled as a chair, mesmerized by the view of Alma's extraordinary breasts, as she was surely meant to be. Why else would that gigantic image be positioned there? Mind you, she mused enviously, if I had those tits, I'd wallpaper my house with them too. She briefly recalled stumbling into an early 2000s party Juergen Teller had thrown at a stripped-bare townhouse in London. Each of the four floors was fly-posted with his images of naked supermodels and the makeshift bar in the basement, was two claw footed bathtubs filled with sponsored vodka and ice.

Forcing herself back to the torturous present, she sat nervously rear-ranging her hands for what felt like a lifetime until, overcome by the piercing silence, she blurted out, "I l-l-love your office, Alma; it looks like an art gallery."

"Yes, Astrid Beyer did it." Alma's words rose, crisply audible from behind the chair. "You know her? Probably not. She did the Bick Gallery and Franck Zeger in New York. And once I found out that she put a drive-in car elevator in that building on 11th Avenue, I simply had to have her. It wasn't easy, but everyone has a price, and hers was Jeopardy. She, Alex, and I had dinner after one of the shows. Marvelous woman. Though she couldn't put a drive-in for me, damn Beverly Hills and their tiresome regulations. But I did, at least, get my mezzanine area with a private elevator down to my parking spot, so it wasn't a complete bust."

Belinda, enjoying this unexpected intimacy with the back of Alma's chair, turned and looked admiringly at the sculptural raw concrete stair-case, edged with an anthracite spiral rail that wound to the upper level. Alma spun back around, fixing her unblinking charcoal-rimmed eyes on Belinda, her narrow crimson mouth stern. "Now, let's get this over with." *Annnnd she's terrifying*, Belinda squealed inwardly, reflexively crossing her fingers and wondering if she too could rock a dirty, smudged eye remi-niscent of Kate Moss at 3 am.

Tapping her nude-manicured nails on the desk, Alma spoke in her clipped hybrid British accent, "Janie is uncomfortable with you bringing up money with her. She feels it was inappropriate of you to put her on the spot." Softening, she added, "Now I, my dear, understand this is your *profession*, and of course, you should be remunerated according to your *worth*, but the question is, what are you worth? More appropriately, perhaps, what is your *market* worth? Sell yourself to me, Belinda."

"Um, well, um, I'm sorry, I don't quite understand?" Belinda stumbled over her words. An atrocious negotiator at the best of times, she sat silenced by her tongue pretzeled to the roof of her mouth before eventually forcing out, "Um, well, Janie already agreed to a one thousand a month raise? I th-th-thought we were only discussing, you know, additional expenses?"

"Well, you are talking to ME now, Belinda, so humor me. We can get to expenses later."

"Okay, well, I asked for a raise on my retainer because it's been the same for seven years. The workload has quadrupled, and Janie doesn't pay for out-of-pocket expenses, which include tailoring, assistants, gas, dry cleaning, etc. Often, she needs red-carpet outfits twice a week. Occasionally, there's a studio or designer paying, but mostly not. She lives a two-hour round trip from Hollywood, and my assistant Jasper almost lives in Calabasas some weeks—between fittings and getting her ready. I'm losing money at this point and—"

"Belinda," Alma cut her off, "I asked you to sell yourself to me, not whine. Why do you deserve a raise? There must be so many others waiting in line behind you. My god, some would do it for free and be thrilled to have Janie on their resume. She does ad campaigns occasionally. Why, she has that limp dick one this month. You make money then, don't you? What have you brought to her career that any other fashion-obsessed person couldn't?" Alma fluttered her hands dismissively.

"Well, to be f-f-f-fair," Belinda stuttered, shocked at the blatant contempt for her career, "aside from all the hours it takes, I . . . I . . . I've curated a whole image for her for years. She is now an established red-carpet and street-style presence, which she was not before. The media impressions alone must be worth—"

"Media impressions!" Alma snorted dismissively. "Oh puh-lease, that's utter drivel." She paused to read something on her phone, which was pinging incessantly, her face darkening further until it became as frigid as the environment she presided over. "This week needs to end," she muttered, eyeing her brass Howard Miller grandfather clock.

"Well, Belinda, I've wasted seven minutes on your trivial matter." She paused and pressed a number on speed dial before scooping up her purse and walking briskly to the staircase, where she stopped and said urgently to the unknown person on the phone, "They're okay? Right, wait, please." She turned to Belinda. "At any rate, it's already been decided. Janie will give you a $500 raise per month. She is not willing to pay expenses. You decide. We need the contract signed ASAP. This one includes a non-disclosure. Dustin will facilitate." And with that, she disappeared up the concrete spiral stairs, leaving Belinda in silence, save for the receding sound of Alma's aggrieved voice and clacking Louboutins.

★ ★ ★

Belinda trembled at the memory and protectively hugged herself. "I was so shocked I ran out of her office and was waiting for the elevator when I realized I'd forgotten the contract. I saw it on the desk when I arrived. Dustin had stressed beforehand that it was there—and I was to take it—to remind her if necessary. I texted my assistant, Jasper, because he's friendly with Dustin—they used to bartend together at The Cock in WeHo. He got in touch with him, Dustin even answers his phone at Barry's Boot camp, who knew that was allowed? I was instructed to go back *very quietly*, grab it, and go." She started searching through her phone. "I've never done anything faster in my life, let me tell you. It's ludicrous to be 41 years old and that terrified of a work colleague. Here's the text conversation." She showed it to Cheryl. "I can screenshot and text it to you?"

Cheryl nodded and recited her number. "Thank you."

"Do you want to see the contract? It's in one of my tote bags. I'm not sure where it is—might still be in the car. I haven't had a day off for 23, possibly 24, days and I'm losing my mind."

"I don't need to now, but I'll let you know if that changes, okay?" Cheryl made a note.

Belinda nodded.

"So, what happened after that?"

"My phone rang, scaring the shit out of me, and I ran out of the office to the elevator. Jasper was waiting in the car, circling to avoid getting a ticket, so I was outside for a couple of minutes. I'm sure there must be cameras in that building, or could you track my phone? I got to eat dinner with my child that night, which almost made the *'only seven minutes' of Alma* worth it."

"Yes, the cameras show you leaving, so we won't need to check your phone for now. Lastly, did you see anyone else on the way out?"

"No, no one, just the security desk guys, I think. I was so upset. That woman has got dehumanizing down to an art form, and I wasn't paying attention, honestly."

"Okay, this all seems consistent with what we know so far. Thank you for your time. We'll be in touch, and if you think of anything else, you can text."

"Of course, no worries. Thank you!" Belinda closed the door, relaxing as she sighed with relief, "Hopefully, that's that." She smiled and headed towards Rose's bedroom, shouting, "Darling, get the globe out. Let's plan more of our European vacation!"

"Borrring, Mom!" Rose yelled. "We did that soooo many times my teacher Marie says I know more about Europe than she does." Rose skipped out of her room into the hallway. "I wanna see pictures of the Oscar dresses since, meanie—that's YOU—won't take me to work. Do you have any big diamonds I can try on? And I don't care that Daddy's in Greece, I still want pizza, I don't like Greece food, I wish he'd stayed in Italy, *he's a fucking loser!*"

"ROSE!" Belinda barked sharply, trying desperately to cover a snort of laughter. "Only swear in your bedroom! You know the rules! And even in your room, you shouldn't talk about him like that; he's your dad."

"Okay, Mommy, but I heard Paola say only deadbeats leave their kids for two years, and she's nice about EVERYONE."

*"Power doesn't corrupt people.
People corrupt power."*
—Unknown

Chewing It Over

RIDING IN CARS WITH DETECTIVES
Leaving the home of Belinda Grant. 11:55 am

ORTIZ SLOWLY PULLED AWAY from Belinda's succulent-heavy garden, popping cinnamon gum into her mouth and starting to chew noisily.

"Who's Pedro, and why'd he make you so mad?" Cheryl asked bluntly, genuinely curious about her partner and acutely aware she knew nothing yet. "Boyfriend?"

"Brother. And you eavesdropping, girl?"

"Of course! Shocking, what with me being a detective and all."

"Fair. He's my baby bro and he's fucking annoying. I'm a lesbian. And that's all you gettin' today."

"Sure," Cheryl replied, satisfied. "I'll get more tomorrow. But back to the case—whaddya think so far?"

"You'll get nuthin' else outta me if I find out you repeat my personal shit at the station, and, as for the case, as I predicted, they are all freaking crazy. Elephant shit coffee! I ain't never heard of anything so *loca*. But then again, now I know a bit more about how to contour," she nodded approvingly. "You reckon she'll give us those free samples?"

"Yeah, no." Cheryl shook her head mockingly. "Anyway, seems like Alma's pretty high profile, and the media is all over it. Upstairs are already up my newly arrived ass, so privilege says we gonna have to sideline every-thing and make this case number one."

"Color me shocked," Ortiz shrugged. "Welcome to Hollywood. Next, we gonna be interviewing those crazy actors? *I can't wait.* Get ready, girl." She spat her gum out into a tissue. "Hate gum when it loses its flavor—same way you gonna feel about celebrities real soon."

"Rumors aren't interested in the unsensational story; rumors don't care what's true."
—*John Irving*

Tantrums & Tulle

Juliet Hunt Photo Shoot
Milk Studios, Hollywood. 1 pm

BELINDA WAS STARING ABSENTMINDEDLY IN THE MIRROR, diffidently twirling a piece of her hair, when she heard their voices. "Only 45 minutes late," she whispered to Jasper, peeking around the door of the dressing room to watch Juliet march her snakeskin Saint Laurent platforms into the cavernous, bright white studio, tiny body wrapped in a men's toweling bathrobe, her haughty demeanor giving the bathroom basic the illusion of a mink. A slight girl in a worn Reebok sweatshirt was trailing immediately behind, hunched over a phone, tapping it desperately, pushing lifeless mousy hair out of her welling eyes and whispering, "Please work, oh god, *pleeease* work."

"*FOR FUCK'S SAKE*, Kara. Make. It. Work!" Juliet spat out, not turning around. "He's calling me in 30 minutes from the yacht in Croatia, and it better fucking work by then, goddamnit." Her voice switched to a girly whine. "Where's my *Daneee*?"

"Here, sweetie. Never fear," answered Daniel, his head, with its grey-rooted ombre-colored hair appearing through the door behind her, followed by his muscular, tattooed body. Belinda jerked her head out of sight as the group headed towards them. Daniel, who was wheeling monogrammed Gucci luggage, raised his voice a notch. "Juliet, thank *god* they organized these two shoots today in adjacent studios! Marco is a publicist extraordinaire, although how this stylist is going to top the exquisite Vanity Fair clothing selection from this morning, I do not know. Who's the stylist again, Marco?"

Marco, tanned, well-preserved, and clad in all-black Prada, was expertly switching between an android and an iPhone, replied without looking up, "Don't you people ever read call sheets? Belinda Grant."

Daniel cocked his head, eyes widening, as he stage-whispered, "*Alma!*"

Marco rolled his eyes. "Yes, I, too, heard that she was the last person to see Alma alive, but let's not dwell on that today. She is an excellent stylist, not to mention FEMME'S go-to Freelance Editor in LA. We will get this cover done and go home. I assume you all have lives? Now excuse me, guys, I have a situation in New York." Marco scanned the studio before striding to a black director's chair in the furthest corner and sitting down.

Daniel, glancing at Marco and assessing he was out of earshot, persisted cattily, "I know everything, you guys; nothing gets past MY salon. I hear Belinda's retainer renegotiation with Alma did *not* go well." He paused for dramatic effect and smiled smugly, "So *she* is so very lucky to be working with you today, Juliet, you perfect human. Imagine if she *did it*! Oh, what fun, being styled by a murderer? Dra-ama! *Pleeease* can I come to wardrobe with you to pick outfits, and *spy*?" His hand splayed out and flew excitedly to his chest. "Darhling, I simply must get the goss and, of course, be inspired about how to perfectly style your already-perfectly-styled hair."

"As I never stop telling you, darling, *my* hair is *your* hair, you perfect boy and, duh"—Juliet batted her lashes and wrinkled her famously altered nose—"*you*, the bestest gay pal a gal gets to have, can decide *all* the things I wear."

"Jesus. Did you hear that?" Belinda turned to Jasper, nauseated, the pupils of her hazel eyes dilated in shock.

"Yes, Bels, he's a nasty, reeking queen, I can smell his Tom Ford Noire Extreme from here. And best gay pal? Best employee, more like! Let's avoid them for as long as possible and grab a coffee in the cafe while they set up. We can split a Xanax."

"Can we leave the jewelry, though?"

"Honey, remember the armed guards from six jewelry houses stationed immediately outside the exit? These diamonds are in Fort Knox." He wrapped an arm around her protectively, swiftly guiding them towards the exit at the far end of the dressing room, admiring his work along the way; just an hour earlier, this room had been a white, soulless, empty cube, and it now resembled a mini-Neiman Marcus. Equidistantly spaced racks showcased the latest in haute couture: cascading white fringing, whimsical feathers, delicate pearl beading, intricate corsetry, and voluminous embroidered tulle. Perched on rudimentary shelving were countless shoes and show-stopping hats. Velvet jewelry trays housed diamonds worth more than their combined lifetime income. Jolting out of self-admiration, he grimaced, hearing Belinda mutter in shock. "*Murderer*? He really just called me a murderer?"

"Look, boo, Daniel's a nasty, botoxed queen. No one listens to him. Every client fired him when he got busted for selling celeb gossip to Together Weekly. That's why he's always available to the delightful Juliet. He doesn't have a choice, nor does she, after the abuse she's given hairdressers in this town."

"Oh, I remember now," Belinda recalled, "Didn't she, mid-tantrum, wrestle Jose's curling iron from his hand, give herself a second-degree burn and then attempt to sue *him*?"

Jasper nodded, his dark curls bouncing. "Exactly! It was thrown out of ambulance chaser court and got her a (long overdue) glam shadow ban. I think this current Juliet-Daniel work marriage is what Buddha would call '*Karma*.'" He pulled a foil package from his pocket and popped out a Xanax, biting off half and handing her the other. "Take this and try to ignore them. Also, you've got lippy on your teeth."

"Jesus, Jas, is there rehab for Xanax? Oh, fuck it, this isn't the week to go down that road." Belinda threw the half-pill in her mouth and swallowed it dry. "Let's also get them to put a shot of CBD in our coffee. And to think I could have spent the day with Rose instead of this shit."

"Well, my love, 'no' is not a word you're very familiar with."

Tell that to Rose," sighed Belinda. "She would not agree."

"You are just more scared of your agent than of Rose. Let's be honest: the world won't end if you don't do every FEMME cover, Bels. Why do you think they book you on all these bitches? Because you absorb the abuse and don't make a fucking fuss. Their Editors always do the nice ones—you ever noticed that? Maybe one day you'll give both of us time to detox from our cocktail of self-prescribed anxiety meds."

"Oh, fuck off, Jasper. Devon is the best agent in town and very persistent. If I start turning them down, they'll just hire someone else. And you are just as much of a workaholic as me. Don't pretend you aren't."

"Not true, Bels. I would love nothing more than to spend my days floating around Fire Island, sipping ice-cold Verve Rose in embellished kaftans. I could begin my remote crusade against overhead lighting and mullets while crocheting sweater vests for my four-legged rescued harem."

"Nope."

"*YES*," he nodded adamantly. "I do all this for *you*."

"No, you don't, Jasper. That's bullshit. Nobody lives for someone else. And if they do, it's their boundary issue." Belinda was getting agitated now. "God knows I have enough experience in that area."

"Well, you are welcome, bitch!" Jasper huffed, irritated. "And yes, our boundaries are all tangled like a cheap chain—but one that *you own*."

"Fuck Jasper, let's not take this out on each other, today is bad enough already."

"Yes MA'AM." He saluted resentfully, slid off his stool, marched his pert booty to the bathroom, and scrolled thirst traps on Instagram to calm down.

Ten minutes later, they slipped into the dressing room, medicated, caffeinated, and wordlessly back on the same team. They unobtrusively watched Juliet, who stood, personifying ennui, in front of the display of designer footwear. Daniel sashayed to her side, stiff leather pants creaking, draping his arm over her shoulder.

"What a sinewy old cat," Jasper muttered as Daniel asked loudly, "Whaddya think honey? Anything you likey? I'm positive FEMME magazine will want to gift their upcoming cover star something beautiful!" He looked expectantly at Belinda, who looked away, busy doing nothing with tiers of gossamer silk ruffles.

"Well, Danny"—Juliet systematically jabbed at different shoes—"got 'em. And those. Got those Gucci pumps in every color. Got similar but

Penny Lovell

better from Saint Laurent. Got those Balenciaga boots in Brunei—remember, Danny, when that Sultan loaned us his fabulous jet?"

"That gold, mirrored, mink-trimmed restroom, honey. Who could forget?"

"Got 'em in leopard. Ugh, I would never wear those. So many clunky crystals. And these?" she sneered at a cream pair of Saint Laurent boots, "Yuck, clunky and UGLY. What am I, a Midwestern white influencer?"

Juliet spun round and, spotting Belinda, looked her slowly up and down, assessing her Stella-for-Adidas black wide-leg track pants, chartreuse floral Gucci blouse, and silver Air Jordans.

"Well, hi, you must be the *stylist*? You certainly look like one. *Finally*, you are here. Do you have anything else? I'm so bored of these shoes already. No color, no print, so dull. You know what, let's look at the clothes. Hand me something. What is the Magazine asking me to wear? I assume *they* decide?" She smirked and dramatically shrugged the robe off her shoulders, letting it drop to the floor to reveal her naked, famously revered body.

"Tell me I can wear body makeup with these samples? I'm so tired of having to be white for this role. I told Steven so many times that drug addicts can have tans too—like they can afford sunscreen. But no, the director thinks he knows better." She rolled her celebrated green eyes. "Such a mistake, and Alma was no fucking help. God rest her soul."

"Amen," agreed Daniel, miming a cross and staring pointedly at Belinda.

Je-sus, Belinda thought, fixated on Juliet's hairless naked form, vaguely familiar but no longer instantly recognizable minus the deep golden spray tan, careful lighting, and photoshop. Speechless, she continued staring as Juliet turned back to the shoes to muse over a nude Givenchy bootie, revealing a fresh and angry hand-shaped bruise covering the entirety of one tiny butt cheek—so perfectly outlined it might have been painted on.

"Um, hi Juliet, yes, I'm the stylist. I'm Belinda, and this is Jasper, who works with me. And, to answer your questions, this is a spring cover, and Sarah, the Editor-in-Chief, wants you to be in white couture pieces. It's a big trend from the recent couture runways. I know your team approved this. And although FEMME requires Chanel, Henri LeRoque, or Dior on the cover for advertising reasons, there is plenty for *us* to choose from." Belinda paused, realizing she was nervous, and her voice was becoming shrill. She took it down two octaves and continued, "I'm sorry, but we can't use body makeup. It can potentially destroy the pieces, and they are straight off the Paris runway, thousands of hours of work, and worth hundreds of thousands of dollars." Belinda smiled beseechingly at Juliet. "But with your pale skin, all white will be really modern, so edgy, and very FEMME." She spun to point at a look: "Jasper, can you hand me the velvet and metal sculpted tutu from Dior. It has matching white tights and opera gloves, it's so *strong*. *And* no one has seen you this way before."

"I agree!" Marilyn, the makeup-free makeup artist, chimed in, "Virginie only allowed natural skin at Chanel this season; all the white models were so pale. No blush, just a bold brow, gorgeous skin, and a screaming red lip. It's beyond chic and really on trend."

"The *red lip*! I've been dying to tell you how much I loved what you did with Jacinta for The Gilded Orbs, Marilyn," enthused Jasper, blowing her a kiss. "Divine. Everyone is raving about how it iconically offset her tangerine Dior."

Juliet, agitated at hearing the name of another actress, cocked her head and screamed, "*MARCO!*" at the dressing room door.

Marco appeared within seconds. "Yes, Juliet?"

"No body makeup, Marco? What in the actual FUCK?"

"Juliet, I told you, just like Vanity Fair this morning, they'll retouch to your 'normal' skin tone in post, and we have photo approval for this. It's not a big deal. Hi Belinda, Marilyn, Jasper."

"Well, it is to *me*. I need to feel myself, *TO BE MYSELF*" she yelled as he reversed out smoothly.

"It's called acting, Juliet!" Marcos's words wafted back into the hostile dressing room.

Wow! Fifteen love Marco! Thought Belinda as Jasper mouthed, "*Love him!*"

Longtime experts at dodging the eye of celebrity tantrums, the room got to work focusing on pretend tasks at hand. Belinda and Jasper turned to the racks and shuffled through the clothes. Marilyn looked intently at shades of red lipstick, and even Daniel started to clean a brush. They remained this way until the silence was violently broken by a phone ringing at full volume. Hiding in a corner, Kara jumped in shock, watching in horror as Juliet's vibrating, Prada-encased iPhone tumbled from her shaking hands and bounced on the concrete, leaving shards of broken crystal glittering around her Chucks.

"*OY! FUCKING FUCK!*" screamed Juliet, striding to Kara, naked. "You'll pay for that!" She plunged into an expertly executed forward fold and scooped up her phone. (Jasper, behind her—perfectly positioned for the front row seat to her vulva—squeezed his eyes shut, desperately trying to strike the memory.) Stabbing the green button, Juliet took a deep breath, and squealed in high-pitched saccharine, "*ARE YOU THERE*, my sexy Popppa? Oh, *THANK GOD*. I miss you so much. Baby girl needs you to come home soooon—No, I miss you more, I *neeeed* you Poppa, I can't *breathe*, your sweetie needs some discipline from her daddy—*Poppa*? POPPA? Oh, my fucking god Kara"—Juliet turned and hurled the phone at her assistant, narrowly missing her ear—"it's stopped working again. What the fuck is wrong with you? You are a clumsy, nervous *IDIOT*! I don't ask for much, just that my *shit works*. Why did I fucking hire you? Did your parents pay Columbia for that degree you say you have? You are so fucking worthless!"

She turned and paused, noticing for the first time the palpable shock in the air and the sympathetic looks surreptitiously aimed in Kara's direction. Taking a deep, dramatic breath, she tugged her robe back on and changed tack. "Oh, *sweetie*, I'm sorry. Really sorry. You know how much I miss my big boy Poppa, and it just drives me crazy not to hear his voice. You understand, right, Kara? You know me *so* well. It's just something I can't help. Forgive me, baby. I told you my aura still isn't cleansed from my relationship with my daddy, and it overtakes me sometimes. Tell me you forgive me, Kara? You forgive me, *right*?" She glanced around to confirm everyone was listening. "I tell you what—to make it up to you—I'll invite your mom to my foundation's Oscar night party. Also, you can have that monogrammed Gucci bag they sent yesterday. You can paint over my initials. Okay? Are we good? If it makes you feel better, you can take a few minutes in the restroom to cover your red eyes. Marilyn must have concealer for your tone."

Crouched down, still scooping broken crystals with trembling bare hands, Kara nodded without looking up, her face flushing crimson. Then she stood and bolted from the room, leaving a trail of glittering shards in her wake.

Juliet pouted and turned to Marco, who'd entered the room silently during her meltdown. "Oh, this is too much for me. Why do you *force* me to do this stuff? It's sooo hard, and I'm so tired! Look what it makes me do." She gestured to the door Kara had just exited. "I had to pretend to OD like 20 times this week; Steven is *a monster*, and now this grind on the weekend. If only the world knew what it takes to be me."

Marco, sitting in the makeup chair, stopped writing emails and looked up. "Juliet, I know you are busy, and Steven's movie is a challenging and draining topic, but shooting two top magazine covers in one day is excellent publicity for both you and 'Woke Queen'—a movie which, I might add, you are also producing. If you think about it, you contracted yourself to do this press." Unperturbed, he returned to his phones, silent and focused within his invisible office.

Hiding behind a rack listening, Jasper grabbed a Valentino white tulle skirt, placed it on his head, and whispered to Belinda, "I want to marry him!"

Belinda, grinning, selected a Stephen Jones pearl-trimmed floral fascinator and held it reverently at her chest with both hands like a bouquet, mouthing, "*Same!*"

"Oh fine, Marco, you win," Juliet pouted sullenly. "But I need a break. I'm going to nap in the talent suite for 30 minutes. Daniel, just work out with *her*"—she pointed at Belinda—"what I should wear. You know me so well, and I am over it. Also, Marco, make sure *they*"—she gestured carelessly around the room—"have signed NDAs."

"I think that every religion says to love your neighbor. In Hollywood, they add, but don't get caught."
—Anita Ekberg

Mad & Muted

RIDING IN CARS WITH STYLISTS
Leaving Milk Studios. Hollywood. 7 pm

JASPER PLACED THE LAST OF THE GARMENT BAGS in the trunk of his white VW Atlas—which ensured he could no longer see a single thing from the rearview mirror—before climbing wearily into the driver's seat. Belinda sat bolt upright, cross-legged in the passenger seat, making room for the multiple bags squashed below and behind her.

"Well, that was not fun!" said Jasper, starting the engine and swigging leftover coffee from a Coffee Bean cup. "And I can't even sit here and gossip about Vapid Barbie's hideous white, pimply, kink-games ass and her fucking weird-ass relationship with that Gucci devoted hairdresser. You will just have to do it for me bitch. How come *you* didn't have to sign an NDA?"

"I dunno, Jas. Maybe because I run a—*CLASSY OPERATION*," they both yelled in unison, laughing at Jasper's custom-made gold-embossed sign, which was just visible on the dash. "But no wonder she doesn't want anyone to talk. That bruise looked very fresh to me. Hasn't 'Poppa' been on that yacht for a couple of weeks?"

"You're right! How did I miss that? They obviously aren't doing any ass-play on FaceTime. But, oops, I should shut it, signed NDA and all. In my world, NDA—'no dicks attached'—is *way* more friendly" he sighed, "Okay, spill the tea, what does your super-agent have to say about them?"

"Devon said it's rare they ask personal stylists to sign since we are the proprietors of our business or something. I wasn't really paying attention. I do remember him saying that they are occasionally required for the paranoid ones or those experiencing rampant tabloid abuse."

"*Janie!*" they both asserted, thinking of their neurotic action star client, who routinely dated famous men. Marriages (theirs or hers) never seemingly getting in the way.

"But I've never been asked to sign one for her until Alma yesterday. Oh god, Alma, I've been trying to forget about her all afternoon. You don't think anybody believes I, you know . . ." Belinda's face paled, thinking of the speed of Hollywood gossip. "You don't think it will be a thing, right, Jas?" Adding hopefully, "The police were cool."

Discreetly crossing his fingers, Jasper replied, "Of course not. Jeez, honey, everyone knows you. You're a pussy. A yes person, no offense, but you are. Who else would take on as many clients as you and keep the permanently ungrateful almost pleased? You can't even get mad at your ex, who abused the shizzazzle out of you and then fucked off to get his selfish kicks. *You*, murder? God knows I wish you would sometimes, but what a fucking joke of a rumor—no one in their right mind could possibly believe it!" He pushed back his next thought, *but is anyone in this biz in their right mind?*

Belinda, clinging onto this seed of hope, shot back, "Well, fuck you, 'Mr- I secretly wanna be a designer and hide in my apartment sewing incredible pieces of art that will never see the light of day.' I'm not the only pussy around here."

"Yeah, let's not do me right now, bitch, and we shouldn't say pussy anymore. Getting back to work. Emily, bless that angel, said the Lanvin suit fits perfectly and that we do not need to go to her to button up a blouse tomorrow. So tick that one off the list. The Oscar fitting with Janie is late afternoon Wednesday at the Calabasas Estate, and, before you ask—I tried to get her to come to our office, NOPE. So now Wednesday is nuts. We have Caroline in Brentwood before her, and Janie will take HOURS.

Just an FYI, her whole team is coming to weigh in. Why don't we go full American Idol and bring them scoring cards?"

He swerved around a slow-moving weaving Prius, yelling, "*WE DON'T ALL HAVE ALL FUCKING DAY,*" at the driver, who was on her phone, applying lipstick. "*AND THAT'S A TERRIBLE COLOR FOR YOU.*"

"Jasper, she can hear you! Your window's open."

"So? Someone should tell her." He sped up and ran a red light.

"Now be sure to take a picture of your child to remember what she looks like this week, and make sure Paola has an overnight bag on standby. Shall I text her?"

"No, it's okay, I'll remember. Do you think Rose is gonna start calling Paola mommy?"

"Probably. And do not forget like last time. We can't have her at fittings this week, being beautifully honest with people. The 'Rose with Lara's rabid dog' incident was a nail-biter."

Belinda smiled proudly. "Toto decapitated Barbie, deflowered Kit, then peed on Ken. She was well within her rights to banish that dog to the garden and tell Lara to train his over-groomed arse. Let's be honest, she could teach both of us a thing or two about balls or, more accurately, vaginas. Anyway, changing the subject completely, I can't believe Janie's divorce is still going on! It's been even longer than mine!"

"Oh yeah, well, who can blame her for dragging it out with *that* living arrangement? Who wouldn't want to live in small, gated country inside Calabasas. Oh, just fyi, they said this fitting will be back in the ballroom."

"Really? She must have gotten rid of the ice rink then. She couldn't have got the Kristi Yamaguchi role."

"Err, maybe because—spray tan aside—she's white?"

FIRE THE STYLIST
Dishing Daily Doses of Fashion Justice

JASON BIRD Walk of Shame.

Posted on February 24, 2018

The internet has been polarized by the announcement of Jason Bird as Locust Man in the next installment of the comic book franchise. Love or hate him, he will be in charge of the upcoming swarming! And here he is, Firers, in, WELL, suspicious circumstances, caught leaving an unknown house in East Hollywood at 5 am yesterday. To be fair, this must be his previous evening's outfit, so it would explain why it's a little rumpled and why his handsome face looks so—dare we say this about a man?—haggard.

We couldn't BEGIN to speculate what this **married** man was doing in the wee small hours, but his attire does leave something to be desired… He may be wearing $750 hand-graffitied jeans, $550 Lanvin leather sneakers, and a priceless, one-of-a-kind Saint Laurent cashmere sweater (which—forgive us if this was a style choice—seems to be inside out), but he still looks 'homeless-adjacent.' No wonder the meme about 'each generation getting the Locust Man they deserve' is trending. What do you think, Firers? *Is there trouble in his pants again?*

As always, leave comments below!

> **@proudmotherofboys** does he have a gut or is that just the sweater? He's gonna need to start working out if he wants to command those grasshoppers
>
> **@chilychiken** the only thing I see swarming is his trouser snake
>
> **@fembotwoke** so we can only age shame women then? Equality loses yet again
>
> **@mamatojacee @fembotwoke** nobody should be calling anyone haggard, if you were woke you would know this, but you are probably just a bot
>
> **@bear** love a man with meat

Busy Saying Nothing

Re: COCOTTE 48-hour Lip Stain/WORLDWIDE AD CAMPAIGN FEATURING LARA WHITE.

> From: Devon Dalton Devon@stylistsonly.agency
> To: Belinda Grant Belinda@BGstyle.com
> Cc: Jasper DLC Jasper@BGstyle.com
> Date: Feb 24, 2018 at 7:45 pm
> 🔒 Standard encryption (TLS)
>   Learn more

Belinda and Jasper,

See wardrobe notes below.

Please confirm receipt. They want to set up a Zoom with you and their team. When do you have an hour to spare?

Let me know ASAP.

Thanks, Devon

————————Forwarded message————————

Please ensure Belinda knows the wardrobe instructions below from Jana, our Creative Director. Let us know when she can shoot over a presentation of the items she is suggesting. Heads up, we are looking for her to pull about <u>six</u> racks.

Thank you.

Jose B
Senior Art Director
artproductionsNYC

*After speaking with Lara, we can confirm the featured lip colors will range from bright red to dark burgundy. As such, the wardrobe palette is revised to **ONLY** white or off-white/very pale cream.

*We will **ONLY** be shooting her from the waist up. The goal is for her to be *'everywoman'* in a top that is *casual* yet *dressy. Interesting* yet *simple. Aspirational* yet *relatable.*

Please follow the **'COCOTTE'** guidelines below.

***We need to see skin**. But this ad is running in all territories and, as such, it is imperative **that the top feels season-less**.

No long sleeves (too winter), no summer straps (too summer)

No cap sleeves (too summer)

No scoop necklines (Lara finds them uncomplimentary)

No V-necks (our CEO feels they are too casual)

No turtlenecks (too winter/no skin)

No buttons, trim, or detailing

No sophisticated fabrics - silk knits, etc

No sporty styles/textures

Yes to subtle texture in the fabric (but not overtly visible)

Yes to aspirational fabric (better than regular cotton knit)

We will circle back with any additional instructions after we see images of Belinda's suggestions. **Dropbox** is preferable for us.

Lastly, Lara has requested complimentary pants and heels. Per Lara: *"The shoes must be high for posture but comfortable like sneakers."* (These items will **NOT** be seen in the final product, but we want to ensure she is comfortable and happy while shooting.) We do not want to waste much budget on this, but as Lara does **not** wear fast fashion (as

I'm sure Belinda is aware) perhaps she could loan these items from acceptable designers?

Thanks all.

Best

Jana

SUNDAY 25TH FEBRUARY 2018

"The CEO knew cocks were bad for business. Breasts she could get away with. Women knew their place, but with men, it wasn't as simple."
—Sarai Walker, Dietland

A Wandering Wanger

JASON BIRD, STARS & US MAGAZINE PHOTOSHOOT
Venice Beach studio of Dan Daniels. 9:45 am

"WELL . . . GOOD MORNING. HAVE WE MET BEFORE?" Jason, stroking Belinda's hand softly, tilted his head, and gazed at her intently with his deep-set Oscar-winning brown eyes.

"Morn—"

"Did we *fuck*?"

"What? *No*, Jesus. *NO!*" Belinda replied, recoiling.

"Shame." Jason shrugged lazily. "Well, we got all day." He ambled away laughing as Dan, Leica in one hand, joined him and slapped his back with his other. "Atta boy."

Belinda, discombobulated and momentarily frozen, stood gaping in the center of the drafty studio before bolting to the makeshift dressing area—a corner of the room sectioned off by grubby temporary partitions. She found Jasper on his knees, scrubbing the floor with paper towels.

"Freakin' filthy in here, Bels. Can't put these beautiful items on dirt."

"You mean shoes on the floor? And come on, it's more like dust—"

"Dirt, dust, it's all the same. These sartorial works of art deserve better, and what if something falls on the floor?"

"Sure Jas, you do you, but while you were in here obsessing over the hygiene of designer accessories. I was over there gettin' sexually harassed by an Oscar winner."

"WHAT? Already? Jesus, he got here and got straight to it. No time like the present for the sexual harasser—is he trying to up his anti?" Despite herself, Belinda let out a giggle, which, she reconciled, was better than raging, or crying.

"You gonna tell anyone about it?" He looked at her sympathetically, already knowing the answer.

"That's rhetorical, right? Like, who would I tell? As if anyone would give a shit, and even if they wanted to, he makes too much money, for too many people, for anyone to act on it." Jasper nodded agreement, stifling a wave of shame at their tacit compliance with the system.

"Anyway, I could do without any more rumors this weekend. Besides, I'm almost used to it these days." Her mind wandered backward. "It was way worse when I was styling in New York. Every other 'business meeting' with a photographer turned out to be a handsy date I'd accepted only in their minds. This is nothing."

She turned, shuddering on hearing Dan yell, "Hey Bel, we're going to grab a beer in the kitchen and talk about the photo setups. Bring us some outfit options to choose from, let's show off his muscles, get in as much fun stuff as possible before the—his clammy fingers made inverted commas—'happy family' pics later. I wanna start with hot single shots, oil him up, light the shit of him. You know the drill: six-pack images that make all the girlies and gay boys wet. I know you got this, babe. Send in makeup when they get here. They are LATE."

"Remember I'm *vegan*,' sweetheart," Jason yelled as they disappeared from sight. "Well, my old lady thinks I am, and gotta keep the hormonal baby-mama happy."

Jasper, unusually stern, turned to Belinda. "Since we have to stay here and do this shitty shoot, which quite frankly is *beneath* us, then *I'm* going dress that dick, and I'm going to be the one watching him on set. You are not to go near him until his, ahem, 'wife' gets here, okay? And that's an order."

Fuck, this is gonna be a nightmare, Belinda thought, groaning as she anticipated the passive-aggressive tantrums of an abuser denied today's choice of sexual toy, but saluted Jasper in agreement.

The studio door crashed open, and a towering, flustered blonde flew into the room. They watched as she shrugged off her Max Mara teddy bear coat and dumped her phone, car keys, reusable coffee cup, and massive monogrammed Louis Vuitton tote onto the worn studio couch.

"Erin, remember? A publicist from Marco's office," Belinda mouthed to Jasper.

"BEL! Thank god you are here. Morning Westside traffic is a *disaster*. I hate coming over here. How are you? You got my list of designers preferable for Jason? Which ones are here? You have vegan options, of course? Now, *technically*, he's vegan—but *practically*, we can use some leather shoes and belts. Just don't credit them, okay? How is Jason supposed to maintain his image in a world that just doesn't cater properly to high-end male vegans? It's really unacceptable when you think about it. Don't even show him any cheap shoes. I know we told you to bring some, but he flipped out on another shoot yesterday when he saw a Target bag. Now, how are *you*? Oooh, is that the new wait-listed Bebe Klein bag? AMAZE. Stylists are soooo lucky. How's the baby?"

"Well, she's ten," Belinda sighed—watching Jasper pick up the Kohl's bags and hide them behind the rack—and cursed Devon for persuading her to work with this asshole on a Sunday. Plastering on a smile, she turned back to Erin, who remained breathlessly babbling before her.

"So great you could do this, especially since, you know—she lowered her voice—the 'Alma business.' You have to tell me all later . . . And I know the budget today is, well, zero, but you will love him, he is so charming, and maybe he'll hire you to style a press tour. One thing, though, he has, well"—she cleared her throat awkwardly and whispered, almost proudly—"an oversized penis. So, can you make sure the pants aren't too tight and *it's* not too prominent? Keep a close eye on *it* while we shoot. It is Stars & Us magazine, after all, not GQ. Anyway, I always like to get that out of the way quickly." Belinda stared at Erin's sweaty, blushing face as she plowed on. "Did he arrive yet? Has Dan approved any looks? I should see them too. I just can't stand being late—don't tell Marco—he will KILL me."

Belinda, struggling between the revolting vision of Jason's jumbo cock and the whopper about his alleged charm, took a second to register Erin's silence and quizzical expression. "Oh yes, sorry, he is here, he's in the kitchen with Dan having a beer—"

"*What? Shit, shit, shit, NO!* He's supposed to be *SOBER!*" Erin yelped at a beeping noise, "Jesus, my blood pressure's at 170 already, and it's not even 10 am." Shaking her head, she grabbed her purse and marched toward the kitchen in ubiquitous Aldo suede boots. "Jason darling, I'm here . . ."

Belinda, watching her leave, barely noticed Jasper's arm curling around her shoulders.

"Do we think she's infatuated with him Bels? Cuz Erin is defo wearing rose-tinted glasses for the love blind. And don't worry, I'll be happy to keep an eye on his wandering wanger. So refreshing to get a decisive work directive."

Stars & Us Magazine

SUBSCRIBE

CELEBRITY > BREAKING GOSSIP

DOUBLE CUMMER!
Juliet Hunt's SCALDING HOT BF of six months, Eduardo Quiroz, has been caught today en flagrante with sizzling supermodel Caslina Cummer (20) off the coast of Croatia.

By **Danny Wood**
Published on Sunday February 25th, 2018 11:20 am PST.

The pair were first spotted yesterday aboard the infamous luxury yacht of a certain notorious Russian oligarch. *'Friends'* we initially thought—after all, beautiful men and women can be platonic; it's 2018 people! But this morning, our trusty Stars & Us drone caught the two swapping spit before strip-teasing for an ardent skinny dip. This soon-to-be lucrative sex tape culminated in X-rated, steamy (ahem) 'exercise' on the deck. Evidentially, the two find each other irresistible, and their collective bronzed beauty is blistering.

What says Ms. Hunt (37) of this transgression? Are they broken up? Open? What we wouldn't give to be a fly on the wall of her glass house right now! Calls to her publicist and Ms. Cummer's model agency have not been returned as of posting, but *stay tuned...*

In the meantime, grab yourself some ice and click here for a fiery taster.

> **@huntinghunt** OMG. What an asshole. I mean as a person. Not complimenting his real one. Man, this video is revealing

> **@chicsluvme** Maybe the two lady hotties can oil up and fight it out for a pay-per-view sequel. WHOA! 🌙

> **@alphasingleguy** dudes getting bitch slapped by two chicks. Idiot

RELATED: Juliet Hunt and her (alleged) plastic surgery journey. A Beverly Hills surgeon claims: "You too can climb from a 7 to a 10!"

Caslina Cummer - turning 18! Her overnight journey from teasing teen to legal dream!

"Sometimes you find yourself in the middle of nowhere, and sometimes, in the middle of nowhere, you find yourself."
—Unknown

Safe House

CHERYL STOOD AT THE ENTRANCE to a cavernous bowling alley, momentarily startled by the dirty black carpet printed with neon pink bowling pins tumbling haphazardly into one another and lit by migraine-inducing ceiling panels. She laughed, hearing Ortiz, behind her, mutter, "*Jeeze, this is subtle.*"

They scanned the room, observing its schizophrenic nature: one side showcased twelve gleaming bowling alleys, the action from which was reflected in meticulously polished and angled mirrors. Cheryl noted that they covered the entire perimeter, ensuring, in case there was any doubt, that the always-visible bowling was the only star. On the other side was a tired bar area featuring a crumbling darts board and stained pool table. Wood laminate tables with mismatched plastic chairs were scattered carelessly, and a faux marble counter hosted patched-up barstools and Budweiser on tap. Not one cell of Cheryl's brain could imagine the Alma Astley people described here.

Not open until noon, the place was unnaturally silent and empty aside from one greying woman sitting behind a curved counter in a faded pink shirt, guarding stacked identical used shoes. Above her, hanging on chains from the ceiling and swaying to the rhythm of the A/C, was a pink, fluorescent tube sign announcing Van Nuys Bowl. Cheryl approached and sniffed but couldn't discern the expected odor of feet. She surmised that people in LA probably had more fragrant, aired-out feet. Holding up her badge, she said. "Good morning, are you June? I'm Detective Cheryl Hall, and this is Detective Ortiz. We spoke yesterday."

"Yeah. That's me! So, you are here about Alma—who was it again?"

"Astley."

"Well, I don't know an Alma Astley, but we have an Anna Applegate on our team, who sounds a little like your description."

"Is this her?" Cheryl pulled up a picture of Alma on her phone, striking an imposing pose at the 2017 Gilded Orbs.

"Hmmm, maybe it looks a bit like her?" said June, squinting at the phone dubiously, "but younger? I never seen our Anna with a scrap of makeup, and she always had that baseball cap on. Why would she be at something so fancy? Did something happen to her? Jesus, I hope not. She's our regular five-bagger, *never* does any sandbagging, and her angle of entry is bloody perfection." Seeing Cheryl look at her questioningly, she explained, "Ahh, sorry, detective, it's bowling lingo."

"I'm very sorry to have to tell you this, June, but the woman you know as Anna Applegate was actually Alma Astley, the CEO of AARDA, a primary talent agency in Hollywood. She was found dead yesterday in Beverly Hills, and we are here because she was wearing a Van Nuys bowling team outfit when her body was found."

"Oh, it can't be her," June shook her head. "Anna's a babysitter for spoilt, rich kids. She hates it, but the hourly's good, so, you know, she stays. We all gotta work ain't we? Mind you, those kids must be getting on now; she's been at the same place since I met her. The stories she tells us of their batshit tantrums, we freakin' love it when Anna rants about work. She's real funny."

Ortiz nodded to encourage her to continue. "Her husband Jamie is a chauffeur for some fancy crazy woman—temperamental powerful career sort and always at events at night. It's why he couldn't ever come and watch us, even when we won the local championship! He's quite a bit younger than her—*atta girl*. Still, I felt for her. It's good to have some

Penny Lovell

support, isn't it?" Both detectives nodded, and June sighed wistfully. "Her first husband was an asshole and rapey. She misses that son of hers in the UK so much. Talks about him all the time—she really wishes her dad could have been alive to bowl with him."

"Anyway, come this way, I'll show you the team photo. That might help, right?"

She guided them to a wall of speckless photos in faux gold frames and pointed at the most recent. A group of women proudly smiling and pumping their fists, Alma front and center holding a trophy, beaming from ear to ear.

"That's her"—June pointed—"can't be the same person, can it? Surely not? Mind you, she didn't make the match yesterday, which is *not* like her. We had to do her a blind score. *Oh god.* Is it her?" Her voice broke. 'She's been coming here for years. Every week 'cept when she goes on those little vacations to Cannes and Venice and somewhere in Canada, Toronto? She said they kept the marriage alive and made looking after the brats more bearable. She went at the same time every year." June paused, her crumpled face registering shock. "Oh my god, it's her, isn't it? Ohh, *noooo!*"

She dissolved into tears, Ortiz handing her a tissue, guided her to a beaten-up armchair where grasping onto a furry pink bowling ball cushion, she sobbed noisily, eventually regaining enough composure to ask in a muffled voice, "Oh my god, I just can't believe it. Is she . . . *really English?*"

Cheryl nodded sympathetically. "Yes, she is, and actually, June, despite the pseudonym, I was thinking how you might know more about the real Alma than most."

FIRE THE STYLIST

Dishing Daily Doses of Fashion Justice

Chic Feminist Emily de Vries at ACLU Fundraiser, Los Angeles.

Posted on February 25, 2018

Highly regarded feminist and UNICEF ambassador Emily de Vries (45), seen tonight in head-to-toe Lanvin, hosting a well-attended ACLU fundraiser at her chic Laurel Canyon home. The recent flurry of tabloid interest in her plastic surgery and questions about her sexuality have seemingly not dented her serene demeanor nor affected her exemplary style.

That said, one could argue that navy is a boring color and that having her spectacular blonde locks confined in a French twist is aging, but Firers, this is a serious and smart lady doing earnest things. A prominent supporter of the ACLU (American Civil Liberties Union), she is one of the few female Hollywood stars whose career seems enhanced by her vocal feminist tendencies and far-left political views. We reached out to her stylist, Belinda Grant—asking about the inspiration behind the look: navy-blue shantung pantsuit over a ruffled cream silk blouse; and the minimal accessories: pavé Diamond studs and a slim platinum wedding band—but had heard nothing back by the time of posting.

Anyway, non-responsive stylists aside, we love this choice. Once again, Emily proves activists too can be chic and aspirational, her bold choice of an unsexy silver ballet pump reminding us that comfort is a feminist issue.

Will she take it from the screen and be president in real life one day? Who knows, dear Firers, but an Oscar in the Oval Office would be quite the trophy. What say you, firers? Is she passé or perfect?

As always, leave comments below!

(To review our community guidelines, please click here)

@justice4all I love how she uses her blockbuster reputation for good

@wifeymama She is a goddess. She washes dishes at my local soup kitchen all the time. Nobody recognizes her and she clearly wants it that way. The world needs more Emilys

@7777321yay That couch clearly cost more than my rent for a year. Performative bullshit

@redordead So she's raising money so nazis can speak freely. Go away libtard.

@paris4life This is a fashion site guys. Let's stay on point. The suit is beautifully cut, and no one wears clothes better.

@fempower111 But WHYYYYYY silver shoes? Of course, Belinda didn't comment how could she explain this choice?

@Loveistheanswer She should stay in her lane and stick to lousy acting. She just played a politician, is she confused that she is one?

@Cosplayaway @loveistheanswer Actually, she spent three months interning in DC for that role, so she's more of a politician than you are. She deserved that Oscar. Do your research boomer.

@Lenaloveslittlelenny I hope Zara knocks this look off! I would have to live in it (literally) to afford it

@USA4eva 🇺🇸 LIBTARD CUCK

Styling for a Song

Re: Lara White/Celebs for Changing Climate Change

    From: Devon Dalton Devon@stylistsonly.agency
    To: Belinda Grant Belinda@BGstyle.com
    Cc: Jasper DLC Jasper@BGstyle.com
    Date: Feb 25, 2018 at 6:18 pm
    🔒 Standard encryption (TLS)
    Learn more

Hi guys!

See below email from Marco re Lara. Sorry, you are gonna have to dress her for free. I am attempting to see if we can get an assistant rate paid by her. But no promises. (Remember you will earn BIG COCOTTE money because of Lara—KER CHING!)

—————————Forwarded message—————--

Hi Devon,

Lara is participating in the virtual song-a-thong organized by Brandon Loopner to raise awareness for climate change. The song she will be singing is '*Beautiful World*' by Coldplay. Since this is a cause Belinda supports, Lara is hopeful she will be willing to donate her time. (We understand she regularly posts about climate activism on her private Instagram.)

If so, Lara is requesting that the selection of looks be 100% sustainable and that Belinda's team check (and provide certification) in terms of -

-fabric sourcing

-factories used (must be green and pay a living wage)

-carbon footprint of each item

-compostable

The event is airing live in 10 days: March 6, time TBD.

Will leave it to Jasper and Lara's assistant, Kelly, to schedule fitting as convenient. Thanks.

Marco.

Re:Re: Lara White/Celebs for Changing Climate Change

> From: Belinda Grant Belinda@BGstyle.com
> To: Devon Dalton Devon@stylistsonly.agency
> Cc: Jasper DLC Jasper@BGstyle.com
> Date: Feb 25, 2018 at 6:27 pm
> 🔒 Standard encryption (TLS)
>   Learn more

So they are forcing me to donate my time? UGH.

Ps. Lara is totes tone-deaf. Metaphorically and literally.

Pps. Does Brandon Loopner think winning an Oscar for playing a dead singer/songwriter makes him an actual singer-songwriter? Everyone knows it was dubbed.

Re:Re:Re: Lara White/Celebs for Changing Climate Change

> From: Jasper DLC Jasper@BGstyle.com
> To: Belinda Grant Belinda@BGstyle.com
> Date: Feb 25, 2018 at 6:28 pm
> 🔒 Standard encryption (TLS)
>   Learn more

They will have to AUTOTUNE THE FUCK OUTTA THIS

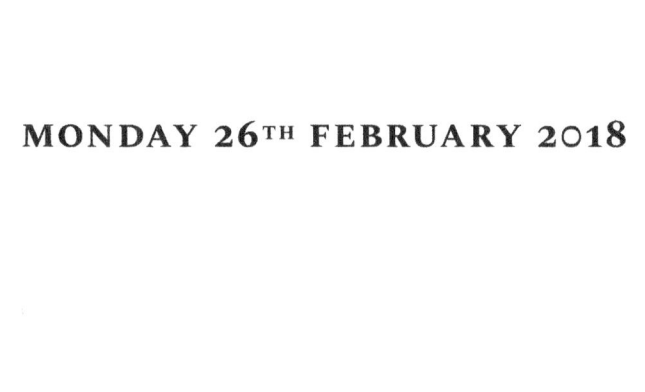

MONDAY 26TH FEBRUARY 2018

"Some natures are too good to be
spoiled by praise."
—Ralph Waldo Emerson

Botox & Bills

SAMPLE RETURN

Home of Belinda Grant. 8:30 am

Text from Emily de Vries to Belinda

> **Hey B,**
> Loved the Lanvin last night! I know they need it back quickly. I'm just around the corner, can I drop it to you if you are home?

> Yes! Omg, that would be amazing.

> Rose just left for school, and I have an hour or so before I need to get going.

> See you in a few!

In a fuchsia beanie and matching oversized cashmere coat, Emily stood in Belinda's doorway, a latte in each hand and a garment bag hung over one arm. "I figured you might need one of these. It's oat milk you like, right?"

"Um, yes! Are you an angel or what?"

"I haven't researched that role yet, but definitely one day." She giggled, hanging the garment bag on the hat stand and tossing her hat on the couch. "Look at this mop. I was so tired I slept in the chignon, and the can of hairspray Richard used has turned it into straw."

"No judgment here. You should see me on a non-work day."

"Oh, shut up, B, you always look chic, even in your pajamas. I'll never forget Paris when I thought you were dressed and ready in those silk PJs."

"Totally missed that I'd overslept and was hungover, perched on the bed trying to unglue my eyes? You are too kind."

"Well, you could have fooled anyone, and sexy, smudgy makeup is so French," Emily shrugged.

"Well, thank you. But I can't take compliments, you know this. I *give* them. Shall we sit and drink these coffees? I have about 30 minutes." Emily followed Belinda into the kitchen, and they perched at the stainless-steel counter.

"Missed you last night. You are great at the political events. I told Grace from the ACLU how much I love your Twitter account. You should go public and let me retweet you."

"Did you also tell Grace I follow politics as a distraction? A respite from fashion? And I'm not as brave as you. One retweet from you to your 10 million crowd would open the gates of hell for me. No offense. And who wants to follow a fashion stylist for politics? I can hear it now; *stay in your lane, Belinda.*"

Emily grimaced. "None taken, but it's perfectly acceptable for you, a multi-faceted being, to have multiple lanes. Just know that if you change your mind, I will be retweeting you endlessly. And you get used to the trolls, you develop a thick skin, well, a partial one, at least. Speaking of, did you see the '*Fire the Stylist*' post about me?"

"Emily, I keep telling you. Don't read that shit! It's toxic."

"It was so dumb. Said I was one of the few actresses whose career was unscathed by my rampant feminism. Or something like that. I think it's hilarious how they attempt to sound woke and then go full patriarchal over my 'unsexy' shoe choice. The comments were also something else."

"Dear god, Emily, have I taught you nothing? NEVER READ THE COMMENTS!"

"I know, I know, I'm sick that way, but it's addictive. God knows I'm aware that they are nasty, nameless—probably styleless fucks. Who hide behind a website, gleefully inciting the public to judge and destroy whatever they put in front of them. I also know from *personal* experience that they will never acknowledge that their targets are human with feelings and families. Yet even *I* can't stop reading."

"Oh, I give up! You know what I think. Now, are you sure you don't want to go to anything this weekend? I'm getting emails every day from designers, offering beautiful looks." She flashed Emily an image on her phone.

"Don't be mad at me, but no. The last couple of years were so full of award-show stuff. I am bowing out this round. The last thing anyone needs is more pictures of me. And much as I'm happy to admit to my plastic surgery, I'm so bored talking about it."

"Did you have to get Botox because the producers said you looked too 'real'? Did you tell me that, or did I read it somewhere?"

"Oh yeah, it was worse, but I didn't wanna say this part publicly; they said that in HD, I didn't look like I lived in a world with the rest of the cast. Not even the men—and we know they're allowed a few wrinkles." She sighed and sipped her coffee.

"Look, the bottom line is I'm a de-wrinkled, privileged, middle-aged white woman who has been ridiculously blessed to have success for looking beautiful. But I'm far *more* fortunate to have parents who urged me to redirect that spotlight onto under-served places. They taught me that my looks and the glare of attention would eventually wane. So now I work to take pleasure from my interior, and I salute my diminishing exterior, for the life and let's be honest—*shit-ton of money*—it gave me."

"Wow. That's profound. I need to write that down!"

"Haha. Pep talks are free. Anyway, how are you doing with the Alma stuff? Are you okay? It's so fucking weird. I feel like Dustin has really been my person for ages, but still, she was the mountain mover, and I'm shook."

"Yeah, I'm sorry for your loss." Belinda touched her arm. "And I'm okay. The detectives seem cool. Two women. They seemed satisfied that it had nothing to do with me. I've always been terrified of the gun toting cops in this country, so that was a surprise. Now, hopefully, it's just the rumor mill I have to contend with." Her phone pinged. "Speaking of which, I have to go in a few. Sorry Emily—Jasper is almost here. Lara's attending the Oscar luncheon today."

"Oh yes, can't be late for her ladyship. Did she pay her tailoring bill yet?"

"Nope, she said (my agent told me via her publicist), and I quote," Belinda scrolled through her email and read, "*The airport looks Lara was persuaded to have altered were not to her taste, which, as a professional, is something Belinda should have known. This is why Lara did not wear them and should not be required to pay for the service.*"

Emily shook her head, muttering, "What the fuck? Also, does she always talk about herself in the third person? You know she wrote that."

"Yup. The studio refused to pay. The designers didn't get pictures to use for press, so they were out. Left me in a shit situation with Yelena. So"—Belinda sighed—"I paid the two grand bill myself."

"Fuck Bee. That's disgusting. You know Yelena has my credit card details on file, so it will never happen with me."

"Narcissistic personality disorder is the only mental condition where the patient is left alone, but everyone else needs treatment."
—anonymous

Gross Expectations

THE ROOM WAS COLD, TENSE, AND SILENT. Lara stared down impassively, only her milky white neck slowly flushing scarlet indicated what was to come. Armed with practiced, neutral smiles, the team looked away and stood perfectly still, hiding in plain sight and wishing themselves anywhere but here.

Lara turned abruptly and scooped the handcrafted Oxford off the reclaimed wood floor in one graceful movement. "Belindaaa," she drawled, with her usual saccharin smile, pivoting the shoe in her direction, "I SO appreciate what you have done, and I see you have *tried*; the laces are indeed the perfect clashing shade I requested, but Belinda, did your team not think to source *unwaxed* shoelaces? Or are waxed laces *all* I have to consider here? How can you not see that this magnificent Celine patent Oxford shoe is a high-shine hard surface and the waxed shoelace is *also* a shine surface? These two things repel each other like magnets—"

She paused unexpectedly, looking round the room anticipating agreement but finding everyone looking awkward. Unaccustomed to anything but total compliance, she pushed on, increasingly adamant. "A soft, UN-waxed shoelace, *Belinda*, would complement the HARD surface, like ying and yang; their very opposite natures would meld into the sublime." Her pale blue, heavily mascaraed eyes hardened as she worked herself up. "How is it that it's always I who have to point these things out? It's just so very disappointing that you cannot put more thought into your work. We have that Cocotte advertising campaign next week, and I know your agent demanded you be paid vast sums of money. I just pray you'll be up to the task by then. Of course, you are European and therefore supposedly more creative, but Jennifer, my previous *American* stylist, had a large, devoted staff"—she glared at Jasper—"perhaps you could try to imitate some of her methods. For example, how hard could it be to find unwaxed vermillion shoelaces with some minor effort?"

Belinda listened to the monologue, everything floating into slow motion as it often did during these moments. How do some people so naturally, almost gracefully abuse, she wondered, Lara's words blurring in her ears. Glancing at an antique mirrored accent table, she noticed a well-worn copy of 'The Curse of the High IQ' casually placed next to 'Living with Joy' and a gilded bowl spilling out moon crystals. She turned her gaze to Jasper for reassurance, thankful for their telepathy, honed by years of working together in this closed, almost impenetrable, world. Devon had once told her that she'd survived for all these years not just because of her ability to curate an image for a star that was otherworldly yet seemingly effortless but—and perhaps more so—because of her expertise in intuiting and combatting the mercurial moods of clients and those who jostled for position around them. Realizing Lara's lecture had ended, she snapped out of her reverie.

"Er, no, Lara. I'm sorry, but you texted at 6 pm yesterday, and these are the only laces we could find overnight. But you know, you are wearing, um, wide-leg pants to this lunch, which will *cover* the shoe, so perhaps you could ying, I mean, wing it this time?"

"Don't be *ridiculous*, my sweet, *sweet* Belinda, it's perfectly obvious these are now unwearable," Lara responded irritably. "I suppose I shall have to help you out *again*. In my second shoe closet upstairs are the perfect Michael Kors ballet flats Jennifer's team picked out for me. You may fetch them. And, while she is doing that, Jacob, finish my makeup. *You* may now use the Cle de Peu."

Walking towards where he was sitting in front of his ring-light mirror, she assessed her caramel French twist. "Perfect." She puckered her expertly painted full berry mouth. "Jacob, do we think this is the right shade? Isn't it like every other berry lip you do? Perhaps you are tired of my face? Start with the eye highlighter while you summon up some creativity."

Hearing her pick at Jacob, Belinda, and Jasper knew she'd chosen today's victim and were awash with relief that the outfit remained in play. Experience had taught them that they were always only a tantrum away from conjuring up a new rack of clothing to cater to Lara's sartorial whim of the second. A rotating emergency selection of designer clothing lived permanently in Jasper's over-packed car. Belinda, barefoot, walked slowly up the hand-carved oak staircase and into the stuffed shoe closet, closing the door and sitting cross-legged on the floor for a moment, grateful for the respite. She closed her eyes, recalling previous disasters . . .

- "At the fitting, this Givenchy seemed like a dress one would want to live in forever, but today, it only makes me want to die."
- "Ugh, this McQueen suit, surely I didn't agree to this? Am I to think you'd like me to be mistaken for an FBI agent?"
- "All 10 of these replacement cream jackets have *pockets*. Could you not have brought even just *one* without? Pockets look so cheap."
- "I cannot wear sequins; I have a rare skin disorder that means they permanently scar my skin. How can it be to so hard to source skin-friendly hypoallergenic sequins that I *can* actually wear?"
- "I had some dreadful news this morning, a death (*of a project*). I can't say more, but this outfit depresses my soul. You have 30 minutes before I leave to find a silky balm for my spirit."
- "For some reason, velvet suddenly gives me a dry mouth and makes me literally GAG."

Jasper, alone downstairs and feeling naked without Belinda, crunched a Xanax and watched Jacob as he picked up the Cle de Peau concealer with perceptibly shaking hands. Jasper blew him a discreet, empathetic kiss before turning towards the door as a loud musical *DING DONG* rang through the lower house. Shocked by the noise, Jacob recoiled, wincing as a box of his Chanel lipsticks tumbled. "Ohh god, so sorry, I'll g-get those cleared up," he stuttered as the door rang again, "but f-f-first can I get the door for you, Lara?"

"Don't be ridiculous, Jacob. We don't need anything *else* to slow you down, do we?" Lara responded, looking down at the rug, adding, in a stab at being magnanimous. "Don't worry about the rug—I don't know why I approved it—I'm not in love."

"Well, all the lids are still on, Lara," Jacob found the courage to say as he knelt to pick up the scattered black cases and noticed a handwritten price tag that somehow remained on the corner of the exquisite azure Turkish rug: $14,000.

"KELLY, get the door. *KELLLLY*, good lord, why is no one available when you need them?"

"I'm here, Lara. I just got back," Kelly announced, cheerfully bouncing into the room on Nike Airs, keys hanging from her white overalls as she juggled, holding a phone to one ear and a haul of dry cleaning in her other hand. As always, she effortlessly balanced everything, answering the incessantly dinging entry phone with her other ear.

"Hello? Yes, this is her assistant, Kelly. Oh, yes, okay. One moment, please—Lara, it's the cops about Alma. I'm sorry, I don't know anything about this."

"Alma's office didn't advise? What is going on over there? Let them in, obviously. AARDA is truly falling apart without her, which reminds me. Please get an up-to-date list of the agents who are courting me. Let's organize lunches in all the new impossible to get into restaurants. So FUN to be pursued this way now I'm *free*. Kelly, tell Elliot I need him down here now. I think he's in the theatre playing that ridiculous 'Night in the Woods' game again. We should face the LAPD together, united as husband and wife. Tell whatshername, the new nanny, to keep the children upstairs. I don't want them sullied with such lurid things."

"Every path has its puddle."
—Old Yiddish saying

Welcome to the Jungle

RIDING IN CARS WITH DETECTIVES
Arriving at the residence of Lara White. 11:50 am

CHERYL PARKED ON THE QUIET SILVERLAKE STREET and joined Ortiz, who was waiting in front of the 16ft ivy-draped gate. She wiped the sweat from her neck onto her pants and irritably pulled at the claustrophobic wool-blend black turtleneck.

"You gotta figure out the weather here, boss," Ortiz rolled her eyes. "How many more times I gotta tell ya? Layers, it's all about layers, *thin* layers, and fuck any scratchy wool unless you a skinny-ass, cold-runnin' bag-a-bones. Which, thankfully, you clearly ain't."

"Ugh, pissah, I'm gonna have to go shopping. I miss the defined Boston weather—I'm fast realizing regular seasons are the shit."

Cheryl sighed, and her eyes widened as the gate opened to reveal a fantastical display of lush, dense greenery—large-leaved mature trees, spiky succulents, towering palms, ivy crawling over every concrete surface, and the centerpiece—a waterfall gently winding its way to a pond containing giant Japanese Koi fish. "How appropriate that 'the witch' has a client who lives in a forest," she drily commented as they walked in single file, following the moss-edged stone path. "I talked to my sister Tracy last night; she's crapping herself with excitement about this case. She'd die to be walking up this Red Riding Hood path. Lara White's been her idol since her teen years; Tracy's seen every one of her movies and award stuff, even the weird art stuff she does."

"You seen any?" Ortiz asked, pushing her way through some low-hanging branches.

"Nah, I prefer crime docs and WBA. Always have since I was a young kid. I know of her, of course, who doesn't? I think it'd be harder to find someone who doesn't know who she is—" She stopped talking as the forest abruptly fell away, and they found themselves stepping into an eclectic open-plan lounge/kitchen—one seemingly missing a wall.

"Detectives! Delighted to meet you," Lara, on a charm offensive, took Cheryl's hand in both of hers and nodded regally at Ortiz. "I so admire what you brave people . . ." She trailed off as she noticed both women were distracted, looking around, searching for the missing wall. "Oh, ladies, don't you love it? It's a retracting window wall. One press of a button, and poof! It disappears. We feel like we live in the jungle, don't we, darling?" She kissed Elliot passionately on the mouth for an uncomfortably long few seconds, ruining 20 minutes of precise lipstick application, then flicked her tongue slowly around his lips to finish. She turned to scrutinize Cheryl and, noticing the foliage in her hair, exclaimed, "Oh, our apologies, it can be a challenge to walk in here—we intentionally have the gardeners keep it raw and wild to invoke a visceral forest experience."

Ortiz coughed gently, rocking on her feet, estimating how many showers she could take with the amount of LA water this would require.

Lara continued, "You look so, well . . . *hot*, detective, I didn't catch your name?"

"It's Detective Cheryl Hall."

"How lovely, Cheryl. Could we lower your temperature with some tea? KELLY, bring us some jasmine oolong from that divine shop we visited in Shanghai."

"Thank you, Ms. White, but just water, please. This is Detective Ortiz." Ortiz flashed a wan smile: "Hi. I'll take the same, thanks."

"Oh, please, ladies. Do call me Lara." Turning her head, she raised her voice towards the kitchen. "TEA Kelly."

"Lara," Cheryl began, "we just have a few routine questions about Alma Astley. I'm sure you are aware of her unfortunate death?"

"Oh yes, it's such a heartbreaking tragedy. What a woman! I trusted her from the very first, you know. And I was one of her first; I joined her at age 12—" She paused as her face suddenly registered confusion. "But why are you here? Was she . . . good god, I can't even bring myself to say it, *murdered*?" She grasped Elliot's hand dramatically, he, having smoked a strong blunt while gaming, stood oblivious—his pleasant face high and serene at the top of his lanky Nike-wearing body.

"This is my husband, Elliot, but I'm sure you already know that."

Cheryl nodded hello to him, responding, "We aren't at liberty to discuss details yet, Ms. White, but we do have questions and are doing routine interviews with her clients who are in town and have seen her in the last week."

"Good lord, you are going to be busy! It's Oscars week, detective, *everyone's* in town."

"And when was the last time you saw her?"

"We had a brief yet delicious lunch at Fred's on Monday. How could I forget? FireTheStylist.com utterly destroyed my choice of outfit that day. Isn't that right, Jasper?"

FIRE THE STYLIST

Dishing Daily Doses of Fashion Justice

LARA WHITE - Leaving FRED'S, Beverly Hills.

Posted on February 19, 2018

And here we have an unusually dour <u>Lara White</u> (33) leaving <u>Fred's</u> today. Maybe she caught a glimpse of her mind-boggling <u>outfit</u> in their <u>infamous mirror wall.</u> (We remind you, Firers, that the first pictures of <u>Angelina and Brad kissing</u> were a reflection on this very wall.) We digress, because how she got out of <u>her house</u> without looking in a mirror is a mystery… but if she did look in a mirror, how did she leave the house? It's a conundrum…

Let us give you one scenario… Lara is starring in a low-budget, historically inaccurate Western. Her character is poor and depressed, as illustrated by the dusty-brown color palette. She walks, crying, to a river, stumbling over her ill-fitting, inordinately long <u>UllaJohnson</u> dress. Using a dirty-red embroidered <u>fabric purse</u>, our heroine begins mining for gold. Frustrated with her lack of success, she accidentally shakes the limited-edition <u>Prada</u> sunglasses off her head and then crashes into the river, frantically trying to retrieve these <u>collectibles</u>. Can she swim? We don't know, but all is not lost as a raven-haired hottie swoop in to save the day. She shivers violently, and he wraps her in his 'its-been-in-the-family-for-centuries' ragged <u>Chloe poncho</u>. The director yells CUT! She dries off her white <u>Gucci plastic beach thongs</u> and aforementioned Pradas, ties her wet hair in a <u>top knot</u>, and rides off into the Hills of Beverly for lunch.

What say you, Firers? Is anything redeemable here? Did stylist Belinda Grant lose her eyesight, or did Lara White go rogue?

As always, leave a comment below!

(To review our community guidelines, please click here)

> @**ilovelara** I would totally watch that movie. Heart her soooo much. Follow my fan site @**lovinglara**
>
> @**lovinglara** SHE IS A CHIC GODDESS ♥ ♥ ♥
>
> @**styleislife** her style person is blind as a bat.
>
> @**culturecurator** You guys need to have some sensitivity training. It's gross how you use famous women to amuse yourselves. Get a life.

@**jenelopyjazz** do you people literally think these fashion stylists live in actresses closets? Maybe give these grown-ass women some credit (good or bad) for dressing THEMSELVES? Don't see you blaming them for famous men in average streetwear, just sayin

@**Vivie_6969** $500 for the first 15 people to DM "STRUGGLING FASHUN" ★★★

"It's a gift of privilege, the choice to ignore what it is inconvenient to see."

Welcome to the Jungle, Part 2

BELINDA, FACE OBSCURED by the five Michael Kors shoeboxes balanced in her hands, walked tentatively down the stairs and was met by Jasper at the base, who took them from her, whispering, "You took your time! You lucky bitch—"

She shushed him and announced, "Lara, these are almost all of the Michael Kors flats I found. Which pair did—"

Sitting as Jacob reapplied lipstick, Lara interrupted in a warning tone, "Belinda, this is Detective"—she pointed at Cheryl—"I'm *so* sorry, what were your names again? They are here about Alma."

"We already met with Belinda this weekend"—Cheryl responded, nodding in her direction—"and it's Detectives Cheryl Hall and Ortiz."

Sitting down an elaborate gold Chinese tea set on the 3-footed African table, Kelly added, "She was one of the last people to see her alive, Lara, I told you."

"WHAT? *Oh my god*, well, you might have *led* with that Kelly. Belinda, I am utterly *shocked*." Lara sniffed in her direction as if she were rancid.

Aghast at this reaction, Belinda stuttered, "Yeah, yes, we had a brief meeting in her office to discuss . . . I . . . well, I thought you knew and didn't want to talk about it." Twisting her hands, she added, "I thought everyone knew. It was in Variety, Breaking Hollywood, and, um, everywhere . . ."

Her voice tapered off. Jasper—having placed the shoe boxes in front of Lara—hooked her pinky in solidarity.

Lara, admiring one of her shoes, took a deep, dramatic breath. "Well, I suppose we don't have time to worry about this for now, it being *Oscars* season. We'll just put it on the back burner until after. It won't bring her back after all. Belinda, has the custom Tatou arrived yet? How long can it take to sew on a few thousand crystals? I am simply dying to try it on."

Slipping into the chosen Michael Kors, she turned to Cheryl. "Detectives, do you have all you need? I must leave now. They will hold the carpet open for me, of course, but one doesn't like to be too much of a bother, you know?" She picked up her #BLM monogrammed Edie Parker clutch, selected Versace sunglasses from a tray Jasper was offering in one hand, and admired herself briefly in the mirror he held in his other. Without a backward glance, she stepped outside and vanished into the curated wilderness. Leaving Cheryl gaping, untouched tea in hand.

Kelly, unperturbed, turned to Ortiz and, prodding her phone, said, "Let me pull up her diary, we'll reschedule."

"A lie is halfway 'round the world before the truth has got its boots on."
—old proverb

Bling, Buzz & Bribes

"BELINDA, JASPER! THANK YOU *SO MUCH* FOR COMING!" a bouncy blonde PR dressed head to toe in L'Agence effused from inside the open penthouse door. "It's okay, Igor, let them in."

"I have to check my list first. For the insurance," growled the 6′7″ security guard, running his immense manicured hand down the list attached to a gold star-embossed clipboard.

"Belinda Grant, Igor, G. R. A. N. T.," she spelled out, as if to a child. "Hurry, let's not keep them waiting. It's such a busy week, and we are simply thrilled you found the time to come by. We have such *great* brands to show you today—Dazzle Diamonds, obviously; 'Carlos'—a *super* emerging talent from Brazil—you will die; 'Save Us,' a line of sustainable vegan pocket squares made by former refugees in Somalia. We love to promote equity so we work for them for free," she added in a whisper, "a whole village could be saved by one placement on a great male celeb! Lastly, we have a new line of clutches from 'Rich Man's Wife'—we can custom-dye, obviously, and the RMW seamstress can embroider initials or slogan of choice on the outside or even *inside!*" She stopped to breathe. "Now, first things first, would you like some champagne? We also have custom

CBD-infused colon cleansing juices and Sprinkles' gold-dusted Oscar cupcakes. So *fun*, right?"

"Just water would be great," Belinda nodded and mustered up a smile, wondering where she would find the energy for the expected small talk.

"Speak for yourself, you boring bitch; I'm gonna colon cleanse and dust off a cupcake."

"*Jasper!*" the bouncy blonde squealed. "You are *too* much! Belinda, how do you cope? Are you just screaming with laughter *all the time*?"

"After eight years, I'm screaming inside, yes . . ."

"Oh, you two!" She swatted Jasper lightly. "Shall we start with the *diamonds*? Gerald! Belinda is here! Are you ready to dazzle her with your bling?"

Belinda turned to Jasper. "I got this; let's split up and save time. Why don't you pop to the Jimmy Choo suite? Get white dyeables—shoes and clutches—for all the clients. I think the email said it's downstairs in the Regency Room. Remember, no ankle straps for Ava-Lily—she's decided her ankles have put on weight."

"Okay, fine, *boss*," he sniffed, "as long as I get a juice first. I'm not gonna let you be the only one to shit calmly later."

Belinda rolled her eyes and turned to Gerald. "Hi, good to see you again."

"The pleasure is mine." He moved in so close their noses almost touched. "Lara and Ava-Lily have been looking phenomenal lately, and we would love to see them in our jewels."

Belinda recoiled at the fermented smoked salmon halitosis and quickly moved to the end of the red velvet-covered table, admiring a large solitaire ring.

"18 carats, Belinda, Asscher-cut, set in platinum with a claw setting. Isn't it sublime? Of course, we could only consider loaning it for the ceremony for Lara or Ava, and it has its own bodyguard, Igor, over there." he added, nodding toward the door.

"Gerald," the bouncy blonde chaperone piped up, "it's Ava-LILY, and I told you already that both those ladies will have *deals*. Am I right, Belinda?"

Belinda, ignoring her, moved on to a pair of cylindrical ruby cage earrings.

"They are superb, but I must let you know that Poppy has confirmed them for the Vanity Fair party for Jazzie Vane, but of course, if you want them for the Oscars, we will be thrilled to pull them from her."

Belinda turned up her mouth at the corners in what she hoped resembled a smile. "So very cutthroat of you, Gerald."

"It's the Oscars! All's fair in celebrity and diamonds, Belinda! We also have these horse-cut diamond cufflinks, four carats each, perhaps for Jonny. Very cool for a musician, no?"

Belinda nodded noncommittally, moving onto a yellow gold necklace set with numerous emeralds.

"Exquisite, no? 77 Carats and the two that drop down are detachable. It's $5.5 million. Emeralds are so fragile, as I know you know. This piece would have to be approved for someone exceptional (and *careful*), plus we would *obviously* want it worn as a set."

"Okay, but do you have an alternative ring and simple diamond earrings because that's a lot of a necklace."

Gerald's mouth dropped open in horror. "I think we would prefer *all* emeralds, Belinda. Having such a magical piece alone would be such a waste of *a moment*."

"Okay, understood." Belinda gave up. "Well, let me take some pictures, and when I have finished my fittings and know exactly what I need, I will circle back."

"Belinda, these pieces are in very high demand, so you can be sure there will be very little left by the end of the day." Gerald adjusted the polka dot pocket square on his vest and stroked his mustache, removing a morsel of onion. "You should grab the pieces under $250k while you can. They are pre-insured and don't need a guard, assuming you have a safe."

"Gerald, of course, I have a safe in my office, but I can't drive hundreds of thousands of dollars of jewelry around in our car for no reason. I don't even know for sure what they're wearing yet."

"Perhaps you could just style a gown around some magnificent jewels? Challenge the status quo? Surely, it is an easy and exciting task for a stylist of your caliber. We could always sweeten the deal with a private, nominal fee for you, of course."

"As you know, that's not really possible, Gerald, unless you are paying the talent." Muttering to herself, "and even then, good luck with that." She turned to face him and was relieved to see him rushing to the door to greet Amy Johnson, his bald spot glinting under the lights as he simpered, "Amy, *darling*, simply divine to see you—"

"*BELINDA!*" Amy yelled from the other end of the suite, dodging him. "*DID YOU MURDER ALMA ASTLEY?* What in the actual fuck, girl?"— cackling—"You are *waaay* more interesting than I thought." Approaching her, she continued loudly, "Sorry, is that too fucking rude? I'd say anything to get away from that man's rancid breath. I swear he can't have brushed his false teeth since the Emmy's suite last September. Anyway, back to *Alma*—tell me all! What did you hit her with? An Oscar? That would be hilarious; it was a head injury, right? She probably deserved it. What a fucking old bitch she was."

"I don't know, Amy, I didn't hear about her head, only read what the press said. The police didn't tell me anything."

"*THE POLICE?* Oh, my effing god, did they arrest you? What's it like in jail? Did the inmates steal all your jewelry freebies? They couldn't possibly have room for all the handbags."

"Amy! Cut it out. I didn't get arrested. They just asked me a few questions as I met her briefly—seven minutes to be exact—that night before she died." Belinda wished for the 100th time in the last five minutes that she hadn't sent Jasper down to the Jimmy Choo suite. He was brilliant at running distraction in these situations.

"Oh, I'm just fucking messing wit' you, gurl. *Perry*, the colorist at that old bitch Daniels salon, does Alma's assistant *Daniel's* hair, and he heard him talking on the phone. *Perry* told *Sally*—his TikTok partner and *my* 2nd intern—who told *me*. I know everything. No one in this fucking shithole town can keep a secret. Come on, let's go in the bedroom and look at that god-awful Brazilian designer's collection. They should pay us for looking at this shit." Amy, who was botoxed, filled, and sculpted to an indeterminate age—bordering on cat face—took one hand out of her zebra tracksuit pants and grabbed Belinda's arm, dragging her through the doorway.

"Amy! Belinda! I, Carlos, am an unbelievably lucky man to show either of you my humble work." He gestured at two racks exploding with a blizzard of shimmering primary-colored feathers. "But it is even more amazing that I get to see you both together! And at my very first Oscars suite. It is an honor." Excited, he smiled as he executed a slight bow.

"How does he know our names?" Belinda whispered to the peppy PR, who was following them in.

"He researched and studied pictures in Brazil. I swear he knows more than me. He's really very sweet," she whispered. "Between us, his family are wealthy—we might be able to get you some money if—"

"Shall I present to you both? How does this work?" Carlos squealed, gesturing with smooth, bejeweled hands.

"Oh no, you go first, Amy," Belinda jumped in quickly. "I'm gonna get a cleanse."

"Ooh, amazing!" exclaimed the bouncy blonde excitedly. "Can we take a photo of you drinking it for our social?"

"No, god no, and pleeeease don't use the ones of me looking at jewelry, okay? I'm behind the scenes for a reason. Sorry to be so firm, but I asked Gerald not to last year, and then there are like 15 images on Getty of me staring indifferently at diamonds worth more than a house. My brother in England made one into a birthday card. He thought it was *hilarious*."

"Totes get it, no worries, Belinda. Sorry about that. Oh look, here's Orlando arriving for his appointment. I'll be right back."

Belinda texted Jasper to get back up there and, standing surreptitiously at the bedroom door, watched as Amy, bleached, greasy top knot wobbling, plowed her way roughly through the rack, yelling assessments at an increasingly distraught Carlos.

"*Ugly, ug-er-ly. So ugly. Ugly-TOWN.* My god, no one will wear so many feathers. This stuff makes fucking Big Bird look fucking paired *down. CARLOS!* Get it together! So many feathers I wanna sneeze just looking at the rack. This one"—she pointed at a black gown—"this one's okay. I could try it on one of the actors' wives; the ones who don't know"—cackling—"which is most of them, let's be honest. Wrap it for me. I gotta go look at diamonds now. Who's got a fucking gas mask for me or an industrial Altoid for Gerald? *OH MY GOD, UGLY,*" she yelled as her swan song, pointing at a burgundy feathered and sequined leather cape. "Alma would probably have loved that if you hadn't bumped her off, right Belinda?" She snickered as she made her way out the door.

Moments later, Jasper crept in and joined Belinda, who was listening to a now fragile Carlos and smiling reassuringly. "*Oh, thank god!*" she mouthed.

"For what?" Jasper huffed. "Jimmy Choo said they are low on stock, and you must tell them which shoes you want. I, apparently, am not sufficient. I've been out there stuffing cupcakes and hiding from Amy. I can't deal with her shit today. Is she really trying to rock Off-White with fluorescent Crocs? Jeeze, talk about white mutton dressed as—"

"Carlos, this is Jasper, who works with me." Belinda interrupted, shaking her head at Jasper.

"He's hawt!" Jasper assessed, just loud enough for Carlos to hear.

Flushing, Carlos continued his practiced presentation, amending his usual ending with a sad, "*But do you think it's ugly?*"

"*No!* So sorry about Amy, she sounds harsh, but I bet she places the dress she took. She just has no filter." Belinda reassured.

"*Like zero!*" Jasper chimed in. "She once called Alma Astley Mrs. Munster, *to her face*. It's a miracle she wasn't banished to the deep valley for life—"

"Um, excuse?" Carlos shyly interrupted. "Would you like to look at the pieces up close?"

"Oh yes, sorry," Jasper responded, mentally undressing him, "um, what was your name again? Christ, we are so rude. And shit, look at the time, Bels! We can do a quick flick-through because we still have Jimmy Choo on our way out." He moved to the rack. "Wow, there's a lottttta feathers here. I'm a little overwhelmed."

"*Sssssh!*" Belinda hushed him, shaking her head furiously as Carlos began to cry. "Amy more than covered the feathers, Jasper. You wanna go and get the car while I pop into Jimmy? The valet here is painfully slow."

"Do I wanna? No. Do I have to? Yes, boss, just stop with the passive-aggressive orders phrased like they are optional." He backed away, still admiring Carlos, before turning and marching swiftly to the exit, where the bouncy blonde accosted him.

"Omg, Jasper," she whispered, "did Belinda *really* have something to do with Alma's death? Amy said she heard the meeting was about Janie's retainer contract, and it did not go well."

"*OH MY FUCKING GOD.* That's insane," Jasper replied angrily. "Why would you even repeat this shit, lady? *Belinda.* This Belinda? Have you fucking met her? She needs *me* for protection, yeah, me, that's why I'm still here after seven years and 11 months. *Belinda murder Alma?*" He snorted and rolled his unusually cold brown eyes, abruptly changing the subject. "Can I get validation for the valet from you?"

"For you guys, of course!"

"Great, because $20 plus tip for parking for 30 minutes is insane." He held out his hand for the ticket, adding coldly, "We'll be in touch about the jewelry."

"Do you want a cleanse juice to-go, Jasper?"

"No, I don't. Not anymore. Gotta run." He walked away, shaking his head, and heard an unknown female voice say, "Did he just say *Belinda murdered Alma?*"

Back in the bedroom, Belinda, watched by a despondent Carlos, looked through his rack, efficiently casting her eye over each dress.

"Look, Carlos, I'm not gonna lie, I think you need to pull it back a little. Well, a lot. But the foundation is there, the beading is gorgeous, and some shapes, like this one, for instance"—she pointed at a strapless ball gown—"are very red carpet. But right now it's veering a little costume house. We want to look at the woman wearing the dress, not the other way around. Do you want to know my honest thoughts?"

Carlos, terrified, forced himself to nod.

"I think it's unlikely you will get a big placement this time. You might be better off rethinking and trying again for the Emmys later this year. TV might be a better match." She looked at her watch and groaned, "Anyway, I better get going. I hope I was helpful. Oh, please don't cry. Oh god." She guided him to the bed and sat beside him. "I'm sorry, this is such a bad week. Everyone is exhausted and irate and sick of fucking movies. I never see Oscar-nominated movies until later because I'm so burnt out with everyone talking non-stop about them for three months. We stylists are all monsters by this stage of award season. I've spent more time so far this year discussing fucking diamonds than I have talking to my child. Anyway, if you want more advice, I'm happy to help. Tell Star PR to give you my email. We can chat after this shit show is over?" Carlos, crying openly now, laid back on the bed. "Okay, I gotta run, sorry. Best of luck, okay?" She touched his shoulder gently and fastened the button on her Chanel boucle jacket, looking around for her purse before realizing it was still on her shoulder. She strode to the exit, oblivious to all the eyes staring at her from around the suite.

"Bye, guys. Thank you. We'll circle back."

"*ONE SEC, BELINDA!*" The blonde chased her down the corridor. "You guys forgot your gift bags. Sooo much good stuff in here." She handed her two white oversized laminated shopping bags fastened with giant gold stars and whispered, "*Good luck with the Alma murder thing.*"

FIRE THE STYLIST

Dishing Daily Doses of Fashion Justice

⚖

JANIE JONES - Leaving Copacopa.

Posted on February 26, 2018

As the world knows, this week Janie Jones (42ish) added yet another ex to her (oversized) bow, and boy, is she showing the world she does not GAF! We would list some of the names on the trail of broken hearts she left behind, but what's the point? Who, in the tiniest of villages, in the world's remotest corners, doesn't know about the always-famous men Janie, ahem, has 'loved'? Seen here last night leaving the feted Hollywood culinary hotspot Copacopa in what passes for clothing in some cultures— and we are quite frankly speechless. No one has yet identified or owned up to creating this look, which is a shame because, well, we have questions. So, if you are out there, designer, please help us out here. (Anonymously if you, quite sensibly, prefer.)

1. Is that an actual dead snake snaking around her and just about covering her nipples?

2. Are the feathers glued or on invisible wire?

3. Are the sequins an applied V-jazzle or sewn onto an invisible netting thong?

4. Did she spill a pomegranate seed into her belly button, or is that a ruby?

5. Was there an audition for experimental musical theatre before dinner?

6. Did she sit and EAT in this?

On the plus side, her hair is, as always, GLORIOUS. Maje envy in our office, MAJE.

Any thoughts or explanations, Firers?

As always, leave comments below!

(To review our community guidelines, please click here)

> **@fashunislife** I think she has just gotten carried away with a new glue gun at Wine Night Crafting. It's the only explanation

> **@davetheonly2** thanks that's my bedtime wank for this week sorted.

@jaceylacey I think that cropped tux jacket over her shoulders is **@YSL** but she cut the sleeves and lapels off to show her tits and stapled the feathers to hide her ass (which is weird cos its gorgeous) the sequins have gotta be panties right?

@femfemfem love the platform, Doc Martins. So different for her. Maybe she's over men, FINALLY.

@jojo49 People hated her for her looks, and now they celebrate her aging. Being beautiful ain't all it's cracked up to be

@moma2moma **@jojo49** Shut up with you're nonsense, her beauty meant she got to shag the world's most eligible men and make a bazillion dollars being a puppet for other people's talent.

@jojo49 **@moma2moma** it's YOUR. Go back to school Moma.

@ladylife 'in some cultures'? Xenophobic much? See also: misogyny. JFC

"They tell you that you'd be more, if you were less."

Star Interrupted

RIDING IN CARS WITH DETECTIVES

Arriving at the residence of Janie Jones. 1:30 pm

CHERYL AND ORTIZ PULLED UP TO A CONCEALED GATE in Hidden Hills. "This is what the sat nav's giving me," said Cheryl, looking around and seeing nothing but bucolic nature and miles of tall wooden fencing.

"Let me check the address. Cos it just looks like a plain old fence to me," said Ortiz, eating chili almonds from a ziplock, scrutinizing the perimeter. "*Aah*, I see it now. Look, there's a disguised entry phone behind the bamboo over there. Jeeze, that's crazy."

"Listen, I've been working here for seven days, and already concealed electronics in front of secluded Disney palaces seem normal, so easy on the surprise, tiger, or I'm gonna take your cynicism trophy."

Ortiz nodded, muttering '*fair*' and throwing the empty ziplock on the floor, noticed a portion of the fence silently opened inward, offering a picturesque view of a long road that snaked down to a chocolate-box village at the edge of a glimmering lake.

"Well, now, someone is invisibly monitoring the entrance, ain't they? She lives in one of them?" Ortiz questioned, pointing at the houses in the distance.

"From what I hear, she lives in *all* of them," Cheryl responded cheerfully. "Who doesn't like a bit of space?"

"Hang on, how'd you know all this, East Coast sports lady?" Ortiz eyed her suspiciously.

"Well, as I keep reminding you, I am a detective, you know, *like you*"—Cheryl laughed—"*but* my little sis called last night, and I had a crash course in tabloid gossip for everyone involved in the case. She even follows the stylist Belinda on Instagram! Not that I need any more crap filling up my brain and distracting from the *real* cases we got, but still, it made her happy and she thinks I'm cool for once, so I'll take it."

Enjoying the rare experience of being surrounded by uninterrupted nature, she slowed the car down, fielding Ortiz's barrage of questions.

"So. Janie Jones. Does your sister think she's a love addict?"

"Yes."

"How many times has she been married again?"

"Four."

"Points for optimism, I guess. How old is she?"

"That's unclear. Seems to go down a year on Wikipedia every other year."

"Is she gonna go back to indie films one day?"

"Also unclear, but ever since the Jane Austin movie a decade ago when she won awards for worst accent, worst kiss, and worst horse riding, she's only made futuristic action movies in rubber underwear."

"Hmmm. Has she ever dated a woman?"

"*ORTIZ!*"

"What? Sorry. She's really hot! I'll keep it in my comfy high-rise work briefs, don't worry."

"Dear god, woman. Yes, you will. I'm definitely asking *all* the questions on this one, and you can call my sister later. Save my ears from you both."

She pulled up abruptly to a gate just before the village. A brawny bald man, immaculate in navy Dickies, appeared from nowhere on a silver golf cart and gruffly asked, "May I see your ID, please, mam?"

He nodded as Cheryl flashed her badge. "Follow me. Ms. Janie is in the meditation house this morning. You will need to remove your shoes to enter." Then he stepped back onto the golf cart, which tilted comically to his side as he hastily drove off.

"Well, alrighty and namaste." Cheryl grinned as she accelerated to catch up to him. "Got clean socks on today, Ortiz?" Moments later, they stood outside a faux British country house, peering curiously at a wind chime that apparently served as an entry bell.

"Do we just shake it?" Ortiz asked. "Where's Mr. Muscles when you need him?" Just as she reached for the chime, the door flew open, and they turned to see an older woman trembling in the doorway.

"Good morning," Cheryl introduced herself and Ortiz. "We're here to talk to Janie Jones."

"Yes, detectives, that's me."

Ortiz flipped her head up and looked skeptically at the slight woman with thinning hair standing before her—nervously toying with the zipper of a grey fleece onesie. She tried and failed to hide her shock, prompting Cheryl—eyes chastising—to push in front of her and say, "Nice to meet you, Ms. Jones. Should we take off our shoes?"

Ortiz, feeling guilty, inhaled the pungent aroma of lavender and sage emanating from the assortment of scattered candles, and distracted herself by studying the spacious room. Aside from the unstained wood floor, it was almost blindingly, spotlessly white. An ample couch, over-whelmed by bleached sheepskin cushions, was positioned in the center with petite shabby chic side tables framing each end. A pristine leather massage chair sat lonely in a far corner. The walls showcased perfectly mismatched, white-framed antique mirrors that bounced natural light around the room, and diaphanous muslin drapes at the floor-to-ceiling windows were moving gently in the morning breeze. The room was centrally lit by a large irregular group of soft white balls floating on the ceiling, *like sanitized grapes*, Ortiz mused, as a barefooted housekeeper in a starched peach uniform appeared as if from nowhere and set a crystal bowl of raspberries on one end table before silently exiting.

"You can keep your shoes on. We won't be going into any of the divine rooms." Janie looked directly at Ortiz. "It's okay. I know I don't look the way you expected me to."

"Oh, er no . . . er . . ." Ortiz stumbled.

"No, seriously, it's understandable. I look like shit. Normally, I would have had my glam done before you arrived, but I have terrible anxiety, and

I took a Mexican Xanax last night. It's so strong I could barely get out of bed today." She paused to chew gently on her ombré acrylics. "Anyway, if you really want to know, my hair falls out because of my condition. We've been using extensions and—more recently—wigs because, well, you can see there's not much to pin it to. I don't think anyone has seen me without two hours of makeup application in 20 years, so yes, I'm unrecognizable without it. My usual heels add half a foot to my height; I had ribs removed for my waist—but I still wear a cinch. My butt has fat added, my boobs are real but lifted, and my face is too many things to list. I take cell growth-accelerating pills that might kill me, and I freeze myself upstairs in my subzero tomb every day—cytogenetics. This is how I get to look like Janie Jones." She stared sadly at herself in the nearest mirror and whispered, *"You are enough, you are enough, you are enough."* She finished with two sharp, deep breaths and turned to them. "The only good thing about being temporarily single is not having to sleep in a wig and full makeup." Ortiz and Cheryl, stunned, stood silently, observing Janie's face as it suddenly fell. "Oh, I'm so sorry, detectives. I cannot believe I just told you that. I'm horrified"—she paused and exhaled—"*although* it did feel good to let it out. Not gonna lie. My therapist will be so proud, she's been wanting me to do this for years." A hint of a smile cracked her unlined face. "Do you mind if I call her quickly? I think this is the breakthrough moment we've been working towards." She clapped her tiny, chemically peeled hands softly.

"Well, sure, but, er, will she be available immediately? Or how long do you think it might take?" Cheryl enquired gently.

"Oh yes, she doesn't have many clients. I needed her so much that I just put her on salary. Actually, I could just go and see her. She lives in the fourth small house on the left—you drove past it—I promise I'll be no more than ten minutes, and then I'll tell you anything you need to know about Alma."

"Okay, um. Sure," Cheryl glanced at Ortiz, who shrugged. "On your return, we'd like to start with the last time you saw Ms. Astley before her death."

"Any girl can be glamorous. All you have to do is stand still and look stupid."
—Hedy Lamarr

Varsity Blues

JANIE JONES WAS NOT THE CONTRADICTION she believed herself to be. As she sashayed up to the entrance of Fred's on this sunny but deceptively cool day, her demeanor was calculated as 'look at me/don't look at me'—but in reality, was more 'look at me, pretending I don't want you to look at me': face lowered coyly, eyes covered by gigantic, elaborate Versace shades, gorgeous jiggling boobs semi-visible through her soft peach ribbed tank, nipples standing to attention, tiny waist and voluptuous derrière molded into sprayed-on chocolate leather pants.

As she reached the door, she whipped off her glasses, handed them and her cream Birkin to a waiting George, and turned, flipping her long layers of luxuriant wavy chestnut hair forward as she expertly posed her torso: Shoulders back, hip cocked, arms positioned to subtly enhance her world-famous breasts. A rose quartz crystal dangling from a thin gold chain trembled at the top of her cleavage as she conjured up her shy Lady Di face for the gaggle of waiting paparazzi (whom her team had called 30 minutes earlier.)

– *"Look over here, Janie!"*

- *"Love it, girl, and your GIRLS look fantastic in that top, Janie."*
- *"Who's your latest boyfriend? Whoever it is, he's a lucky man!"*
- *"Arch your back, Janie. Yeah, that's gorgeous—"*
- *"Can you turn round and show us your ass?"*
- *"Look over your shoulder. Wow, those pants are really something—"*
- *"Can't believe you've got a teenage daughter, Janie. Off to college soon. Isn't she sweetheart? Show us some teeth, honey. Big smile!"*

Having learned early on that silence imbued her with a mystique that her words did not, Janie didn't answer them. However, she complied with each physical request, posing patiently until the cameras had covered all their angles. As the beat paps knew, each frame would be useable and, whenever she got a famous new real or rumored boyfriend, they would sell for good money (great money if he was married). It was dependable income, and they loved her for it.

She sighed inwardly as she saw the photographers wrapping up and rapidly dispersing in pursuit of their next subject (the Biebers entering Prada, she gathered from the yelling). She waved goodbye and blew a kiss to their already turned backs. The fun was over, and now she returned to dreading lunch.

Inside, Alma was perched calmly on her velvet throne, slowly stirring her martini with a gold olive stick as she scrutinized the diners around her and filed away anything she could use. A celebrated director with the author of last summer's smash hit beach read—Lara would be perfect for the lead in that project. A famous couple, holding hands while arguing and periodically pretending to smile at each other through gritted teeth. America's favorite, most empathetic TV shrink yelling about his over-cooked Wagyu steak. She was amused today and therefore less triggered than usual when a waiter notified her of Janie's photo call outside. Alma never took her phone out of her purse when she had lunch meetings and was unreachable during the 50 minutes she allocated, laser-focused on her companion. Most found it to be less respectful etiquette and more of a terrifying torture technique.

Noticing diners' gazing subtly towards the door—even cynical Beverly Hills dwellers snooped celebrity with enthusiasm, albeit in a way that could be plausibly denied—Alma turned to see Janie walking towards her, balanced on 6" tan Saint Laurent heels, followed obediently by George carrying her sunglasses and purse.

Ugh, the gracelessness of these people, Alma thought. *So tacky to treat George like a servant. Janie, of all people, who didn't finish high school and was only saved from a career at The Olive Garden by a pushy, pageant-loving grandmother.* But out loud, she exclaimed, "Janie! Darling. Wonderful to see you. Please join me!" Janie smiled back thinly. *Somewhat of an achievement with her engorged lips,* Alma thought cattily.

"Hi, Alma. Can we do this quickly, please? I need to pick Sara up early from school today." She shimmied onto the seat and took her belongings from George.

"Of course, my dear. My much-preferred style, as you know." She turned to George. "George, your waiter may bring our food."

"But I didn't order yet!" squeaked Janie.

"Oh, Janie, since neither you nor your assistant responded to my office with your choices, we just had them prepare what you ate last time. I trust that will be amenable. I find that it speeds things up considerably to order in advance."

"She's no longer with me, and I didn't see your email, but yes, I guess it's fine." Janie smoothed her hair forward in a habitual move that ensured her aging jawline was rarely seen. "Um, what am I having?"

"Oh dear, another underpaid college grad bites the dust? There doesn't seem to be the right caliber of assistant out there for you, does there? So sorry. It must be exhausting training someone every month or two. And, you are having butter lettuce with two thin slices of avocado and five raspberries dressing on the side for dipping the leaves. Sparkling water with a mint sprig and five slices of lime. Will you need them to weigh the food?"

"No, that's okay. I can wing it today, and I don't need the avocado, but it's fine. I can push it aside."

"How gracious of you, dear."

Janie nodded, wondering if the beta blocker had been a placebo or if she needed to up her dose. At least her hands weren't shaking—her mind drifted to her next manicure design. *Purple ombré maybe . . .*

"Let's get to it, shall we?" said Alma, breaking her reverie. "First, the easy stuff. Your stylist, what's her name again?"

"Belinda."

"Yes, of course. Janie, why on earth did you discuss money with her? You have a whole team who can take care of such trivial matters. I'm not sure why you brought this to me and not your publicist, but since you have—"

"Oh, sorry, I didn't know who to ask, and I was on the phone with you just after she and I talked. Like I told you, I told her I would give her a raise. She's right, it has been a long time, and she and Jasper work very hard. I'm more confused about the expenses. Do I need to spend that much on tailoring? And am I supposed to buy my own bras and thongs? FedEx? Pay for gas? Shouldn't the studio or someone do that? It's not that I mind, and I'm sure she's right; it's just that I've never really thought about it, so I wanted to check with you guys."

"The studios will pay for zero they haven't been beaten into (and by that, I mean contracted). Your bras are not even jotted in pencil on their list. They know you must promote their projects and yourself in order to get cast again, so they have you over a barrel. Such is capitalism, Janie. Just be grateful you have had much success and many rich men and therefore have money. I know it's been *many* years but try to imagine starting out now. It's a costly game for a jobbing young actress, but compete they must. That said, don't waste one more moment of your valuable time on it. Leave it with me. Dustin will review the current retainer and draw up a new one, and I will meet Belinda personally to ensure everything is as it should be. It is important to have a check-in with these people."

"Oh, thank YOU, Al—."

"Now, let's get to the consequential matter," Alma interrupted. "You are contractually committed to Combat Queen 6, and you are going to do it, Janie, so let's not waste either of our time arguing over a rock-solid contract."

"But *my* lawyer says otherwise, Alma. He says there's a loophole. Look, I don't want to wear that god-awful rubber costume one more time. I'm sick of it. Sara says the script is written with a crayon. I can't eat for four months or drink water while we are filming—no bloating allowed.

I don't wanna be back on that dark and freezing sound stage in Croatia again—it's lonely and depressing and it'll set me back months in therapy. Especially as my Sara is preparing for college and can't come with me this time."

"Janie, you eat three raspberries as a treat, and Sara is almost 18. She was always going to leave her mama sometime. I'm surprised she can't drive herself home from school today. But, while we are on the subject, a little birdie told me she had a little help getting accepted into Manhattan U . . ."

Janie sat bolt upright, blood draining from her face as she struggled to retain her composure. *Terrible actress*, thought Alma, before continuing, "Yes, that's right. Don't even start to deny it. I have the contract you signed with the so-called 'fixer.' $250k! My dear, how stupid is your daughter?"

"*NO, no*, she's not stupid! MU is a very fancy school and therefore costs more to um, well, um, fix . . . I mean, I think she would have gotten in anyway. She's a brilliant writer, so smart—people keep telling me—not that I'd be a good judge. Please, we can't tell her. She can't ever know. I love her so much, and she wanted this so bad. Her dad just had another daughter in yet another country. Can't he ever keep it in his pants on location? She's been so down with all the tabloid stories comparing our looks and dissing her weight. This would literally crush her. Oh my god. I only paid him because I thought *I* would be a strike against her getting in. You know, me being a 'slutty commercial' actress. Even though I do have two Gilded Orbs—"

"Oh, those old things? I'd hide them if I were you, Janie, or, if you must, put them in the toilet of your ninth bathroom. The Orbs will never regain their former glory. Whoever respected that bunch of tacky, insanely dressed weirdos, questionably referred to as journalists? All they have is an affinity for white celebrities, freebies, and upmarket hotels—zero idea about what constitutes an award-worthy movie. The Orbs are *somewhat* useful for marketing and encouraging Oscar voters and, thus, I suppose, a necessary evil. If I were Meryl or Barbara, I'd set my nine statues up as pins in Barbara's bowling alley, next to the gift-wrapping room. Now, that would be amusing and befitting. They should play each other. I'm certain Barbara would win. Anyway, where was I? Yes, the contract . . ."

Janie, shaking uncontrollably, tried and failed to hide her tears by sliding on sunglasses, pleading, "Please, Alma. I'm begging—"

"So, it's settled then, Janie," Alma interrupted again. "You will commence filming, as per contract, in four weeks. You need to drop ten pounds before then, just FYI. I know Sara will love Manhattan U; it's an amazing school for her talent. I'll ensure Dustin sends flowers to her dorm for arrival. *So* fortunate we obtained *all* your documentation before the FBI started their investigation into your 'fixer.' Those people can be very helpful to us sometimes. Oh, and don't mention it to any of your friends. It's an ongoing undercover operation, and apparently, dozens of Hollywood parents are implicated. *Insanity*, since most of these kids don't even need to go to college to get a job; just a short call to Daddy or one of his friends." She stopped abruptly as their chiseled waiter approached. "Oh look, our food is here. Let's eat, darling." Alma gazed at their waiter. "You are so handsome, Joseph. Better stay away from Janie here. She'd devour you for lunch and dinner," then chuckled as he smiled flirtatiously. She turned to Janie as he walked away. "He's gay, darling, before you even think of it, and poor. How is the lettuce? My branzino looks delicious. I'm suddenly so hungry now that order has been restored. Bon appetit!"

FIRE THE STYLIST

Dishing Daily Doses of Fashion Justice

JONNY EVANS—Scorching the Hollywood Bowl.

Posted on February 26, 2018

Firers, we are FIRING up the temperature today with <u>Jonny Evans</u> in <u>Henri LeRoque</u> at his <u>concert</u> last night.

This was the gig that anyone who is anyone (and, according to Hollywood, that's everyone!) wanted to see and be seen at, with <u>tickets selling</u> out in just 45 seconds last summer and assistants bartering their lives for them ever since.

We can't speak for the live vibe, Firers, since we have no blackmailing skills or fancy contacts, but we can see from video and <u>images</u> that his wardrobe was on fleek! His series of <u>seven custom metallic suits</u> began with a black tux and ended, by way of increasingly light jewel tones, with him barefoot in glimmering <u>blush mini shorts</u> for the encore. The press release stated this symbolized Jonny returning from the 'dark to the light—a rebirth of his soul.' The accompanying <u>light show</u> progressed through the set, in step with the wardrobe colors: dark and thunderous at the outset and culminating in breathtaking, strobing reflections of hundreds of <u>white doves</u> that covered the whole bowl, audience, and all. MESMERIZING! And by that, we mean the show but also his HAWT-tanned, <u>muscular body</u>! (Click to ogle the video <u>here</u>!)

Henri LeRoque outdid themselves with this choice of ambassador, and, judging by the <u>numbers</u> on 'GRANITE,' Jonny's bestselling aftershave, they're proving that an organic collaboration can rake in cash. Give that <u>CMO</u> a raise!

As always, leave comments below!

(To review our community guidelines, please click here)

> **@ohyeahno** LEGEND. He's the effing MAN. Those doves are NOT crying
>
> **@lightandday777** Transcendent. Spiritually engaging. He is a fragrant designer GOD
>
> **@mizzbizzzz** Can I get in line to be his next wife please? #amblonde #wideopen
>
> **@humannigel** Was there! Can confirm he ATE!
>
> **@stonepatsy** He LEROQUED in those short shorts.

"I like being famous. It can be a bit of a pain, but you get free food in restaurants and people send you clothes."
—Noel Gallagher

To Slut or to Schoolboy?

Running errands. 5:15 pm

BELINDA'S PHONE RANG WITH ANOTHER ANONYMOUS CALL, the third in as many minutes. Concerned, she looked at Jasper, who'd taken one hand off the wheel to flip off a silver BMW. "*Manager's car*," he muttered to himself. "Oh, just answer it, Bels; they're clearly not gonna stop now, are they? Someone must need diamonds or a thong."

"*BELINDA!*" Tabitha's valley girl voice rang out on the speaker. "It's Tab! Where have you been? I've literally been calling *forever*. You know we have the Monte Carlo Music Awards, right?" Belinda looked questioningly at Jasper, and he mouthed, 'Next month.'

"Well, yes, Tabitha, but next month, we have the Oscars before then."

"I know *that*, but the Monte Carlo awards are a *huge* moment for me, him, I mean us. So, I need you to have as much time as possible to get this right. I mean, like, *perfect*."

"U-um," Belinda stuttered as Tabitha continued. "I have two ideas. Do you have time now? Oh, of course you do!" She laughed and continued, "The first one I'm crazy excited by. I'm thinking jailbait boy, androgynous, hot, drug-addicted schoolboy: I'd have Troy pixie-crop and bleach my hair, and you can flatten my tits with graffitied bandages. Jonny and

I will look like two naughty, anorexic, dirty little boys. *Fuck, I'm getting fucking horny just thinking about this photo op.*" Jasper choked on his coffee and, giggling, abruptly pulled over to wipe the liquid off his jacket with a rogue Shout wipe from the floor. "Alternatively, and stay with me here— oh, hang on, our new puppy just shat on the white fur rug—TERESA! Come and clear up Iggy's shit, quick! That's real fucking fur. Does dog shit stain? Anyway, where were we?"

"Alternatively . . ." Belinda offered helpfully.

"Oh yeah, alternatively, I want to go *slutty*, I mean hot, dirty, filthy, empowered *whore*. I want my tits and ass propped up, padded and *out*. Maybe I should get implants? Hmmm. How much time do you need for that? Anyway, I want everyone in the room and on the carpet to want to *fuck me* inside out. Got it? Are we clear? As you know, this night is a lifetime achievement award for, well, for Jonny, but you know it's *so* important to him that I'm happy."

"Yes, of course, Tabitha," said Belinda, shaking her head at Jasper and mouthing, "*Jesus Christ.*"

"Actually, in light of that, you should probably send me pictures of every piece you select so I can approve them in advance. Just my stuff, though, don't worry about his."

"Well—" Belinda was gaping now, and Jasper, trying to stifle his laughter, was doubled up in pain.

"Oh, and lastly, do *not* bring that star-fucker seamstress near us again. I deserve just as much respect and attention as Jonny. In fact, maybe you should bring us one person each for the next fitting? Okay. Great chat. Images by Friday? Thanks, Bel, gotta run, miss you, love you."

"Tabitha! Before you go, the Oscars are this weekend. We—"

"Oh, I'm not gonna go to *that*. I fucking hate gowns. What am I? A prom queen? The show is so long and boring. No thanks. Talk to Jonny's assistant about his shit. 'Kay?" Click.

Flabbergasted, Belinda turned to Jasper, who, driving again, was flipping off a blacked-out matt black Mercedes. "Fucking agent car."

"She's not going? Jonny is performing and *nominated* . . ."

"Yeah, and what's surprising there? Have you met that basic bitch, Bels?" Jasper laughed. "Jonny has literally the worst decision-making cock of all time. And Yelena a star fucker? That's hilarious. That high-rolling queen hates all of them. It's glorious." He drained the last of his cold coffee. "But, *more* interestingly, what's in our Star PR gift bags? I flogged the skincare they gave us last year on eBay and made like $600. A whole car payment. And let's pray to the gay gods there's no more logoed credit card wallets. They don't pay the rent."

"Her absence is like the sky spread over everything."
—C.S. Lewis, A Grief Observed

A Grieving Husband

POLICE WITNESS INTERVIEW: JAMIE DELANCY
Astley/Delancy residence. 1:45 pm

CHERYL PULLED UP TO THE POLISHED REDWOOD GATE of Alma and Jamie's Pacific Palisades home and pushed the recessed button. She looked at Ortiz. "Wow, these agents must make bank. And I thought her office was fancy."

Ortiz, distracted, just nodded her head. "I still can't stop thinking about Janie Jones."

"*M' hmmm.*"

"No, not like that. Did you know they had ribs removed?" Cheryl shook her head as Ortiz continued, "I mean, I heard men did it so they could suck their own dicks, which, let's be honest, is no freaking shock to no one. But for a small waist?"

"Jesus!" Cheryl choked as the intercom sprang to life, "Hello?"

"Good morning," Ortiz answered, "Detectives Hall and Ortiz here to see Mr. Delancy."

"Come in," a heavily accented woman's voice replied, "drive up to the cypress tree and turn right. You can park in the carport. You can't miss it; it's covered in ivy. If you walk from the side, Mr. Jamie will meet you on the terrace."

"Gracias," responded Ortiz, quickly swallowing the last piece of tepid, cut pineapple from the stained Tupperware.

The gates opened smoothly, revealing the crisp cleanliness of the vast Zen-like Garden surrounding the much-lauded house. Daringly built, it comprised three floors of asymmetrically stacked glass cubes edged in polished redwood. "It's like real fancy Lego, ain't it, Cheryl? If Lego could defy gravity."

"Expensive freaking Lego. It looks really familiar. Have I seen it in a magazine or something?" asked Cheryl as she carefully squeezed the car into a shaded parking spot behind a Tesla and alongside a Mercedes minivan.

Opening the passenger seat door, Ortiz untied the scarf from her neck and handed it to Cheryl, muttering, "You gonna freeze in that thin jacket."

"Thanks! One day, I'll get it right. Pretty sure this is the house in that famous rom-com. You know, the old one everybody loves, from the lady director?"

"Nancy Meyers?" offered Ortiz.

"Yeah, that one. Ortiz, you are very surprising sometimes."

"Only sometimes? Whatever, boss." Catching a glimpse of the exhilarating ocean view, Ortiz picked up the pace, rounding the corner and jamming her hands into her pockets to escape the chilly sea breeze, which was winning the battle with the blinding winter sun. *Never gets old*—she reflected, jealous suddenly—*bullshit that these rich folk get to own nature*, but dismissed the thought as she spotted Jamie rocking compulsively in a Perspex egg chair, staring vacantly into the rays.

Coming up behind her, Cheryl greeted him, "Good morning, Mr. Delancy."

"Jamie, please. Sorry," he added, indicating his half-smoked cigarette, which he then tossed into the marble fire pit in front of him. "Since Alma . . . Well, I started again."

"No problem, Jamie, I enjoy me a puff now and then," Cheryl smiled gently. "This won't take long, just a few follow-up questions. We didn't want to keep you after you'd identified her body." They settled into seats opposite him. "Now, can you describe your call at 5:52 pm?"

"Oh yes, our final phone call"—Jamie tried to compose himself—"was about the twins. They had just driven the Porsche into the swimming pool. Jemima is convinced she can drive but panicked and confused the gas for the brake. Thank god they chose the convertible one and weren't hurt at all. They just swam out. God, can you"—his voice broke—"imagine?" He paused to regroup and continued, "I was telling Alma what had happened while she was changing in her bathroom. She said, 'Hold on, Jamie,' and I waited and waited . . . She never came back."

"Could you hear anything at all? Any voices, noise?"

"There were a couple of faint banging sounds and maybe a wail?" He doubled up in searing pain. "I assume that was her dying. I didn't hear anything else."

"I'm so sorry, Jamie." Cheryl paused for a few seconds, allowing him to sit up again before gently probing, "Did you know about her bowling team?"

"Oh yes, although we were together for a while before I did. She's weird that way—was weird that way. Alma wasn't into therapy, but if I were to analyze it, I think it was a kind of pressure valve for her. She used to bowl regularly with her dad in England before he died when she was 14. Anyway, she told me she was going to Al-Anon every Friday for the first couple of years we were dating, but after I caught her in her kit, she came clean."

"The club said you've never been to a match?" Cheryl looked at his handsome, tanned face, stricken with grief, and took in his blue crumpled shirt, buttoned askew over baggy cargo shorts.

"Well, not that she or they knew of. I did sneak in once to watch her for a bit, but then I felt bad because she did take that time seriously, ya know. Like sacred. I'm pretty sure no one from her work world knew at all. Even the girls don't know because they would want to watch her—to have *watched* her." His eyes welled up, and he twisted his titanium wedding ring. "I think Alma was proud she managed to keep it private. It was the one thing that was just hers and she was fiercely protective of that."

Cheryl nodded. "Well, she succeeded. Everyone we spoke to in her office was perplexed by the description of her attire. So much so that most of them didn't believe it was Alma. Now, I'm sorry to have to ask this, Jamie, but can you think of a reason why anyone could have wanted her dead?"

"But it was an accident? I mean, she slipped, right? I mean, this is real life, not the movies. Most of her clients probably loathe her because she calls them on their bullshit, but they *love* her for what she gives them. Selfish fucks. They have no idea what she did behind the scenes to create their megastar careers, and they don't care."

"We cover all the bases until we get the coroner's report. But the evidence points to her being alone, and her injuries are consistent with a fall down the stairs. We don't know the exact time of death yet—your phone call is an indicator—but to double-check what you told us on Saturday, she drove to the Valley on Fridays at around 6:15 or 6:30?"

"Right. She liked to arrive before the game at 7:30 so she could chat with the girls on her team."

"Which leaves her alone in her office after her last meeting from around 6. We don't have camera footage from the mezzanine floor of Alma's office or her private elevator."

"No, she didn't want them in her private space, mostly because of the bowling, I think. She always got ready up there. Not that she'd have admitted that. She'd say it was for the clients."

"Can you tell us about her son from her previous marriage?"

"Yeah, Albert, he's in the UK. They are—were—pretty much estranged. I only met him once. Alma married a much older photographer when she was 19. Not to go into detail, but it was pretty fucked up and abusive. It's why she left her son to be raised by her sister and also why she quit modeling. I used to model, too, so I know that pain. Thank god the shit is starting to come out now about world-famous photographers. All those unpaid test shoots they called 'art.' Nope, not art, just private porn for perverts with camera power. No one protected us in those days. If you wanted to work with big guns, you took your kit off when they clicked their fingers." He shook his head, grimacing. "Anyway, her ex died when Albert was 12, but by then, he was poisoned against her and didn't want to leave England to come to the US. She was devastated. Her motivation was to be in a place— mentally and physically—where she could be a good mother for him. To have a life where she was in control and not a puppet. Alma loved LA from her modeling days. The beach and weather made her so happy, and she dreamed of Albert loving it too. So, she got an entry-level job at JDA.

Hard to imagine, you know? Her, an *assistant*? Especially since they had wanted to represent her as an actress originally. I'm sure you'll hear from people she slept her way to the top, but—as she more accurately used to put it—she worked with men who wouldn't allow her to even glance at the top unless she fucked them. It's so fucked up." He shook his head, tearing up again. "I think that's why she found a younger man. She'd had such a hard time with ones her age."

Ortiz nodded in agreement, muttering "*no shit*" under her breath.

Cheryl gently continued, "I'm sorry to have to ask about this, Jamie, but we hear she retained a suite at the Beverly Hills hotel for the last few months? There are rumors that you guys were having trouble?"

"Oh, not that again, this town's a fucking viper's nest of gossips. We had rows and rough times like any couple. But once every couple of years, Alma would get it into her head that I was leaving. I've been trying to write a screenplay forever, and honestly, I don't think I'm much of a writer—it was more her idea than mine." He smiled sadly. "And that realization pretty much started my midlife crisis. I'm a full-time dad, but now the twins are 14, I don't know what the fuck I'm doing. Mostly therapy and yoga and I've been really low. Alma got it into her head I was leaving—which is crazy—I'm never leaving. Would never have left." He started to sob. Wiping his running nose, he continued, "She just wouldn't believe me, made up her mind I was unhappy with her and nothing I said mattered. She got a suite at the Beverly Hills Hotel about two months ago and stayed there whenever she got paranoid. The last time she did this—about three years ago—she had a private detective follow me for a month. Oh, and she compulsively buys me clothes. I have boxes of them in the basement. *Oh god*"—he started weeping again—"*Sorry*."

"Please, Jamie, don't apologize. We're very sorry for your loss. Just one more question for now, and we will let you go. It's about her will. We understand that it's standard in terms of you and her three children being the sole beneficiaries. The only unusual thing is the numbered safety deposit boxes. She mandated that the contents of numbers three and four be destroyed sight unseen. Do you know anything about this?"

"I don't, I'm sorry. I thought she just had jewelry in the bank. It's probably work stuff. I take care of all the family finances and paperwork."

"Okay, good to know. Well, we're gonna go now and leave you be, but we'll be in touch soon, okay?" Cheryl touched his arm lightly. "Take care, okay? Do you have anyone staying with you and the girls?"

"Yeah, I do. My mom's here."

"Okay, good. Call us if anything comes up, okay? We'll be in touch soon. And again, our condolences."

Praise B

"Life is a disease; the only cure is rock 'n' roll."
—Unknown

FIRE THE STYLIST

Dishing Daily Doses of Fashion Justice.

Tabitha Evans dissing Cafe Gratitude.

Posted on February 26, 2018

Tabitha Evans (25) seen lunching today with a mystery man on the trendy, yoga-loving, yummy-mommy Larchmont Blvd in Los Angeles. Do she and Jonny ever eat out together? She and her averagely attractive companion didn't appear to be flirting throughout the lunch, so perhaps nothing for the HAWT hubby to worry about… Tabitha was wearing a Bebe Klein neon bathing suit with vintage Daisy Dukes, Saint Laurent biker boots, and a white, floor-length Valentino fur, their logo flaunted in giant black letters down the back of the coat in case anyone was in any doubt of its heritage. Firers, we can't believe the diners at this vegan hotspot didn't bombard her with eco-friendly paint bombs. Or, at the very least, swipe her prized $50k white croc Henri LeRoque purse. (Does this woman own another bag? She wears it so often that it appears no one can pry it out of those metallic talons.)

Leaving the restaurant, she posed for paparazzi before hopping into her silver convertible Porsche to pose all over again at the Silverlake Whole Foods.

What do we think, guys? Fur? Sustainable choice or cruel and gross opulence?

As always, leave comments below!

(To review our community guidelines, please click here)

> **@jonnyfan1116974** That's her hairdresser Travis. As all of Jonny's real fans know. She's always hanging with him. You guys are so behind.

> **@madamefop** So grossly disrespectful to go there in that coat. I would have puked my food up. Wearing a murdered animal and flaunting it to the people who are actually humane. B*tch

> **@eviroqween654** Fake fur is just micro plastic. More cash for the oil barons. Real fur is a far better sustainable choice. Do some research, you sheep.

> **@headcoldlife** I would sell a kidney for that purse. Anyone know who her surgeon is? I need those cheekbones, stat!

TUESDAY 27TH FEBRUARY 2018

"You are what you are when nobody is looking."
—Abigail Van Buren

Queen Bee

LARA WHITE, OSCAR GOWN FITTING
Cedric Tatou store, Rodeo Drive. 11:10 am

LARA ARRIVED AT THE TATOU STORE on Rodeo Drive, 70 minutes late. She regally exited the black tinted-windowed SUV they'd sent for her, took her bodyguard's waiting arm, looked down her nose (on which Tom Ford aviators were perched), and smiled left and right to the dusting of waiting fans.

Gliding through the door in a tan cashmere robe, Lara greeted the startled saleswoman like a long-lost friend. "So *kind* of you to offer," she loudly announced to the chic woman, who had yet to utter a word, "but no need to come with me—I know this place like the back of my hand." She walked confidently to the gilded elevator. "Joseph, could you be a darling and hold my purse? I want to greet Lucia with both arms the moment I see her!"

A mirrored two-floor ride later, she strode out into the glass penthouse VIP suite, Joseph trailing discreetly behind her, and spotted Lucia Rosa— powerful in a cream oversized tailored suit—smoking passionately and admiring the Beverly Hills view from the lusciously green roof terrace.

"My darling Lucia Rosa, *CIAO!*" she shouted through the open doors. "*Devine vederti! Mi sono mancato!*" Running dramatically to Lucia, she wrapped both arms around her tightly before pulling back and taking her cigarette. She inhaled deeply, grabbing her hand. "I love Italian cigarettes. They're so delicious!" Lucia Rosa, bemused—her kohl-lined eyes smiling—gently extricated her hand. "But Lara, thees is Marlboro brand. My assistant buys in CVS—"

"Lucia! You bleached your hair! LOVE!" Lara tossed the cigarette into a plant, babbling on ingratiatingly.

Sitting inside, watching, Jasper tried to contain his laughter, whispering to Belinda, who sat on the velvet couch beside him, concentrating on her email. "Well, I didn't know she spoke Italian."

Without looking up, she answered, "She doesn't. I bet you a hundred bucks that poor assistant Kelly looked it up in a rush because I speak a little Italian, and I believe she just yelled to Lucia Rosa that she's missed herself."

"The amount that one thinks about herself, there can't be one fucking *nanosecond* left for her to miss," Jasper muttered, tailing off as Lara approached, dragging a sanguine Lucia Rosa behind her. "Well, hello there Lara—looking fabulous, lady!"

"Why, thank you, Casp—I mean, Jasper, one of these years, I'll get it right! Hello, my sweet Belinda! *Now, my darlings*, have you seen my couture *bebe* yet? Is she," Lara breathed giddily, "magnificent?"

"*MAGNIFICA*," Alessia, VP of Celebrity, announced in her raspy Italian accent, appearing from the mirrored hexagon fitting room. "A *dream* Lara. *Squisito*."

Lara, confused, looked at Belinda, who mouthed discreetly, "*Exquisite*."

"Well, I have no doubt it is EXQUISITE. A woman of this talent could do no less. Shall we enter the zone together, darling Lucia? So that you can witness my utter joy at your exceptional creativity?" Tugging Lucia's arm, she pulled her into the perfectly lit, heated, and scented fitting room, moving jauntily to the discreet soundtrack of experimental Italian hip hop. She kicked off her scuffed cream mules and curled up on the navy loveseat. "Join me, Lucia," she said, patting the seat next to her. "They can present it to us together. Not *you*, Casper, you know how claustrophobic I can be. You can wait outside."

"Alora," Lucia responded, visibly shocked by her rudeness, "but of course I have seen it, Lara."

"Ah, but *alora*, you will see it as if for the first time with *me*, darling." Lucia Rosa reluctantly sat beside her, eyes widening at Alessia as Lara laid her head on her lap and sang in an ear-shattering voice, "*BRING IN THE MASTERPIECE.*"

Moments passed—only the low hum of rapped Italian swearing could be heard as they waited, looking uneasily at each other. Eventually, Lara sighed impatiently and questioned, "Alex, *are you bringing it in*?"

"It's A-LES-SIA, Lara, and *si*, it is coming. Since you were so late, we sent it back downstairs to the Atelier to continue sewing the crystals. We still 'ave around four 'undred to apply on the back, mostly just the train, but of course, it will be perfection by Sunday."

"OH. *I see*. Belinda, may I have a private word?"

"Now? Um, in here? Should we go out on the terrace, Lara?" Belinda conflicted, glanced at Lucia Rosa.

"No, it's okay, Lara, Belinda," Alessia interjected diplomatically. "We have a call to make anyway. She turned to Lucia Rosa. "*Bene?*"

" *Si*." Lucia Rosa stood, slipped off her jacket, pushed up her impeccably cut cream shirt sleeves, and shrugged. "*Anch'io una sigaretta.*"

So chic, thought Belinda, suddenly feeling tired and disheveled as she observed her. Lucia Rosa, noticing her gaze, smiled sympathetically before following Alessia out and closing the door softly behind her.

Lara stood abruptly, shoving her feet into her mules." Belinda," she snapped, "tell me, why am I here if this dress is not finished?"

"It *is* basically finished. Only the remaining crystals have to be hand-sewn onto the train, Lara. The train that we requested to be added just four days ago. Remember it was part of the original design, and we had them remove it? Then you wanted it added again? It's all hand-sewn, and they work in shifts day and night." Belinda fought to keep the terror off her face. By reminding Lara of her involvement in the delay, she was rolling the dice and, from experience, she knew it could go either way.

"Of course, I know that, Belinda. Do you take me for a fool? It's just not relevant. What *is* is that you asked me to come here to try on something that is not even completed. You didn't manage to persuade them to create my burning hologram fabric. Now John, *he*, when he was head of this house, would have achieved my vision. I had his cell, you know,

I could call him any time. And I did. Once—before your time—I had a dream that I was a hot gangster's moll, and I was on the carpet naked but for a couture beige raincoat, six-inch hooker platforms, and a complementary trilby hat. Draped in diamonds obviously, goes without saying." She flapped a hand. "John was excited beyond words at my vision and went to work immediately. It was shipped from Paris three days later, and of course, you know the results. The *world* knows the results, so iconic is that image."

"*Iconic.*" Belinda nodded, though she knew that the image made the cover of every tabloid in the world because it was taken on the night that Lara, hammered, made out with the six-time sexiest man of the year, Raphael Lopez, at the In-N-Out Burger in the Valley, the Trilby shadowing—but not entirely disguising—their faces.

"Anyhoo, Belinda." Reminiscing about the viral image had enhanced Lara's mood. "This is a shambles. It is enough that I have to deal with all the rumors about Alma and you. Do you know I had five texts about it just last night. *Five.* Of course, I support you—it's well-known how loyal I am, how long have I worked with you? Four years? It's absolutely ridiculous for anyone to suggest I would be associated with a violent person. Ridiculous. As if my judgment of people is flawed." She snorted.

"Now, about this dress debacle. I, sweet Belinda, will fix this for you. I suggest I leave now, and Lucia and Alex can bring it to my house with the Atelier when it is *finally* ready. There, it's settled. Oh, and we still have the Prada coming, right? And the gown from the hot London eco designer? Of course, I will never wear that one, but one likes to allow them to *try.* The Gucci custom? Perhaps find me a couple more, too. Okay good. Do you have time for a girls' lunch?"

"Sorry, Lara, I don't. I have to sort things here, and I have another fitting."

"Never mind, probably for the best. You don't need any more pap photos, even with me!" She marched out of the dressing room, surveyed the suite for Lucia, and, not seeing her, took Joseph's strapping left arm (his right one remained carefully holding her purse), waved a brief dismissive goodbye to no one, and entered the waiting elevator.

Alessia silently observed Lara's exit, leaning into a hidden corner and smoking out of a window. As the door closed with a gentle ping, she walked her willowy body to the center of the room. "Darhling Belinda, why does Lara always wear so much 'orrible beige in real life? It eez so unflattering on her anemic skin. I am always meaning to ask you, but I forget."

"Oh, I know! I've tried so hard to get her away from it, but Karl told her years ago—after a show—that beiges, tans, and browns were absolutely her colors, and although one needs to 'explore color for the red carpet,' she should never wear any other shade in her private life."

"Oh, Belinda!" Alessia threw her head back, swinging her thick blonde blow-out and letting out a dirty throaty laugh. "Karl loathed her. Everyone in Paris knows this—he used to call her '*Le gamin vulgaire*.' I never worked with him, but still, I miss him. He was *cosi cattivo*."

"Fucking hell! For real? Jasper, did you hear that?"

"Oh sister, did I ever! Oh lord, please allow me to rise temporarily into fashion heaven so I may talk further shit with his sartorial Highness on this sacred day. Bless you, Karl." He mimed a cross.

"Alora," Alessia chuckled, "let us sip champagne. Necessary medicine during this hellish week, no?" She beckoned the waiting model/waiter. "Now Belinda, let me give you a bag—to replace the Chanel you have there—god knows you deserve one." She opened a cream-ruched leather wall panel, revealing a hidden accessories display. "What color, *amore*? Blush would be so chic for you, I think. Also, we have drinks soon at the Castilian? We can play 'Spot the John,' and you can tell me about the strange story of dead Alma, no?"

"When you are in the ocean, you must swim."
—Pedro Almodovar

Patriarchal Play

POLICE WITNESS INTERVIEW: GEORGE BOIS
Manager of Fred's. 10:45 am

TO THOSE WHO PAY ATTENTION TO THESE THINGS, Fred's unremarkable mustard doorway is one of the most recognizable in the world. The portal to Tinsel Town's historic and legendary restaurant stands demurely and anonymously in the background of decades of paparazzi pictures. It is as infamous as the Viper Room door, but Michelin-starred, discreet, and less tragic.

Standing outside the entrance on this chilly morning, George, its almost-as-famous manager, was waiting for Cheryl and Ortiz. Seeing them approach, he nodded respectfully and used both hands to shake each of theirs graciously. "Good morning, detectives. I am George. Please come this way. We are just setting up the tables for the early lunch crowd. Shall we sit at the bar?"

"Sounds good," Cheryl nodded, showing her badge and following him as she rattled off their names. "Thank you for seeing us."

"*De rien.*" He pulled out two tall brass and auburn velvet bar stools for them, positioning a third for himself to complete the triangle. "I am so distraught about *ma chère* Alma. I cannot believe it is impossible." His grief-stricken eyes flickered to her booth, empty save for a wild arrangement of velvety burgundy-black dahlias. Noticing the detectives following his gaze, he clarified, "That was 'er booth. She detested traditional arrangements—they reminded her of funerals and weddings. She liked wild and rare blooms, always critiquing my choice of flowers for the restaurant as 'pedestrian.' *'Flowers should remind us that one must allow oneself to grow in all the places people never thought you would.'* Of course, I would remind her that she was not my only customer, but as it turns out, in my heart, she was . . ." George blinked rapidly, visibly pained. "*Pardon.* You are not here to witness my grief." He dabbed the corners of his melancholic blue eyes with a linen napkin. "How can I be of service to you?"

"We just have a few routine questions, Mr. Bois," Ortiz jumped in, "while we wait for the autopsy results. If you could tell us the last time you saw Alma?"

"Please. Call me George. She came in for lunch on Friday with Janie Jones. Her preferred time was 12:50. It seemed amicable enough. Ms. Astley doesn't seem to care much for Ms. Jones"—he shrugged his chalk-striped shoulders—"these clients can be so difficult, but it was not *compliqué*. Not like the lunch on Tuesday with Lara White."

"Complicated?" Ortiz questioned.

"Yes, *pardon*. On Tuesday, she sat down with Ms. White for a few minutes, and the conversation looked very tense—to me at least—but detectives, I know her very well since 25 years. She rarely leaves before eating. However, that day, she had her order sent to her office and left Ms. White to eat alone. Insisting, in fact, that she do so. From my position close to the table, I saw that Ms. White was trying to leave, but whatever Ms. Astley said forced her to stay. I did not hear this. It is imperative in my line of work to be discreet—and I learned early—the less you hear unintentionally, the better. Ms. White ate her lunch awkwardly and rapidly. From observing her, one could reasonably assume she never dines alone."

"So, they'd had some kind of disagreement?"

"*Oui*—yes. That day, Ms. Astley did not want me to wait outside to greet Ms. White as I did for all her VIP guests. She told me to '*leave the child to the hostess.*' I had the impression that Ms. Astley expected disagreement."

"You say you've known her very well for 25 years. Just from her coming here?"

"Non, but at first, yes. I was new here from Paris, and she was from London. She worked for that horrible man at JDA—this is a big Hollywood agency—in case you are unfamiliar. He demanded everything and *tout suite. Mon Dieu* he fired women even for a little weight gain or bad skin. One day, she forgot to reserve his 'standby' table for the evening, and we were fully booked—as we always are. She came here in person and begged me. She was then—as now—well not now . . ." He faltered briefly. "Impossible to refuse. *Monsieur* Eastwood was not happy that night, and the revolting JDA CEO did not even turn up."

"Wow, she was something, even for this town," Ortiz blurted. "Sorry, I can't believe I said that out loud. Jesus. Ignore me; please go on."

"Yes, yes she was, detective," He smiled. "Please don't apologize. It is nice to hear. Well, from that day, we became friends. We missed our origins and loved culture similarly—art, fashion, food. She was utterly stunning, wild, and sensual. Every rich man wanted to possess, control, and hide her in their mansions for private consumption. I'm sure you must know of her reasons for leaving Europe?" They nodded sadly. "Alma was fragile then, mourning leaving her son and yet to harness her untethered power. Sadly, she had to endure more abuse in her journey to control access to her body and to gain the protection self-earned money could afford. From the beginning, Alma knew the way she was going to do this was to run the most successful agency in Hollywood. She was ruthless in her pursuit of autonomy. I gave her what I could. Even as an assistant—she was the *only* person in town who was guaranteed a table at Fred's. And, detectives, you must understand it is *impossible* to get a reservation, and to be seen here is to be *seen*. I would place her prominently, often next to clients she was cultivating. As for me, when my contract was being renewed, or the owners were in town, Alma would ensure a superstar dine here and vocally sing my praises. She made Fred's synonymous with George. I am now a well-paid co-owner because of her. In the early days, she would often come by at closing, after work or an event, and we would supper together, plan her takeover, and play chess. Now, of course, she has taken over. We are old, have partners, and mostly play a chess game over our phones. *Played.*"

"You have a husband?" Cheryl asked, observing his impeccable style and wedding ring.

"Ah, *non*. I have a wife."

"Oh, my bad. Sorry."

"*Non*, it's fine; it 'appens all the time. This whole town thinks I am gay because I am private and dress with finesse—so few men here know how—in France it is *expected*." He sniffed, spinning one of his mono-grammed cufflinks. "She flew me home twice. The first time—before my wife we were always friends, never lovers, you understand—one of her male clients (I forget who) was in a campaign for Dior, and we went to the show. I adore Dior. The next time was with ma femme, Andrea. Alma took us to Cannes for *Le Festivale*, with Jamie. We didn't see her much—she was so busy being powerful—but it was an exceptional, cham-pagne-drenched weekend. How do you say it here? Such a gauche phrase, but truly a bucket list moment."

He looked over at her booth and said softly, "*Je ne peux pas croire qu'une telle beauté soit partie.*"

"Oh, pardon my language, detectives, I was just saying—"

"No need, George. Pretty sure we get the idea."

"Los Angeles is a large city-like area surrounding the Beverly Hills Hotel."
—Fran Lebowitz

U-Hauling

RIDING IN CARS WITH STYLISTS
Leaving Cedric Tatou. 1:15 pm

SLUMPED IN THE PASSENGER SEAT, Belinda sighed as she rammed down an organic almond energy bar and then haphazardly applied more red lipstick before rubbing most of it off. "Lara wants to try more dresses, Jas. Jesus Christ."

"Are you *kidding me*?" Jasper swerved into the inside lane. "Do you think she's going to nix the Tatou? *FUCK!*"

"God, I hope not. Alessia has a temper on her like no other. She loves me, but she will lose her shit, and who would blame her? Remember the 2016 Met Ball when she called as I was about to take off for New York and bellowed about Ava-Lily randomly dying her hair pink?"

"Oh yes, teenage mega-stars dying their own hair is always a winner. Add bonus points for her matching cat."

"Yup. Ugh. Who could blame Alessia? The hair did clash horrifically with the neon yellow couture. But am I supposed to babysit 24/7? How much power am I supposed to have? Thank god she raged in Italian, so I didn't understand most of it. But she was so loud that the woman in the next seat started comfort-stroking my arm." Belinda grimaced. "The amount of time Tatou has spent on this dress already, fuck, I hate making custom for Lara. Oh, and she *also* nixed the eco gown from London. So much for that fad."

"Saving the planet lasted two months. That's a lifetime for her."

"The amount of money they must have spent making this dress, it's so complicated. I'm pretty sure they got a loan to do it. I *told* Lara they were a young brand, and we shouldn't go ahead unless she were serious. So idiotic of me to think she'd wear it to the Vanity Fair party at least."

"Aw, your naivety is sweet. But maybe you could persuade her if, for once, you'd turn your volume *on* and *up*! *IT'S A STOP SIGN, BITCH!*" Jasper yelled at a woman in a brushed gold Bentley. "*ARE YOU BLIND?*" He glanced at Belinda. "Mind you, she might be, looks like she's 80, which in this town means 100 plus."

"Beverly Hills! The more expensive the car, the fewer traffic rules you follow—you *know* this—stop signs and traffic tickets don't apply."

"It fucking sucks," Jasper grumbled, "but back to the other privileged bitch, let's go positive and assume she's gonna wear the Tatou because Alessia will put a hit out on her otherwise—which, thinking this through—might be a better outcome for everyone."

"Also, Jas, she brought up Alma. People are texting her about me, apparently. She told them she wouldn't work with anyone violent. Can you fucking believe this? Me, violent?"

"Oh honey, try not to focus on it, yeah? It'll blow over. You know this town. Someone will have a large lunch mistaken for a pregnancy or their deleted racist tweets from ten years ago will resurface, or, best case scenario, Ben and Jen will get engaged again and the gossip will roll on. Now, are you ready for Ava-Lily?" He pulled up to a line at the valet.

"Who the fuck tries to valet a U-Haul at The Beverly Hills Hotel?" Exasperated, he sighed as he waited. "*Shit*, is that Chanelle?" Opening the window, he yelled, "Babe, what are you doing in that thing? I told you to rent a minivan!"

"Oh yaaaa, hi guys. I tried, but I couldn't rent one as I'm not like, 25. The guy told me all I could rent was this. It makes literally no sense at all—waaay harder to drive—I already reversed into a wall. Don't worry. My family has great insurance. Anyway, I tried to call you and you're like always telling me to show initiative." Chanelle shrugged, and Jasper turned to look at Belinda, who was typing furiously. "Do you need a Xanny? I for sure do." Belinda lost again in emails, ignored him, so he swallowed half a one dry as he watched Chanelle totter back to address the head valet.

"I don't know your problem, but I've got to valet this ugly van. I have an important Oscar fitting here, and the clothes are literally tied up in the back. I can't be late, so stop being so difficult." The valet was shaking his head, clearly disgruntled, and Jasper couldn't quite catch his words but could easily make out Chanelle's haughty tone. "Look, will I have to call Daddy to talk to Edward? You know him—well, maybe you don't—he's the general manager. My family might as well live in this place. Jesus, we had my christening, my sweet-sixteen, and, last month, my 21st here." Jasper strained to hear another muffled response from the increasingly flustered, uniformed man. "Look, if you can't park it downstairs, just leave it here. Be much better for me anyway. Like, way quicker when I leave. Just bring three carts and three bell boys. Here's the key. They can unload the back." Seeing him still hesitating, she sighed, "Look, stop giving me shit, we both know I'm literally gonna win. Here's $100. Now can you *hustle*?"

Jasper, mesmerized by this side of Chanelle, nudged Belinda. "Hey, you don't want to miss this, it's fucking fantastic. Chanelle rented a U-Haul. Now there's a reality show. Hey, HEY. EARTH-TO-BELS. Christ, look at your face. I'll ask again—do you need a Xanax?" Finally hearing him, Belinda shook her head.

"Thanks, babe, but I think I'm okay. I drank half a bottle of CBD oil sitting on Tatou's heated chrome loo. That's why I took so long. It was hard to move after that, to be honest."

"I did wonder what was blocking you, well, at least you got a new bag."

Classy Operation

The Beverly Hills Hotel. 2:45 pm

"AVA-LILY WILL BE WITH YOU SHORTLY," announced Jackie, her stocky body compressed into a black stretch Amazon Basics pantsuit. She added in her raspy, smoker's New Jersey accent, "You can set up in here." She beckoned them to follow and stomped in her steel-toe-capped boots to the end of the suite, gently stroking the white Persian cat asleep in her arms. Opening gold-painted double doors, she revealed an opulent French baroque bedroom, saying gruffly, "This should be enough room." Belinda and Jasper nodded as Chanelle—and the three bell boys behind her—struggled to maneuver unstable vintage hotel carts teeming with designer garment and shopping bags. "Do you have the mirror?" asked Jackie, with a hint of panic. "The special mirror? You know, the one that makes things look better?"

"Yes, Jackie," Jasper responded soothingly, "the same one we brought last time."

"Yeah, okay, great, sorry, I shouldn't have asked," she said, beginning to thaw, "you guys run a *classy operation*, unlike some others."

"Thank you," they said simultaneously, stifling smiles.

"Yeah, anyways, I don't know if I told you yet about Sabine. The last stylist and the whole Cannes mess?" Gently releasing the cat, she perched her sturdy 6ft frame on the edge of a velvet armchair, pushed up her ill-fitting, hair-covered sleeves, and settled in to watch them set up.

Jasper glanced at Belinda, who was typing furiously on her phone, and without looking up, they said in unison, "Yes."

"*Well*," she plowed on, oblivious, "that dress from that French place *Lav*-something hadn't arrived."

"Lanvin," Jasper interjected.

"Yes, that one. You guys know your shit. Well, my Ava was understandably freakin' stressed. I mean that Cannes event is very prestigious. Sabine brought her nail person to Ava-Lily's room and was getting a freaking *manicure* while this was going on. *No* assistant. She wasn't even bothered—just smoking and yelling at people in French on her phone. Such a loud voice on that long stick of a body, and get this, telling me in a rude voice to stop worrying and mind ma business"—she paused to puff on her vape—"as if everything to do with Ava isn't my business. I've saved her from stalkers nine times and ordered her lunch every frigging day since she was 14, give or take a sick day or two. That's five years now, in case you creative people are no good at math." She shook her yellow bleached ponytail stub, smiling fondly. "Can ya believe she's 19? My little Capricorn's gettin' all grown up."

Jasper, efficiently unzipping garment bags on the racks, egged her on: "She adores you, Jackie."

"Well, I don't know about that. I'm just here to serve. I'm lucky to have this fancy gig after 22 years in the force. My girls are still excited even now—don't see them much, of course—with all the traveling. She can't stay still that Ava. Can you believe she came to my Jenny's wedding at a golf club in Hoboken? Well, she stopped in to pick up this one"—she gestured at the now-sleeping cat—"I'd been cat-sitting Ulysses while she took that residential needlepoint course. But still nice of her to say hi and try the disco fries. It wasn't her fault she didn't know the gravy wasn't vegan. She didn't mean to spit on my dress. The stain did come out eventually, and she paid for the dry cleaning, of course," Chuckling, she continued, "Anyway, back to Cannes, this Sabine, can you believe it, she starts to tell Ava she'll just have to wear a different dress. There were about twenty boxes with other frocks in them in the guest bedroom, and she calls a maid from the hotel to hang them up. I mean, who wudder thought? The maid was pissed, I think, but then those Frenchies always look pissed, don't they? Anyways, it turns out Sabine's pop mighta owned the hotel. I wasn't sure what with all the foreign talk, and I didn't like to ask. Not my place, of course. Anyways, I call her a stylist loosely 'cause she weren't no stylist now I've met the likes of yous. She's some kind of social person—skinny and pretty— famous for something, I never did find out what. Anyways, the dress from the Lav place turned up in the end, and pretty great it was too, but what doesn't look great on my gal, eh?" She smiled maternally. "Well, that Sabine, you'll never guess! She goes in the other room and puts on a long gold dress herself—with a train and *everything*—then waved at us and says, 'I am so late for *my* red carpet,' and left! Can you friggin believe it? Ava's gold dress wasn't even *steamed*. I did it, of course, and thank god the hairdresser tied the big bow right, put on the nipple covers, and figured out the weird bondage shoe. I had to pack up those twenty boxes, which was a freaking nightmare. Like I said, it's a classy operation you guys are running here. Long may it last!"

She stood up, puffing on her vape again and surveying the room, taking in the six skillfully arranged racks and heels in every color that snaked around the perimeter. Chanelle was anxiously organizing tiny black and nude bras and various styles of child-sized Shrunx on the ornate four-poster bed. With a flourish, Jasper removed straps holding a gifted black cashmere Ralph Lauren blanket in place and unveiled the $24 Target mirror. He balanced it on the wall opposite the windows for maximum light and announced, "*TA DA! Behold 'The Sorcerer.'*" The Sorcerer had been an improbable last-minute purchase on the way to a fitting with Lara on location a couple of years previously—a mirror that miraculously conjured up an almost imperceptibly trimmer and longer reflection, help-fully countering the omnipresent body dysmorphia in Hollywood—thus making their job immeasurably easier.

"Looking good, guys! Let me check on Ava," Jackie growled, jogging out of the room.

"Where's Yelena?" Belinda whispered to Jasper urgently as soon as she was out of earshot. "We said 3, right?"

"Yes. Let me text her. You know how crazy Oscar week is, and she's in one of her moods." He mimicked quotation marks and pulled out his Gucci phone case, startled as they heard loud banging. Belinda rushed to open the door. "Yelena! Are you trying to break into the Beverly Hills Hotel? We told you to text, not knock. Ava-Lily naps in the afternoons."

"Oh, fock's sake. I am up ALL the nights sewing these beetches dresses. How can I remember all this stupeed shit?" She dumped her bag on the floor and carefully placed her sewing machine on the table by the entrance. "Why do I have to bring the machine, huh? Stupeed. Will not get sewing done here, this crazy beetch so tiny I have to recut *everything*, taking focking hours and all my girls' time."

"We've been over this before. You know Ava-Lily feels safer if she can see you with a machine. A costume designer dressed her for years, so she still doesn't understand how we work."

"Why I do this, I don't know—just for you two—you not beetches like the others. All celebrity stylists are *beetches*." Yelena paused, her face softening as she looked sadly down at them. "One day you two will also be beetches, is not possible to no be beetch after working years in crazy town." She turned and stared at Chanelle. "Who is this?"

"Chanelle, our new intern. Chanelle, meet Yelena." Yelena reluctantly grunted hello.

"Actually, Chanelle, you should go now. Ava-Lily only meets staff she has agreed to in advance. Can you grab Lara's newly dyed shoes from Jack please. There should be three different shades of red. Drop off the rings to Tiffany: Jasper, can you give them to her, please? Caroline has decided today that the Shrunx that have always worked '*don't work*' and wants to try an old-fashioned corset at our fitting, so please do something about that. Collect the Ralph Lauren tux for Emily, and Lara wants her bodyguard to have a designer bag to carry her flats, deodorant, raspberries, and weed for the husband on the day of the Oscars. She wants it to be—and I quote—'*chic but manly*.' Go to Ferragamo and see if they have a plain black tote or something, but for god's sake, DO NOT tell them it's for the bodyguard." She sighed. "As if we don't have enough to think about. Are you writing this down?"

"No need, I'll text her the list in a second." Jasper turned to Chanelle, smiling reassuringly at her shocked face and handing her a brown paper bag worth $300,000.

"Put this in your purse and NEVER lose sight of it. You might wanna get yourself a backpack before the weekend; it's safer. Anyway, go to Tiffany's first, give these to SARA, with no H, and *only* Sara, and get her to text me to confirm receipt. Now get going before Ava-Lily sees you, babe. Text with questions—I can't talk in a fitting—be back here by five, okay?"

As Chanelle tottered from the room, her fingers, with their impossibly long ombré acrylics, tightly clutching the latest Celine 'It' purse, Yelena snorted: "She vil last four minutes, with those platforms and false eyelashes like she on red carpet. I bet she drives Mercedes, no?"

"A Porsche. Family money: how the fuck else could you afford to be an intern in this town?" Belinda shook her head as she pulled diamonds out of more brown paper bags and deftly arranged them on black-velvet-lined trays. "So few of them are like our Jasper here, who worked at a dazzling downtown factory four days a week when he first started interning for me, right Jas?"

"OMG, Bel, staaapit!" Jasper swatted her shoulder. "But yes, Yelena, my delicate fingers bled, designing Swarovski crystal art on costumes for whip-cracking, show pony riding-bitches. Yes, they did—honestly, it wasn't terrible prep for this batshit world—and my designs were A-mazing."

"Yes, they *were*! They *are*!" Belinda agreed. "His work is *insane*. Tell her how Carrie Underwood wore one of your jackets on tour."

"Oh my focking gods, I LOVE Carrie Underwood music!" Yelena squealed, uncharacteristically animated. "I play *all the time*. I want to do tailoring for her, but her beetch person says I am rude."

"Surely not, Yelena," Jasper deadpanned.

"Exactly. Rude. Me? No."

"Yelena, sssh." Trying to keep a straight face, Belinda pointed at Jackie, heading back towards them.

"So sorry, you guys. Ava-Lily is just so tired. Can you come back in two hours? Between us, knowing her as I do. I think it'll go better—if you catch ma drift."

"Um, I guess, Jackie,' Belinda exhaled, adding reluctantly, "I think that should be okay. Let me try to move some stuff ar—"

"Great! Thanks guys. Like I always say, classy operation." This time, neither Belinda nor Jasper found it amusing.

"And all who told it added something new,
And all who heard it made enlargements
too."
—Alexander Pope

Chatty Cops

Leaving Ava-Lily

The Beverly Hills Hotel Lobby. 3:15 pm

"Fock dis," Yelena yelled, tugging her sewing machine on wheels down the tropical trompe l'oeil corridor. "This teenage beetch is the *WORST*."

"I don't know why you just didn't leave the machine in the room, babe," Jasper shrugged.

"How you think I focking sew without it? You think I got 100 machines? I got a million dresses to fix before Sunday, most of them yours. No way I can take two hours off. I'm *NOT* bringing it back, okay? No way. Stupeed little girl understands nothing but that ugly fat cat."

"Yeah, we get it, babe," Jasper pacified, knowing how much they relied on her this week—and all the weeks. "Can I carry it for you?" he offered.

"Are you joking? I am twice your size," Yelena replied gruffly but softened a fraction.

"*Belinda Grant*?" Hearing her name ring out as they reached the expansive, packed lobby, the three turned.

"*Detective!*"

"Whatcha doing here?" Cheryl asked. "This is Detective Ortiz. She was outside your house yelling if you remember."

Belinda laughed. "Oh yes, good to finally meet you."

"Same," nodded Ortiz and stepped away to answer her phone.

"One of our clients is staying here. She's napping, so we're just leaving, coming back to fit her for the Oscars later. This is Jasper—he works with me—you probably saw him picking me up on the security footage."

"Oh, we did. Good luck this week. I'm getting to know a *lot* more about your world and I had no idea. Hats off to you both," Cheryl grinned, adding, "You don't work with Jason Bird, do you?"

"Why thank you, detective," Belinda laughed, "And no, I do not. Funny, you should ask because we did a one-off shoot with him this weekend. I take it you met him—hope you aren't too traumatized?"

"Piece of work. Ortiz has been buggin' about him all day—"

"He's a POS"—Ortiz, hand covering her phone, interrupted—"but she destroyed him, and it was fire"—then returned to her call.

"How did she hear that?"

"Apparently, as I'm learning, nothin' gets past her. Anyway, gotta run. We will update you when we can, okay?"

"I appreciate that, detective. I'm getting swallowed by rumors, stalked by tabloids, and that's before I start work . . ." And as the words came out of her mouth, she spotted Daniel, Juliet Hunt's hairdresser, in her peripheral vision. Unmissable in a tight tan leather jumpsuit with matching Gucci work case, his trout lips were wide open, staring at them.

"Oh, *fuck*. Sorry, detectives, um, I have to go." She turned and realized they'd already left and that Jasper was alone. "Where's Yelena?"

"Oh, you didn't notice? She just kept walking when you stopped to talk to the cops—her face turned ghostly. Maybe she robbed one of those casinos she frequents in her spare time? Such a dark horse. We must interrogate her one of these days."

"You are so dramatic, Jas! And you wouldn't *dare*—she'd skin you alive—besides, who knows if she's legal or maybe just terrified of guns like us? *Ugh*, I can't believe gossipy Daniel saw me with the cops." Belinda turned to wave at him, plastering a smile on her face as she hurried out of the foyer. Daniel moved his wrist unenthusiastically in her direction and pulled out his phone, typing, 'OMG, YOU WILL NEVER GUESS WHAT I JUST SAW! Cops were questioning Belinda Grant *AGAIN*.'

FIRE THE STYLIST

Dishing Daily Doses of Fashion Justice

LARA WHITE, OSCAR NOMINEES
luncheon, Beverly Hilton Hotel.

Posted on February 27, 2018

We missed this one yesterday, perhaps because we took one glance, fell asleep, and didn't wake up until today: the 33-year-old actress in yet another wide-leg pantsuit. Despite it probably being the 100th pantsuit she has worn in the last year, we still, for you dear reader, dutifully report that this cream double-breasted silk version is from the fall Gucci runway, worn with a scarlet Edie Parker clutch and Martine jewelry. The accessories, at least, are interesting!

What does Lara's stylist, Belinda White, have against this woman's legendary legs? Has she stopped shaving her legs as well as her armpits? How could anyone forget her luscious pits at the Critics' Choice Awards last month? Not Versace and not us; it's burned into our eyeballs. We may still be (definitely are) debating whether her hairdresser applied serum to those smooth and shiny underarm tresses.

Belinda, we beg of you, WAKE US UP. And, for the love of god, what were those generic Michael Kors flats doing anywhere near a Gucci suit? Is her body lunching in Beverly Hills while her feet work at Macy's?

This might be an unforgivable crime. What do you think, Firers? Should Lara White #FTS?

As always, leave comments below!

(To review our community guidelines, please click here)

> **@juicyanddelicious** That's a great suit. Nothing wrong with classic style, you guys. Also #FREETHEHAIR

> **@laraliveloveslaughs** We are not worthy! Also Michael Kors is expensive, fuck off with this snobbery

> **@jolearnstoday** Please read about this subject before you make such thoughtless comments. The history of body hair removal in the US is racist. Current beauty norms keep all of us feeling inadequate and corporations rich. #nothingwronghair

> **@metalman** I'd still bang it

"People need to be edited;
life needs to be edited.
I need to be edited."
—Andre Leon Talley

Pay to Play

RIDING IN CARS WITH STYLISTS

3:20 pm

"HI, DEVON, IT'S BELINDA. Hang on one sec, I'm getting in the car." She threw her Chanel bag on the floor, unperturbed by the lipsticks and receipts tumbling out. "The phone's just connecting to the speaker."

"Hi Belinda, hi Jasper," said Devon.

"Hi, handsome," Jasper said, starting the car. "Made that hottie your husband yet?"

"Ha Jasper, mind your biz—and why are you two in the car? Aren't you with Ava-Lily?"

Belinda, staring dejectedly at herself in the sun visor mirror. Pinching her cheeks, to test for signs of blood flow, answered, "Poor little darling is *tired*. She pushed the fitting by two hours. It's a fucking nightmare logistically. This week is the absolute fucking worst, Devon. I'm so over this bullshit. We're only human. I'm not a fairy godmother and don't have a dream dress-conjuring wand and teleporting skills. No, I have traffic, nightmare logistics, a million egos to massage, and finite hours." Belinda grabbed her bag from her feet and rifled through it, pulling out CBD oil and chugging it from the bottle.

"Belinda, I hear you and understand it's a rough week. The Oscars is the worst, you know that. It will be over in six days, okay? Just six more days of award season and think of the money!"

"Devon, I'm making the same money doing Janie's ad job next week."

"Now that's not entirely true—"

"Fine," she huffed. "Did we get a figure for my fee from Lara's jewelry deal?"

"We aren't finished yet. Lara wants so many extras: two cars all day, separate hotel rooms for her nanny, and a glam suite. They all come out of the budget after her fee. We will have to see what is left, but we have been told that, *as always*, Lara absolutely refuses to pay for anything out of pocket. As you know, she's just presenting this year, and with no current movie to promote, there's no studio to hang all the costs on—just this jewelry deal—hair and makeup are also paid from it."

"But what if there's nothing left? Why the fuck can't she get ready at home? It's 15 minutes away from the Chinese Theatre. *Ugh.*"

"Well, both things are unlikely, but we'll just have to deal with whatever comes. You have an excellent rate for the Cocotte campaign next week, which Lara's publicist Marco pointedly pointed out when we discussed earlier."

"Are you fucking kidding? Those are two separate jobs. What does one have to do with the other? Lara makes bank for wearing Dazzle Diamonds to the Oscars; her family gets hotel rooms and cars they won't use; she gets $3 million a season for Cocotte, and they are commenting about *my fee*?"

"Hang on—how do you know about her Cocotte fee?"

"Oh, I meant to tell you, she accidentally pulled it up on her iPad last week when she showed me images that apparently illustrated how much more *creative* Ellie's stylist is than me."

"Oof. She really is a gem. Look, my lovely Belinda, regardless, it's still a chunk of change. Most people don't earn this kind of money, so let's focus on that. As I often remind you, it's a job, not a hobby. Sometimes, you will be unhappy."

She pouted at Jasper as they both silently mouthed, "'*Sometimes*.'"

"Lastly, about Alma," Devon's tone turned serious.

"Oh god, Devon, not you as well. I just bumped into the cops in the hotel. They were chill and know I had nothing to do with it."

"Well, you know Hollywood and gossip. It's my job to let you know what I'm hearing, but don't worry, hopefully it'll blow over."

"Hopefully?" Belinda yelped.

"Yes, hopefully. To paraphrase the words of the great Ru Paul, '*You must see the darkness, just don't stare at it.*' Why don't you get your Oscar credentials since you have two hours? I'll email them and have them put you on the list for access. Go to the parking garage behind the Chinese Theatre. And remember that since you have backstage access on Sunday, you must wear black. It's a mandatory dress code."

"You think we can get over to Hollywood and back in two hours?" she asked Jasper, raising an eyebrow.

"Yes! If you drive the way I do, honey!" Attempting to pull out, he was cut off by an aggressively speeding black Land Rover and flipped his middle finger as the car swerved around him.

"Holy shit! Was that David Beckham?" gasped Belinda.

"Yup. Scores like a god. Drives like a demon."

"On that note, bye, Devon. Tell everyone I'm not a murderer."

"I will! Now stop thinking everything is dire—that's an order—I'm emailing you the farcical wardrobe demands for Janie's flaccid dick campaign. They, at least, should make you laugh. Bye, girl."

Orgasmic Ads

Re: WARDROBE BRIEF /PENICLE CAMPAIGN WITH JANIE JONES

> From: Devon Dalton Devon@stylistsonly.agency
> To: Belinda Grant Belinda@BGstyle.com
> Cc: Jasper DLC Jasper@BGstyle.com
> Date: Feb 27, 2018 at 4:12 pm
> 🔒 Standard encryption (TLS)
> Learn more

See below the email from the ad agency. Please confirm receipt. Thanks.

Ps. Happy Oscar week. LOL.

Hi Devon,

Just a few pointers for Belinda for the upcoming shoot. First off, we are thrilled Janie has agreed to become our spokes(wo)man, she so perfectly **PENICLE.** We want (and of course the contract dictates) wardrobe to ultimately be her decision. But if we could *please* bear in mind the following:

Previous **PENICLE** ads have all heavily featured **red**, and we would love to continue this theme. **Burgundy** is a viable alternative if necessary.

Janie will hang playfully, and sometimes upside down, off a waterbed, therefore a dress that molds to her body and stretches easily would be ideal.

We would love to see a hint of cleavage but **not**, perhaps, her usual amount. See below the one picture we have found of her with subtle décolletage. Lastly, we want to avoid masculine items (eg pants and shirts.)

Obviously, Janie is stunning, but we do **NOT** want this to be overtly sexy. We want the men to be turned on, not knocked out. Our next initiative (stage two of Janie's contract) will target women, encouraging them to order **PENICLE** for their men. It's essential she appeals to these wives, and her beauty does not alienate them but inspires them to take charge of the multiple orgasms in their relationship.

Over to you. Let me know if I can help in any way. I look forward to seeing images.

Cheers all.

Oscar

Re: Re: WARDROBE BRIEF /PENICLE CAMPAIGN WITH JANIE JONES

From: Belinda Grant Belinda@BGstyle.com
To: Devon Dalton Devon@stylistsonly.agency
Cc: Jasper DLC Jasper@BGstyle.com
Date: Feb 27, 2018 at 4:14 pm
🔒 Standard encryption (TLS)
   Learn more

OMG, this is hilarious. Why TF is she even doing this? Don't get me wrong—I'm not complaining—I love the money, but wow!!

Re: Re: WARDROBE BRIEF /PENICLE CAMPAIGN WITH JANIE JONES

From: Jasper DLC Jasper@BGstyle.com
To: Belinda Grant Belinda@BGstyle.com
Date: Feb 27, 2018 at 4:15 pm
🔒 Standard encryption (TLS)
   Learn more

She's taking charge of orgasms Bels! OR doing it for the lawyer fees.

D.I.V.O.R.C.E: Sing it, gurl.

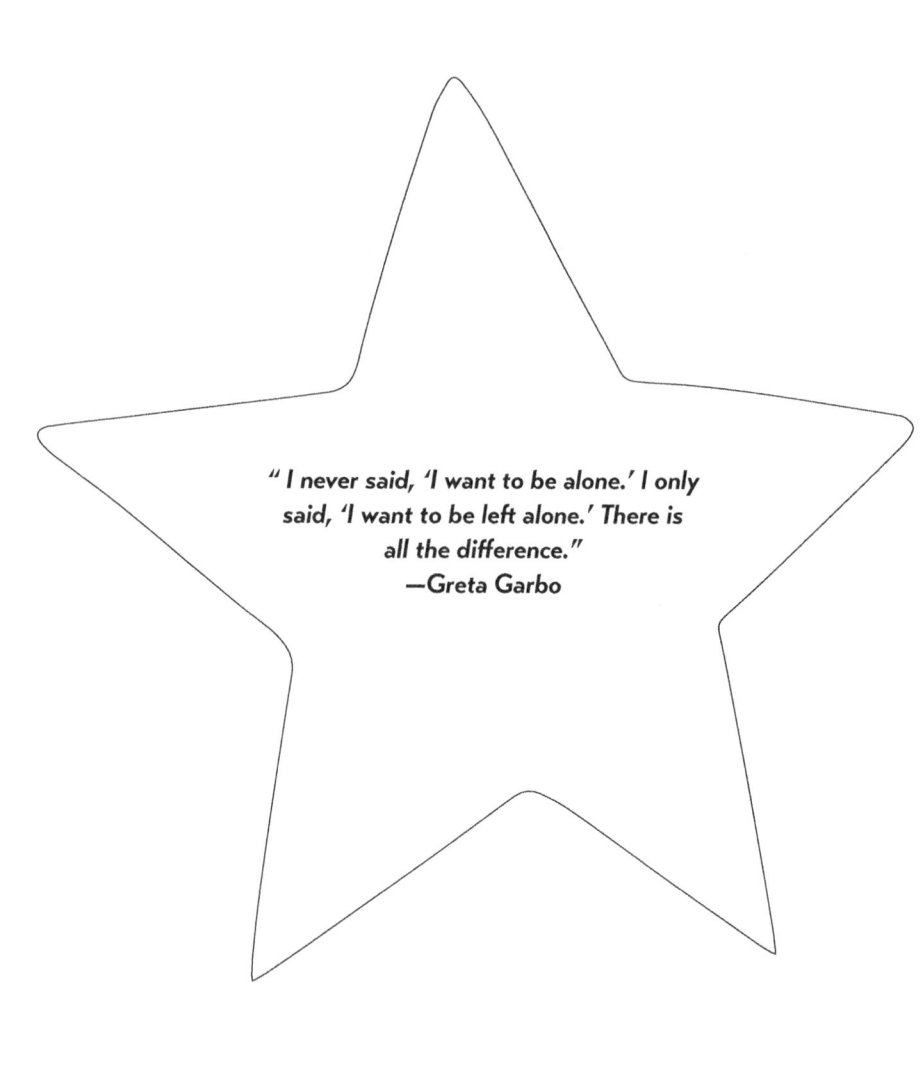

" I never said, 'I want to be alone.' I only
said, 'I want to be left alone.' There is
all the difference."
—Greta Garbo

The Devil Wants Couture

Ava-Lily Oscar Fitting

Round two. 5:15 pm

'We're back.' Jasper texted Jackie from the other side of the suite door, which she opened immediately, speaking in hushed tones. "She's up now. Go on through and wait, okay?"

"She naps like a toddler," Belinda whispered as Jasper and Yelena crept into the bedroom and sat beside her, in a line on the couch, waiting.

"Hi!" Ava-Lily's timid voice announced from the doorway. "Sorry to make you come back. Was that okay? I'm so tired from all the award show stuff and that trip to Milan. Press isn't really my thing." She slipped into the room carrying Ulysses, who, viewed against her tiny frame, looked like a tiger.

"Um, Belinda—did you get my sketch idea for tomorrow's party?"

"Oh, I'm not sure, Ava-Lily. Actually no—sorry—I don't think I did."

"It's okay, I'll get one—I did a few. Jackie, could you bring the drawing I did of the outfit?" Ava-Lily curled herself up on a mustard velvet chair, kissing Ulysses.

"Sure, honey. Is it on the desk? Also, Pat just arrived, Ava-Lily."

"Tell her to come in, and yes, I think it's next to the Scorsese script." Pat, Ava-Lily's publicist, a middle-aged dyed brunette with the energy of a frazzled bulldog—uncomfortably stuffed into a grey wool shift dress—marched into the room gripping two Bebe Klein garment bags and a pristine monogrammed mustard Goyard tote.

"Guys! So happy you could rearrange so I could be here!" She air-kissed Belinda, handing the garment bags to Jasper. "These were sent over to me today from Alma's office. Poor Alma!" She shook her head, then stared for a protracted moment at Belinda. "Anyway, she was in negotiations for Ava-Lily to be their face next season, so it would be advantageous if she could wear one. I've looked at them. They are quite, well, French and avant-garde, but I'm sure you can work it out somehow, Belinda." She pursed her lips into what Belinda supposed was her smile.

"It's not a done deal yet, but placing one of these looks on her could help, so . . . no pressure, but well, pressure. Don't mind me, I'll sit here and be quiet; I'm so *busy*! The press is going insane about your performance, Ava. They won't leave me alone. I've had over 200 emails about you in the past hour." She plopped down on the couch they'd just vacated, kicked off her pink kitten heels, and used her calloused left foot to rub her right swollen ankle.

"Here's the sketch." Jackie hurried back into the room and handed it to Ava-Lily. She passed it straight to Belinda, who pretended to study it intently as she figured out what to say. "Um." She pointed at the pencil drawing of a stick person. "So, you are thinking a boxy two-piece—is that shorts or a skirt?"

"Oh, sorry! It's a skirt. I forgot to erase that line in the middle. Do you think it's a good idea? I thought it seemed very 'you,' Belinda."

"Show me," Pat glanced at the picture. "Brilliant, Ava-Lily, such a chic silhouette. You really are very talented. Why didn't you tell me you have an interest in design?"

"Oh, I've only recently thought of it. Maybe I could go to Parsons? Or St. Martins in London? Although Ulysses hated all the rain there."

"And deny the acting world?" Pat sucked up shamelessly.

"Well, I was thinking part-time . . . Oh, I don't know"—she turned away and walked to a rack, mostly talking to herself—"I'm not sure I even really like acting. It's weird. My parents chose my career when I was eight, and now I'm permanently followed by 15 old men with cameras and need a bodyguard. I can't choose to *un*-fame myself." She unzipped one of the Bebe Klein garment bags, which was bigger than her, and pulled out a taupe plaid balloon-sleeved shirt and a black ruffled satin mini, oblivious to the knitted zigzag-patterned metallic vest falling to the floor.

"Jerome is very particular about whole looks being worn together," Pat announced, "but obviously, you don't need *me* to tell you that, Belinda."

"Of course," Belinda replied, bending to pick up the top. "Can I ask you, Pat, what event are these looks suggested for?" She unzipped the second bag to reveal an aqua, chocolate-edged belted '70s-style stretch viscose suit. Echoing Jasper's widening eyes she continued, "For the Oscars, I thought we'd agreed it was between the gold Chanel couture look (which we've held since the show) and the custom Tom Ford?"

"The embroidered train Tom added is AMAZING," Jasper added, excited.

Pat stared at him coldly. "Let's not have too many opinions today, please. We don't want to confuse or influence Ava-Lily in her choice. If you can't make the Bebe work for the Oscars, Belinda, then I suppose we'll have to go back to the *old plan*. You have other choices just in case, correct? For a nominee, we must cover all our bases. Who else do you have?"

"There's a one-of-a-kind Calvin—"

"No." Pat interrupted, putting down her phone. "She already did a campaign for them, so that is out."

"Er, okay, I wasn't aware that was a thing—Also, Valentino sent—"

"Would it be exclusive? If Ava-Lily were to wear them, we couldn't have anyone else in Valentino."

"Well, no, Ava texted me the runway image a couple of days ago and asked me to request it. Apparently, her yoga instructor told her it would be perfect," Trying hard to keep her tone even, Belinda continued, "Valentino kindly flew it in Worldnet from Milan. They are already dressing one other actress. It's been planned since before nominations. They didn't say who, but she's not in the Best Actress category, and it's not a remotely similar dress."

"The same collection?"

"Yes, I believe so, the latest one. I can check, of course. I didn't push because I was told it was only between Chanel and Tom for the ceremony. The other looks are only for the Vanity Fair party."

"Is it couture? I don't think she should be in anything less than couture, even for Vanity Fair."

"No, Pat, but like I said, this was a direct request from Ava-Lily." She looked at her client for validation but found her oblivious—AirPods in—swaying to the music and stroking Ulysses.

"Let's not bother her with this. Justin, can you pack that dress away? Belinda, if she even remembers, you can make some excuse. You need to keep her on the right track. Thank god I'm here."

"His name is Jasper, Pat."

Ignoring the correction, Pat plowed on, "And what else do you have?"

"There's also Armani Prive, three looks."

"Too OLD for her, don't you think? She just played Jessica's young teen daughter!"

"I don't think it's old. Emma wore it to the Emmys, and Zara wore that amazing red tulle to the opening of Cannes. Armani has a very elite young following these days."

"Any Prada?"

"No. They have an ambassador exclusive."

"Hmm," Pat snorted, "well, if this is all you've got, we have no other choice. I'm not thrilled, I gotta tell you. She needs to look like a *princess*."

"It's not all we've got, Pat. There's also Viktor&Rolf, Lanvin, Off-White, Chloé, Burberry, and three vintage Givenchy dresses from their 1960s refrigerated archives. Ava requested them after she met Greta Thunberg, who inspired her to pursue environmentally friendly options." Belinda, losing it, paused and took a deep breath before continuing. "Look, Pat, I'm sorry if there's been a communication breakdown, but Alma was very clear—via Dustin—that she wanted Chanel or Tom for the ceremony, so we've worked everything around that."

"Well, Alma and I didn't get to discuss any of this because *she* micromanaged Ava-Lily and didn't think I was *important* enough to be included," Pat snapped back. "Ignoring that I have to spend the whole weekend answering the question on everyone's lips: *what is she wearing*? I could also have advised on what the other female clients we represent are wearing—which you'd think would be helpful—but not to Alma, *oh no*. She was also going to take me off retainer after the Oscars, for god-knows-what reason. But hopefully, Alma's replacement will be sensible. Ava-Lily NEEDS ME!"

Realizing her voice had risen, Pat glanced uneasily at Ava-Lily, who was quietly humming along to her music as she doodled artless flowers onto her fashion sketch. Seeing her oblivious, Pat continued with full force.

"And I hear, Belinda, that you might know something about that tragedy? Have the police cleared you? I assume you'd have recused yourself if there was something we should know. Or that Devon would have told us? Because absolutely nothing can jeopardize the magic of what probably will be Ava-Lily's first Oscar."

Belinda's face flushed scarlet, but Ava-Lily pulled out one gold ear pod before she could respond and said, "Oh, Belinda, I keep meaning to tell you, that ring you need back, the one from the Milan event on Sunday. I think I gave it to Bulgari when they picked up the stuff Pat made them send. Or I might have left it on the coffee table in the room. Sorry, I was in a rush. And Ulysses was in a crappy mood—he's so grumpy where we travel—was it very expensive?"

"Um, approximately 70," Jasper answered, realizing Belinda was close to tears.

"70 dollars?" Ava-Lily looked confused.

"70 *thousand* dollars."

"Don't you worry, lovely girl," Pat interjected. "No need to bother yourself with trivial things on this exciting week! I'm sure Belinda's assistant can sort this in a nanosecond, right?" She turned to Jasper and whispered, "*Was it insured?*"

"Cinderella had it easy – she just had one woman and a few mice telling her what to wear to the ball."

Loans & Losses

RIDING IN CARS WITH STYLISTS
Heading home. 8:40 pm

SITTING IN THE CAR AT THE BEVERLY HILLS VALET, Jasper tapped his phone's red button to end a call. "*FUCK*, Belinda, the Jelany ring is not at the hotel in Milan. I'll email Bulgari US when I get home. See, this is what happens when Pat decides to get involved. The small selection we packed for Ava-Lily was perfect and confusion-free. Doesn't she fucking know the teenager loses anything surplus to her requirements? And we signed for that ring Bel. So—as always—it's *us* they will invoice if I can't find it."

"Oh no problem at all—I'll just remortgage the house," Belinda said sarcastically. "Pat makes our one-word 'yes' or 'no' email dealings with Alma look like a walk in the park. Did she really take off her personal jewelry and give it to Ava-Lily to wear? Gross! Why is that girl so fucking compliant?"

"Poor thing hasn't been around someone her age since the maternity ward. She's clueless about what the young ones do *or wear*. Knowing Pat, that jewelry was a freebie, and by putting it on Ava-Lily, the ante for her next Von Speer Christmas gift just went waaay *UP*."

"And that princess comment. Ugh," Belinda retched.

"Goddamn princess propaganda—*whyyy*? Cinders couldn't run in heels and was apparently unrecognizable without her face on; Sleeping was roofied, and Beauty was giving total Stockholm syndrome. *JESUS, LADY*, how many lanes does a Prius *FUCKING NEED*?" Jasper honked his horn. "*OH YEAH, FLIP ME OFF, YOU BLIND, TANK-DRIVING BAT. OH, WHAT NOW*?" He yelled, putting in his earpiece as his phone rang. "Hi qween, I'm driving and putting out fires—what's up? Sorry, what was that? Bright PR's address—are you kidding me with this question, *Chanelle*? There's this amazing thing we have now: *it's called Google*. Might I suggest you use it? I've gotta go." Stopping at a red light, Jasper, irritated, turned and looked at Belinda. "For fuck's sake, can't we hire another proper assistant? One that we pay. These rich, overeducated-to-do-nothing bitches are torture."

"Come on, Jasper, that's not fair. She's actually pretty good. The U-Haul alone was amaze! But yes—I want to get us a proper second assistant. I tried to get an experienced freelancer for award season, but the only one available wants $500 a day, and I just can't afford it."

"$500? She charges the entire Netflix outfit rate? I'm in the wrong gig. Who can pay that?"

"People who have partners that pay the mortgage maybe. I dunno, but *he* works a lot. I hate not paying interns, but I don't know how else to do it. Chanelle knows to keep track of mileage and her food receipts, though, right?"

"Yes, of course. But she'll forget—the rich ones always do. Just know I might die from stress before this week is out. Oh shit, sorry, my subconscious is death obsessed." He turned the car abruptly, pulling into her driveway. "Well *TA-DAH*! You are home, a mere hour and fifteen after Rose's bedtime."

"*Success*," she replied sarcastically. "And thanks, Jas. Try not to email all night, 'kay?"

"Yeah, like I'm going to sleep when there's a 70 grand uninsured ring AWOL in Italy. Kiss that gorgeous sleeping girl goodnight from me. Auntie Jasper will be stealing mommy again at 8 am sharp. Don't murder anyone before then."

FIRE THE STYLIST
Dishing Daily Doses of Fashion Justice

CAROLINE PORTER-JONES -
Bristol Farms, Sunset Blvd.

Posted on February 27, 2018

Firers, you, like us, might do a double-take, but believe it, this is indeed Caroline Porter-Jones, former svelte teen queen and daughter of the indomitable Sophia Porter. Click here for the infamous poster every teen boy (and some of their fathers) had over their bed in the '90s! Rumor has it that in all these years, only KK has knocked her off the Hollywood Plastic surgeons' top 'requested bootie' spot.

Caroline's image single-handedly created a wave of teen girl body hatred because despite most of them trying (the red and white polka-dot thong bikini sold out 93 times), it was impossible to live up to that iconic image. Women were disgruntled, and men were disappointed. Jerry Springer even had an episode blaming her for a wave of eating disorders! Ah, the patriarchal '90s.

Fast forward to this morning at the Bristol Farms grocery store, and a red-faced Caroline pushing an overloaded cart. This former icon is now 44 and a regular Range Rover-driving, Alo Yoga-wearing, Chanel purse-carrying mom of five kids. She has piled on the pounds in the 30 years since she rose to fame: we're guessing a size ten now? On the bright side, although it's a tad lower, her butt remains resplendent! Apparently retired from acting, only occasionally appearing at charity events with her multi-millionaire businessman husband, there's simply no need for her to starve herself into a thong anymore. Free the fat, Caroline! Bravo.

As always, leave comments below!

(To review our community guidelines, please click here)

> @chadlives gross. This fatty needs to go on a diet before her man moves along

> @luvinlives she's so unhealthy. She literally needs to call a trainer, she can afford it

> @jenniem @luvinlives seriously? I took a brief look at your profile, and you are bigger than her! I'm a size two and look thin, but I

have a condition which means I can't put on weight. I'm way less healthy than she probably is, but you wouldn't know that bc you are 'literally' no one's doctor. Stop lifting for the patriarchy—luv yr life—and mind your own

@jewelthief she should put half that food back or at least run some laps with the cart ☺

@bae666 she must cry every time she looks in the mirror. I'd never let myself go that way

@susegrad @bae666 girl, you are an arrogant baby. Don't doubt it bc, unless we REAL unlucky, aging comes for us all. If you continue to base your worth on your outside, your eventual downfall will be just as hard as you think hers is.

@poachedpeaches the comments here are horrific. The post itself is cruel and reductive. The woman is just living her life, shopping for her family. She should not be target practice for anonymously written misogyny masquerading as fashion feeds

WEDNESDAY 28TH FEBRUARY 2018

"Fashion should be a form of escapism and not a form of imprisonment.
—Alexander McQueen

Lose a Rib

CAROLINE PORTER-JONES FITTING
Home dressing room, Brentwood. 11:45 am

CAROLINE PULLED A FACE AT HER REFLECTION in the last of the designer gowns. "I hate the goddamn Oscars. Have you ever been, Bee?" Belinda shook her head distractedly as she aggressively tugged at the back zipper on Caroline's dress, aided by Jasper, who was having difficulty pulling the two sides together. "Yelena, can you come and give us a hand, please?"

Yelena, quietly concentrating in the far corner of the vast custom-built cedar closet, paused Cashman Casino, put down her phone, and padded over the plush cream rug in her mismatched sports socks. "Give to me!" she ordered Jasper, her powerful hands pulling the seams together. "You grab at the bottom." The three of them fought silently and valiantly to close the scarlet silk Prada gown to no avail. "Is too small," announced Yelena, beads of sweat forming on her forehead.

"Nooo!" Belinda mouthed at her as Jasper slashed his neck with his hand. *How many times do I have to tell her?* Belinda thought despairingly. *It's too small! Blasphemy.*

Caroline's face flushed with shame as she sucked in her stomach and, using her hands cinched her waist aggressively. "Now, can we *try*? Belinda, why aren't there size 8s that fit me? Peter and my mom said I should try other stylists after the Dior disaster at Hollywood for Child Literacy. I don't want us to part ways, but we must get the Oscars right!"

"That's not fair, Caroline. You insisted on wearing the Dior to HFCL. We didn't even get to tailor it. I only brought it to show you how beautiful it was and wait for the size 10 to arrive this week. I planned on it for the Oscars . . ." She tailed off. "Is everything okay? You seem very edgy today."

"I'm NOT a size 10, Bee, that's impossible. I'm a 6/8. I have to be. Peter says he didn't marry a heifer."

"There! Dress almost closed," Yelena triumphantly announced as she zipped it to two inches from the top and deftly fastened it with a safety pin. "You just lose one of the ribs, or I recut top of back of dress and be good. Also, you layer two pairs of the power Shrunx."

Ignoring her, Caroline continued, whining sadly, "*Oh*, why didn't you make me listen to you, Bee? It was a horrible night, and it all started with that dress." She turned, eyes darkening, and shuddered as she looked at the creased, carelessly hung, black and gold strapless sheath. "Just take it away, Jasper. Give it to Decades to sell. Take the shoes too. The Ferragamo clutch you lent me is in the beauty room—it's so nice to be loaned things. Peter says it's a lot to pay your fee and pay for clothes too. He says I should just go to Rodeo Drive and do it myself."

"Caroline, we've been over this. You are not a sample size. The models who wear those dresses on the runway are adolescents—or the size of them, at any rate. It's getting a tiny bit better. There's starting to be a token size 6 or 8 models and, equally amazingly, an older supermodel or two in some shows. But even so, the designers you love have European PR teams who are very specific and rigid about who they loan to. It's a cutthroat business, and they are ruthless about getting maximum clicks."

"Did we get a picture of this one yet?" Caroline, no longer listening, had been staring sadly at herself and pinching the jelly rolls at her arm joint as she slipped on the pink satin Chloe Gosselin ballet pumps in front of her. She walked uncomfortably to the 'photo corner' and stood before a stark white wall on the red rectangular rug. "Does this look good? Do we like the lighting? Cost me a fortune to get a photographer to set it up." She posed one leg in front of the other and cocked her left hip.

"It's perfection! Cash well spent, lady. Just a bit more hip action from you, and we're good to go," Jasper advised, standing on the designated mark, iPhone ready and crouching slightly, ready to shoot her slightly from below (to make her look taller.) "Great, Caroline, you look A-MAZE in red. Now from the side . . . and the back. Can we get one more straight-on with you smiling, please?"

"Ugh, do I have to? Bad enough that I have to go to the Oscars and stand there all day grinning like I'm still on kids' TV, watching Peter brag about that performative inner-city indie he produced like he's some racially healing guru. He's never given one single shit about race or reparations in his entire white life. But now it's all *BLM*, this *BLM* that. Can we make sure my clutch can fit a hip flask in it? I won't survive that day without wine. And I've also heard that cannabis cream numbs your feet, so you can wear 5-inch heels for a *whole* day. Or do people really get Botox on their feet? I need something because my feet are fat and useless in heels since the last baby, and Peter won't let me wear wedges." She walked to the far side of her enormous shoe wall and stood before at least a dozen pairs of equidistantly displayed wedges, longingly stroking the pristine bejeweled Miu Miu pair.

She has a wedge section, thought Belinda. *I didn't notice that one before—a new addition to the pump section, the pumps with ankle straps section, the peep-toe section, flip flop section, sneaker section, color section—Just so many shoes sitting there immobile, a vision of limitless excess.*

Kicking off the pumps, Caroline sighed with relief and took a bottle of sparkling Badoit from a chunky glass tray, pouring it into a crystal tumbler. Sipping, she walked to the satin loveseat by the window and gazed at the vast, perfectly sterile lawn below. A distant shriek rang out as two of her white-blonde children belted onto the grass kicking a ball, pursued by a uniformed nanny, who was trying—and failing—to shoo them back inside, the children remaining giddily, joyously defiant. A second, matching nanny, called in for reinforcement, ran out of the children's guest house just visible at the far end of the lawn, and Caroline watched helplessly as her kids, now sad and dejected, were dragged off the forbidden green.

Belinda, Jasper, and Yelena exchanged questioning glances as they waited patiently, wondering if they should start to pack up but not wanting to disturb her. So, they just watched as she stood silently in an ill-fitting twelve-thousand-dollar crimson dress, staring miserably down at her recently vacated garden.

"At least Alma won't be at the Oscars," she spun around, brightening. "There's that at least, I suppose. *OH SHIT*. Did I say that out loud?" she choked on bubbling water as she came out of her reverie, shocked to see other people in the room. "So *sorry*, Bee! I was trying not to mention it. Are you doing okay? The rumors and stuff? Obviously, I know it wasn't *you*. You're always so calm. I've never even seen you raise your voice."

Jasper and Yelena looked at each other, their eyes widening in disbelief. "Well, I raise my voice sometimes; I just don't usually do it with clients. But are you suggesting that anyone seriously thinks I might have . . ." Belinda faltered, oblivious to the Jimmy Choo clutches falling from her shaking hands.

"Oh gosh, NO Bee. Of course *NOT!*" Caroline interrupted. "Just the Hollywood gossips chattering. No one *seriously thinks* that. I mean, you're still here working, aren't you? The police released you, didn't they? And what could you possibly have against Alma? Why, I'm sure she barely knew you. Surprised she had the time to . . . What were you meeting about anyways?"

"*YOU—TAKING OFF DRESS*," Yelena interjected loudly. "Before it get more stretched."

"*Excuse* me?" Caroline turned to face Yelena, noticing her properly for the first time, taking in her impassive face, choppy, bleached hair, and bulky, towering frame. "Are you wearing your *pajamas*?"

"Yez." Moving behind Caroline, Yelena swiftly unzipped the dress and pulled it down to her waist, revealing her immobile, spray-tanned breasts. She pulled a piece of ribbon from her tattered fanny pack. "Now I make belt to put on body under dress, to make waist here."

As she aggressively cinched the ribbon, Caroline winced and squealed. "Ow! Can you let me breathe?"

"No breathing—is breathing or waist. Also, I sew hook on this now, you keep on and wear all the time; you ladies get too fat for dresses because you always wear the yoga clothes." Disgusted, she continued, "Is too comfortable, you forget and eat all the food." Adding under her breath, "Food is for fat people like me."

Jasper, picked up the clutches at Belinda's feet and, seeing her still immobile, stood up and gently put his arm around her shoulders as she blurted out, "Caroline, I wasn't arrested. They just came to talk to me. I—I think it's important you know that . . ."

"What? Oh yes, of course," Caroline waved dismissively. "Forget I said it. Shit, shit, shit." She glanced at her Cartier Tank watch. "The police are coming to talk to me, like, right now."

Yelena quickly hooked the belt she had been sewing onto her waist, and Caroline pulled on her black Alo yoga onesie, breathlessly demanding, "Bee, send all the pictures from today to Peter. You guys can discuss it, and he can decide which dress I should wear. I don't care. The Oscars is his day, after all."

"No, Caro . . . I don't think—that's not a good idea—I don't even have his number," Belinda, looked horrified.

"Jenel, our housekeeper, can give it to Casper."

"Umm, it's Jasper," he corrected quietly and sighed, wondering again why he bothered, as he began zipping the gowns into their garment bags. Lost in organization, he barely noticed Jenel's skittish voice announcing. "Caroline, Detective Hall is here to see you."

"Oh god!" She pushed back her shoulders and took a few yoga breaths. "Okay, yes, I should go straight down. Thank you, Jenel. And please, can you give *him*"—she pointed at Jasper—"Peter's second number?" And she disappeared through the double door, biting the French tip of her manicured thumb.

"Which of my important nothings shall I
tell you first?"
—Jane Austen

Pain & Privilege

JENEL SHOWED CHERYL AND ORTIZ to the pristine sitting room nearest the front door. Standing by the entrance, they studied the large, uninviting space with its polished concrete floor, untouched cream suede couches, gigantic oval marble coffee table displaying precision spaced books, and a flashy bejeweled box of Cuban cigars.

Ortiz groaned and muttered to Cheryl, "I'm getting sick of all this wasteful luxury. Aren't you?" Cheryl shrugged ambivalently. "I mean, who the fuck actually uses this room? No TV, I don't see no music. The books have clearly never been touched, let alone read," She picked one up, '*The Widow Clicquot: The Story of a Champagne Empire and the Woman Who Ruled It.*' I see why they are all still in their plastic wrap. What is the actual point of these four walls? To do sewing or some shit and learn about champagne?"

"And mount the heads of dead animals," Cheryl added, pointing at the moose head above the gleaming electric fireplace. "But it's pretty obvious, Ortiz, it's their pianoforte room. Just waitin' for the piano." She shrugged, grinning.

"What the *eff* does that even mean?" Ortiz responded grumpily.

"Freaking hell, lady, watch a period movie one of these days. Or better still, read a novel."

"Hours of wimpy chicks in corsets marching after men in fields and fainting? No thanks."

"Ortiz, they were the opposite of weak. In fact, they were total hardos. That's the whole goddamn point. They fainted because they couldn't breathe—laced to within an inch of their lives, boobs hiked up to their chins. And *starving*—a lifetime of boning shoved organs into their lower abdomens—no room left for food. Freaking patriarchy and their demeaning, sexist uniforms. Have you ever tried getting stuff done in a corset?"

"Of course not. And when did you wear a corset?"

"When I got hitched, that's when. Man, you are in a bad mood today."

"I'm jus' gettin' tired of this bullshit. Alma Astley fell down those steps and busted her neck. We all know it. And yet, we still have to interview these ridiculous folks who think they are better than us because they got money. We have got a *lot of* other cases. You are still finding this shit funny cos you are new; I, on the other hand, am freakin' over it—wait, you got *married*?"

"Yes, I got married. Nuff said 'bout that. I do still feel like I'm living a series of MTV cribs. It's true. And if it makes you feel any better, I don't think it will be long now. I put in a call to the M.E. this morning to push them. And C.S.I. just emailed there was nothing on the photocopier memory after 4 pm, so Dustin was right. She didn't use it."

Ortiz nodded and was shrugging her shoulders as if to say, *tell me something I didn't know,* when Caroline—still biting her nails—entered the room, cowering. "Um, good afternoon, detectives, I'm Caroline Porter-Jones. Welcome to our home."

"Hello, Ms. Porter-Jones. Can we call you Caroline?" asked Cheryl. "Beautiful place you got here."

"Of course you can. Do you like it?" Caroline looked surprised. "I think it looks like Restoration Hardware. That's a home shop. It's such a waste of a room, and no one ever comes in here. I mean, it's pretty obvious there's nothing to do except read and look at that gross dead animal, but Peter—my husband—doesn't like us to sit on the couches, so even that's out. If leaving the plastic wrapper on them wasn't so tacky, I think

Penny Lovell

he might have done that." She laughed nervously, looking behind her to check that no one had heard. "He's not here. If you need to talk with him?"

"No, Caroline, we just need to talk to you today."

"Okay, um, shall we sit?' Caroline twisted her hands nervously.

Cheryl couldn't work out if she was more anxious about the interview or sitting on her couch. "If that's okay?"

"Oh yes. I'm sure Peter will be okay with the police sitting on them. I'll have Jenel vacuum straight after. Maybe just don't eat?"

"Wasn't planning on it," Ortiz snipped as she sat awkwardly on the couch nearest her, sliding beef jerky bites back into her pocket. Cheryl took the sofa opposite, and Caroline perched nervously on the furthest one. They sat for a second, acclimatizing to the uncomfortable distance between them.

I'll just shout, Cheryl thought dryly, but figured it would send this jittery woman over the edge. "So, I understand you last saw Alma at the Children's Literacy event?" Cheryl observed her shrinking into the couch as if she'd rather vanish than remember. "Yes, what a hideous night that was." Caroline whimpered and started tearing into her nails again.

"It's our understanding that you had a difficult conversation with her and—"

Caroline, on the verge of tears, cut Cheryl off. "Yes, I know, I said that terrible thing. Oh god, it's all so horrific."

"I'm sure this can't be easy, Caroline," Cheryl acknowledged, "but it would be very helpful if you could tell us about the conversation and everything you remember from that night, starting at the beginning."

Zsa Zsa Gabor, when asked which of the Gabor women was the oldest, said, "She'll never admit it, but I believe it is Mama."

Mean Girl Prom

FLASHBACK TO HFCL
(Hollywood for Child Literacy) Santa Monica

CAROLINE TOTTERED UNCOMFORTABLY OFF THE RED CARPET and through the door into the Santa Monica aircraft hangar. Like the rest of the rich and generally jaded guests, she was wholly unprepared for the flamboyantly transformed interior: a wonderland lavishly reimagined to evoke Alice tumbling down an expertly lit, flower-decked hole into a Hogwarts classroom. Even by the usual, overarching socialite standards, this set was insane. Custom oversized wooden desks with elaborate crystal settings for twelve were reflected in gigantic Tom Dixon mirror balls strategically placed around the perimeter. Rainbow-hued flower arrangements and fluorescent fruit sculptures festooned the tables, and hundreds of pencil-shaped gold candles gave off flickering auriferous light. At the center of the room stood a hand-blown glass wall, each of its 48 bricks displaying a first edition of a classic children's book and a cursive handwritten sign denoting the starting bid, bidding number, and (if requested) donor name.

Caroline, needing a drink to numb her nerves and feet, scanned the room and spotted miniature Moet champagne bottles spilling out of vividly graffitied vintage lockers on the back wall. Dismayed at the distance to relief, she hopped uncomfortably from one foot to another.

"What's wrong with you?" Peter asked scathingly, his eyes bitter. "Can't you, just once, get shoes you can walk in for Chrissakes?" He switched to a smile for Alma, who had just nodded a hello from across the room, then continued through gritted teeth, "Jesus, I pay that stylist enough, don't I—will you be able to sit in that dress?" He looked her up and down critically. "Looks like a seam might burst any second. You better not eat tonight. I don't want any wardrobe malfunctions. And when did you stop asking for my opinion on what you're wearing? Not okay, Caro, don't do it again, 'kay?" Staring at the floor, Caroline began to stutter inaudibly, but Peter was already moving away. "BOB!" he yelled, smiling broadly at a short, bronzed, and botoxed man in a sapphire velvet tuxedo. "What the fuck, man . . . *Snazzy!*" And they disappeared, laughing, into the crowd.

Caroline, crestfallen, stood alone, staring at her distorted reflection in one of the mirror balls, new boobs spilling out of the breathtakingly expensive strapless Dior gown. Opening her metallic clutch, she frowned at her face in its interior mirror before extricating the Barbie sticker-decorated phone and walking to the nearest corner.

"Mom, it's me—No, I'm not crying—My dress is what—? How do you know? You're *here*?" She spun around, stumbling slightly, astonished to see her mother standing behind her.

"*Darling!* I didn't realize you'd be here, or we could have gotten ready together!"

"But I told you yester—"

"Now, darling, it's hard for me to listen to *everything* you say. You talk so very much. Anyway, I'm here now, they just begged me this morning, and I threw this old thing on. I think I wore it to the Gilded Orbs in '93. I lost that year, of course, but regardless, it's a fabulous piece, Ralph custom-made it for me. *And* it was wildly expensive, the fabric was spun from real gold!"

Caroline stared dejectedly at her mother, resplendent in the exquisitely-fitted lamé fabric jumpsuit—her famous hourglass figure shimmering and luminous under the extensive candlelight. They looked like sisters, but she was the sad, dreary, fat one.

"Mom, did you get your lips done again?"

"*Ssh* darling, must we tell everyone?" She glanced regally around her to confirm no one was in earshot.

"They look amazing! When will you tell me who you use?"

"Oh darling, a lady never, *never* tells! Liz gave me that advice decades ago, along with how to buy emeralds, and I've never wavered. Mind you, her advice about getting married was clearly terrible, so she wasn't all-knowing. Speaking of which, where's that dreadful husband of yours? Has he been up to his tricks again?"

"Well, he told me I can't eat tonight because my dress is too tight. And he's only called me a whoring, lazy C-word once this week, but then he has been in Vegas for four days. He may have been trying to kill me with his insane driving tonight—or he can't drive a Ferrari—the jury is still out."

Sophia winced as she replied, "Oh darling, I'm so sorry. If I had any money left after those blood-sucking, Liz-approved five husbands, I would pay you to leave him. We simply must get you back to work. Did you talk to Alma again? If we can get you on a good show with lots of publicity, he won't dare try and steal my four fabulous grandkids. It would be so *fun* if we were both famous again."

"Five grandkids, Mom."

"Oh, silly me, I always forget about your middle girl. Does she still have those rolls of puppy fat?"

"*MOM*, Delphine is 9!"

"Yes, yes, of course, I know that," Sophia responded, unperturbed. "Let's get back to what's important. Alma is here—"

"I know. I saw her earlier. And, as I told you already, I spoke to her last week—she said she was looking into representing me again. Making some calls to see what she could come up with."

"Well, she *should*. I made you sign with her when she was a junior agent, and we made her a considerable amount of money back in your heyday."

"Heyday? *Mom!* Again, I was a teenager!"

"And how stunning you were then . . ."

Caroline, for the first time, brightened fractionally. "Okay, well, let's go and find her . . ."

"Oh honey, you go. I've got so many people dying to catch up with me. But do stand up straight and suck that stomach in, my sweet. Perhaps you should fire that so-called stylist you insist on using. I loathe him, but Peter might have a point there. And, of course, *I* have never needed one . . ." Sophia wafted away, waving her heavily bejeweled arms and nodding left and right at the adoring people who were reflexively clearing a path for her to pass.

Crestfallen and alone once again, Caroline visibly sucked everything in and tentatively raised her chin, eyes darting around the glittering room.

"Caroline, darling!" The unmistakable transatlantic lilt of Alma's voice floated before her—a warning—but Caroline still jolted skittishly as she appeared, bedecked like a gothic Louis Vuitton couture bride, in a second skin of blood-red leather, overlaid with a diaphanous black floor-length cape that floated majestically behind her. *She loves to wear things that make it impossible to stand near her*, Caroline thought, trying awkwardly to sidestep the silk cape that had landed and puddled on the floor.

"Your iconic mother said you were looking for me?"

"Oh yes, Alma. I was wondering if—"

Alma cut her off. "If I had considered our conversation last week? Yes, dear. I have. Not that it needed much consideration, if I'm honest." She paused to light a cigarette nonchalantly. Aghast yet thrilled, Caroline hungrily inhaled the forbidden smoke.

"I was going to call you tomorrow. It's just tacky to talk shop while we give to charity—but I'm so *bored* by this overwrought and ludicrous event. Dear god, why don't we just give the money it costs to produce this inanity directly to the illiterate children? The expense of decorating this nonsensical, garish place; flying and insuring first editions from all over the world, not to mention the dresses. How much was your constricting off-the-rack Dior, for example, Caroline?"

Looking down her angular nose, Alma gestured—her hand covered by a fingerless silk glove—at the people around them. "Most of this crowd might be phenomenally rich, but they are not relevant enough to be loaned a designer dress. Half of last week's receipts for Rodeo Drive are in this cold, drafty, ostentatious shed." She laughed lightly at her joke and carelessly dropped her cigarette—just missing the train of her dress—stubbing it out with a patent black 5-inch Manolo. "Anyway, I digress. Back to business. I want to be straight with you, Caroline—you deserve nothing less. Although you were, of course, once *the* focus of teenage masturbators everywhere, you are now, sadly, *old* for a woman in Hollywood. Unlike your ageless, patriarchy-approved mother, you left the scene, you've had less than average work done to combat aging, you have a bloated body, ravaged by nonstop children and—I'm guessing here—pasta, white wine, and no discipline. In short, by Hollywood standards, you are no longer interesting or sexy. Aside from a couple of weird left-over fans from the '90s, Caroline, men do not want to fuck you, and nor do women, for that matter. Could I get you a starring role as, say, a relatable mom or someone who only wears overalls? Yes, of course, I could. One phone call. But do I want to? Well. No." She paused to acknowledge someone across the room with a curt nod and a hint of a smile. "Two reasons. Firstly, there's a rumor that you want to leave your deeply unpleasant husband. I don't blame you for that; it's long overdue, from what I hear. Perhaps it wasn't the wisest to marry for an oversized, under-decorated mansion in Brentwood? There's always a price, my dear. Always. Oh, listen to me, who am I to give you advice? You stopped wanting my advice many years ago. I apologize. Obviously, you haven't been paying attention to your significant other since you don't seem to know that Roger and I are in talks to bring him on as an investor at the agency?" Scrutinizing Caroline's horrified face, she continued. "It seems you are *also* unaware that he prefers that you don't go back to work. What was it he said again? I believe it was, '*at home with the kids, organizing closets is where she belongs.*' Secondly, but more importantly, YOU LEFT ME, Caroline. Could I find another investor for the agency? Of course. And would I, if you were a client? Absolutely. But you're not a client anymore, are you, Caroline? I'm sorry, what was it you wrote to me? Do you remember? A brief message on embossed Tiffany notepaper—a gift from the deal *I* got you. A note, not a lunch, not even a phone call. '*Sorry, Alma,*' she imitated Caroline's voice, '*but Jonathan Blackwell is just more my vibe.*' And what a vibe he didn't turn out to be, am I right?' She stared coldly down at Caroline's quaking cleavage. "Two more clients left immediately after you, Caroline. Your careless words and the implication that I was incompetent gave me the stench of failure. I only hung in there by a thread *and* had to provide unthinkable, sometimes illegal, services just to keep my job as a junior." For a fleeting second, genuine pain showed in her eyes. "I framed that note, you know. It sits in the top left drawer of my desk and has been a constant reminder and inspiration. Only Chris Jackson has left me since that day." She brightened and continued, "As it turns out, I may—in part—have you to thank for my illustrious career."

"I was 18, Alma!" Caroline pleaded.

"Old enough to vote, Caroline, and to sign contracts." Alma's voice turned hard and pragmatic. "Anyway, it's been fun thwarting your attempts at comebacks all these years. What? You didn't know? Oh! I made sure you couldn't make a return, though you made it easy for me, of course, by being—and looking—permanently pregnant for a decade." She shuddered briefly. "Anyway, I'm done now. It's so easy it's not even fun anymore. Consider us even. One final piece of advice: do yourself a favor and give it up. You won't work again. You are fortunate to be rich and married. Amuse yourself with a handbag or jewelry line, like all the other bored wives of affluent men."

Alma—catching Jamie's eye as he hovered just to her right, looking bored but handsome in his Tom Ford tux—beckoned him closer. "I've had enough. Let's call the car."

"Babe, we haven't even had dinner."

She glanced at him, amazed. "No one actually eats at these things."

"No, Al, most people do, or at least they pretend to, only you don't know that because you—*we*—always leave." He sighed but pulled out his phone and texted the driver.

Fighting back tears, Caroline watched the pair exit without a backward glance. Standing alone in the crowd, suffocating in her dress as Sophia floated up, flushed and woozy, spilling champagne out of a crystal coupe glass.

"There you are. Oh, darling—what on *earth*?"

"I hate her, mom. And I wish I was dead. But mostly, *I wish she was dead*."

Penny Lovell

"The best time I ever had with Joan Crawford was when I pushed her down the stairs in Whatever Happened to Baby Jane?"
—Bette Davis

Crazy-Driving

Between fittings. 1:10 pm

"OKAY, YOU READY FOR JANIE?" Jasper swung an illegal left out of Caroline's driveway. "Eat a protein bar. Shall we stop for a CBD Latte? We might just have time. You're going to ignore Caroline, right? She's terrified of everything and everyone. Especially that controlling asshole she remains hitched to. And *imagine* growing up with that mother."

"Yeah, growing up with that mother is how she came to marry that asshole. Being abused is what she knows, as I well know. She doesn't mind taking it out on us though, does she? Happy to make *me* deal with him! Ugh," she shivered. "He gives me PTSD. You'll text him, right? I get it, I do. I feel empathy for her mind-fucking teen fame and evil family. But frankly, she's giving 'abused people abuse people,' and I feel sorrier for *us* right now."

"That's fair, babe, fuck her then. And *FUCK YOU* and the three lanes you drive in!" Jasper yelled out of the window, his curls flying in the wind as he sped up to tailgate a red, flag-flying monster truck.

"You'll get us killed one of these days."

"Might be preferable to the small deaths you have us die daily. Tell me we can fire Caroline after this, so I can have fun texting the diminutive dick, at least?"

Belinda shook her head. "And how will we afford another assistant if we fire—?"

"Yeah, yeah, I know. But a boy can dream, can't he?" Jasper stuck his tongue out at her and swerved between lanes, honking at an Audi.

"Better the devil you know Jaspe—"

"Oh my god! I totally forgot to tell you in all this madness! I found the Jelany ring!!!"

"*YES!*"

"But before you get too excited, no one wants to pay for it to be shipped back, and it's being held hostage by an Italian security company until someone does. I called Pat's assistant who just laughed maniacally, possibly cried and hung up—I reckon *she'll* be gone by next week. Jelany, rightfully, also laughed, but more politely. Devon said the studio didn't even respond. I mean you can't just standard FedEx seventy grand—"

"How much is the shipping?"

"About 2k. It needs a specialized service to get through customs etc."

"*Oof.* Well, that's another problem for next week. We are at max capacity right now."

"I dress for the image. Not for myself,
not for the public, not for fashion,
not for men."
—Marlene Dietrich

Callback

Round Two. BHPD. 12:45 pm

"IS SHE REALLY COMING TO THE STATION FOR THE INTERVIEW?" Ortiz asked in disbelief. "Why the fuck would she do that?"

"Yup, and I have absolutely no idea," Cheryl answered without looking up from her computer. "Her assistant said she wanted to make the lives of the women in blue less complicated and it would be her honor to come to us since we came to her last time. Or something like that."

"It's not a goddamn dinner party," Ortiz shot back.

"Oh, for Christ's sake lady, does nothing make you happy? It's traffic we don't have to sit in, for one thing."

"Oh fine," Ortiz accepted grudgingly. "Anything to get this over with. She'll be late, I betcha."

"I'll take that bet," Cheryl said, looking up for the first time. "Ten bucks?"

"Might as well burn it, but you're *on*." Ortiz glanced at her Apple watch and leaned back in her seat, propping her black Nikes up on the desk. She grinned. "Three minutes, Chez. Get ya money ready."

"It's Cheryl, and oh, looky here. I just got a message saying she's on her way up with the boss, who *accidentally* bumped into her downstairs."

"That star fucker can sniff a celeb from a thousand paces. He'll be pretending to get a picture for his wife—does it every freaking time."

The elevator doors opened, and Lara, arm-in-arm with the chief superintendent, exited majestically. Pushing white Fendi sunglasses onto her head, she tossed her shiny caramel hair behind her shoulders and surveyed the slick glass and metal modernity of the Beverly Hills PD. "Jim," she said, turning to the superintendent and handing him her tan cashmere coat and plaid scarf, "I've always wanted to see the inside of this building. To see the lifeline of our city at work—and to thank everyone personally. Also, it will be SO helpful for my next role as an unhinged officer with PTSD. I can't thank you enough for hosting me." The superintendent stood dumbfounded, his doughy face and bald head reddening.

"Has anyone ever called him Jim before?" Cheryl whispered to Ortiz.

"No one would dare. He's an arrogant, people-hating bastard, I avoid him like the plague and only ever call him boss. Who knew he was a coat check?" Ortiz chuckled. "This is better than Real Housewives."

Lara spotted Cheryl and Ortiz and shrieked, "Ladies! So great to see you again! I'm just dying to pick your brains and soak up your vibes. I know you will be key to my understanding of the depressed, complex mind of my character."

Wow, she just zings 'em naturally, thought Cheryl, saying aloud, "Hello, Ms. White, thank you for coming. If you follow me, we can discuss *the case* in one of our meeting rooms."

The entire office watched her stride over, proudly modeling the look she had curated for the visit: a grubby 70's embroidered tan suede vest over a brown striped tee, beige skinny jeans, and leopard-print Chanel ballet flats. On reaching Cheryl, she threw her arms out and hugged her tightly. "Cheryl? Is it Cheryl? May I call you Cheryl? Could I take a quick snap of your outfit? It's just so perfectly 'working woman in a man's world,' with a marvelous disregard for style—such a difficult thing for a costume designer to imitate well."

Ortiz, who at the first sign of a hug had bolted to the meeting room door, couldn't hold in a belly laugh. Attempting to cough over it, she said, "You should take a picture of me. I'm dowdier than her. You can do that in here if you come this way." She entered the small, window-free room as Cheryl and Lara followed, their colleagues still staring after them, transfixed.

"Excellent." Lara looked around as she walked, saying loudly, "I can sign autographs before I leave. Jim, we can FaceTime your wife Miranda as well. Take good care of my coat, will you? It's my new favorite, gifted to me by Gucci, of course. I couldn't afford such an indulgence—$8000! Why, one day, I'll have to put my children through college . . ."

Cheryl, memorizing the words to dissect with her sister later, closed the door, and the three of them sat down. Lara placed her mustard, monogrammed Gucci tote on the laminate table and pulled out a copper water bottle. "I don't like to use plastic cups, officers. I am so passionate about the environment. I met Greta last year when I was in Europe. I invited her to my house for dinner, but she said she only traveled by boat—and who can make arrangements that far in advance? Now, what do you need from me? Actually, first have a crucial question for you. I was experimenting with makeup today and wondered if you think this cat eye would be too much for a working cop. Will it detract from her character? She's a deeply caring soul. Her spirit animal is a pit/doodle mix, but—and I think it goes without saying—she is *terrified* of the human condition."

Cheryl and Ortiz studied the liner painted on her sapphire-blue eyes. The left eye was noticeably more prominent than the right, drooping down while the other swooped up. "Um, well—"

"It's too much. I knew it. My instincts are so good, and my effort wasn't wasted because I'm thrilled to conquer the cat eye. It'll save me a fortune in makeup artist fees for small events. Anyway, I digress. How can I help you?"

"Lara, could you tell us about the last time you saw Alma?"

"Yes, yes, it was at Fred's, of course. So tedious of Alma to never go anywhere else."

FLASHBACK TO LUNCH WITH ALMA
Fred's Restaurant.

That Thursday, Alma left her office at 12:25. It was exactly four minutes to Fred's, and she liked to be just early enough to imply her companion was late. This wasn't necessary with Lara however, as she was one of the few who dared to arrive a fraction past the appointed time and act oblivious to the pointed glare Alma would give her Jaeger Le Coutre watch.

"'Allo, Ms. Astley," George greeted her as he opened the entrance door. Taking her arm, he escorted her through the lunchtime crowd—as he always did. Alma strutted regally alongside him—as she always did. When they reached her elevated booth, centrally located on the back wall, she climbed the two burgundy carpeted steps, tossed down her Saint Laurent python tote, and positioned herself on the chocolate leather banquette.

"Merci, George. My usual lunch, please, and whatever my office called in for Lara." She removed her black Tom Ford sunglasses, placing them on the table.

Absolutely, Ms. Astley."

"Oh, George, do call me Alma."

"Ms. Astley, as I always tell you, I shall only do so off duty!"

They both smiled, comfortable in the familiarity of this almost daily banter. A waiter entered, delivered a dirty martini in a Riedel glass that balanced four olives on a gold cocktail stick, then exited. She continued with their patter, "Oh, I miss Europe, George. How is it that you and your lovely Andrea don't long to run back to Paris?"

"And leave you? *Jamais.*" George bowed slightly, looking fondly at her, then glanced at his Patek Phillipe watch. "Enjoy your lunch. I should go and wait outside for Ms. White?"

"Oh, absolutely not, George. Let the staff deal with that tardy, irritating child." He nodded in agreement, and she watched him walk away, admiring the exquisite quality of his Savile Row suit. It reminded her to order a new one for Jamie—*maybe that would make him less sullen and more accommodating.* Alma grimaced briefly at the possibility of another divorce. Brushing the thought aside, she scanned the room from her dais. It was the only booth in the room and, over the years, had been customized to her taste. She liked to be seen by all but heard only by the chosen few, and thus, the tables surrounding her were positioned more spaciously than in the rest of the restaurant.

Alma's eyes arrested at the entrance where Lara now stood. She was instantly recognizable, even with oversized Prada sunglasses and a wet top knot. A picture-perfect blonde hostess immediately ushered her to the table, and Lara (knowing all eyes were on her) shrugged off her well-worn poncho and handed it to the girl with sugary politeness. "Thank you SO MUCH, HONEY. You are *adorable*," bestowing on her and the restaurant at large her distinctive toothy smile before turning and stepping up to the booth.

Good lord, Alma thought to herself as she took in her outfit. *Stevie Nicks would be utterly horrified to have inspired that* and made a mental note to have Dustin email the stylist about improving Lara's abysmal street style.

"*ALMA!*" Lara exclaimed loudly for her audience, "*I've missed you.*" Taking a seat, she threw her vintage crimson and gold embroidered pouch beside her and, noticing Alma glance at it, said, "Isn't it divine? I'm getting so good at vintage shopping. It was only $45! I told my stylist I'd give her a lesson."

"Well, it smells vintage," Alma sniffed dismissively. "Now, Lara, let's get business out of the way so we can enjoy our lunch. We must discuss your incessant and unrealistic requests to be on the *Also Me* Hollywood board. People are starting to talk. Why, Page Six called this morning. Even they have wind of it."

"Unrealistic? Excuse me, Alma, I am a very prominent feminist, as everyone knows."

"Lara. Please, my dear. That's patently untrue."

"Alma. I'm beginning to wonder if you even know me *at all*. I've worked with at least two female directors in the last ten years and fought hard for them. On the cancelled HBO debacle, I agreed to the lady DP—I forget her name now—even though the top men were available. All my assistants have been female—except the gay one, *but he practically was*," she tittered. "I told Keisha that I supported her and that, with decent notice, she could stay (discreetly) in my New York apartment. And, lest you've forgotten, I played Gloria Steinem—"

"Lara, please." Alma, toying with the gold stick in her Martini, laughed. "You've starred in three Woody Allen films and publicly supported him. You said, and I quote, 'One can, and one *must* separate the controversial genius from the art.' I know it's a common opinion in this town darling, but one doesn't say it out loud. You listed 'Last Tango in Paris' in your top five films for your last New York Times profile. Chris Brown played at your wedding. You are mentioned in the Epstein flight manifest *seven* times. And we can't ignore the supportive email you sent to Harvey, which, *thankfully*, I managed to suppress. Need I go on? Now, you must stop contacting the members individually to plead your case. They forward me your emails and texts, and it's just embarrassing Lara. *Also Me* is a serious organization for an urgent and vital cause. We are doing excellent work, and it's absolutely unthinkable that we would jeopardize our progress to satisfy yet another of your vanity schemes."

Lara, her neck flushing angrily with red welts, retorted coldly, "*NO!* You do not get to fucking talk to me this way. *I am Lara White.* It's inconceivable that I am not on this committee. Why, every other actress of *my* caliber—and *so few* of them are—has been invited. That's what's embarrassing, and *you*, if you were the power agent you believe yourself to be, would have fixed it by now. What's actually unthinkable is that you are the committee Chair. Unbelievably hypocritical of *you* to talk to *me* about supporting rapists, given how frequently you cover things up and allow the lawless dicks *you represent* to carry on abusing."

Alma sat silently, her unblinking eyes focused on Lara's face, before slowly and softly responding, "You don't have a clue about what I can do, *or* what I know Lara." She sighed. "I didn't want to do this, but since you have, unwisely, decided to cross the line." She sipped her Martini slowly. "Remember Brad? That first little boyfriend of yours? Well, to label him more accurately, your first almost baby Daddy. Remember all those drug-fueled underage pool parties? '*Love puddles*' as you called them. I imagine it's fuzzy for you; this was pre-rehab, and you couldn't remember your name between 17 and 20. It was ghastly. I had to hire a full-time fourth assistant whose sole responsibility was to tail and discreetly babysit you."

She was satisfied to see Lara's face draining of blood. "You didn't know that? Why do you think you were never arrested? How do you think the designer clothes you wantonly stole were paid for? The cars you crashed were fixed? Even the girl you thought was your drug dealer was one of my assistants. The press was kept far away. Every time they so much as sniffed near you, we fed them dirt on another *lesser* client. *Lara's sacrificial lambs,* we called them. My team did so well until"—Alma shuddered—"your boy-friend recorded those poking puddles of yours. (Sadly, there was no one there to stop him. It was too far—even for this town—to list 'orgies' as a job responsibility.) Dear god, I still feel sorry for the innocents who used that pool to *swim* . . ." Alma retched a little. "Yes, Lara, shocking, isn't it? What's *more* shocking is that for all these years, you had no idea. Didn't you wonder why big-dicked, little Brad abruptly left you alone? Why his incessant calls and demands for money ceased? Did you ever wonder how a 22-year-old unemployed Midwestern boy—without even a GED—pur-chased a vast farm in the outback of Australia to follow his sheep-like dreams? Of course, you didn't because you've never, ever thought beyond yourself." Alma drained her Martini. "Well Lara, if you're finally wonder-ing—as I assume you must be—let me enlighten you. *I own the farm, and I have the tapes.*"

Alma sat serenely enjoying the unprecedented moment of defeated silence from Lara, before she stood and announced, "Well, I'm no longer hungry." She picked up her tote. "And I'm so very tired of you, my dear—twenty years of your supercilious, unearned superiority and your faux, vapid intellect. The only thing that is *not* average about you is your avarice and your colossal ego."

She buttoned her black McQueen blazer and concluded, "It could be an immense relief to throw those tapes to the tabloids, repossess my beauti-ful Antipodean farm, and finally be done with you." She blew Lara a kiss and looked around to her right. "George?" she said loudly, knowing he'd be waiting to escort her, "*unfortunately*, there's been an emergency at the office. Would you have my lunch wrapped and delivered? Lara will stay for hers, of course. Thank you, darling."

Lara, grabbing her smelly bag, moved as if to stand.

"Oh *no, no, no*," Alma hissed, discreetly pushing her down. "You stay. You courted this audience when you arrived, with that ridiculous, oxy-gen-sucking display. So, sit down, eat your exquisite little lunch, and finish their show," she gestured discreetly at the other diners. "While you do that, ask yourself this question: do you really want the *A-List Lara show* to be canceled? Let me know what you decide. We'll meet again next Monday at my office. Dustin will call to confirm details, *darling*." Turning, she slid on her glasses, took George's arm, and swiftly exited. Leaving Lara with no place to hide, performing solo for the lunchtime diners.

★ ★ ★

It took Lara less than three minutes to recount to the detectives her clumsily edited version of the lunch. "... *and* as I might have mentioned, Fred's infamous dirty Martini, which (god rest her soul) Alma favored, is simply *filthy*—"

"Yes," Cheryl interrupted, "we've established the restaurant is great and which cocktail we absolutely must order. Do you know the emergency that took Alma back to the office?" She was jotting down notes.

"I don't, unfortunately. She's such a busy woman; I imagine she has, she *had*, fires to put out all day long. It's an unbelievable, *unknowable* world we inhabit, Cheryl. Sometimes, I wish I could be anonymous and go to Whole Foods to buy my spirulina like an average woman—without a care for my image. But then, we all have our crosses to bear."

She continued to answer their questions for the next few minutes, but it was glaringly apparent that Lara knew absolutely nothing about Alma, or her life, unless it pertained to her career.

"Oh! I do remember one thing! Did you know she loved quotes? Forgive me, I should have told you that earlier! Let me recall which one I loved recently." Lara closed her eyes and placed her fingertips on her temples. "*Life is flavorless* . . . no, that's wrong . . ."

Ortiz, bored, mouthed to Cheryl, "Can we wrap it up? She's *loco*."

In agreement, Cheryl stood, pushing her chair back and announced, "We don't want to keep you, Lara. So lastly, do you think anyone would want to harm Alma?"

Lara's eyes flew open. "Gosh, that's very dramatic. I thought we created the drama, not actually lived it. I don't think so. And—for what it's worth—my stylist is highly unlikely to have, you know, *murdered* her. I've worked with Belinda for several years and am an excellent judge of character."

"Okay, noted." Cheryl was already hovering at the exit.

"You see, detectives, it's reflecting on me quite badly, the ugly rumors. Do you think you'll have this sorted soon?"

"We can't comment on that, unfortunately." Ortiz opened and slurped a Diet Coke.

"Yes. Of course. Well, thank you, detectives. Can I grab a picture of your outfit, Detective Ortiz? I think you're right; yours *is* the more unremarkable of the two." Lara snapped a shot of a grinning Ortiz and then swept out the door. "*Darling*," she cajoled a woman working nearest the elevator, "could you be a love and show me to Jim's office?"

As she disappeared behind the closing doors, Ortiz turned to Cheryl. "That was nuts! Never had fancy cocktail recommendations in an interview, and I thought I'd heard every freakin' thing. What *did* they talk about at that lunch? Cos' she sure as hell ain't tellin'."

"Yeah, she's terrible at improv. But she's got a rock-solid time-coded alibi. That woman is photographed by people, all day, every day, evidentially."

"She was a waste of time, but it was totally worth it for the Jim humiliation. Let's get a coffee. Look! Everyone's in the kitchen mocking Superintendent Coat Check. This'll keep morale up for weeks!"

"Nah, I'm going to write up this menu she gave us. But go bask in Lara-reflected glory girl. Grab me a water?"

Ambling back to her desk a few minutes later, Ortiz glanced out the window, stopped abruptly, and yelled to Cheryl, "Hey, Chez, get over here. Quick!" Annoyed at the interruption, Cheryl pulled out an earbud and reluctantly rolled her chair over to witness Lara holding an impromptu photo call in front of her Land Rover, answering questions as a gaggle of paps furiously snapped pictures.

"*Yes, I'm here to help in any way with the death of my beloved agent, Alma, and I would like it to be known that I fully support my stylist, Belinda Grant, in her quest to be proven innocent. I wasn't there, of course, but it simply couldn't have been her. She's very placid and mostly unflappable.*"

"Beauty is a gift, just like good health or intelligence. The only thing is not to be proud of being beautiful. Because you didn't do anything—it was given to you."
—Monica Bellucci

Three's a Crowd

JANIE JONES FITTING
Her residence. 2:30 pm

CLAD IN SCANTY NEON YOGA GEAR, Janie stood at the center of her huge ballroom in the makeshift fitting area: six empty racks arranged around a three-piece mirror and a velvet podium. She glanced at the unused skate ramp to her left, sighing at how short her daughter's fad had been, and, walking to her right, slumped down on one of the jewel-tone velvet chairs scattered around her gleaming speakeasy bar.

"Teresa, put the food out," she ordered. "The guard texted that they're on their way in, so they'll be here any second—Jasper drives like a maniac."

"Yes, Miss Janie," Teresa rapidly positioned exquisitely arranged platters of hors d'oeuvres along the polished bar. She was finishing up meticulously spacing bottles of water as Jasper tumbled into the room, almost hidden behind the stack of garment bags in his arms. Chanelle, tottering behind him on towering platforms, dragged a battered trunk.

"Hi Janie, hi Teresa. Good to see you."

"Hi Jasper, where's Belinda?" Janie was flustered. "She's coming, *right*?"

"She's here! Just finishing up on a call."

Belinda, standing outside, had been on hold for five minutes and was irritated. To pass the time, she studied the white yacht bobbing in the middle of a field-turned-man-made lake and contemplated how many famous men must have been shagged on it.

"Hi, Devon—*finally*. I read your text. Why the fuck is Pat calling *you* about Ava-Lily's dress? There is no way I can tell Chanel that their *finale* gown, which we have held for *five weeks*, is no longer in play because Alma is dead and Ava-Lily has a tasteless, controlling publicist who's clawing onto fifteen minutes of power. Don't even get me started on what Tom Ford will fucking do to me. *CUSTOM TOM FORD!*" Realizing she was yelling, Belinda paused to regroup.

"Look, both houses know it's only between them, and neither will tolerate another designer in the mix at this late stage. If Pat is going to renege on this, then I quit. I can't blow up this level of designer relationship. Feel free to pass that on to Pat. Let her know *she* will be dealing with the fallout—of course I don't want to Devon—anyway, I have to go. I'm literally standing outside Janie's ballroom—no, she never does fittings in the main house; it's either the Olympic-sized gym or here. Keep me posted, and thank you Dev."

Switching her phone to silent, Belinda pushed open the door and mustered up her most reassuring voice (perky top notes with subtle mom undertones). "Janie! Hi babe, sorry to keep you waiting! *OOH*, look at all this delicious food. I'm so excited for today—we have so many beautiful things to try!"

"Oh, I hope so," Janie whined, self-pityingly. "I'm so *ugly* at the moment. Did you see this pimple on my chin? Because 'Stars & Us' totally did." She picked up the magazine from the bar and threw it in Belinda's direction. "No solid food for me this week." She sniffed a plate of deviled eggs longingly.

Belinda squinted at her face, seeing no blemishes under the full face of makeup, but understood that Janie, like so many women, saw flaws where there were none.

"You look gorgeous. I don't see a single pimple, and your body is banging!"

"Oh, thanks," Janie responded doubtfully. "I've been working out six hours every day for a month, and I'm running out of colonic places I go so often. I might have to drive to San Diego next time—god forbid. Do you think it's working? I would die for some carbs, but this is my life."

"So, you think you will end up presenting again this year?" Belinda asked, watching Jasper and Chanelle speedily unzip the garment bags of gowns they had placed on the racks.

"Oh, I imagine so. Someone *always* cancels at the last minute. Only in 2014 did everyone turn up. That is why I have to work out all the time. I've still got half an inch to go on my stomach." She pinched non-existent flesh on her exposed waist. "See?" Janie turned and glanced at the racks. "Do you have anything—"

"Fairytale? Yes, Janie, of course," Belinda nodded. "*Although* we have some amazing sleek options that would look insane on you and are so on-trend! Also, hear me out—how about a sensational, fitted tuxedo?"

"Belinda! How about we wait for me to find a new man before we dress me like a lesbian?"

"Um—" Belinda stumbled with words as Jasper choked on water.

"Perhaps that was a bit mean. Sorry Jasper, I'm just so nervous. I love lesbians—obviously—just not, you know, *that* way. I tried it seven or eight times. Some men love a threesome, but it's *hideous* not being at the center of it all. And I don't like watching other people fuck—I just start comparing myself. Jesus, I'm rambling. Anyway, my team will be here in a minute. Are we ready?"

"Almost." She eyed Jasper on his knees, arranging rows of shoes. "Who's coming this time?" Belinda tried, and failed, to keep her voice and face neutral.

"Well, obviously Eve, my publicist; Daria, my manager; her assistant Ken, because she says he has great taste; George, my New York publicist, is popping in for a second; and maybe Ian, my British agent—since Alma is, you know, *dead*—but he's 50/50. What's really important, since I'm currently *temporarily* single, is that I don't look *desperate*. So many of my exes are going, so the pressure is on, Belinda. But hopefully, between us all, we will get it right."

"Well, sometimes too many chefs can make it harder . . ." Belinda responded, her voice trailing off as she saw Janie making a call.

"Oh, and the other thing, Belinda"—Janie covered the phone with her hand—"they, like me, don't care about the clothes for Penicle, so let's save that for another day. I don't give a fuck whether old men can fuck or not;

I just need the money and to pretend it never happened. Can you believe I have to host a live stage event and walk on stage to a man singing, 'I can't get no satisfaction, I can't get no hard erection'? How does Mick allow it? You know what—let's decide wardrobe on the shoot day—Yelena can tailor on set. That would be much easier for me."

"But we brought it all here. Jasper has set it up, and the client—"

"Oh," interrupted Janie, "just have your intern put it back in the car. The client will be fine. They literally begged me to do this. Let's dedicate these hours to me looking amazing at the Oscars. It's a hot man-fest, and you know how I can't be single."

Might be best not to look like a fucking desperate bride whenever you wear a gown, Belinda's thoughts yelled, as her face smiled reassuringly. "We got this, Janie, don't worry." She added conspiratorially, "Which exes are going?"

"Oh, the usual suspects and some you don't know about, Belinda, so best not ask. You might know their wives."

"Hollywood is a door leading to
a thousand doors."
—Kensington Roth

Looting

Riding in Cars with Stylists

5:30 pm

JASPER, SIGHING, SLAMMED THE CAR'S BACK DOOR. "That's all I can get in here unless I leave you behind. Chanelle was waiting to pick up the Tom Ford from Yelena, but I told her to abort until later tonight, so she will be here soon to collect the rest."

"Don't leave me in this hell for one more second. Can you believe fucking Eve demanding we give her the Givenchy dress to show another client?"

"Oh, I forgot about that. Every memory from today has been obliterated by Eve and the manager woman dividing up—and stealing—the designer gifts they *assumed* Janie would not want. *I mean*—Janie was only out of the room for five minutes—*brazen*. The speed with which they put the stuff in their cars." He shook his head so hard his curls swung. "I'm so disgusted that I'm mildly impressed."

"Who the fuck sent her an air fryer anyway? Like she eats. Love that they left her the platinum vibrator, though"—Belinda giggled—"such a low-key burn for the newly single. It was *gigantic*."

"Quite frankly, I'd be surprised if Eve had a clit, and she be trippin' if she thinks those yoga pieces will fit her in this lifetime. They would barely fit little Rose."

"As far as I can tell, Eve is permanently on the latest cleanse." Belinda pulled a sad face. "Maybe that's why she's such a raging bitch. It's so gross that they couldn't give a fuck we were in the room to witness their thieving. Like it never occurs to them that we would say anything."

"Which we won't."

"Yeah, yeah, I know. I feel dirty, but what good would it do? Just fast-track us to unemployment. Speaking of which, I'll let Devon know about no fitting images for the Penicle campaign. Let him troubleshoot that."

"It's what he's good at!"

Belinda pulled her phone out of the new Tatou purse and recoiled as countless new notifications jumped out at her. Terrified, she read the first two before scanning down. "*SHIT*, Jas, I've got about 400 messages that Lara did an impromptu interview about Alma outside the Beverly Hills PD. She said, and—I quote the Daily Mail—'*I fully support my stylist Belinda Grant in her quest to be proven innocent.*' *WHAT IN THE ACTUAL FUCK*. How could she not know this will make everything 5000 times worse?" She tossed the phone on the dash and closed her eyes, breathing deeply, only to open them again as her phone rang. 'Flox Corp' popped up on the caller ID.

"*FUCK!*" she shouted, jabbing the decline button and bursting into tears. "The tabloids are on it already."

THURSDAY 1ST MARCH 2018

Services Rendered

Thursday 8:45 am

> Hey B, I saw the Lara thing. Why is she such an ass? So sorry. Let me know if there's anything I can do xxx

> Thanks, Emily. Means a lot. Seems I'm in the tabloids more than you this week. How the fuck do you do it?

> I pretend it's not me. Did you know that tabloid Emily currently has anorexia? The stress from being an activist is killing her, AND she is having a torrid affair with her last female co-star, (Josie) they are living a double life (they had a hike together last weekend and hugged. Close-up photo of leggings touching is incontrovertible evidence)

> Oof. You win. Btw did you Venmo me $2000?

I did! For the ACLU event.

But that's charity!

Yes, but mine, not yours!

I'm blown away.

And I'm appalled that you are blown away about being paid correctly for a job I hired you to do!

Penny Lovell

*"People see me and they squeal
like tropical birds or seals
stranded on the beach."*
—Carrie Fisher

Flirting with Fans

JONNY EVANS OSCAR FITTING
Henri LeRoque store, Rodeo Drive. 10 am

BELINDA AND JASPER PULLED UP TO THE PUBLIC VALET under the 1920s Tiffany building in Beverly Hills. "We'll be about an hour and a half," he said, handing his keys to a man with a wizened face, slicked-back hair, and a burgundy vest.

"Thank god for Jonny today. This fitting is going to be so fast. Imagine being done with any of the ladies in an hour and a half?"

"Excuse, sir, parking is free for one hour."

"Yes, I know, thanks." Jasper glanced at him briefly, then turned to Belinda. "And $400 for the next hour. How much do you pay for our parking a month anyway?"

"Fuck knows. Another thing I can't change and don't want to cry over, that's for sure. And as for Jonny, we haven't done the fitting yet for chrissakes. Don't jinx it. Besides, what we get in relief from him is more than compensated for by his wife. God, I wish I could ditch her."

"You know his publicist keeps it a two-for-one because who the fuck else at your level would put up with her, Bel?"

"Whatever," Belinda was tapping on her phone. "Hopefully, she won't be here today stealing purses like last time."

"Did Jonny end up paying for that?"

"Yup, but she thinks it was a freebie. God help us all." They took the elevator to the ground level and jay-walked across Brighton Way towards Henri LeRoque, dodging tourists posing for photos in the glaring winter sun. Looking up from an email, Belinda glanced at the Harry Winston window display and stopped, distracted by a 6-row diamond choker suspended in front of a red velvet backdrop. "*LOOK, JAS*," she yelled excitedly, pointing and taking a hard right, oblivious to the disgruntled shoppers swerving out of her way. She waved her phone in his direction, waiting for him to catch up, then thrust a headless image of Janie modeling a slinky peach silk-knit gown in his face. " Look at this! This is *perfect*. For Janie and the Calvin Klein, *too simple*, we thought, *but* if she was wearing an insane million-dollar diamond necklace, *BOOM*! Not simple anymore!"

"Jeeze, Bel, each of those stones must be four carats at least. That must be a squillion mil."

"So? She looked at him in genuine confusion. "It's the OSCARS! It doesn't matter what it's worth as long as they'll loan it and send a guard or six. Better if it's crazy expensive anyway; Janie, or more truthfully, Eve, loves that shit. Do we have time to pop in?

"Er, no, I don't think we do, Bel, look."

Belinda turned in the direction of his finger to see a commotion around a car outside Henri LeRoque. "Oh fuck, I tell him every time to park around the back."

"Since when does he ever listen? And he can't leave his car to get towed again. I'll sort it." Jasper yelled back, sprinting his Air Jordans towards the green vintage Porsche, his silver bomber jacket pushing through the crowd gathered around the car.

Belinda trailed him as fast as she could manage, berating herself for the 20th time that day for wearing 4" stack-heeled ankle boots just because Rose said they looked *rad* with her outfit, her gorgeous face flushing with pride when Mommy took her advice.

"Belinda!" Jonny called out in his inimitable smoky voice. "Babe!" He threw his arms around her as she approached, totally immune to the fans' iPhones and, more importantly, a paparazzi clicking away beside them. Belinda lowered her head, pulling away as quickly and as casually as possible, raising her voice to say, "Great to see you, Jonny. Shall we try on clothes?"

"Ripper," he responded, grinning for a selfie with one ecstatic tourist and signing an autograph for another, "Can't wait, mate. Let me just sign a few."

Belinda stood by the door, scanning 49 new emails from the last hour, half watching the familiar scene. Jonny chatting, posing, and laughing. Charming the crowd with his Australian humor, sexy-eyed flirting with the women, and bro talk with the men.

"Do you know him? Like, are you friends?" A flushed, breathless girl asked, grabbing Belinda's arm urgently.

"Yes. Well no. I'm his stylist."

"*Oh my GOD*. Have you touched him? Seen him in his underwear? Like, in *PERSON*? She looked at Belinda in total awe and squealed, "Can I get your autograph?"

"What? No." Belinda winced at the girl's crestfallen face. "But why? I just work with him."

"But you know him! Pleeease? It would mean a lot."

Looking at her beseeching face, Belinda capitulated, "Okay, sure, quickly though." She grabbed the pen and signed on Jonny's face:

Belinda Grant
STYLIST to Jonny Evans
(clothes, not hair)
xoxo.

"Shall we?" Walking up from behind, Jonny put his arm around Belinda's waist, causing the autograph hunter to almost faint. "Belinda, are you signing *autographs*?" he chuckled, pulling her into the store.

"Only because I know you. Your sweet fan only wanted one because I have been close to the air you breathe. I tried to say no, and she almost cried. Dear god."

"I am pretty great, Belinda. Admit it."

"Whatever," she deadpanned, wriggling out of his arm. "You pay me."

Dazzle Dosh

RE: LARA/OSCARS/JEWELRY DEAL WITH DAZZLE DIAMONDS

> From: Devon Dalton <u>Devon@stylistsonly.agency</u>
> To: Belinda Grant <u>Belinda@BGstyle.com</u>
> Date: Mar 1, 2018 at 11:59 am
> 🔒 Standard encryption (TLS)
>   Learn more

Hi Bels,

Per her manager, Jeremy, Dazzle Diamonds has won the bidding war for Lara's neck. Please set up a fitting ASAP. The good news is the amount is enough for you to get a rate. Working on it but at least $5k. I am trying to get assistant paid as an additional fee, BUT it's 50/50.

Will circle back ASAP. See contact info in the attachment.

NOTE SHE MUST WEAR A NECKLACE. It is contractual and not negotiable.

Pls confirm receipt of this email.

Re:Re: LARA/OSCARS/JEWELRY DEAL WITH DAZZLE DIAMONDS

From: Belinda Grant Belinda@BGstyle.com
To: Devon Dalton Devon@stylistsonly.agency
Date: Mar 1, 2018 at 12:08 pm
🔒 Standard encryption (TLS)
Learn more

OKAY, you and I both know $5k for her is shit. Devon, this has taken me ten days at least, and the same for Jasper. After Tax, expenses, assistant rate, etc. It will work out at about $200 a day FOR THE OSCARS. Jesus. I might weep. Also, does she know about this? She thinks Dazzle Diamonds are tacky AF and *never* wants to wear a necklace.

Re:Re:Re: LARA/OSCARS/JEWELRY DEAL WITH DAZZLE DIAMONDS

From: Devon Dalton Devon@stylistsonly.agency
To: Belinda Grant Belinda@BGstyle.com
Date: Mar 1, 2018 at 12:11 pm
🔒 Standard encryption (TLS)
Learn more

Yes, she knows. Jeremy says she chose them. As for her change of heart on the necklace, I heard the number was HIGH (approx $250k) through the grapevine.

I will fight for more $$$ for you and Jasper, but you know how reluctant she is to pay for styling. Again, remember you'll make more on the advertising, she has no control over that budget.

"More is more and less is a bore."
—Iris Apfel

Be You

STYLISTS LUNCH HOSTED BY DAISY DUPONT
Her residence in Hollywood Hills. 12:30 pm

"DAHLING", DAISY DRAWLED LOUDLY, sweeping her floor-length coral silk dress coat through the crowded room to Belinda, who was scrolling her email, oblivious to the goings on in Daisy's opulent Hollywood Hills mansion, "remind me of your name again?"

Startled, Belinda looked up. "Oh hi—hi Daisy. It's Belinda Grant."

"Ah yes, Bee-linda." She traced her mahogany, bejeweled index finger up Belinda's cheek, and stared intently at her for a few seconds before announcing loudly, "SO *fresh*." She turned with a dancer's pivot, smooth silver hair swinging as she glided away, and asserted without looking back, "You will sit with me at my table, *of course*."

"That's amazing, Belinda. Daisy wants you to sit with her. She must really like you. Let me take you to her table." Janet, the peppy PR, gently took Belinda's arm.

"Hi Janet, I didn't see you hovering there." Jasper returned from the bathroom. "Your look is divine as always. Is that your own waist-length hair?"

"It is! Who can afford extensions this long! And I always hover around Daisy. This dress is from her new collection. Don't you just love?" Janet flushed with pleasure and looked down at the one-shouldered saffron silk-tiered maxi dress, which completely overwhelmed her starved body.

"I could see any of your ladies in this collection, couldn't you? Daisy's recent trip to Bhutan so inspired her that she just insisted the Atelier scrap everything and start over. After lunch in her terrace garden, I can take you to the conservatory and show you the full line. There are some sensational custom gowns for Oscar parties, if you guys haven't confirmed all your looks yet, of course."

"Great. Would love to see them," Belinda responded. " Jasper's sitting with me at lunch? We are so busy, and I need him close."

"Well, I don't know if assistants *usually* sit with Daisy, but since it's you, maybe we can squeeze him in this time. Let me double-check. One quick sec." She dashed out of a side door.

"You have to go to the bathroom, Bee. It's fucking insane. A hand-carved waterfall that I assume/hope was the sink, and a sheepskin-covered lamb sculpture are highlights. Oh, and it's entirely wallpapered in shells. Real ones."

"Oooh, maybe I'll go now—" Belinda was thwarted by Janet frantically waving them over. They followed her outside onto the terrace, where low, carved wooden tables covered the stone-tiled floor. They were set rustically, folded terracotta linen napkins centered on hand-woven layered placemats, embossed bronze cutlery, gilded glasses, and clashing tribal-print poof cushions in place of chairs.

Standing in front of her table overlooking the terrace, Daisy gestured widely with gold-adorned arms. "Ladiees, sit down. And the non-conforming and the men, of course."

Awkwardly, the stylists started to lower themselves onto the poofs. "Quite comfortable once you get down here," Jasper heard style presenter Dylan Moore say to uber stylist Jolly Jaden.

Rushing back to them, Janet squealed, "It's okay, Belinda! Jasper can sit with you! It will just be a bit of a squash." She pointed at two poofs balanced on one another, positioned at the corner of Daisy's regular-height wooden table.

"Well, Belinda," Jasper whispered, "I see it's a core exercise class for me today. Are there no spare chairs in this mansion? God, I hate these events."

He turned and looked at the room of power stylists trying, with varying degrees of success, to lower themselves graciously onto the poofs. *Well, maybe it's worth it for the entertainment,* he thought, cheering up and giggling.

"*BEE-LINDA*, here." Daisy patted the seat next to her. "We have had to improvise for your helper, but it is done, of course."

"Thank you, Daisy, I appreciate it. Oh, what a beautiful bracelet." Belinda lightly touched Daisy's Bulgari double-wrap 'serpenti' bracelet, one of many she was wearing.

"Isn't it, dahling? I found it under my pillow this morning. My dahling Teddy had left it there. He is so utterly romantic. It is the secret to marriage: a great husband. And you, Belinda, are you married?"

"Getting divorced, actually," she shrugged sadly. "No bracelets under my pillow."

"Oh, then he is not a great husband, my dahling. One little divorce is not a problem. Is being married all that you are? Is being divorced? Nobody cares. Do your thing. Don't dwell on the dark, look for the light and build around it. You will always be with yourself. So, *you* must be *you*. In all of your marvelous glory. Tell me, do you have children?"

"Yes, one daughter, Rose."

"You see, you've already created a light, a magical floral force. What an energy you two must be in the world, my dahling."

Belinda, strangely reassured, flushed and tried to put together words of gratitude to respond to this world-renowned woman, but Daisy was already on her feet, announcing, "Thrilled to have you all in my home. Lunch is self-serve. Please make your way to the conservatory on the right. The one on the left has the new collection, which I hope you will all browse after lunch and love."

There was a flurry of frustrated sighs from the room, as many had only just lowered to the floor and now, reluctantly, had to stand again.

"There's just no elegant way to do it," Jasper whispered to Belinda, not quite succeeding in stifling a laugh. "It's worth balancing for an hour on unstable, upscale cushions to witness this. Do you think I could get away with filming it?"

"No!" She bit her tongue to stop herself from laughing. "And stop, or I'm gonna lose it!"

Fifteen minutes later, seeing the room seated and farm-to-table organic salad being pushed around plates, Daisy rose again, clapping her hands, bracelets jangling.

"Once again, it is a pleasure to have *me* in my humble palace! I mean *you!*" she tittered. "Now, please, everyone, I want to get to know you, hear your issues, and answer your questions. Who would like to go first? Yes, Amy?"

Amy Johnson stood up, wiping her hands on her yoga pants, her expansive cleavage wobbling in a corseted Balmain tube top. "Well, Daisy, I've been in the industry for a long time. As you all know, I practically invented celebrity styling—yes, you're welcome, everyone! And I have seen everything, but the recent nickel and dime-ing the studios have been getting away with is next-level disgusting. Cutting our rates, refusing to pay for expenses. And then we have to come to designers such as you, Daisy, to ask you to pay for the tailoring, our fees even, and I have to—"

"Dahling," Daisy interrupted dismissively, "no one wants to hear of your money problems. Please sit down. Now, who is next? Oh, hello, Pansy"—she smiled at the late arrival, a wafer-thin, blonde-bobbed super stylist—"Dahling did you eat? You must get yourself a plate. I hear the food here is *marvelous!*"

"Um . . . isn't this her house?" Jasper whispered in Belinda's ear and then giggled uncontrollably, almost choking on the marvelous food. "Do you think she knows?"

"*Sssssshhhh*"—Belinda gently slapped him—"she can hear you."

"No, she can't. She doesn't even know I'm alive."

"JOLLY!" Daisy pointed at a stylist dressed in a silver-threaded kaftan with Margiela Birkenstocks.

They stood up, flipping their waist-length fuchsia hair. "Daisy, I'd like to ask if you will be offering more inclusive size runs in the near future? Several clients of mine have chosen not to succumb to societal Hollywood pressure to be a size 2—or 4—or even an 8. I also have one singer who is a size 20. I know you offer limited pieces in bigger sizes and occasionally have a token plus-size model in your show, but do you plan to expand on this?"

"Dahling Jolly. Of course, you use hilarious puns and ask all the best questions! I will talk to my team at length on this issue. My shantung silk kaftans (I see you are enjoying one today) were among the first designer items to fit many sizes, and I would tell you when, but a lady doesn't reveal her age!" She tittered, "But you are right to take me to task, and I will rise to your challenge for those brave ladies or people. Now, who is next?" Daisy indicated that Jolly should sit.

"Oh yes, *you*," she said, pointing at a slight male who, with his neon-yellow buzz cut and pinstriped Thom Browne shorts suit looked barely older than a teenager. Janet, jumping in, whispered in Daisy's ear, "*Adam.*"

"ADAM! What have you to ask of me?"

"Oh, hi Daisy, thank you for inviting me today. I was wondering what you think of Breaking Hollywood's Uber Stylists Top Ten list. It occurred to me that it is very divisive to *number* artists such as us. It seems obvious to me that, on this list, you can only be as powerful as your clients are famous, and creativity is not an important factor. Further to that, I understand a very powerful agency (I won't mention their name in case they shadow-ban me) successfully lobbied to have the number one and two stylists on the list switched out in the final moments before publication last year. This seems to counter the recent industry claims to be more transparent and inclusive. What do you think about this?"

"Oh, dahling Ian. Sorry, *Adam.* I agree that one cannot number creativity, especially with the depth and breadth of the talent in this room. However, Karen, the editor of Breaking Hollywood, is such a dear friend, and I find it impossible to believe such a rumor could be true. Perhaps we should not discuss here what we do not know to be correct. Disinformation is the scourge of our era. Now, who is next?"

A striking, cropped redhead in military pants and an asymmetrical peach button-down stood up. "Hi, Daisy. Since many of us are here today, I want to discuss the idea of forming a union. We all know how unstable our world is financially. The studios lowball us endlessly, one I worked with recently even has a policy to never pay stylists. The rates haven't gone up for years—I think I got paid more a decade ago! And of course, our income can easily be kneecapped on the whim of a client or their team. Maybe, if we stood together instead of competing with each other for clients, we could get some protections.

There was a smattering of impromptu applause, and conversations burst out noisily around the room.

- "We talked about that a couple of years ago. Everyone is too scared to rock the boat—"

- "No shit."

- "Come on now, we know they would fight it—they studios only agree to our rates if they are forced into it by a BIG client. They pay whatever they feel (or don't feel) like paying."

- "AND they take months to *actually* pay! 90 days on my last press tour! After I had to work as a local and pay for all my own flights and hotels."

- "Yeah, and if we ask the clients to pay anything, they get mad because why should they pay to promote something that makes the studios millions? And then *we* get caught in the crossfire. Ugh"

- "NOBODY wants to ask anybody to pay for ANYTHING."

The volume rose as the tables debated, and Daisy stood, waving her hands to silence the room, replying loudly, "Dahling Amanda, I believe in any uprising against this brutal late-capitalistic world as I write about extensively in my latest biography. (One will be gifted to each of you on departure.) I am and always have been, for the people. I privately support you in this endeavor and wish you the best," she glanced at another waving hand. "Yes, Orlando?"

Orlando, remaining seated, his ring-clad fingers toying with a knife, drawled, "Daisy, as I'm sure you know, *everything* I touch turns viral." He paused, staring pointedly at Belinda. "For high *fashun* reasons, I might add. I have 1.3 million unpaid followers on social media." He stroked his pavé septum piercing. "As such, I don't think it's unreasonable for me to ask to be *paid* for exposing your brand to the masses who worship me. How do you feel about this? Other brands are jumping on it, so will you keep up?"

Daisy, visibly bored, sighed. "You know I *adore* you, Orlando, but, as I said earlier, discussing financial matters at lunch is terribly inelegant. Please email Janet if you wish to take this further. Now, I understand you are all very busy this week, so let's finish lunch and for those who can't stay for the dessert—which I'm told is delicious *and* gluten-and-lactose free—please don't forget to take a small token of our appreciation for your time. Janet has gift bags for you by the door. All we ask is that you don't sell them on eBay. And, of course, we welcome any social media support you care to give us!"

Jasper leaned into Belinda and whispered, "100 bucks there's a purse in that shopping bag."

Stars & Us Magazine

CELEBRITY > BREAKING GOSSIP

CHEATING JONNY?
WOAH! Is Oscar nominee Jonny Evans Exchanging Blondes Yet Again?

By **Emerald Woosly-Jones**

Published on March 1st, 2018 3:39PM PST

Earlier today, he was seen outside Henri LeRoque on Rodeo Drive in a very intimate embrace with an <u>unknown strawberry blonde</u>—a blonde who was most definitely not his current wife, <u>Tabitha</u>. One onlooker said Jonny, wearing his signature skinny, ankle-skimming suit, looked giddy and excited when she arrived and couldn't keep his hands off her, wrapping her in a tight embrace, only letting go to sign autographs for his demanding fans. A second onlooker added that, although charming as always, Jonny seemed distracted and couldn't stop looking at his (new?) lady.

After hastily satisfying his admirers, Jonny immediately returned to his friend. He intimately wrapped his arm around the waist of her on-trend leather jumpsuit, walking her masterfully into the store. His lady, sporting oversized sunglasses and Bridget Bardot bangs was coy and reserved, hiding her face from the crowd and the cameras. I'm sure we will find out this mysterious beauty's identity soon enough!

And what of Tabitha? Is she proving the old adage that when a man marries his mistress, he creates a job vacancy? We shall see, but no doubt his last wife, <u>JoJo Evans</u>, will enjoy her <u>20 million settlement</u> more gleefully this week.

The only question is, which blonde the hunky pop star will bring as his date on Sunday? Only three days until we find out...

RELATED: <u>Jonny Evans a complete A-Z of his dating history (guess which two letters are missing!)</u>

<u>Jonny Evans, the HOTTEST MAN ALIVE: getting sexier with every wrinkle!</u>

Affairs to Forget

JFC B,

WHAT IS GOING ON OVER THERE?

Assuming, of course, you are not shagging JE?

E xoxo

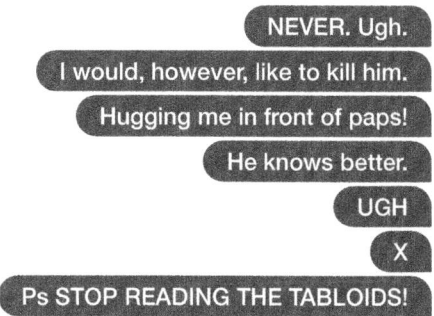

NEVER. Ugh.

I would, however, like to kill him.

Hugging me in front of paps!

He knows better.

UGH

X

Ps STOP READING THE TABLOIDS!

But then I wouldn't know that tabloid-Emily is having a raging affair with Brandon Loopner. Apparently, a bloating, heavy lunch earlier this week might be his child. He's been in Australia filming for four months, but no matter...

Do you even know him?

No! Not great news for our upcoming child.

"*I saw the world from the stars' point of view, and it looked unbearably lonely.*"
—*Shaun David Hutchinson,*
We Are the Ants

Musing Life

AVA-LILY DRESS REFIT
Beverly Hills Hotel. 4 pm

"PAT IS RUNNING LATE. CAN WE WAIT FOR HER?" Ava-Lily asked timidly, walking barefoot into the suite, tugging at an oversized beige sweatshirt dress falling off one shoulder. "And Jackie isn't even here. She took Ulysses for a hike. I'm trying to teach him to use the toilet and he's depressed about his lack of success. I thought getting out would be good for him. Even though he hates the leash, she took the stroller too, just in case."

"Oh, I'm so sorry, Ava-Lily, but we're actually on a really tight schedule today," declared Belinda firmly, trying not to smile at Jasper, standing behind Ava-Lily, silently whooping in joy.

"Ya!" Yelena added, "I have many dresses to sew. I have to leave, so we must start." She winked at Belinda and mouthed. "*Fuck that beetch.*"

Belinda sighed happily as she unzipped the Chanel Couture garment bag. Not dealing with Pat was an unexpected bonus. "If she doesn't make it in time, we'll send her images, Ava-Lily. We have to send them to Tom Ford and Chanel anyway."

"Okay . . . I guess. Pat might get mad with you, but okay." She shrugged her tiny shoulders. "I probably won't be working with her for much longer. I might travel around India for a year—see some real life—and be like a normal 19-year-old girl. Do you think I should take Jackie with me? Maybe I should ... just in case I get recognized ... and Ulysses would totally miss her."

"Um," Belinda was trying to keep a straight face. "It's quite unusual to backpack with a bodyguard/personal assistant and your cat, but—didn't you plan on doing this last year? And the one before too?"

"Oh, that's right, I did, but maybe I'm serious this time." She shrugged her shoulders. "I dunno ... I could write about my experience, you know, for magazines or start a blog, so an assistant would be a big help."

"Belinda used to write a column for FEMME Magazine," Jasper remarked as he hung up the Tom Ford jumpsuit.

"REALLY?" Ava-Lily's eyes grew large as she turned and looked at Belinda. "That's so *hot*. Why did you stop?"

"Oh, it was just online. I loved it. But it was unpaid and weekly. It took up so much of my time. I couldn't keep going and still have enough hours to sleep," Belinda made a sad face. "I do miss it though. Writing is—"

"I totally love to write, too. When my tutor assigned me essays on set, it was a very happy time in my life."

"You are a child; you have had no life." Yelena startled herself by muttering this out loud and hurriedly moved on. "OKAY. No time for all the words, ladeeez. Just put on dress, please, Lily."

"It's Ava-*Lily*, Yelena," Belinda corrected.

"Yez. Whatever you say." She thrust the gold unzipped Chanel gown in Ava-Lily's face. "Here, poot this on."

After removing and dropping her dress on the floor, Ava-Lily—topless in kitty-cat cotton panties—stepped gingerly into the sequined halter-neck gown. Yelena swiftly closed the zipper before hooking on the 6-foot train. Jasper, sitting at their feet, slid on matching custom-made heels.

"*WOW!* It fits like a second skin," Belinda gasped, momentarily elated by the vision before her. "Yelena, this is fucking perfect. *WOW!*"

"Of course," she snorted. "What else you think it would be? Chanel, don't let just any fucking idiot cut up their shit."

Jasper laughed as he stood and ushered Ava-Lily to the wall. "Pictures, ladies! We need to get a wriggle on, so let's photograph all the angles for Chanel and then quickly switch to the Tom Ford."

"He also wants to avoid beetch lady," Yelena, once again, tried and mostly failed to whisper to Belinda, "smart!"

"No shit. He's right, and no need to whisper, Yel. Look—she's got her AirPods in again."

FIRE THE STYLIST
Dishing Daily Doses of Fashion Justice

⚖️

JONNY EVANS' New Lady, STYLIST BELINDA GRANT (Age unknown), HENRI LEROQUE Store, Rodeo Drive.

Posted on March 1, 2018

In an unusual turn of events today on #FTS, we are discussing the outfit of celebrity *STYLIST* Belinda Grant, rumored new paramour of her client Jonny Evans (not to mention the last person to see Alma Astley, 56, alive). Boy, this gurl is having an Oscars week!

Seen earlier today intimately embracing Jonny outside Henri LeRoque (his sartorial home since their 2017 contract), Belinda was sporting a chocolate brown Phillip Lim Fall 2016 belted jumpsuit with Celine 2015 tan stack ankle boots, tortoiseshell Prada sunglasses and a 2017 cross-body white fringed Proenza Schouler bag. (How has she kept *that* clean all these years? Tips, gurl, we need tips!)

But we digress. Let us return to the look. Overall, we think it works (better than her professional morals, apparently!) Despite all the pieces being older season, they fortunately still look current. Though as avid followers know, we are not generally fans of brown here at #FTS. That said, mixing up the shades with the tan boots and throwing in the white bag might just have saved the day.

What do you guys think? *Should she fire herself?*

As always, leave comments below!

(To review our community guidelines, please click here)

@mommyof2 She is a home wrecker. What a slut.

@Ilovestyle23 @mommyof2 HE has wrecked all his marriages with affairs, look it up, and while you are at it, do FEMINISM as well. #SMDH

@freestyling didn't this hottie get accused of murdering that agent lady? Man, this man likes trouble. LOL

@manu4eva she's a bit old for him

@llovestyle23 @manu4eva JFC He's 50 (I think). I don't know how old she is, but she doesn't look a day over 35.

@normcorenever the devil wears Celine! So, NOT a girl's girl. Shame on her, but I like the bag, clearly polished with Tabitha's tears.

FRIDAY 2ND MARCH 2018

Tabloid Whoppers

10:15 am

Hey B,

I just thought you'd want to know that Tabloid Emily's husband is filing for divorce because of her 'DIVA DEMANDS'. No actual example of the aforementioned behavior, but two whole pages of word salad, illustrated with images of the couple looking mad or sad. ♀☹

WTF?!

It's impressive, actually bc they usually forget I even have a partner since he's not famous, I didn't 'steal' him from another woman and he doesn't wear eye candy on the red carpet...

I can fix that! Just let me and Jasper at him

Then he would divorce me! Lol.

Speaking of diva demands.

I'm getting offered some hardcore 'Everytown' donation money to attend the Bebe Kline Pre-Oscar dinner tomorrow night.

Is it possible to swing a fitting? I don't think I can, in good conscience, turn it down. If you don't have time, I could go by the Atelier myself and send images for your approval?

Got it. Could the Diva do a fitting later on today? I have jewelry fitting with Lara, but I have some time after that. Tomorrow, however, is nuts.

What's a jewelry fitting?

LOL. More wasted hours with Lara alternating between berating my taste in stones with lectures on how deeply spiritual she is:

"Princess-cut diamonds are not chic." and...

She is 'terrified of the current human condition.'

"Rubies upset her chi."

But...

We all need to 'deprioritize the self.'

Tell that to tabloid Emily, okay?

No words.

Jasper has some.

"*Everybody wants to be a diamond, but
very few are willing to get cut.*"
—*Unknown*

In the Doghouse

JEWELRY FITTING WITH LARA
Her Residence. 11:45 am

BELINDA AND JASPER FOUGHT THROUGH the untamed greenery outside Lara's house. Today, like many days, this was problematic since Jasper was piled high with garment bags and Belinda was hauling a massive trunk of shoes over the rickety stone path. Two black-suited, grizzled security guards carrying brown paper shopping bags containing four million dollars of diamonds followed them discreetly. "Jasper," Belinda spoke quietly so only he could hear, "do *not* mention the impromptu press conference she had outside the police station, okay? I know you are furious for me, but it's just not worth it, okay?"

"God, I hate her," he answered, lifting his chin in an attempt to see over the bags in his arms. "It's just *so* wrong. But okay, for you, I'll keep it zipped. Now, let's change the subject. We're almost in the house. *OW*—" he yelled as he crashed into closed glass. "*Shiiiit*. What the *fuck*? This bazillion-dollar 'jungle experience' moving window is always fucking open. *Fuck*, I hope I haven't broken my toe. This was not the day to be wearing my Proenza Birkenstocks." He hopped backward as the glass started to move.

Lara, standing behind it, announced, "Sorry, guys, Kelly has taken Toto to canine therapy, so I had to open the door myself. It took me a minute to find the switch." Noticing Jasper wincing, her eyes widened behind oversized tortoiseshell readers. "Casper, are you okay?" She looked down at his swelling painted toe. "Anyway, let me know when you finish setting up. I shall be in my office. I'm writing now, you know. Creating my own material to counterbalance the rampant sexism in this town and shocking lack of female projects." She spun around and disappeared from sight, her chocolate silk kaftan wafting behind her.

"Her dog is in therapy?" whispered Jasper. "They don't mention that on his Instagram."

"Haha. A fake dog life. It's probably not a moment too soon for that poor pooch."

"No human or animal escapes the trauma. Fuck, my foot hurts." Jasper carefully took off his shoes.

"Sit down, Jas. I'll get the Tatou dress out. Let's keep the back-ups in the bags unless she demands them."

"No, babe, let me do it—I can hop. Thank god it's not my driving foot."

"Shit, Jasper, should we go to urgent care?" Belinda guided him gently in the direction of a chair. "I can't believe she didn't even get you ice. I have ibuprofen." She rifled through her new Daisy Dupont' Liberation' purse. "Fuck, I must have left them in the Tatou bag. Sorry, Jas. I'll go ask Lara."

"Don't do that! I'll be fine, Bel." Jasper, refusing to sit, hopped outside to take a hit on his vape. "This weed should do it. Although I'll probably be mute for a bit, I warn you."

Acquiescing, Belinda turned and instructed the guards where to set up, observing their gloved hands methodically placing the jewels on velvet trays.

"Please be careful on that table!" Lara's voice pierced the industrious silence as she re-entered. "It's a family heirloom. Well, my mom bought it in 2000, but still, another two years, and it's vintage oak."

"Yes, of course." one of the men gruffly responded, backing away. "We'll wait outside to give you privacy."

"Thank you," Lara nodded." There's quite a comfortable tree stump just around the corner if you want to sit. You probably passed it on the way in." Unperturbed, the guards gave a thumbs up and walked out into the foliage.

Walking to the table, Lara inspected the gems and turned to face Belinda. "*Not* what I would call breathtaking. Who designed this mediocrity?"

"Dazzle Diamonds," Belinda responded, glancing at Jasper, whose face reflected her confusion.

"Is it not tacky to wear Dazzle Diamonds, Belinda? Why on earth would you choose this brand for me? *No one* wears them voluntarily. Should we just stick a SOLD sign on my forehead?"

"Jeremy, *your manager*, advised that this was the deal you chose, Lara. I wasn't aware that I had a say. Also, virtually everyone gets paid for jewelry at the Oscars."

"That's irrelevant," Lara snapped. "It's one thing to be paid for, say, Tiffany or Chopard, but Dazzle Diamonds? I might choke saying the name if the necklace doesn't do it first. And I loathe things around my neck. Why weren't you communicating with Jeremy more closely, Belinda? Perhaps you were too busy dating your other clients?"

"Lara! I'm not dating Jonny. He's *married*. Surely you, of all people, understand the lies of the tabloids?"

"Yes, it's possible I was a tad harsh, but really, between him and Alma, what is happening with you? Do you think these distractions are affecting your focus? I need your A-plus game for the Oscars, Belinda, so tell me now if there's any problem."

"No, no problem, Lara. Let's try stuff on. And wearing a necklace is a contractual requirement, which I was advised you understood. This one looks sensational with the dress. The teardrop diamond subtly echoes the shape of the crystals. I chose it for that reason. I, like you, was nervous about the selection they'd offer, but I think it worked out perfectly."

Lara looked skeptical. "I think you're wrong"—she cocked her head at the scarlet couture gown laid out on the couch—"but we will see." Checking the security guard was out of sight, she wiggled out of her kaftan and stood naked in the center of the room. Belinda held the body of the dress open, and Lara stepped in. Jasper limped over to wrangle the train while Belinda fastened the 24 minuscule crystal buttons. Six minutes later, she gently positioned the necklace, expertly closing the invisible clasp.

"Shoes, Casper?" Lara demanded, kicking the fabric at the hem.

"I'll get them," Belinda walked to their trunk, cracked it, and pulled out their chosen pair, closing the lid immediately, lest Lara see any others and steal further hours dissecting them.

"Are they exactly the same color, Belinda?" Lara scrutinized the sky-high Jimmy Choo peep-toe heels.

"Yes. They were dyed to match a swatch of the fabric."

"Do we like an ankle strap? Hmmm . . . since it's a delicate width, it won't shorten my leg too much. Yes, I think it will do"—she nodded—"but perhaps we can glue a crystal on the back of the heel. Wouldn't that be chic?"

"You know we won't see the shoes, Lara? The train is 6 feet long."

"Yes, but I'll know, won't I?"

"Sure. I can ask Tatou for extra crystals, no problem." Belinda looked down at Jasper, fastening the shoes and wincing—from pain or the unnecessary work, she couldn't tell. Probably both. Refocusing, she picked up a delicate ear cuff and two-carat studs and handed them to Lara, who didn't allow anyone to touch her ears. She selected and stacked four diamond bands on Lara's right hand, which she was allowed to touch. "*Ta-dah!*" She announced theatrically, standing back to assess Lara's look. She wanted to cry with relief. It was breathtaking.

Lara turned slowly to the mirror that Kelly, on her return, had quietly placed in the room. Belinda and Jasper stood behind her, holding their breath, waiting for the verdict dictating how terrible their next 48 hours would be.

"Well, now . . ." There was a long pause, followed by dramatic breath, as Lara regarded herself in the mirror." Is it so utterly annoying to always be *right*?"

Belinda sighed with relief and coughed to try and cover it up. "Um . . ."

"No need to respond, Belinda. You were right. I was wrong. I'm gracious enough to admit my mistakes."

"Well, it is my job, Lara."

"Yes, yes, I suppose it is. Thank god the diamonds are so exquisite with the dress. It might make it more palatable to say their name. They really are paying quite well. Now, Belinda, what is happening with all these rumors about you? They don't seem to be going away. I read something on Page Six yesterday. I forget what it—"

"*Jesus!*" Jasper interjected. "Lara, you did a mini press conference outside the police station on Wednesday. You mentioned Belinda. It went viral. It *was* going away, but you headlined it again. *How don't you know this?*"

"Excuse me!" Lara spluttered. "What are you talking about, Casper? I *defended* Belinda and take great offense to you talking to me this way." Her neck reddened as her face and demeanor turned frigid. "Belinda, take your required pictures. I have to get on with my day. Make sure we have exquisite backup gowns should I change my mind before Sunday. And obviously, you will have alternate jewelry on standby—" Lara paused, unsmiling as Belinda snapped a photo. "I'm sure that will be adequate. Now, get this off me."

"Can I just get the back for the atelier? Those buttons took them days."

"No. And in fact, I will have Kelly help me take this off. Wait here for her to bring it back to you." Lara stomped across the room and up the stairs, leaving Belinda and Jasper wincing at the sound of crystals smashing against the walls.

"It takes two to speak the truth,
one to speak, and another to hear."
—Henry David Thoreau

Fashion Fighting

RIDING IN CARS WITH STYLISTS
Leaving Lara. 1:15 pm

"FOR FUCK'S SAKE, JASPER. I told you specifically *not* to mention the press conference!" Sliding into her seat, Belinda slammed the car door, her face livid.

"Well, excuse me for FUCKING DEFENDING *YOU*," Jasper yelled, slamming his door. "I am not a fucking ROBOT. I hate how that bitch abuses us. And *YOU*, you're so controlling. Do this Jasper, do that Jasper, but don't do it that way Jasper. Say that Jasper, don't say that Jasper. Be everywhere Jasper, but don't be seen."

He slammed his hand on the steering wheel. "Make sure the five million things that need to be done every fucking day are done. Who cares about sleep, Jasper? Who cares about your husband, Jasper? I haven't fucking slept a full night in like six years."

"NO, that's not fucking fair, Jasper," Belinda's voice cracked. "I'm always telling you to turn off your phone and go home. And I do ask about Bobby."

"Oh, you do, do you? Tell me when you've mentioned him even *once* this week. You can't answer that because you haven't." He started the car, blasting up the heat. "*AND* who ends up in the shit if I don't get things done? Who is it the publicists call and give shit? *ME*, that's fucking who. You, they keep sweet, with me they fucking let rip . . ." He paused, thinking. "Except for Eve, that one lets it rip 360."

Cooling down a little, he continued. "I've been doing this for eight years, Bel. You can't still be micromanaging the shit outta me. Lara is the devil, and she is making it hell on earth this week. It doesn't just affect you; it affects me too."

Belinda nodded, suppressing tears and listening silently.

"Bels, I'm so fucking tired of this red-carpet-lined hamster wheel. Same shit, same sexism, same power struggles, same *people* year in and year out." He inhaled and, on a roll, kept going. "Same rigged game: *Oooh*, look, she's wearing new season Bebe Klein, so she's cooler than you. Her stylist must be better than yours. FEMME magazine claims she's best dressed. For fuck's sake. It's all bullshit. An A-list famous person, in an A-list designer outfit, is featured in an A-list magazine because said magazine makes massive ad revenue from the aforementioned A-list designer"—he took a hit of his vape—"It's a fucking commodified racket: a stone-cold, women-hating business, controlled almost entirely by men. Men who cynically propel the fantasy of Hollywood to perpetuate unachievable dreams and sell billions of dollars of perfume and lipstick."

Belinda, wincing, continued listening.

"And all the talk of empowerment? Empowered my ass. The day they can turn up on a red carpet in whatever the fuck they want, that will be empowerment. The day they can proudly announce, 'I got paid $250k to wear this. I am, in fact, an advertising space, and I fucking own that.' Now, *THAT* would actually be empowered and *honest*."

"You are right. I—" Belinda whimpered.

"Let's not even start on the tabloid sites and their followers who get high on eviscerating us and our clients. We are clickbait for the bitter, jealous, and mean."

He looked at Belinda as the anger drained from his voice. "Jesus, Bel, I'm so tired of living in constant fear, always waiting for the other shoe to drop. I started with such excitement, thinking it was gonna be so creative. My *dream* job—but in reality, I'm nothing more than an underpaid, insomnia-afflicted lackey with a probable Xanax addiction. It wouldn't surprise me if my husband took off. I'm no fucking fun, and neither are you." He had tears in his eyes. "I know I'm preaching to the converted, but this is no way to live, Bels."

"I know, Jas. I know." She wiped her nose on her designer sleeve. "But you're not a lackey. *You* are the reason that everything works. And the thrill of the climb was *real*. But the clients got bigger, we got bigger and busier, the stakes got higher and everyone's thirst for power and money, including ours—*mine*—squashed the joy. We couldn't have known that back then. How could we? Like everyone else, we started out assuming that proximity to celebrity—and therefore the best in fashion—was a golden ticket. I really miss that naivety, don't you? Jesus, with my first A-list client, I thought I could just point at any dress on any model and they would jump off the runway to loan it to me. So *stupid*."

Jasper leaned in to embrace her. "And I'm sorry, Jas." She sniffed. "Thank you for defending me to Lara. How fucked is it that I got mad? I don't want to ruin your life or your marriage. I sure didn't help mine."

"Oh, babe. You did nothing to destroy yours; that absent narcissistic prick did that all by himself." Handing her a tissue, they blew their noses in tandem.

"Ow," his face contorted as he stubbed his injured toe on the brake.

"Let's stop by urgent care for your foot, Jas."

"No time. I've got a spare."

*"Clothes make the man.
Naked people have little or no influence
on society."
—Mark Twain*

Pay for Play

EMILY DE VRIES FITTING
Bebe Klein VIP suite, Rodeo Drive. 4 pm

EMILY AND BELINDA HUGGED before accepting crystal glasses of sparkling water and turning to Ines, Bebe Klein's VP of VIP, a permanently scowling, blonde Parisienne of indeterminate age, wafer-thin in a black leather sheath and mesh biker boots. She stood in the center of the room, her style perfectly in sync with the luxury white and chrome suite. Situated on the store's top floor, it was two thousand square feet of rarely used, stark opulence, exclusively reserved for couture customers and celebrities.

"Emily, we are 'appy you can join us tomorrow. Jerome is insisting you sit with them, *bien sur*. They are fascinated by your brain, and, of course, so few wear clothes like you, with such chic purpose." She harrumphed to indicate her disgust with the world.

"Well, thank you, Ines," Emily replied politely. "Should we look at some clothes? I know Belinda doesn't have much time."

"Oui. We have put a selection of unworn samples in the dressing room for you. Come this way." She ushered them towards a front corner, stopping briefly to pick up a remote and turn down the Leonard Cohen track. "Just so you know, amongst others, the finale gown from last season is included. It might seem over the top, but many of our other guests have opted for black tie. It's simply stunning, even without the train, and Jerome adores it for you. Particularly with this season's boot." She looked down at her feet. "*Tres modern.*"

Nodding in bemused agreement, Belinda and Emily also stared down at her feet.

"As you can see, we also have a 360 mirror out here, with excellent lighting for photographs if you feel comfortable in public. Or, if not, the dressing closet is mirrored, of course. Jerome only requests that I send photos. They are still awake."

"But it's 1 am in Paris?"

"Yes, but Jerome is so excited you are attending. They cannot wait until the morning! And they leave early to get on the jet."

"Oh, I see. We'll be quick so he, I mean they, can sleep."

Closing the dressing room door, Emily turned to Belinda, laughing. "Why do brands always act like it's a personal invite or something? Not one person will reference in any way that I'm getting paid to do this."

"Dirty fashion money." Belinda quipped.

"Guns off the streets money. They should be shouting it from the rooftops . . . Now, what should I try? Assuming we're on the same page about the gown? No one in the current climate needs to see me eating $100 spaghetti in a $40,000 hand-beaded dress, train or no train."

Rifling through the rack, Belinda pulled out two items. "How about a cream silk sweatshirt tucked into gold lame cargo pants?"

"Done!"

"Great, you put them on. I'll quickly go and seek out accessories in the store. Keep control freak Jerome at bay."

"Sleep! Ha! We all know they are almost definitely wasted in a club." Emily giggled and pulled off her leather pants.

Thirty minutes later, Belinda left the sanctuary of Emily's company—her outfit sorted and photographed—and walked back out into madness. She tapped anxiously on her almost dead phone as she hurried down Rodeo Drive.

"*Belinda!*" A tall, sophisticated man with dark-cropped hair and gleaming teeth bounded over to her on the corner of Rodeo Drive and Brighton Way. "What an absolute joy to bump into you! Feels like we've been rescheduling drinks for two years!"

"Oh my god, Luke! You are a sight for tired fashion eyes. You just missed Emily. We were at Bebe doing a fitting." Excited, she hugged him, adding, "Our schedules never align!"

"Oh, sorry to miss her, of course, but what are *you* doing now?"

"Amazingly, I have about 30 minutes. Jasper was coming to grab me but is currently waiting in line to pick up diamonds at Star PR. It's a Mad Friday Oscars rush. You don't have a phone charger by any chance?"

"I do! Let's swerve into Coffee Bean, madame! Or something stronger elsewhere?" Luke took her arm, and they strolled along contentedly.

"Oh, I wish! I only stop working to sleep briefly this weekend. We'll have to make do with a coffee break this time. How are you, Luke? Enjoying LA? Who are you dressing on Sunday?"

"Love the weather, New York is glacial. But getting a dress placement this weekend has been *BRUTAL*. I love it at Henri LeRoque, but when you had your start at Chanel, it's well—"

"Uh-huh, I get it. But change is good! It hasn't been long. You'll turn it around—you are one of the best PR's out there!"

"Speaking of which. Off the record, I have a couple of custom dresses Henri designed for award shows. One of them is awful, but try telling him that. The other is pretty great. If there was a way you could get it on the back of one of your A-list ladies this weekend, I could make it very worth your while."

"Oh, you know I always want to help you, Luke, but I don't know about that. They are pretty set—"

"$30,000 to be un-set?"

"Jesus."

"Yeah, I need it pretty bad. If it's a private, no reps involved deal, I might even be able to stretch further. I just don't have two hundred grand to pay talent. Look, I'll send you an image of the dress and think about it, yeah? For me? I can bring it to you any time of the day or night."

Filler

> Janie is confirmed as a presenter. Zoe Jacobson dropped out. Apparently, she's at the ER with pneumonia, although I will never understand why she doesn't get a shot and power through. Anyway, her hypochondria is our gain. Make sure you kill it, okay, Belinda? No room for error here. I've seen pictures of some of our other clients' dresses, and they are magnificent. I'm praying you can finally rise to the occasion.

> Got it. We will do our best.

> Best? Perhaps try for better than that. I've called in a few extra dresses to our offices. Have your assistant pick them up first thing? Don't bother Janie tonight. She's at the emergency plastic surgeon."

SATURDAY 3RD MARCH 2018

Last Minute Looks

Hey B. Decided I will go to Oscars tomorrow w. Jonny. Need something to wear obv. Going into a pole dancing class for an hour—will call you after.

PS I don't want to buy anything and don't want ANYTHING BORING (like a gown)

Love ya!

"It is not possible for a man to be elegant
without a touch of femininity."
—Vivienne Westwood

Matchy-Matchy

JONNY EVANS DRESS REHEARSAL
Chinese Theatre. 2 pm

JONNY WALKED INTO ROOM 14 in the basement of the Chinese Theatre on Hollywood Blvd, where Belinda and Jasper sat, waiting, on dirty plastic foldaway seats. His three tailored Henri LeRoque suits and shirts were hanging, steamed, on the solo wobbly rack pushed up against the back wall, two pairs of Oxfords balanced on the bar beneath them.

"Fucking hell, guys, what a shit show to get in here! I must have shown my ID about six times. I should have taken them up on the driver, but I couldn't resist driving my new Ferrari. It's silver and *killer*. By that, I mean hard not to kill someone with how fast you have to race it. Don, my manager, texted he's also having problems. He's gone walkabout on Hollywood Boulevard for some reason, probably still drunk from last night. *And* he continues to be a dag." Jonny laughed affectionately, looking around. "Mate, who knew down here would be this fucking ugly? My guys decorate all the backstage areas in my venues before I get there. They did leopard print, fake fur, and stinky musk candles for the last tour. It was like a fucking fragrant safari vomited everywhere. Tab's creative direction, as if you couldn't guess, I forced her to keep the Space Invader and Pac-Man games, so she wallpapered the sides to match. Never did

☆ 325

come off." He sighed. "*And yes*, before you say it, I am a spoilt bastard!" Still bemused by the decor, he glanced around at the bare, grubby white room again, throwing his keys and tattered silver blazer onto the solo table. Slumping down onto a third fold-up chair beside it, he absently toyed with a diamond cufflink from the velvet tray displaying his jewelry choices. Uninterested, he softly rolled it back Vegas style and turned to them.

"Did you see the purple walls outside? Purple? Gross. Let's not do selfies out there. Mind you, the blue metallic suit could look weird and cool against it. . . . Oh shit, I forgot. Tab wants to wear my spare suit tomorrow. She said she likes the blue one best?"

"No, Jonny, Henri LeRoque would lose their mind," Belinda rebutted, unusually aggressive. "Not to mention, the performance lighting is structured around it. She can take the white one or the black one, though. You can wear the other on the arrivals carpet and change back after you perform, before they announce the winner of your category."

"Yeah, I thought so." He looked deflated. "Can you tell her? She's gonna spit the dummy. I can't cope with that drama today. I'm hungover as fuck as it is. She wanted me to tell you to get a matching blue suit for her so we could be the same on the carpet even though I told her, 'fuck off, Tab, I'm not that much of a pussy."

"Yeah, well, that suit is custom in every sense, down to the thread, so that wouldn't have been an option anyway. You won't have a back-up suit if Tabitha takes one, Jonny. I'm just putting that out there, okay? It might be safer, stain-wise, for you if she wears the white. Does it even fit her?" Belinda tried to keep the frustration out of her voice.

"Yeah. We're the same size. Except for the tits, though I could buy some of those too, of course." He grinned and pulled off his t-shirt, revealing his spray-tanned, sinewy six-pack. "Let's get that suit on so I can soundcheck and be done." He removed a hip flask from his back pocket and swigged. "God Bless tequila. I just need a tiny bump from Don, and I'll be right as rain. Jasper, can you go quickly find him while I get dressed?"

Jasper nodded, grabbed his phone, and exited the room.

"Bels, do you reckon I could get a helicopter to the carpet tomorrow?"

FIRE THE STYLIST
Dishing Daily Doses of Fashion Justice

TABITHA EVANS Sullen at Coffee Bean.

Posted on 3rd March, 2018

Well, Firers, we are all fired up about <u>Jonny Evans</u> potentially winning an <u>Oscar</u> for his incredible original song for the movie '<u>Driving with Dogs</u>' and even more fired up for his performance. Maybe his <u>raw sexual vibes</u> can bring some, ahem, heat to this traditional broadcast…

Not evidently excited, however, is his current wife, <u>lingerie</u> model <u>Tabitha Evans</u> (25); why do <u>these women</u> all take his name? Seen here yelling at their <u>cute dog</u> outside <u>Coffee Bean</u> in Hidden Hills, wearing what appears to be Jonny's faded <u>striped pajamas</u> with <u>Vivienne Westwood' Pirate' boots</u>. (We haven't seen those dusted off in a while!) Now, much as we are still fans of the <u>nightwear-as-daywear</u> trend, this perhaps literally takes things too far. Not helping, of course, is her <u>greasy top knot</u> and, evidently, <u>last</u> <u>night's makeup</u>.

What do you think, Firers? Does she need a shower?

As always, leave comments below!

(To review our community guidelines, please click here)

> **@laceyjacey** maybe if you get to f**k him every day, you never bother getting dressed. Lucky bitch.

> **@fashunisfukked** they probably all take his name to try and get more cash when they split. From him OR the tabloids

> **@loveyourmuffintop** that POOR BABY. Someone should rescue that delicious fur muffin from this monster.

> **@crystalstar** she might be channeling Pirates of the Caribbean, but her vibe is giving all is not well in Rock Paradise. Is she on her way out?

*"Fame is a fickle food
upon a shifting plate."*
—Emily Dickinson

Clueless

CHLOE 'NIGHT BEFORE' DINNER GLAM
Villa Carlotta, Hollywood. 5 pm

"OH, HI BELS. UM, I DIDN'T REALIZE YOU WERE COMING—" Chloe glanced in the mirror at Belinda's reflection as Richard removed rollers from her red hair. "How's it going? Are you still sane? You must be nuts before tomorrow, right? I thought you'd be with Lara or Ava-Lily tonight. I didn't think you would come . . ." Her low voice trailed off awkwardly.

"Ava-Lily bailed on tonight two hours ago after *all* that sewing. I can't bring myself to tell Yelena—there can't be any more Russian swear words. And I sent Jasper to Lara. If I see her every day this week, I might end up rocking incoherently in a corner."

"Good for you honey, save that sanity. But poor Jasper," Richard chimed in. "That woman has always been vile to me. I refuse to work with her. Did a couple of press tours during the teen years, which was enough." He pushed his glasses up his nose and teased Chloe's hair with a mint green comb.

"I avoid her as much as I can myself," Marilyn agreed, testing Chanel lipstick colors in strips on her hand. "I don't know how you do it, Belinda."

Chloe jumped on the bandwagon. "You're such a saint. Is she wearing something amazing to the ceremony?"

"Well, hopefully, custom Cedric Tatou, but you didn't hear it from me because who's to say I won't get a text at midnight demanding more options?" She slumped down on the mid-century velvet couch and pulled out her phone. "It would be so much easier if she would let a designer pay her, but no, she likes to be able to change her mind whenever the wind blows her mood."

"What a luxury to have the choice," replied Chloe. "I do miss that freedom already, although I shouldn't moan because of the money and all. Do you have to dress her husband, Bels?" Chloe enquired. "What's his name again? Isn't he, like, a massive stoner?"

"Elliot."

"Oh, that's right. Ed met him once at a party. He said he stood there high as a silent but grinning kite."

"Sounds about right—we don't see much of him, but when we do, he's charming. I don't usually dress Elliot, but Jasper organized for him to wear Tatou to the Oscars this year. Another reason we pray that she wears their dress is because they have made him a bespoke suit. Speaking of which, is Ed not coming with you to the dinner?"

"Nope, he had to go to Vancouver for work last minute. He's bummed. He got to sit next to Bruce Springsteen last year. They fell in love."

Richard giggled. "This is the *only* correct emotion for the boss. If you couldn't tell"—he pointed down at his outfit—"I'm a big fan."

"Is Elliot coming with Lara tonight?" Chloe asked.

"Um, yes, I think so," Belinda mumbled as she chewed over why Chloe was so forced and gossipy tonight. Her thoughts were interrupted by a text from the Cartier security guard saying he was in the lobby downstairs waiting with the jewelry. She texted him back and announced to the room. "Hey guys, the jewelry is on the way up. Richard, they would like the antique diamond broach in her hair tonight. Can you make it work?"

"Of course, my love, they're paying the bills. Shall we use it to pin up one side?"

"Perfect."

"Burgundy or scarlet lip, Bel?" asked Marilyn, holding up both the backs of her hands.

"Ooh, I like the idea of burgundy. The fourth one down on your right hand."

"Perf. Done. All good with the cat eye? Vogue loves a sexy eye. Harriet, the beauty editor, will be thrilled." Marilyn winked at Belinda.

"Oh yes, I forgot you guys are doing behind the scenes for Vogue. Do you need me to take some more pictures? And I love it all. You guys are the best. Not that you need me to tell you that."

"Aw, thanks, sweet cheeks," Richard responded. "Right back, atcha. And yes, please, snap away. Just send them all to me, and I'll put them through the filters before we forward them to Vogue."

"Tell me you don't use 'Featurefix'?" Marilyn questioned. "We need her to still look like a real person, not CGI."

"As if," Richard sniffed disparagingly. "This new crop of so-called influencer *experts* needs to step back and learn some skills outside of the Apps."

"Sorry, Rich, I don't know what I was thinking saying that to *you*." Marilyn was sheepish. "I've just had to work with too many filter experts masquerading as makeup artists recently. Did you see Jazzie's face last night? She looked like a tanned teenager on her Instagram but as white and old as a ghost in the red-carpet images."

Belinda half-listened to the familiar griping of the glam squad as she opened the door and signed for the diamonds, agreeing that the security guard and his hidden gun could wait outside the apartment door.

She handed the delicate broach to Richard, who carefully pinned it to Chloe's hair. After he had finished, Belinda put three diamond studs in her one exposed lobe. Chloe, reading something on her phone, was oblivious. Taking a compliant hand, Belinda slid on a selection of rings before settling on a statement 'Tressage' ring, which she then removed and placed with the clutch.

"So, Chloe? You like everything?" Marilyn asked, combing her brow again.

"Oh sure," she said, not looking up from her phone, "if you guys do. Which dress did you end up choosing, Bels?"

"The pink floral appliqué mini. Your legs are divine."

"Oh, that reminds me, my shin got bruised training today, Marilyn. Can you fix that?"

"For sure," Marilyn grabbed her foundation pallet, threw down a cushion, and got down on her knees as Belinda's phone pinged again.

SHIIIIT! All hell is breaking loose here. But don't worry - the dress is still currently in play. She had a makeup meltdown. I am hiding behind our favorite life-sized fertility goddess sculpture and spying. Do not want to get in the FIRING LINE.

SHIT

Who's doing it again?

Alexander Dubois. I've never met him, you might have in Europe?

French. Old but hot—Just told her he can and has made her face look beautiful, but he 'cannot be 'eld responsible for her not liking her own face.' And the piece de resistance?

'Self-love is your voyage en voyages.' I can't decide if I'm more turned on or terrified...

Oh, hold, please...

Well, the makeup is OFF

All of it?

Yup. Lara is currently doing it herself

USING HIS KIT and instructing him step by step on how to 'sculpt' her face

She's instructing Givenchy's beauty director on how to do makeup? Are you fucking with me?

NOPE, she just told him how to hold the eye pencil. His face has turned purple, and there is steam. I honestly cannot tell who will die first in this battle.

Oops SORRY! I'm seemingly obsessed with death now.

> SAME. Ugh.

> Did I tell you Jonny's trying to get a helicopter to the carpet tomorrow?

LOL. Well, gods don't drive themselves to the center of the universe, now do they?

Giggling, Belinda looked up at the room. Richard and Marilyn, finished for now, were sitting quietly, working on their phones.

"Shall we get dressed then, Chloe?"

"Sure." She stood up from the vanity and, not meeting Belinda's eye, said, "Oh, sorry, I don't have any good underwear, Bels. Do you have a thong?"

"Yes, of course." She dug one out of her kit bag and handed it to her.

"I'll just pee." Taking her phone, Chloe slipped into the bathroom.

"Is it me," Belinda whispered, "or is she being weird with me?"

"She does seem a bit off tonight, babe," Richard whispered back, "but it's probably not you?"

"She can't hold my gaze at all."

"Darling, Marilyn's been doing her makeup. It's hard for her to look at anything."

"I think it's the Alma thing. But it would be nice if she would just *talk* to me."

"Yeah, babe. She's sweet but not the bravest. Has Lacey not said anything? She's her main publicist. Aren't you guys friendly?"

"I thought so. We're business-friendly at any rate. I did go to her baby shower last year. She hasn't returned any of my calls this week, which is also weird."

"I've been doing this for more years than I will ever admit, honey," he said, pointing at his black slicked-back hair. "I bet you didn't realize this was dyed! And to remind you, friendships in our world are mutable and often go *poof* when the business moves on. Lacey is Chloe's publicist. *If* something is going on, which hopefully there isn't, she can't say anything until Chloe pulls the trigger. She's scared of getting fired too. Sorry honey, is this too much tough love?"

"No! I know you are right, but naively, I still hope for better. *Stupid.*"

"No, not stupid. *Human.* There's so much duplicity in this town it's impossible to know who to trust. And as for Alma, I know it's been rough, but it'll blow over. Something else more interesting will happen."

"That's what Jasper's been telling me every day."

"That young hunk is a blessing, Bel. Anyway, Chloe has been with you for how many years?"

"Nine."

"Exactly. You've been through city changes, fiancés, babies, and her ascent to fashion royalty. Just remember that. It will all be fine."

"Yeah, well, you would hope." Much as she wanted to sink into his reassurance, Belinda couldn't shake the feeling that something was wrong.

"Okay, I'm ready." Chloe returned to the room in the thong and bent over, touching her toes to stretch her lower back. Richard flew over to protect her hair as Belinda handed her the unzipped dress to step into.

"One last thing, Chloe," Belinda said, buttoning the collar, "I'm still waiting for Bebe Klein to get back to me about your outfit for their handbag launch next weekend, but weirdly, no one has responded to our emails. I even copied Lacey." She walked around the front of her, kneeling to slide on embellished mules. "It's probably just Oscar madness, so I'll text you directly on Monday to schedule?"

"Um, sure," Chloe's face flushed. "Monday . . . um, I should probably go; my driver's been here since four. God knows why."

"Of course." Belinda stood, slid the ring on her finger, and handed her a metallic pink clutch. She snapped a quick full-length image with her phone and said goodbye, feeling queasy as she watched her leave.

"Okay, honey, that *was* odd."

Richard looked at her sympathetically, shaking his head. "This business—no skin thick enough. Can I give you a ride home?"

"No need. Lara released Jasper, so he's on his way. But thank you. I'll cheer myself up and depress my followers by posting about politics while I wait in the lobby."

"You are one strange lady, but good on ya." He kissed her cheek and returned to packing away meters of red hair, layering the pieces meticulously in a custom Bebe Klein case.

Sneak Peak

Saturday 6:03 pm

Hey, tabloid queen! Can we give CBS any dress credits yet? Any client will do, but they REALLY want to talk about Lara and Ava-Lily on the pre-show tomorrow. Could you just rattle off the three top choices of designers in the running? They don't need the actual one, just anything, so they can sound 'in the know' for their four straight hours of bullshit speculation while the carpet is still empty.

Wow, Dev, you are cynical today. Are you okay? And no, I can't. I'm too superstitious, and my clients are too mercurial. I know a million others won't mind giving up info. Let them do it.

You're not the only one being harassed, lady. I'm booking a vacation in Iceland after this. I need to look at some actual fucking stars and regroup.

Ooh, can I come?

No.

"We live by the golden rule.
Those who have the gold make the rules."
—Unknown

Losing Luster

Leaving Chloe. 6:10 pm

"FUCK FUCK FUCKITY-FUCK." Belinda, standing outside the Villa Carlotta, climbed into the car as her phone call ended, threw her phone into her new Tatou bag and turned to Jasper. "Harry Winston has sold Janie's necklace. FUUUCK."

"*FUUUCK!*" he echoed in tandem. "That's a fucking fuck of a nightmare, not gonna lie to you. But how? Who the fuck to? It's like ten mil."

"To a Texan collector who does not want it touched by anyone else. They asked if she could make an Oscars exception, and the answer was unequivocally no. She also bought the matching bracelet and earrings, so make that approximately $20 mil. I better call Janie and Eve. Maybe I will email first to forewarn. Ugh, we had to fight so hard to get her out of tits-forward bridal wear and into chic minimalism. You know she's gonna use this to change the dress."

"Oh, sweetie, she still has 16 hours. She'd probably have done that anyway. But why don't I quickly text around the other jewelers before you call and see what I can find that is similar?"

"I worship you, Jas."

"I know, as you should." He handed her a tub of CBD gummies. "Have some Dutch courage. Or do you want a shot of tequila? I took a couple from Ava-Lily's minibar. They're in the glove box."

"Tequila. Definitely tequila."

"It's not the having, it's the getting."
—Elizabeth Taylor

Histrionics

CONFERENCE CALL WITH JANIE AND EVE
'Coco' aka Jasper's Car. 6:35 pm

"HOW COULD YOU LET THIS HAPPEN, BELINDA?" Eve dove straight in, not bothering to say hello.

Belinda, defeated, bailed on pointing out the obvious—she had no power over commerce and a billionaire from Texas—and instead answered. "It's unfortunate, I agree. But we've been texting and calling all the jewelers non-stop. Harry Winston has another, only slightly smaller choker that's almost identical. Cartier also has a vintage emerald cut choker, but it's two strands, Lorraine Schwartz has a pink diamond four-strand, and Dazzle Diamonds has the biggest one; it's almost identical, and they can also pay you $50k, Janie."

"*Ooohh*—" Janie responded but was interrupted by Eve.

"Obviously, for the Gilded Orbs, Janie could suffer and wear something from *them* for money, but this, this is the *Oscars*. What's wrong with you, Belinda? *NO*. We will have to change dresses. I am right, Janie?"

"Yes, Eve, of course." Janie agreed reluctantly, not really agreeing at all, still thinking of the money.

"I believe the Clara Jank cream crochet-knit gown is perfect," Eve opined. "Yes! It is stunning, and the train is magnificent. So bridal, I mean Oscar-worthy. Same thing."

Belinda, chugging the last of the tequila, undid her seatbelt and made a face at Jasper. They were thinking the same thing: Clara had made Eve's wedding dress last summer (she never wasted an opportunity to brag about it) so she must owe her a favor.

"Really? But I thought Janie wanted to change it up and be sleek and modern . . . oh, never mind." Belinda gave up, capitulating to Eve and ignoring Jasper, who was shaking his head vigorously. "Although I want to point out, you guys, that it's not lined. I think just a nude bodysuit would be best, Janie?"

"I've got my period, Belinda. I don't feel comfortable," lied Janie, still trying to summon the courage to argue with Eve.

"One would think that you, being such a feminist, Belinda, would be more sensitive to Janie's female needs and modesty. These are the things we pay you to solve. I have to go. I have better things to do than discuss semantics. Janie darling, call me later."

Modesty! Jesus, thought Belinda, fuming. *Janie had been naked on the cover of almost every magazine in the world. Why was this the one time she got shy?* "Okay, we will figure it out. Janie, before you go, did you get a spray tan? So that I know for the color of the lining?"

"Oh yes, I did, just a refresher, but I'm pretty much the same color as always."

"Okay, great. Text you later when it's done and figure out a time to try it on this evening." She ignored Jasper, who was mouthing, "Yelena will have a fucking shit fit."

"Oh, I can't do tonight. I have a date in a minute. Probably best in the morning, first thing, after my 5 am workout?"

"Sure, Janie. But it will be Jasper. I can come tonight, but not in the morning."

"Great." Janie, distracted, was looking at the time. "Gotta go. My date's gonna be here soon, and I need to do some kegels! Thanks, guys!" And with that, she was gone.

"Well, Jasper," Belinda turned to him. "I'm sorry about the early morning tomorrow. You know there was no point in battling Eve."

"There was every point, Bels. The money clearly tantalized Janie, and we might have won if we'd backed her. Are we just giving up now?" He glared at her, his disappointment evident.

"Yes, I think at some point you have to quit trying and just endure. Now, can we get off this side street and go home, please?

"*You* can go home. I have to take that dress to Yelena. *Pray for me.*"

Jitters

Sunday 2 am

> Are you awake?

> Duh

> Knew it

> Do you think Yelena got the lining right? You were right; I should have gone to bat for the Calvin Klein.

> I'm such a wimp.

> As I told you four hours ago, she said the color was the usual one she uses for Janie, so it should be fine.

> That said, maybe we should get one of the chokers in case she has to go back to the Calvin? And yes you are a wimp, but I appreciate that you know this.

Ha Jas, you so funny. But yes, let's do that. I feel bad, though, cos she probably won't, and they'll have to send two guards for such a high value.

They can't be in the game if they're not on the court.

Now GO TO SLEEP

Look who's awake and talking...

Night (or almost morning).

Love you. For real

Same girl. SAME

SUNDAY 4ᵀᴴ MARCH 2018

"Arguing with a narcissist is like getting arrested. Everything you say can and will be used against you."
—Unknown

Toxic

BELINDA JOLTED UPRIGHT as her phone roused her from a nightmare—a cobalt-blue tsunami enveloping a red carpet and sucking up everything in its way, her house, Rose and Jasper spinning furiously into a black, star-dusted hole, leaving her alone in a soaking wet wedding dress, eating cold vegan oatmeal at the Beverly Hills Hotel buffet. Discombobulated, she kicked off her weighted blanket and rubbed her mascara-smudged eyes. It took her a few moments to realize her phone was buzzing. "Oh god, what already?" She could feel her furiously thumping chest as she grabbed it from the bedside table, seeing '*Rose Dad*' flashing across the screen. She pressed the green button and said in a croaky voice, "Hey, it's 6 am here. Is something wrong?'

"Yeah, something is wrong, Belinda. And don't pretend you aren't already awake for the fucking Oscars."

"I didn't get to sleep till 3. What's wrong? Please, can we not fight? Not today."

"Oh yeah, of course, as *per usual*, your job is the first consideration. I'm in fucking Holland, and even I've heard crap about you and the dead agent. That client you hate has been talking to the press about it. I thought

I should check in and find out what in the actual fuck is going on? Tell me, Belinda, how is this good for Rose?"

"*Rose?* Rose, who you haven't seen in person for two years?" Belinda involuntarily pulled the covers up her neck to protect herself from a man 3000 miles away.

"Oh, here you go, changing the subject. Deflection should be your middle name."

"Rose is fine. It's a stupid rumor because I coincidently met with Alma just before she died. The police are fine, and Rose knows nothing about it."

"Yeah, but for how long? And what about you fucking Jonny Evans? Whoring your way around Hollywood now? That fancy industry school you insist on sending her to, those networking parents will find out and tell their kids, and then what? Poor Rose. I feel sorry for her. Her mother's shit job is ruining her life, like it did our marriage."

"Are you f-f-fucking kidding me?" Belinda attempted to formulate words that would adequately illustrate her anger and frustration. But once again, fear shredded every thought, leaving her stuttering as she tried and failed to stem tears. "I'm not fucking him. You . . . you aren't even here. You don't even send money anymore! You can't call and do this. *It's not—*"

"Jesus, are you crying again, Belinda? When will we have a grown-up conversation? God, you are so self-centered. I have to go. But clean up your shit, yeah? I'll never forgive you if you fuck up our kid, and I'm sure she won't either." He disconnected the call, and she stared, heart racing, at her home screen, an image of 3-year-old Rose on a premiere red carpet, dressed head-to-toe in daffodil yellow to match the life-size Minions. Now wide awake, she sobbed until the fear of puffy eyes in the coming pictures induced her to stop.

Werk-It

> Good luck today! Text me with outfit credits ASAP and creative behind-the-scenes photos.

> Recapping the ones we agreed on—

> Instyle.com—Lara

> Vogue.com—Ava-Lily

> Vogue Australia—Jonny

> GQ—Jonny (must be different from Vogue shots)

> Red Magazine (UK)—Janie

> (Where possible, get Jasper to take them. You are a shit photographer, LOL)

Ps. I know you hate being on camera—you live in the wrong town—but they all want you featured in the pictures/video. This is not negotiable. Remember to wear something cute (haha) and BLACK FOR BACKSTAGE. They will not let you down there otherwise. Lastly, we need pics of you with each client for our agency social—also not negotiable. Go get it for us, gurl!

"Must I always wear a low-cut dress to be important?"
—Jean Harlow.

Color Blind

Calabasas. 7 am
Red carpet arrival time: 2:30 pm

JASPER SAT WAITING AT THE BAR in Janie's ballroom, clutching his second large coffee. The cream-crocheted dress that Yelena had unwillingly lined overnight hung on an otherwise empty rack, its hem protected from the spotless parquet floor by a garment bag he'd placed below it. Yawning, he heard his phone ping. Belinda.

> Did she see it yet?

>> Patience. She's probably having a massage after the workout.

>> She has him here until she leaves. He might even go in the car with her. Contracted to massage her for every free moment she has. It drives glam mad.

> But why?

Jasper turned to face Janie, trailed by her housekeeper balancing a
silver tray with matching pots of green tea and coffee. "Morning, babe.
Happy Oscars Day!"

"What the hell is good about this day?" she grumbled. "Sorry, Jasper,
my date was terrible last night and I'm bummed. Teresa, I'll take my tea
now, please. Jasper, would you like more coffee?"

"Um, sure. Thanks." He did a double-take at Janie. "I thought you said
you had your *usual spray tan color*?" His face grew increasingly horrified as
it sank in that her skin was, in fact, terracotta and the dress's new lining
was many shades too light.

"Thomas said I looked pale last night. Well, that was one thing he said
before he told me he was totally into some French supermodel he's dating,
but he couldn't resist my tight wet pussy."

Jasper choked on the fresh coffee.

"So I came home and used some of the Kate Somerville self-tanning
wipes I got in a gift bag. They're excellent, actually. Why am I bothering
to pay hundreds of dollars to have women come to the house every week?
But I admit I couldn't see it working immediately, so I applied it three
times. That might have been a bit nuts."

"Um, can we exfoliate it off?"

"No, Jasper. And even if we could, why would we? I like this shade—it
highlights my muscles better."

"Well, because the lining color is totally off now." He pointed at the rack.

"*Whoopsie*, I didn't think about that."

"Should we maybe move to the Calvin dress?"

"Oooh . . . Could I still get the money from Dazzle Diamonds?"

"Yes, I think so. Let me text Belinda." He couldn't keep the excitement
out of his voice.

"Actually *no*." Janie paused. "*Shit*. I don't know what I'm thinking. Eve
will never allow it. I'm not strong enough to fight her today. She terrifies

me more than my grandmother, and that's saying something. There's no Alma to protect me anymore." Grief registered on her face briefly. "What happened with Belinda about that, by the way?"

"Nothing bec—"

"Sorry, I'm getting us distracted, so how are you guys gonna fix this?"

"One second." Sluggishly walking to the rack, he lifted the dress, held it next to Janie, and snapped a picture. "I'll text this to Yelena now and go outside to call her." He added under his breath, "No point in both of us going deaf when I tell her she's going to have to line it *again*."

Ten minutes later, rubbing his ear, he came back into the ballroom and searched for Janie, whom he could hear but not see. He finally found her—headphones on—furiously doing crunches behind the bar. Kneeling on a barstool and leaning over, he waved his arms until she saw him and paused the music.

"So, Janie, I have good and bad news. She does have a lining in your new skin color, but it's not a four-way stretch, which is the type of lining that does not move under fitted garments. I've texted the owner of Fab Fabrics to see if they can open up today, but I haven't heard back yet, and it's unlikely. If we go ahead with what Yelena has, it *will* ride up a little when you walk."

"What kind of a store closes on Sunday?"

"Humane ones," Jasper muttered in response as she talked over him.

"Well, it's not ideal."

"No, it's not, but what are our options, Janie?" Jasper was frustrated. "You could wear a skin-colored bodysuit. We have every skin tone Shrunx offers in our office. Or you could return to the gorgeous and sexy Calvin dress. Do you even have to tell Eve? Why don't we wake your therapist and get her to weigh in?"

"Oh, I don't know Jasper. I'm so confused. But yes, it is a good idea to wake her up. You go and have the dress lined and I will have a session and let you know what I decide. Can you leave the Calvin one here?"

"Sure, I'll grab it from the car. Just let me know quickly, okay? We have to get jewelry delivered, nail accessories down, and we don't have long."

"*Of course.* You think I don't know that?"

"Any actress who appears in public without being well-groomed is digging her own grave."
—Joan Crawford

Bush Whacking

RESIDENCE OF LARA WHITE
Silverlake. 10:15 am
Red carpet arrival time: 3:30 pm

JASPER AND BELINDA FOUGHT THEIR WAY AGAIN through the wild, lush garden leading to Lara's house, lugging two plastic Ikea bags full to the plastic-covered brim with a (pared down) rainbow of designer shoes. Rain gushed from the foggy sky, draining, mercifully, through the sieve of vegetation above them.

"What's with this hurricane?" Jasper, wrestling an ineffective umbrella in a futile attempt to shield his monogrammed Gucci blazer, added, "Why did God have to break the California drought on Oscar day? She evidentially hates us, but then, who can blame her? This bitch of a town must be due a tsunami of karma. On the bright side, at least the Tatou team carried the dress here. It's terrifying to be responsible for couture in these weather conditions."

"I made them," answered Belinda, muffled by a sopping wet hood, "when I found out Lara had decided to bypass the two hotel rooms at her disposal. But I have long since given up trying to understand her logic. The backup dresses are in the car, right?"

"Yes, m'am. I put them in the car while you were begging and bribing

Yelena on the phone. Did it work? Has she crossed her own picket line and resumed sewing?"

"I believe so. But she doubled her rate for the Janie dress, which is entirely reasonable in any other world, but in this one, means another Janie fight on another day."

"Maybe madame Janie can buy one less pair of shoes this week? Or post another ad for laser hair removal? She gets a hundred and fifty grand a post, I heard. That would easily cover the tailoring."

"Ugh, you know I'm gonna end up footing this bill." She cursed as a gust of wind-sheeted water over her. "How the fuck is Lara gonna get in the car?" Belinda's frown deepened as she visualized the voluminous scarlet dress drenched in raindrops. They turned a corner in tandem, narrowly avoiding two gardeners shearing off foliage to widen the pathway.

"Wow, the visceral jungle experience has been Oscar'd," Jasper laughed despite shivering in his now-soaking jacket. "Do you think they'll also lay down a red carpet?"

"Well, she'd rather hack down her garden than stay in an event-adjacent hotel room this weekend, so fucking nothing would surprise me." Entering the house through the crack of the sliding door left open, they were puzzled to see every person in the room positioned, without shoes, in an attempt at a circle.

"What the . . ." Jasper mouthed, humming under his breath, "Ring-a-ring-a-Rosies . . ."

"OH GOOD. You're here!" Lara's voice rose grandiosely from the center. "I was going to start without you since you are late. I hope it had nothing to do with the Alma investigation. Take off your shoes and come join my ring of thanks. Lucia, bring another two glasses of the Dom Perignon or, if there isn't enough, Casper can have some open Prosecco from the fridge. It's from Trader Joe's and terribly good for 12 dollars."

"It's Jasper, and we're not late," Belinda protested, accepting the crystal flute Lucia placed in her hand. "Also, I've told you so many times I had nothing to do with Alma's—"

"Invite the gardeners in to join us," Lara, ignoring Belinda, barked at Kelly.

"Oh no. Lara, I don't think that's a good idea; they've only got three hours to clear the pathway before you leave. They couldn't work through the night because, you know." Kelly gestured towards the window. "The torrential rain."

"Well, surely one can join for two minutes on my special day, Kelly? Go and choose one. Quickly now."

Belinda mentally roll-called the uncomfortable crew as she joined them: Alessia from Tatou, her assistant Francois, and a seamstress from their atelier; Deepra, the makeup artist; Zane, the hairdresser and his assistant Dani; Lara's parents; her obviously bombed husband Elliot; her PA Kelly; their un-named nanny and the primary housekeeper, Lucia.

Kelly returned, having swiftly secured the presence of a sopping, visibly baffled gardener, who, after he removed his muddy work boots and bucket hat, she pushed into the circle. Shrugging his shoulders, he drained the crystal glass of Prosecco he was handed in one gulp.

"You inhale champagne like it's Mexican coke," Lara chided. "Now, everyone, please link arms and look at me." They all did as she asked, staring at her standing barefoot, wet hair scraped off her makeup-free face. Once satisfied that she was the focal point, Lara gestured 'welcome,' theatrically extending the draped, floating arms of her taupe silk kimono and ignoring the champagne spilling from her overfilled glass. Alessia, owner of the most effective poker face Belinda had ever met, barely managed to stifle a guffaw.

"I am so very thrilled to have you all here on my special day. I wanted to toast you all and say how I cannot do this alone. Without you, I am nothing. To the marvelous people from Tatou, I say bravo for your talent, patience, and exquisite artistry. I only hope I can make you proud—"

"Shoulders back, darling." a clipped voice ordered loudly, and the circle turned in unison to look at Lara's mother.

"They look like they're back to me," Lara's father immediately disputed.

"Oh, what do you know about it, David?"

"Your posture is marvelous, pumpkin. Don't listen to your mother."

"You think she would be where she is if she hadn't listened to me, David?" Lara's mother snorted and drained her champagne. "Lucy, can I get some more, please?" Lucia unlinked her arm from the gardener and shuffled to the kitchen in her socks.

"Darling, this will be your third. It's only 10:30."

"And who's counting, David? It's a very special day. My baby is at the Oscars *again*."

"Your baby is in her *thirties*—and if drinks in the morning are the measure—then all days are special days," he retorted under his breath, just loud enough for Jasper, by his side, to hear.

Flushing, yet obediently rolling her shoulders further back, Lara continued, "So I would like to extend my heartfelt thanks to each and every person here today. All of you are in this room because you are vital to *me*, and I would like each person in this circle to stop for a moment in this ever-spinning world and take the time to toast each other." She walked slowly around the circle, taking an uncomfortably long moment with each face until she reached the gap where Lucia had stood.

"Lucia, what's taking you so long?"

"I open the champagne for Mrs. White, Miss Lara."

"Jeeze, *Mom*, why do you always have to ruin my moments?" Lara slumped forward, her posture unconsciously mimicking her first audition at age seven.

"Oh, stop being so dramatic. Always so dramatic." Lara's mom held her glass out to Lucia for a refill. "Thank you, dear. I apologize for my daughter." And, turning back to Lara, "Carry on. You can finish now, darling. I'm sure everyone has something to do. I'm positive the lovely Deepra here is dying to do something about your pale face. You look a little ill. Are you feeling okay, baby?"

"I'm fine, Mom." Defeated, Lara raised her glass. "*SALUTI* and again *Grazie* everyone."

The circle, arms still linked, attempted to raise their glasses, and Belinda observed the usually unflappable team from Tatou struggling to understand what was happening. They were relieved to be distracted by the gardener coughing awkwardly and gesturing towards the door.

"Oh, gardener, please feel free to resume your duties. Belinda, may I see you in my main closet, please?" Lara pushed past her mother and swept up the stairs.

"I might have just peed myself a little bit, trying not to laugh," Jasper whispered to Belinda and Alessia.

"Is madness. I don't understand the Americans at all," Alessia rasped quietly, "I need a cigarette. I will be out in the drenched wilderness if anyone needs me." She threw her bespoke tan raincoat over her shoulders and glided outside.

"Love that she refused to take her shoes off. I'll take rebellion in any form in this house." Jasper took Belinda's glass and drained it. "You are a terrible day drinker. I can't have you all maudlin this afternoon."

She nodded in agreement as the in-house intercom sprang to life, "Belinda. Are you *COMING*?"

Belinda found Lara, rigid, perched on the sheepskin loveseat in the corner of her closet, staring miserably into the gilded mirror that faced her. "Do I look pale, Belinda?"

"Sorry?"

"Oh, never mind. Shut the door, please. Where's Alessia?"

"Oh, she's outside in the garden smoking."

"Disgusting yet delicious habit, but I'm glad she's out of earshot." She looked at Belinda pityingly and softly announced, "This is going to devastate you, but I don't think I can wear the Tatou today."

"What? I don't understand—"

"Well, technically, I don't need you to understand, just to facilitate."

"Lara, they are in your house. Seriously, they will never work with you again if you do this. Also, and more importantly, the dress is astonishing, like, truly. It might be my favorite of all the award show gowns I've worked on."

"*Really?*"

Belinda sensed weakness. "Yes! Let's try it on again now, just us together here."

"More beautiful than Ava-Lily's dress for today? You like it better?"

"I do. Please don't ever repeat that, okay?" Belinda lied seamlessly.

"Okay, fine, I shall try it. Don't leave me; just text or intercom Casper and have him bring it up immediately."

Ten minutes later, dressed and posing extravagantly, Lara appraised herself in the mirror for an excruciatingly long time. Standing nervously behind, Belinda and Jasper waited, praying silently. She spun around abruptly—numerous layers of scarlet tulle, romantically swooshing as the hand-sewn crystals bounced shards of light around the room—and exasperated, announced. "Once again, you are *annoyingly* right. How could

I even think of not wearing this unparalleled gown? It is so phenomenal; I've decided not to change for the parties later. With consumption in the world at record highs, it's only appropriate that I lead by example and not encourage fast fashion sales."

"Well, Lara. You were going to wear the sustainably resourced dress from London to the Vanity Fair party tonight, which is also an excellent way of raising—"

"No, Belinda. It's decided. Please thank them for *trying* and explain my position. I'm sure they will understand and support me since they are also for the planet."

"Sure, Lara. Consider it done." Belinda struggled with the opposing feelings that consumed her: utter relief for Cedric Tatou and equal horror for the phone call she now had to make. She barely noticed Lara shedding the gown—leaving a priceless, twinkling red pool on the floor—and, after tugging on her robe, dancing down the stairs to start glam.

"Do you want me to call them Bels?" Jasper asked, reading her mind as he carefully placed the dress on its cushioned '*CT for LW*' monogrammed hanger.

"Oh god, would you? Sorry, I know I'm being a coward."

"It's fine. Go downstairs and discuss the '*controversial*' coral lip Deepra likes, and I will take care of it."

"Oh, how I heart you."

"No need to keep saying it. You just owe me BIG in this life and the next five."

After a fraught call, Jasper returned to the lounge to find Lara, loudly critiquing images of the braided bun Zane was suggesting. "Hmmm, it's not radical . . . but maybe if we add matching crystals for pizazz. Belinda, you have them, correct?"

"Yup, Alessia brought a bag of spares."

"Also, Belinda, I've had a genius idea! Kelly is asking the gardener to loan us a leaf blower so Elliot or Marco can elevate the tulle for the perfect picture. Isn't that amazing? Then my bodyguard Joseph can pop it in the handbag you borrowed for him. How brilliant to have my own wind for the night."

"Um, Lara, I think industrial leaf blowers are huge—and are you even allowed to do that on the carpet?" Belinda mumbled in response.

"What did you say? I didn't catch it; Zane was deafening my ear with his dryer."

"She said *what a great idea*, Lara." Jasper interjected, pulling Belinda to the door and whispering, "Let it go gurl. Are you crazy? Don't fight other peoples battles! Do nothing that will jeopardize this dress."

"Okay, okay, you are right. I must be losing it already. How did the phone call go?"

"Awful. As expected, I was on speakerphone, and they both cried, like real tears. They borrowed money from their dentist to make this dress," he said sadly. "I told them we would place it on another actress soon. That kinda eased the pain, but not really. Now you have to go. Chanelle is waiting outside in the car to take you to your next hell. Oops, I mean Oscar nominee, Ava-Lily."

"There is nothing original about advising others to be original, if one hasn't done anything original oneself."
—*Abhijit Naskar*

Designer Desecration

Heading to the Loews Hotel. 11 am

BELINDA, SILENTLY DEBATING THE DANGERS of Chanelle driving a Porsche in 6-inch Gucci platforms, decided that maybe death would be preferable to this day—this week—this month. On cue, her phone started to buzz furiously, and she clicked the sound back on as she answered, "Good morning, Jonny!"

"It's Tab, Belinda. I knew you would answer *his* phone straight away. So, here's the thing: since I can't wear the blue tux. Ugh, the white one is just *so* fucking boring—*why* is Henri LeRoque *so* difficult? But, before you shit your fancy pants thinking you have to find me something in a couple of hours, I've fixed it. I've fucking made it hot. I'm a genius. I cut the trousers into shorts! And it's way fucking cool without a shirt, a bow tie hanging around my neck—like a choker, kind of. One thing, though, the shorts are a bit wonky. I like the raw edge; it's like literally edgy, but they should probably be *even*, right? Can you send a person to fix them? You know what time we leave for the carpet. Love you, miss you, byeee."

"Is everything okay?" Chanelle asked in her valley girl drawl as Belinda threw the phone into her black Balenciaga bag.

"On today's scale, sure. Actually, didn't you go to Parsons?"

"Yaaaa."

"For design?"

"Yaaaa, for a year, but then I switched to marketing."

"Okay, great, I have a task for you and—no pressure—but you can't fuck it up."

Sold

Check your emails. Ava-Lily has a last-minute jewelry deal. Nigel Jolly Jewels. Something to do with a cat shelter. Yes, you guessed it... she is contractually required to wear A NECKLACE. Sorry babe, hope it doesn't fuck up the vibe, but I know you will deal, pro that you are. You must call Nigel ASAP. He is ready and waiting with images and will bring you anything you need. They will cut you in privately as a gesture, so this is good news! The amount is still TBD. I'm trying for 10k. I will let you know ASAP, but are you open to partial payment with jewelry?

All Clear

Belinda, I just wanted to inform you that the autopsy results came back.

They ruled Alma Astley's death accidental. The Chief will be doing a press conference soon, but I thought it might help you to know this today. Good luck, and my sister would LOVE it if there's any tidbit you can share in advance. No pressure, obviously.

OMG. I'm so relieved. You have no idea how bad the rumors have gotten. THANK YOU!

PS see below a picture of Ava-Lily's outfit for you and your sister's eyes ONLY! YAY

TEXT FROM BELINDA TO JASPER

See below from cops!!!!

OH YAY, OH YAY! OH YAY, OH YAY
INNOCENCE IS HOT, HOT, HOT.

Wait, you think they coordinated this
with the Academy?

Fucking perfect Oscar Day timing

Cool, it conspiracy qween

It's a dynamic ending for her biopic

*"No pressure, no diamonds.
Little pressure, little diamonds.
Great pressure, great diamonds."*
—Matshona Dhliwayo

The Bling Keepers

Ava-Lily Glam

Loews Hotel, 20th floor. 11:45 am

Red carpet arrival: 3 pm

"Hey guys, happy Oscar's day!" Belinda, smiling broadly, didn't have to force her bubbly tone as she walked into the perfunctory space masquerading as a luxury suite, wondering—as she always did in these types of corporate hotel rooms—which beige-fixated interior designer had signed off on the mass-market art and instantly forgettable faux-something furniture?

She air-kissed Richard and Marilyn, who were finishing setting up. "So, I got the email about the jewelry deal. You have to wear a necklace, so the halter-neck Chanel gown is out. Are you cool with that, Ava-Lily?"

"I guess so, yes, although gold is my favorite color. It's a massive amount of money for Purr Protection, and they have vintage jewels, so Greta and the environment will approve." Ava-Lily's face flashed doubt. "We do like the Tom Ford, right? Pants are sick."

"Yes. It's amazing. I mean, we couldn't lose either way!" Belinda reassured her, adding, "But it seemed Pat wanted the Chanel more."

"For a handbag, honey," Richard quietly deadpanned as he tousled Ava-Lily's hair.

"What was that, Richard?"

"Oh, nothing, baby. Pop those earbuds in and relax."

"Oh, okay, thank you! You guys decide on my hair and makeup, yeah? Belinda knows what Tom suggested."

Belinda nodded in response. "I sent this to you guys the other day, but here's a print-out. "Tom is suggesting this dark '60s eye with a pale or nude mouth and, for hair, a modern take on an elaborately braided chignon. Sort of Twiggy—meets Breakfast at Tiffany's—via British Vogue."

"*LOVE!*" Richard and Marilyn chimed in unison.

"Okay, great. Be back in a second." She walked outside the room, scrolling down contacts to call Nigel's cell. He picked up on the first ring. "Belinda! Been waiting for your call. What do you need, honey? We are ready to bring anything and can be there within the hour."

"Great, Nigel. I'm texting you over a picture of the look. Can you send me images of necklace options first, preferably a choker if you have one? Let me know who's delivering ASAP so I can organize access. It's insane here today."

"Oh we know! On it, darling! Give us fifteen minutes!"

Belinda looked regretfully at the security guards lining the hallway, waiting patiently with her assiduously selected jewelry options from Tiffany's, Cartier, and Harry Winston. "Sorry, guys, but her team just did a last-minute deal. Thank you for your time, but you can go."

The host of armed dark suits shrugged indifferently, nodded at her, turned, and strolled towards the elevator, chatting.

- "A short day! Nice!"

- "Nah, I gotta go back to the safe and switch out for a drop in Malibu. I think you gotta come, Mikey—it's over three mil."

- "The pop princess's beach place?"

- "Must be Vanity Fair party run."

- "Cartier are loaning a bunch this year?"

- "Yeah, I'm exhausted."

- "Dude, get on the Chanel run next year. It's super chill."

Tan-talizing

TEXT FROM JASPER TO BELINDA

12:01 pm

> Hey B, just tried the dress on Janie.

> The lining color is spot on, BUT as predicted, it does ride up when she walks/sits. Luckily, we have some Shrunx in the exact same color, so it's not super noticeable if it rides ALL the way up to the vadge, but she's really nervous.

>> There's no way she will switch back to the Calvin Klein?

>> If anyone can persuade her, you can!

> NOPE. Eve has blown a tsunami of fear up her fake-tanned, colonic-drained ass, and she is ADAMANT.

> Hold, please; Eve is now furiously squawking on Janie's speakerphone...

The upshot of it all is that Eve must owe that designer big. And I personally think she must be blackmailing Janie—cos that one ain't never cared about showing skin before. Janie is clearly freaked out. Looking ghostly underneath that chestnut tan.

They want you to meet her at the carpet when she arrives to check the lining before pictures and then meet her backstage before she presents. They know you have an all-access pass because of Jonny, so ♂

I said we needed to check the timing to make sure it's all doable, but...

But I have no choice...

That about covers it, yup (hopefully the lining will, too... BA BOOM!)

Ugh

Laugh Belinda. Do it, girl. Remember you are a free woman now!

HA

The excellent news is Chanelle is coming here to (wo)man this fort and provide ventilation with her eyelashes. I can now go back and be tortured by Lara. HAPPY OSCAR DAY!

Press & More Press

The Daily Mail wants to ask you about Janie's red-carpet process. Pass?

DUH.

Duh yes or duh no?

Daily Fail? PASS

MY, aren't we grumpy today?

Devon, they called me a middle-aged 'alleged' home wrecker yesterday JFC

Oof. Now is the time to delete that Google Alert girl.

What? I've never googled myself ever. Jasper, on the other hand, he knows more about us than we do, you should tell him. Sigh.

"Forget glass slippers – this princess wears boots."
—Unknown

Taping Tatas

TABITHA AND JONNY EVANS GLAM
Loews Hotel, 12th Floor. 12:45 pm
Proposed carpet arrival time: 2 pm

OH MY GOD, BELINDA. WHERE HAVE YOU BEEN?" Sitting on the bed, Tabitha yelled over Radiohead as she stubbed her half-smoked Marlboro in a clean martini glass, draining her Bacardi and Coke. "I don't know if any of these shoes are gonna work."

Tabitha stood, fully made-up and barefoot, wearing Jonny's now cropped white suit. The open jacket revealed half of each flawless breast, and a loose bow tie was hung over a long double-wrapped diamond chain. Her hair was waxed back into a ponytail at the nape of her neck. Jonny, smoking a massive joint, lying on the bed in boxer shorts and a threadbare Rolling Stones tee, looked up briefly and lazily said, "Hey, B."

Belinda nodded in response and yelled over the music to his wife, "Tab, you wanted a sky-high platform with an ankle strap!" Her eyes skimmed the number of shoes Chanelle had lined up by the wall. "There are 12 pairs here for you to choose from."

"Well, maybe I want boots now," she whined, "Doc Martins could be cool." Grabbing her black glittery phone, she turned the music down.

"For the *Oscars*? No, Tab, I don't . . ."

"Who are you to say *no* to me, Belinda? Hmm? Right? I don't think so. Just because you are a red-carpet sheeple like all the others. Why can't I wear whatever shoes I fucking want? I'm rock'n'roll. Jonny is rock'n'roll, so why can't we do what *we do*? Perhaps you're so blinded by the system you've forgotten how to fuck it up? And here I was thinking the British were fashion *anarchists*."

Momentarily floored by the accuracy of this statement, Belinda stood silent, an unexpected wave of shame washing over her before she pulled it together.

"Okay, Tab, I understand what you're saying, and actually, I agree with you. Of course, you should do you, but perhaps you could have told us yesterday? I can't read your mind, and as you just correctly assessed, we are sheeples, so Doc Martins aren't something we have on hand for the Oscars red carpet."

"Yeah, I thought so. Well, luckily for you, I popped down to Hollywood Boulevard earlier, and *voila* (that's *French*, Belinda), look what I have here." Tabitha dramatically threw open a mirrored closet door, revealing a pair of crystal-encrusted white worker boots. "Fucking spectacular. Jonny loves them, don't you babe?"

"Yeah, totally, babe." Jonny didn't look up from the miniature game of Space Invaders he was playing.

"Well, okay then," Belinda sighed, "So this is *sorted*?"

"Yeah, I guess so. I still need a bunch of bling on my fingers and for you to tape my tits to look perfect and then tape the jacket to my perfect tits."

"Your tits are already perfect."

"No, they need to be a quarter inch higher." Tabitha shrugged off the jacket and threw it on the nearest chair, laid down next to Jonny on the bed, and pulled one breast up. "You've got good surgical tape, right?

Bending over the bed, Belinda deftly cleaned Tabitha's chest with alcohol wipes before taping her boobs up, carefully ensuring that nothing would be seen if her jacket accidentally swung open. Which, knowing Tabitha, was virtually guaranteed. Jonny lying on his stomach, distracted by his game and cursing periodically, paid zero attention.

"Also, do you have a pad to put in my shorts?" Tabitha stroked her crotch. "You know I hate wearing underwear, and I don't want to sweat into them. Plus it stops camel toe, and who doesn't love a smooth pussy line?"

"Um, no. I don't have one," Belinda said, rubbing her forehead, "but I'm sure the hotel can bring one up."

"Okay, cool, give them a call, will you, and while you're at it, ask for some more Bacardi and a giant hot dog with chili on the side. But before you do that, how's my makeup? I can't fucking believe I had to have it done at 8 am this morning. Like, what in the actual fuck? I'm not important enough to have a later time slot. Jonny's groomer arrives soon, and *she* stays all afternoon . . ."

"You look beautiful, Tab!" Belinda gushed before deflecting, "Jonny, should we try on your suit and pick the jewels?"

"Nah, we know it fits, and that rich girl steamed it earlier. I'm not fussed about bling. Whatever you gals think is good for me."

"Don't ask me," Tabitha looked taken aback. "That's what Belinda gets paid for. Wait until after you've called room service, Bel. Tell them to hurry. We are hitting the carpet early at two, so we can come back here and get wasted before his performance."

Belinda, on hold for room service, watched Tabitha, who, having turned the music back up and thrown her jacket on a chair, was dancing wildly on the bed next to Jonny.

"HEY, BEE!" she yelled over the music. "*WHO WAS THE FANCY BITCH WITH A RARE CROC BIRKIN THAT FIXED MY SHORTS?*"

Let the Fashion Hunger Games Begin . . .

Text from Jasper to Belinda
1:45 pm

Janie IS IN THE CAR.

Let the games begin!

(Well, in an hour or so, depending on traffic.)

You have to go and find Norm, the limo arrivals wrangler, in like 40 minutes. He will tell you where to wait for Janie. You won't have much time when she arrives because the cars have to keep moving, like two minutes tops.

JESUS

Oops, I nearly forgot these!

Wardrobe Credits

Gown—Clara Jank

Pumps—Stuart Weitzman

Clutch—Chanel (she bought it yesterday)

Jewels—Lorraine Schwartz

WHAT, she changed the clutch? Why didn't you stop her?

That's a joke. Right?

Yeah, I guess, but also no.

I have already sent the credits to the evil witch masquerading as her publicist. She is also unhappy about Janie making a decision by herself. She wants to schedule a call to bollock us for that later. ☺

*When it comes down to competition,
it's not always about the best skater,
it's about who skates best
in that competition.*
—Gracie Gold

Misery

BELINDA, SHUFFLING THROUGH MULTIPLE KEY CARDS, walked into the elevator, searching for the one to Caroline's floor.

"*Belinda!*"

She looked up to see Orlando beside her, the muscles of his face managing a thin smile despite competing Botox and filler. "Good to see you, Mama," he drawled.

"You too." she responded politely." How's it going today?"

"Oh, you know, the same. *Crazy*, as always. My roster of A-List divas is the personification of insanity for the Oscars, as I know *you know*. I wish I had the time to work with more relaxed actors—like yours. But can't complain about being in demand!"

Belinda nodded, used to the grotesquely inflated self-confidence. "Well, at least award season is only a few hours from over."

"Yes, mama. *Yes!* But there is no rest for me. I am so in demand! I'm off to Paris in the morning and then Milan. I have a camera crew following me, too. I don't know how I do it. My assistant is calling in runway looks for *me* these days—" He continued his self-reverent monologue, and Belinda, mentally running through the rest of her day, tuned out.

The elevator halted on the 18th floor, and Orlando swept out into the corridor, his flat-ironed grey hair and fuchsia silk trench flowing behind him. Belinda, relieved at the silence, slumped against the carpeted wall, watching the doors close, and was horrified to see Orlando's diamond-encrusted hand snake back in, forcing them to open again.

"I just wanted to say, Belinda, that I love the '*no hard feeling*' vibe you are giving about Chloe. You put in *so* many years and created some radical looks. Bravo, mama." He clapped slowly, holding the door with his Cuban boot.

"I don't speak any French, so god knows how I will cope with Bebe Klein. I'll have to hire a bi-assistant, I guess. That's lingual, not sexual." He giggled, and his face contorted into a terrifying, plastic smile. As he spun around and walked away, she heard him say, "*Wish me luck!*"

Numb, Belinda got off at the next floor and, pacing, dialed Jas's number. "Pick up, Jas, pick up! Aarrggh, fucking voicemail—"

"Jas, it's me. Where are you? I just saw Orlando. I was right about Chloe; he told me they are working together now. The smug asshole assumed I knew." Seeing a tuxedo exiting a room at the far end of the corridor, she lowered her voice and, head down, walked in the opposite direction. "Jesus. Did they have to hire that arrogant fuck? And fuck Chloe and Lacey for not telling me directly, or even Devon. Christ, even an email would have been some kind of cowardly fucking gesture. *Fuck fuck fuck.*" She paused, watching the tuxedo enter the elevator, and checked the time. "Shit, I've got to go to Caroline." She braced herself. "So don't call me back, we can talk later. Or, maybe it's best not to talk about it at all today. So I don't cry."

"When in doubt, wear red."
—Bill Blass

Glamming with the Enemy

CAROLINE GLAM
13th Floor, Loews Hotel. 2:10 pm
Proposed red carpet arrival time: 3 pm

"WHERE HAVE YOU *BEEN*, BELINDA," Caroline whined as she opened the door. "Oh, thank god! I was wondering who was going to dress me." Belinda, confused, pointed at Chanelle, who was perched awkwardly in her Versace micro mini on the luggage stool, thighs pressed firmly together to hide her La Perla underwear.

Belinda watched Caroline turn and look right through Chanelle before panic engulfed her. "Chanelle, why are you still here and not with Janie?" she pulled her to the nearest corner of the sitting room.

"Oh yeah. You, like, didn't know? Jasper told me he totally bribed Yelena to go to Janie's. Caroline wouldn't let me go. She literally grabbed my hand—wouldn't let it go—when I tried to pick up my Birkin. Something about me not leaving her alone. She's totally buggin'—"

"Oh phew, so Janie is good—hang on—isn't Caroline's husband here?"

"Yaaaa, he is." Chanelle pulled a horrified face. "But, like, it all makes more sense now that I've spent 45 minutes with them."

On cue, Peter—dressed in a loosely belted standard white hotel robe that, on him, was almost floor length—swaggered barefoot out of the bedroom, talking loudly on the phone and slurping champagne that he held in his spare manicured hand. "YEAH, I get it dude. Producing 'woke' is such a freaking MONEY spinner. Love it! Who *knew*? My dad was horrified I was doing this originally, but now he's like, fucking impressed. Fiscally it's a fucking dream. If I'm raking in right-wing-style money, I'm happy with all my lefty snowflake stuff." He drained his champagne and handed the glass to Caroline to refill. "Anyway, stop by the suite for a quick one if you have time . . . Yeah, I know, frigging cool, we got a suite. I booked it a year ago. I just knew this one was gonna go. Speaking of which, I gotta go. Staff are here to iron the threads. Catch ya later, dude. Come and kiss my gold." He turned his tanned face to look contemptuously at Belinda, his ever-loosening robe revealing a waxed chest and black Versace silk boxers almost knee length on his little muscular legs. "You . . . um . . ."

"Belinda?" she responded.

"Yeah. Come with me." Belinda tentatively followed him into the bedroom, where he handed her his shirt.

"Iron this, please." Belinda handed the shirt to Chanelle. "Babe, can you steam this?"

"I said I want it *ironed*."

Looking down at him, unsmiling, she held his gaze and repeated in an even tone, "Babe, can you *iron* this, please?"

Caroline entered with his refill, and Belinda walked swiftly out, followed by Chanelle with the shirt. Through the open door, they heard him say nastily, "What is that color on your lip, Caro? Red? Do you really think you can carry that off? I knew I should have stayed here this morning instead of working out when you were getting dolled up. You have no idea what suits you." Hearing Belinda cough, he softened his tone. "Look, on the bright side, you have dropped a couple of pounds, so you're gonna look much better in the photos than usual. Your hair looks great, and it hides your jowls too. Get dressed now. Let's hit that red carpet before all the big stars steal my thunder. Also, that stylist is rude."

Caroline, fighting back tears to avoid ruining her makeup, shuffled back into the lounge. "The lip is *great*, Caroline," Belinda murmured encouragingly. "It goes so well with the dress, excellent call. And you have lost some weight. Not that you needed to, I might add."

"I haven't eaten for five days, Bel. Well, nothing solid. I want a drink so bad, but I'll probably pass out. I'm already dizzy, and I feel so sick."

"Why don't you have an energy bar? I'm sure there's one in the mini bar, or I have one too."

"NO! I can't bloat before the pictures. I'll put one in my purse for after. Oh god, I can fit one in my purse?"

"Not the one we originally chose, but I have spares, so let's swap it out for a bigger one." Belinda's tone grew strict. "You have to eat something. It's a fucking long ass day."

"Sure, Bel, *thank you*," Caroline replied weakly, with so much gratitude that Belinda wanted to cry again. Chanelle, examining the iron in the hall closet as if it were a relic from a prehistoric age, waved to catch Belinda's attention.

"Um, Belinda, how do I—"

"Just plug it in, babe. You know how to do that bit? I'll show you how to iron when it's heated. In the meantime, bring me Caroline's dress and shoes, please. Also, the spare clutches are in the blue Rimowa case."

She turned to Caroline. "Where's the corset?"

Caroline opened her robe. "Here, I've had it on for three days straight, you know, to encourage me not to eat."

"You slept in it?"

"Well, yes," she admitted sheepishly. "I remembered what Yelena said about comfortable clothes and eating more. I'm a big night grazer."

"Christ. I'm surprised you got any rest."

"Well, I didn't really, but it'll be over in a few hours, and then I can sleep forever."

Belinda shook her head as Caroline turned to step into the crimson Prada gown. She zipped it up and secured the satin-covered buttons as Chanelle helped Caroline slip her feet into gold, peep-toe Stuart Weitzman platforms.

"Well, the good news is these are voted 'most comfortable of the uncomfortable' by almost every client I've ever had, so hopefully, you won't be in too much pain."

"Oh, I've got CBD cream on my feet. Now that I'm getting a bigger bag, I can take some with me," Caroline responded more happily. "And my jewelry is gorgeous. I told Jasper that Peter wanted to buy my jewels for this. You heard, right? He thinks it's tacky for me to borrow pieces since we are so, well—*so well off.*"

Fucking loaded might be more accurate, thought Belinda, who said out loud, "Yes, I heard. Exciting. Can I see?" Caroline handed her a leather box. "I mean, I'm sure you'll think the stones modest, but Bee, this movie is about poor people, so it would be wildly inappropriate to flaunt our wealth."

Assessing the delicate necklace and earring set, consisting of a slither of ruby and the tiniest of pavé diamonds, Belinda announced with as much sincerity as possible, "Beautiful," then handed the earrings to Caroline and fastened the chain around her neck.

"TA-DAH," Belinda exclaimed, gesturing with both hands at a fully dressed Caroline as Peter walked out of the bedroom in his pants. He turned and looked her up and down briefly, his face indifferent. "The jewelry is great. Where's my shirt?"

"Everyone shines,
given the right lighting."
—Susan Cain

Wardrobe Malfunctions

Limo Arrivals Area. 2:40 pm

BELINDA FLASHED HER ALL-ACCESS CREDENTIALS for the ninth time in twelve minutes as she finished the final stretch of her walk to the limo area. She was overwhelmed by the deafening cacophony of a thousand or so members of the tanned and embellished media, lined up behind red ropes in the tent in front of her, fawning over the nonstop parade of gilded demigods, otherwise known as actors. She spotted Eve watching the limos roll slowly in, waiting with one orthopedic stiletto on the concrete road and the other on the red carpet. "This lining had better work, Belinda," Eve snapped spitefully as a hello. She tossed her fake brown ringlets, bitterness visibly emanating from her satin-encased body. "Luckily for you, it's stopped raining. Get ready to jump in her car on the far side. You will have to be very fast and don't let the audience see."

Belinda said nothing and nodded in agreement. She looked at the hundreds of fans, winners of the lottery for a ringside red-carpet seat. Most of them had already been there for hours and, despite the tent, were dressed for the inclement weather.

"I would supervise you, but my Clara Jank dress has no stretch. I, unlike you, made an effort today."

Belinda looked down at her vintage YSL tuxedo in amusement. "Yes, that's *quite a dress*," she quipped, just managing to keep the sarcasm out of her voice.

"It is, isn't it? I did wonder if the mink trim was too much on the cape, but what the hell, I'm in the background on TV all afternoon, so why not?"

"Does it tickle your face?"

"We all have to suffer for fashion, Belinda. I'd think you'd know this by now. And, as I have to remind you—sometimes weekly—black is such a dull color, so unphotogenic. It needed a little fur magic to make it special."

"Well, try not to tread on it. Mink is very fragile. And come find me if a seam splits; I have magic stuff for that." Belinda, buoyed as she channeled her inner Jasper, found herself giving zero fucks.

Eve opened her mouth angrily but was interrupted by Norm, the limo wrangler. "Ms. Jones incoming, 30 seconds. Are you ready?"

"Oh yes, Norm. Thank you!" Belinda waited in position on the far side of the lane as the car pulled up. She stood, wondering why the door wasn't opening, then realized in horror, as the car rolled slowly away, that Janie had gotten out of the wrong side and was waiting at the edge of the lane for all the world to see. Belinda rushed to her side as Eve whispered with a public-facing smile, "Well shit, Belinda, you were on the wrong fucking side. Check the lining quickly, and I will try and block you as much as possible. Thank god for my cape!"

Belinda groaned, knowing she had no time before all the cameras would turn their way, if they hadn't already. She sank to the ground, knees cracking.

Locked & Loaded

2:45 pm

She is in the dress and has LEFT THE BUILDING!!!

I could cry with relief

Credits below

Dress - Cedric Tatou

Jewels - Dazzle Diamonds

Shoes - Jimmy Choo

Clutch - Tatou

I already sent this to Marco and the rest of her publicity team, FYI.

BELINDA TEXT CONVERSATION WITH DEVON

See below for Lara's credits

Dress - Cedric Tatou

Jewels - Dazzle Diamonds

Shoes - Jimmy Choo

Clutch - Tatou

Awesome. Jasper sent them already, but thanks.

I just saw you on TV! Janie looks HAWT. But why were you

on the floor with your hands up her gown? And WTF is going on with the fur shroud evil Eve is wearing

Oh FFS.

DO NOT ASK

"Thick skin is prized so abusive people don't have to see their targets flinch."
—Unknown

Barefoot Finish

Belinda ran back from carpet arrivals to Ava-Lily's room in the Loews Hotel, a route that took her from the front of the Chinese Theater through the security points of the shopping center and the cavernous areas of the corporate hotel. Halfway there, she removed her satin Marc Jacobs platforms and finished barefoot, ignoring the curious and judgmental looks along the way. She crashed into the open room, and, breathless, waved a weak hello to Chanelle, who was teetering next to a full-sized steamer.

"Oh," she exhaled noisily. "Hi Pat, I didn't realize you'd be here. Aren't you usually on the carpet at this point?"

Pat stared coldly at Belinda's bare feet. "I"—she extended the syllable for multiple beats—"*devoted* this momentous day to Ava-Lily. Unlike *you*, it seems. Where have you been, Belinda? You think that on this, of all days, you would be present for her. Is someone else more important?" She paused, staring, barely blinking. "And look at you all in black, just like a publicist. Are you mourning Alma?"

"It's a backstage requirement, Pat."

"And how do you get a backstage pass?"

"I work with Jonny Evans."

"Oh yes." She paused. "Didn't I see something salacious about you and him?"

"You might have. A tabloid taking a photo of me and him hugging hello at his Oscar fitting and running to the moon with it."

"You should know better after these years, Belinda. You seem to have become very careless. And, as for Alma, we never did get to the bottom of that!" She shuddered.

"But Pat, the Police have told me it's nothing—"

"Oh, we don't have time for your excuses. Now, let's get Ava dressed. She has to leave in 20. Her glam is divine. But of course, *they* got here early."

"Reality is like a fruitcake, pretty enough to look at but with all sorts of nasty things lurking just beneath the surface."
—A. Lee Martinez

Working Girl

DRESSING JONNY

Dressing room two, Chinese Theatre basement. 3:45 pm

BELINDA STOOD AT JONNY'S DRESSING ROOM DOORWAY, catching her breath again and fixating on an antiquated metal cart against the purple corridor wall, stacked edge to edge with gleaming gold statues.

"Bloody hell, Jas, they just leave them here like this?"

He stuck his head over her shoulder and laughed. "*Baffling* that we could just wheel it away. It's taken everything I got, and I mean *EVERYTHING* to not play chess with them."

"So incongruous against this vinyl hellscape. Jonny was right!" They surveyed the corridor before them, painted a dull mauve shade on one side and a dark peeling purple on the other. The drop ceiling was missing all its panels, just metal bars remaining, with exposed cables dropping down like electrical bunting, the floor an afterthought of cheap beige vinyl.

"Thank god they put that one cheap Office Depot burgundy chair there to jolly up the place," Jasper laughed again, pointing at a random chair pushed up against the wall further down the corridor.

"What a design scheme, Jas! I just love the dance between the glamor above and the neglect below. The Oscar statues are a simple yet effective way to tie it all together."

"Well, Belinda, *wait* until you see the inside of the dressing room again." Jasper stepped aside, gesturing with both hands. "TA DAH! You see! Nothing says Oscars like a dank, dingy white dressing room last painted circa 1995, complete with matching era TV."

"I particularly love the low ceilings, Jasper, an intimate design choice. The hard, dirty plastic chairs keep it earthy and real. Okay, we watch way too much HGTV."

They both giggled as Jasper looked at Belinda properly for the first time. "You look nice, girl, but why are you carrying your shoes?

"Oh, I had to run here. Didn't want to miss watching the carpet. What in the actual working-girl fuck was I thinking wearing heels today? Ava-Lily was rolling around on the floor with her cat just before she was leaving, and we had to lint-roller the hell out of that couture jumpsuit. It took forever, and cat hair is *gross*. It's not normal to love a pet that much."

"No comment, you cat-hating bitch. I have been here for half an hour, enjoying the magnificent ambiance. The suits are steamed and ready, and the jewelry is in its tray on that old fold-up table, where it absolutely does not belong."

Belinda glanced at the small rack in the corner and then at the table. "I see it doubles as a glam station, too."

"Yes, once again, it features the high and the low, the ying and the yang. Maybe some fancy performer had this room last year and left this top-of-the-line Hollywood mirror here."

"Had to be Mary J. Anyway, all this design fun aside," Belinda sighed, pulling out her phone, which had been pinging incessantly for the entirety of her run. "Christ! My battery's down to 20% already. Can you turn the volume up on the TV?" She slumped onto a plastic chair, catching up with her messages as low-volume red-carpet commentary broke the room's silence. "Shit, Jas, I need to post about a thousand things, and I forgot to tell you, Pat was so fucking mean about Alma and that tabloid shit with Jonny, plus I have another missed call from fucking Flox Corp. They keep sending emails, too, which I don't read. And Chloe—No, don't talk about Chloe, I'll fall apart."

He hugged her tightly. "I heard your message, and I promise I will not bring up that C-word today."

"I just don't know if I can do all this. Can I just go home? I feel like a slow boiling frog."

"Oh no, no, no, honey." Jasper gently wiped away her tears and wrapped his arms around her. "Look, you can do this. Don't let the bastards win." He pulled a chicken salad sandwich from his Balenciaga backpack. "It's warm, sorry. But I knew you wouldn't eat, and you know you have to, or you get nutty—and by that, I mean unbearable."

"Everyone gets nutty when they don't eat," she sniffed, a hint of a smile forming as she munched her favorite sandwich. "I just admit to it, unlike some people—"

Jasper, one eye on the TV, interrupted, shrieking, "Look, it's Ava-Lily! Does this thing even have a remote? We need to turn up the volume!"

"The camera makes everyone a tourist in
other people's reality,
and eventually in one's own."
—Susan Sontag

Titillating Teen

AVA-LILY STEPPED CAREFULLY UP the three scarlet-carpeted steps in her five-inch stilettos, accepting the steadying hand of the ubiqui-tous, sexually ambiguous presenter Brian Landmarck. They stood on their marks as he lifted the crystal-encrusted branded microphone to his baby-smooth, bronzed face and announced in a bubbly TV voice: "Well, next up, we are honored to be talking to the *STAR OF THE NIGHT*, the one person everyone along this 900-ft red carpet has been waiting for . . . Ava-Lily Manderson! Ava-Lily, you look absolutely *SENSATIONAL*, and what a stunning and utterly riveting performance you gave in 'Loaded.' Truly deserving of your Best Actress in a Motion Picture nomination. Is it true you filmed the entire movie completely makeup-free? So *brave*. Now, the big question on everyone's lips is, obviously, *WHO ARE YOU WEARING?*"

"Thank you, it's Tom Ford, except the jewelry, which is"—she stood awkwardly for a few seconds, biting her glossed lip—"um, hang on." She glanced at Pat, standing at the base of the stairs, who mouthed the answer. "*Nigel Jolly*! I can't believe I forgot! I'm so thrilled because they are making a massive donation to my charity, Purr Protection, as a thank you!"

☆   *415*

"Yes, Ava-Lily, I think it's common knowledge that you have always supported kitty organizations. What an extraordinary human being you are! How is Ulysses, by the way?"

"Oh, he was upset that I had to leave him today."

Brian screeched his famously fake laugh. "And such a funny lady too!"

"Well, he truly is upset. But that's pretty nice of you to say."

"Of course, the feelings of pets concern all of us animal lovers." He flashed a sympathetic smile directly to camera. "Now, Ava-Lily, tell us, what's next for you?"

"I'm glad you asked, Brandon."

"It's Brian, you forgetful little minx—"

"Because I have a big announcement to make today. I've decided to take a year-long sabbatical—and maybe retire completely from acting. All I really want to do is work with deprived cats. I'm so excited to finally, for the first time, be choosing my own life. You're the only person I've told so far."

Brian's face flashed gleeful excitement at this extraordinary scoop, his voice rising an octave, "Oh no! What a *loss* for us in the entertainment business, but what a *win* for cats! The world needs more young people with your heart and exquisitely sympathetic soul." He tilted his head and stopped smiling for a beat in an effort to look benevolent, before once again flashing his infamously blinding, toothy smile. "NOW, since you are sharing life choices, are you *also* open to sharing your elegant, soft hands with our mani cam? I see you've chosen a deep red manicure, very *sexy*."

Ava-Lily giggled uncomfortably as Pat, just in frame behind her, stood looking at her with her jaw dropped and eyes frozen open.

In the basement, Jasper and Belinda stared in shock at the TV. "*HOLY SHIT*, did she tell you she was going to do this?"

Belinda shook her head. "Nope. Nor to Pat, clearly: look at her puce face!"

"Pat needs to file down those horse teeth. What about Ava's next movie? She's not gonna promote it?"

"Well, if she is really retiring at 19, she's not going to give a single shit about pissing off the studios. Fucking insane how the meekest client

I thought we had just told Hollywood to fuck right off in front of the world. I don't know whether to laugh or cry."

"Oh, Belinda, there'll be other clients, babe. Especially with how rad they all look today." Jasper wrapped his arms around her. "ALSO, what the freak is she talking about with '*the only person she's told*,' the only person being Brian and the whole fucking world! He nearly creamed his pants with that exclusive, and while I'm on that subject, did he just basically jerk off to her teenage hands on live TV? To be expected, I suppose, remember the eve of her 18th birthday and the gross media salivating about her finally becoming 'legal.' I guess for the pedos, she's old now."

Belinda mock vomited as she emptied her purse on the floor, grabbing CBD gummies.

"Fuck that Bels have some hard stuff," Jasper ordered, handing her a Xanax as she scooped up her belongings. Belinda obeyed, staring blankly at the TV, oblivious to the din of peppy voices sucking up to couture-clad painted humans, and waited for the numbness to kick in.

"I have nothing to declare but my genius
and this four-kilo bag of cocaine."
—Oscar Wilde

Breaching the Line

JONNY COSTUME CHANGE
5:30 pm

"HEY, GUYS." JONNY CAME BOUNDING into the changing room, reeking of booze, pupils so large his eyes were almost black. "I'm so *pumped* for this performance." He shed his black tux in a frenzy and stood naked, bar a black Calvin thong, waiting to be dressed.

"Hi, Jonny. You guys looked great on the carpet." Belinda walked behind him, holding the electric blue shirt open and guiding it onto his arms while Jasper fastened the buttons from the front.

"Ah, thanks, mate. Have you seen images already? Cool! Hey Bel, can you grab the wrap out of the pocket of that jacket, please." Jonny asked, sniffing.

"Sure," she said, handing the stage pants to Jasper and grabbing the baggie.

"Anyone want a line?" Jonny asked.

Zipping up Jonny's pants, Jasper looked tempted, but Belinda immediately shut it down. "Very kind, Jonny, but we've still got a bunch of work to do."

"A cheeky line would help, no?" he said, grinning like a naughty kid.

"Not really, not for our line of work anyway. Speaking of which, Jonny, where's your groomer?"

"Oh, she was partying with us upstairs and put this blue eyeliner on me up there. Fucking rad, no? Anyway, she and Tab were *ahem* having a very good time, so I told her to hang out there. There's makeup people backstage, right, if I need powder for sweat?"

"Yup." Belinda deliberately didn't look at Jasper, who was mouthing '*sexual unicorn*' as she slid on Jonny's blue jacket.

"Well, you boring fucks, I'll just rack one up for me then," Jonny leaned over the white table and expertly tapped out and inhaled a long fat line. "*Riiiiight*. Shoes, and then I'm ready. How long before I go?"

"Five minutes before they take you up and another five before you go on. I think that's what they said, but it's not really my area. Where's Don?"

"Oh, time for another line then. *Sweet*. He's up in the room too. Too tame down here for my crew."

"Well, the PA will come and get you," Belinda wondered why she was doubling as his manager as she watched Jasper sitting at Jonny's feet, lacing his white-pointed Oxfords.

"Have you been watching the show, Jonny?"

"Nah, mate. Those speeches fucking kill me. Bunch of pompous, self-important fucks dressed like royalty, thanking a bunch more pompous, self-important fucks and god."

"Um, you realize you might have to make one of those in about 30 minutes?"

There was a knock on the door, and as it cracked open a fraction, a female voice announced quietly, "We're ready for you, Jonny."

He walked out the door, answering Belinda, "Jesus, I hope not. I mean, it would be nice to have an Oscar and all, especially for the loo," he cackled, "but mate, what the fuck would I say?"

FIRE THE STYLIST
Dishing Daily Doses of Fashion Justice

Early Oscars Edition!
Ava-Lily Manderson in Tom Ford.

Posted on March 4, 2018

FIRERS! What a day in Tinsel Town, and the show isn't even over yet! There have already been some fantastic highs and some horrendous lows; see mass market retailer Lowbop having a stab at Oscar dressing and causing everyone's eyes to bleed cheap red sequins.

Yes, we KNOW they donated one million to climate causes. However, can they leave their performative philanthropy for other lesser events next year or maybe invest the money in learning how fast fashion f*cks the planet?

Anyways... Back to the matter at hand, let's talk about Ava-Lily (19) because, frankly, who isn't? Resplendent in Tom Ford, she stole the carpet in her modern take on a Hollywood goddess. Some more old-school critics might consider a jumpsuit risky for the ultimate award show, but it's 2018, people! Every single thing about the look was sublime, and we hope she gets Tom Ford to design the wardrobe for her next role as a philanthropic cat ambassador.

Stylist Belinda Grant pulled out all the stops on this one, and in our opinion, with this look and Lara White (33)—a knockout in Tatou (to be discussed in an upcoming post)—she has reached a career-high. Rumors of alleged murder and infidelity clearly agree with her creative side. (Click here for links.)

As always, leave comments below!

(To review our community guidelines, please click here)

> @fassssshunDL is she f*cking CRAZY. Who in their right mind would give all this up for a CAT? Great look, though. Props for that.

> @stylestarflorida I'm sorry, but I have to disagree. No one wants to see an actress in trousers at the Oscars; it's disrespectful and unattractive. Leave pants for the men

> @rachelrules @stylestarflorida bullshit. Go back to upholding the patriarchy where you and your man-pleasing fake tits belong.

@stylestarflorida **@rachelrules** Oh, please take your jealous feminism elsewhere. Bitch at least I know how to please a man.

@speakznoevil Who cares about Alma? BG MURDERED these looks... as well as JE's marriage. #triplethreat

@dogslife **@speakznoevil** you live evil! What a terrible thing to say. This platform is dying.

Cocaine & Carats

JASPER PICKED THE LEATHER SUIT UP FROM THE FLOOR and hung it up carefully. "Maybe I'll just steam the lining. Man, there is cocaine all over this fucking thing! I'm getting a contact high." He sniffed harder, dipped his hand into the wrap pocket, and rubbed his gums.

"Yeah, well, he's always stoned when he performs, so nothing new there," Belinda responded glumly. "No idea how he's still alive. Look, they're coming back from the ad break. He's up next."

Jasper dropped the steamer and rushed to her side. Mesmerized, they watched Jonny on the stage, a floor above their heads, silenced by his orgasmic voice and frenzied gyrating, sweating blow all over the stage. "It's wild that even after all this time, I still can't take my eyes off him," Jasper said admiringly, his expression turning to horror as Jonny dramatically ripped open his shirt, roughly pushing up his sleeves, a visible glint of a four-carat diamond cufflink flying into the air and bouncing off camera.

Belinda squealed. "*Shiiiit!* We have to get that back, Jas; it's worth like $20k."

"Don't worry, honey, I'll talk to the PA. She can find it. She can retrieve his jacket as well. At least this loss is on tape if we need evidence for insurance purposes."

Press for Pay

5:45 pm

NYT OBSESSED WITH AVA-LILY in Tom Ford. YAYYYYYY. SO CHIC! They are probably running her as the cover pic for their Oscar roundup. Can you hop on a call when you get out from under the theatre? Sarah at 212 445 6792. Give me an estimated time so I can give them a heads-up. I told them NO questions about Alma, but she's a serious fashion journo, so that's unlikely anyway.

Also...

Vogue GAGGING for BTS ASAP. Chop chop.

Also...

You MUST post a close-up of Lara in Dazzle Jewels in order to GET PAID!

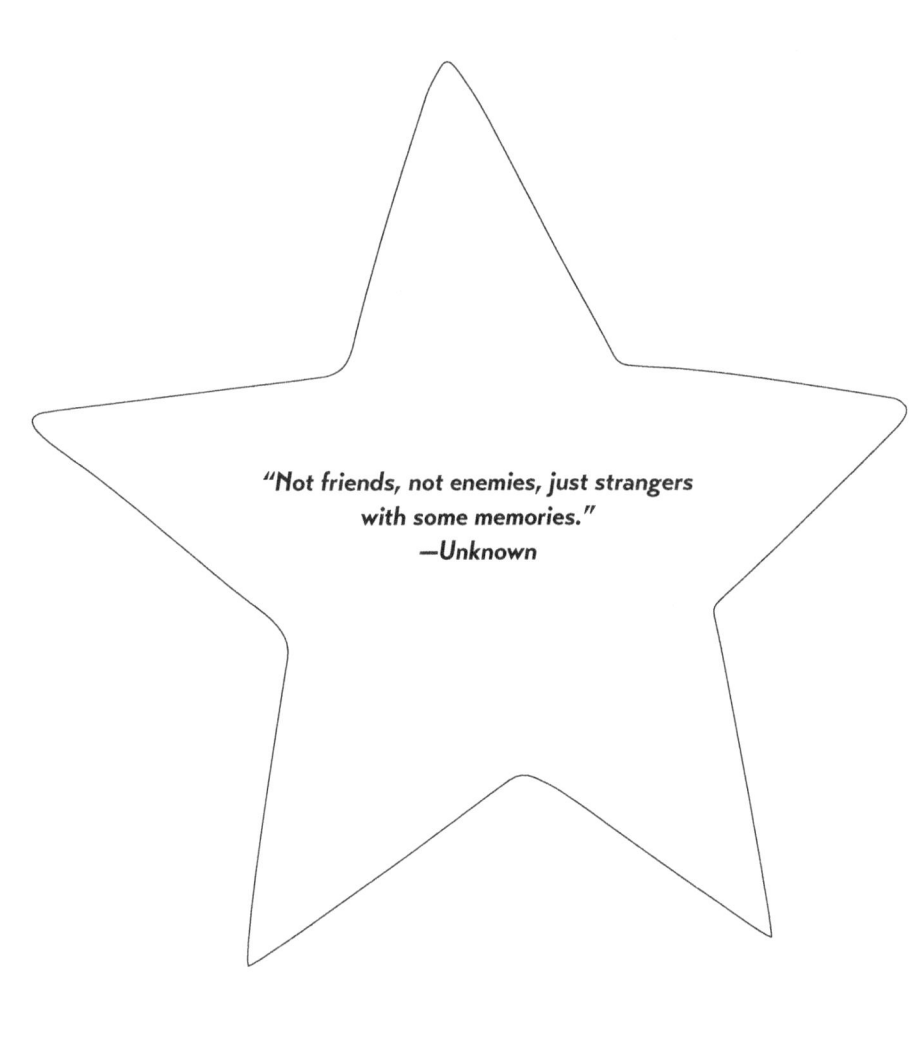

"Not friends, not enemies, just strangers with some memories."
—Unknown

Contact Lows

JONNY'S DRESSING ROOM
6:20 pm

"IS THERE A TOWEL IN HERE?" Jonny asked, looking around the room, his hair and torso soaked with sweat.

"I think there's one in the bathroom, one sec," Jasper disappeared through the tattered door.

"Jonny, shouldn't we get your groomer down here? Just in case?" Belinda asked, feeling like his mother.

"Nah, mate. I'm not gonna win. Those fucks will have voted for one of their own."

"I dunno, Jonny. Most people have been saying you've got a shot."

"Whatever. Who cares what I look like anyway, right?"

"Well, lucky you for being a man. Imagine the uproar if a woman was on stage with wet, sweaty hair and running makeup."

"Yeah, babe. I'm a lucky bastard, fuck being a woman, it sounds terrible."

"Can confirm," Belinda agreed.

"Oh plu-easse, Belinda," Jasper disputed sarcastically, "you love all those purses."

"Well, why can't straight men carry cute purses, too? Or maybe they should give everyone pockets?"

"Yeah, much as I love this equality convo, can I put on my suit now, guys?" Jonny stood before them limply as Jasper fastened his leather pants, and Belinda, standing behind him, slid on the jacket and switched out his jewelry.

"Hey, Bels, mate." Jonny rocked awkwardly from one foot to another. "Um, this isn't easy to say, so I'm just gonna blurt it. Tab wants me to hire a new stylist. It turns out she is bothered by the tabloid shit, and she's chucked what feels like a million wobblies about whether or not I think you're a spunk. (You are, obviously, but I don't shit on my work doorstep, so to speak. I'm a dog, not a drongo.) Anyway, my hands are tied, I've already had a gutful, and she won't fucking stop yakking about it." He turned his head to look over his shoulder at her. "Sorry, babe."

"But Jonny," she spluttered, "we've worked together for longer than you've known her, and everyone knows that was just tabloid bullshit."

"Yeah, yeah, I know, but you have been in the press a lot lately with the agent and everything, and it's making the Missus even crazier. She gets very jealous when people get more press than her. Look, I really am bloody sorry, and I'm gonna miss you." He turned his head back, unable to look at her pained expression. "Aw, mate, don't get upset. I know I'm shit at doing this stuff. Too blunt, as every wife so far has told me, but I wanted to tell you myself, you know, to your face, be straight up . . ."

"But Jonny, the police are announcing Alma's death as accidental today, so the press stuff will blow over fast—"

A knock at the door interrupted her. It cracked open again, and the PA whispered, "Are you ready to go, Jonny? We cut to commercial in four minutes, long enough to get you back in there."

"Yeah, sure, I'm ready, right guys?" He looked at them, ignoring the mirror right in front of him. Belinda nodded, not trusting herself to speak, and Jonny walked to the door, turning just before he exited, his face wistful. "Listen, babe; it was always tough with you and Tab. She hates hot women around me unless we can fuck them together. If I get divorced again, which, let's be honest, seems statistically likely, I'll hire you back pronto. I promise. Okay, mate? It's shit, I know, but it's the best I can do right now. Sorry." He put his arm around the anxiously waiting PA and allowed himself to be guided back to his seat.

"Chin up, Mary Poppins." Jasper gently dabbed her face with a tissue, pulling the makeup bag out of her purse. "No more tears. We will survive like we always do. Today's nearly over. Well, only four-ish more hours by the time you've done all the press. Now, let's quickly fix those gorgeous red eyes." He gently wiped away her tears, muted the TV, and reapplied her eye makeup.

They sat silently for the next 20 minutes. The room devoid of Oscar's excitement was back to its usual state—depressing and stifling. Jasper worked intently on his phone, keeping one eye on the screen. Belinda was deep into Twitter, reliably distracted by politics, her feed Hollywood-free, a whizzing conveyor belt of pernicious Trump antics.

"Bels"—he nudged her gently—"Jonny's category's next. If he wins, d'you want me to go up there and check on him? You can stay here. No one will care."

"Devon will kill me. Listen, a man actually killed himself outside the White House today, so I can go up there and futz with a fucking perfect suit. What is there to do to a leather suit anyway?"

"You go, girl! That's the attitude. Now put on more lippy in case you need to snap a selfie with an Oscar and a thoughtless, gutless, rockstar wanker."

He unmuted the TV, just in time to catch Talia Berry and Turell, in expertly co-ordinated looks—hers a gold-embroidered sheer mermaid gown, him a custom Adidas metallic gold tux with white stripes—announce, "And the winner of the Oscar for Best Original Song for a Motion Picture is"—Talia, smiling broadly, ripped open the envelope and they both yelled—"*JONNY EVANS!*"

"Oh, *SHIT. WOW!*" Overcome with involuntary excitement, they hugged, jumping up and down, and were immediately halted by the PA, who grabbed both their arms and pulled them into the dark corridor. Using a flashlight, she swiftly guided them upstairs to the stage wing while Jonny, onstage, made his speech. They waited for him to finish—roll-calling the dimly lit famous faces around them—so they could check his suit before he hit the backstage press room and pose for more images that would ricochet around the world. *Where's press-whore Tab now?* Thought Belinda scornfully, whispering, "Hey Jas, maybe I should snap a picture with Jonny and the Oscar and post it immediately? A giant final fuck you to Tab?"

"Yaassss gurl. That's the salty spirit. Oh my god. Stars & Us Magazine will *freak*! I'm getting my phone ready. Let's photobomb it before we even touch his suit. And I want you to hug him tight. If you're feeling really brave, kiss his cheek."

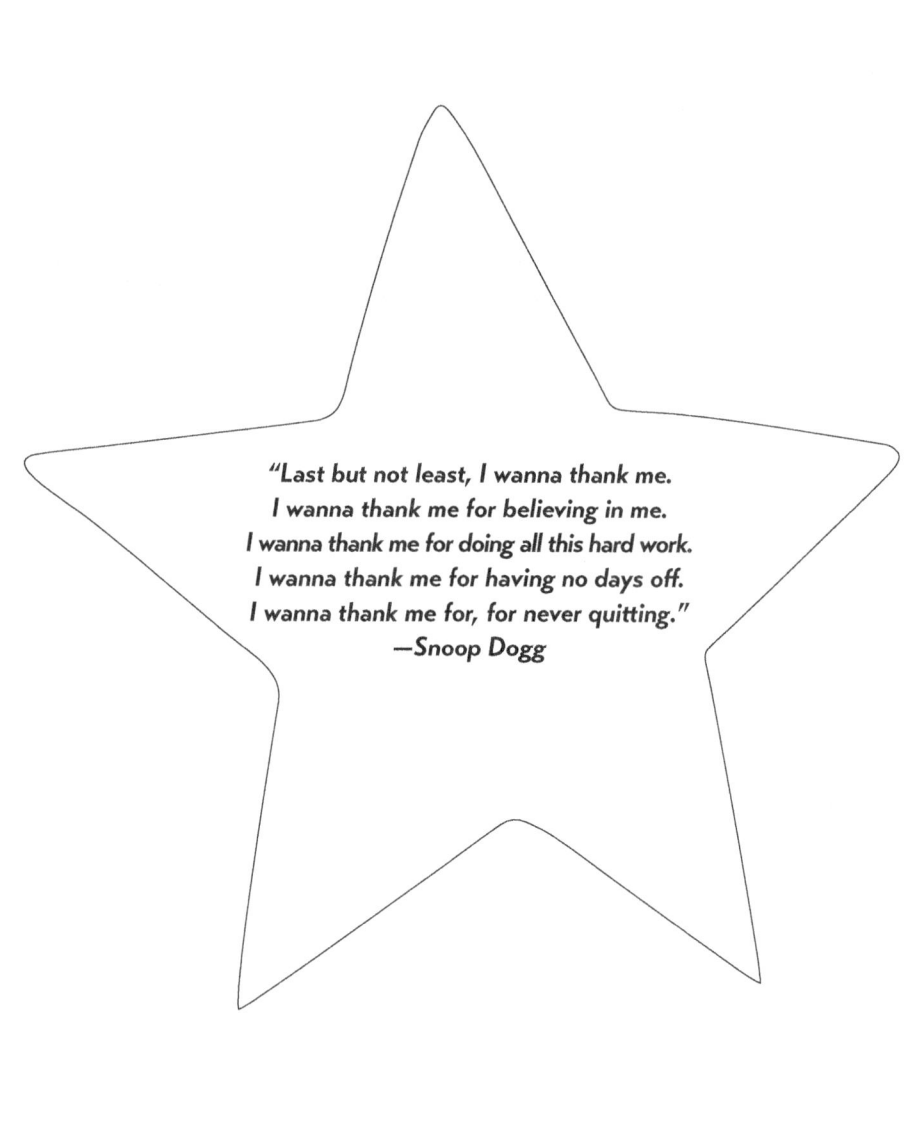

"Last but not least, I wanna thank me.
I wanna thank me for believing in me.
I wanna thank me for doing all this hard work.
I wanna thank me for having no days off.
I wanna thank me for, for never quitting."
—Snoop Dogg

Speech-Less

JONNY BOUNDED UP THE STAIRS in three coked-up strides, a broad grin consuming his face as he arrived on the extravagant stage, 45 million Swarovski crystals and 3250 hours to evoke a live-action 'Frozen' set. He pulled Talia Berry close, pausing abruptly as he faux-whispered, "*Shit, consent,*" and immediately pivoted to Turell, whom he kissed full on the mouth before pushing him laughingly away. Turell muttered, "It's a good job we're friends—but don't ever do that again." Jonny grabbed the Oscar from Talia's outstretched, perfectly manicured hand and raised it above his head, turning to the microphone.

"*MAAAATE!* I was just backstage saying there was no way I would win or have to make a *BLEEP* speech, so I don't have one ready! *BLEEP*. Anyway, I always think most speeches are as dry as a nun's nasty, so I'll keep it quick. Firstly, I don't thank god, but I do have to thank the current missus, Tab, or my life won't be worth living." He stopped to wipe his nose, and his tongue flickered over his teeth and gums. "Love my kids, all of them, love the band, love Don, my manager, my label, love me, of course—and thanks to Henri LeRoque for the threads and Bels for making them make sense. The movie was pretty good, too. Plus, of course, all the other nominees. Love ya. *CHEERS! BLEEP!*"

He started to walk off stage before turning to add, "Do I get the jet ski prize for the shortest speech? Did Jimmy mean that? They should honor what the host promised, right?"

Revenge is Spicy

GET PHOTO OF YOU WITH THE OSCAR (and Jonny)

NOT NEGOTIABLE. WILL KILL YOU IF YOU DON'T - all the GQs want it.

I CAN NOT BELIEVE HE MENTIONED YOU IN THE

SPEECH!

> Literally just posted

What the fuck is up with you today. You posted a shot KISSING him? The tabloids are going to freak out.

> Fuck 'em and fuck him. He fired me just before he won.

> His wife is jealous apparently.

LOLOLOL

Never would you doing this have been on my bingo card. Ballsy.

Revenge is sweet, my friend.

He'll get divorced and be back.

That's what he said.

Penny Lovell

"A smart girl leaves before she is left."
—Marilyn Monroe.

End of an Era

JIMMY KIMMEL TOOK HIS PLACE at the center of the glittering stage for the final moment of the broadcast, his face solemn. "We've heard much about the late, great Alma Astley tonight from two of our winners and many presenters." He paused as the camera cut to Ava-Lily in the audience, holding her Oscar and hastily putting down her phone. "Tonight, in the last hour while our show has been airing, it has been confirmed that Alma's mysterious death was, in fact, a tragic accident. We know that she is looking down on us all, happy in the knowledge that her run continues with two Oscar wins tonight." He waited for the applause to die down.

"God bless you, Alma. We dedicate this show to you. Hollywood won't be the same without you." He saluted at the sky.

"And that's it from the 90th Academy Awards, coming to you live from the historic Chinese Theater in Hollywood! *Good night!*"

"It's always darkest before it turns absolutely pitch black."
—Paul Newman

Diamonds & Dive bars

Riding in Cars with Stylists
Hollywood. 9 pm

"That place looks like somewhere no one in Hollywood would lower themselves to visit," Belinda pointed to a windowless, partially boarded-up bar, wallpapered with peeling flyers, in a dimly lit mini-mall on Santa Monica Boulevard.

"Perfect! Let's fucking do it. *FUCKKKK YOU* and your shriveled-schlong monster truck, you *ALPHA DICKHEAD!*" Jasper yelled, doing a rapid U-turn and narrowly avoiding a crash.

"Technically, Jas, that was his side of the road. The cock insult might be a bit low."

"Whatever. Driving a monster truck is *asking* for insults. Anyway, I've never needed a drink more in my goddamn gay life. Ugh, we will need to take the spare jewelry in with us. If only they knew that this old backpack contains diamonds worth more than most will earn in a decade."

"Ugh, it's so gross and terrifying when I stop to think about it, which I mostly don't. I wish we could drive home and put it in the safe, but if we do, we'll never leave again. You just keep that on your back the whole time, Jas. Let's drink a few margs and I'll finish doing the press."

"Devon wants to know if you can make one more call to the LA Times?" Jasper threw open the door to the dingy, mostly empty bar. The lighting

☆ *441*

was dim and red: a solo middle-aged bartender slouched over the sink, washing glasses, her thick, bleached hair-tinged pink in the light. Her only company was a guy in a sports shirt playing on an antiquated pinball machine and two crumpled men splayed on patched-up armchairs, nursing on-tap beers and arguing lethargically in Spanish.

"This place is perf," Belinda exclaimed. "Although how the fuck you are gonna see to edit the photos for Insta, I do not know."

"Oh, gurl, I did most of it while you were catatonic in Jonny's dressing room. Devon already has them. I also pretended to be you and sent your quotes to the NYT, FEMME, Marie Claire, and British Vogue. Don't worry, I just regurgitated what you said to American Vogue and Elle but shuffled a few words. You know, the same but different. Can I say no to Devon about the LA Times? Save it for the morning?"

Belinda nodded, fatigue overwhelming her as she slumped onto a scratched wooden bar stool, dumping her Balenciaga purse on the sticky and stained counter.

"Okay, *good*"—he looked at her approvingly—"because I already did!"

"Oh my god. Thank you."

"No more tears, lady, and that's an order. I'm not doing your makeup again today. Also—dear god—hand me your purse! That's insane dollars you just plonked into damp, 90 proof old gunk. Anyway, yes, it's true! You are freaking fortunate to have me. Now *let us drink*."

"Just one, okay, Jas? Two max. Rose went to a sleepover at Halo's, but I don't want to be super late. And who fucking cares about the purse? These days, they are just memory bombs of misery." She paused as the deep, leathery cleavage of the bartender appeared in front of her. "Oh, can I have a *large* resposado on the rocks, please, and he will have a Margarita, right Jasp?"

"Yep, blended and skinny. Should we eat?"

"*Meh*. Maybe after this drink?"

"It takes only one drink to get me drunk.
The trouble is, I can't remember if it's the
thirteenth or fourteenth."
—George Burns

"I'm gonna be *fiiine* to drives, Belsie boo. I ate an energy bar and Doritos, so that soaks up at least three of the margs, right?" Jasper slurred his words as he stumbled and crashed into the car. "It's okay! I'm okay! The diamonds are okay!"

"I dunno, Jas." Belinda, stumbling behind him, smeared red lipstick haphazardly on her lips before tossing it in the general direction of her bag and missing, oblivious to the Chanel case bouncing into the gutter. "I think we might be *reeeally* hammered."

"Iss not far to your house. I'm so fine. Could drive in my sleep, and I park *SOOO* mush better when I drunk," Jasper said, flopping sideways onto the driver's seat and pulling his legs in after him.

"*Oh my god*," Belinda squealed, looking in the wing mirror. "Why have I got blood all over my face?"

"Lipstick, you silly bitch. Get in the car. Why is this seat so *uncomfortable*?"

"Diamonds, Jas," Belinda giggled, pointing at the backpack. "You are leaning on them. Let's give them to homeless perrsson. I mean unhoused— no homeless—shit, I don't know the right word." She pointed to a human curled up in a filthy sleeping bag on the sidewalk, head hidden inside a cardboard box. "This rich town is horrible. No one gives a shit, and it's so fucking cold at the moment."

"Bishhhh, the world is horrible. But Dazzle Diamonds will not send me to jail, you wasted Robin Hood wannabe."

Jasper pulled out tentatively and then braked aggressively at the edge of the parking lot. "*OH SHITZ*, forgot to call the hubster." Picking up his phone, he stabbed randomly at the screen, turning on the speakerphone.

"*JASPER!* It's 1 am. Where the fuck have you been?"

"Oh, I loooooove you, babeeee!" Jasper slurred, dropping the phone onto his lap and pulling out of the lot. "We just had little drinkies. Terrible day. They're a bunch of cunts. Jonny is a fucking *BIG* diiiick, who Bels is not fucking, jus' to be clear, in case you saw the Instagram post or any tabloid goss. Tequila is the best, tho. We lurrrve tequilas, don't we, Belsie?"

"Yesss. We love sooooo mussh. Oh *shiiit*, Jassie, I think you missed the turn."

"*WAIT . . . ARE YOU FUCKING DRIVING, JASPER? PULL OVER THIS MINUTE. JESUS CHRIST YOU TWO. WHERE ARE YOU? I WILL COME AND GET YOU*," Bobby roared.

"Oh. That's so sweets, baby. Can you jus' hang on?" Jasper swerved rapidly into a U-turn, his phone tumbling to the floor.

"Okay, going the right way now. Juss a few mins, Bels." He turned to look at Belinda, who was drooling, cheek pressed against the window, her eyes closed. "Now, what was I doing?" He thought for a second, shrugged, flipped on the radio, and started swaying, singing along "... 24-carat diamonds in the *CAR-A-ARRR*, head to toe drunk *PLAYA*. Something, something. Next bit for the *FUCKERS*, bastard clients, *AND YA SHITTY UGLY ASS AWARDS*."

His off-key singing drowned out the faint yelling coming from under his seat, "*FOR FUCK'S SAKE, JASPER, I WILL FUCKING KILL YOU. IF YOU DON'T DO IT YOURSELF FIRST.*"

FIRE THE STYLIST
Dishing Daily Doses of Fashion Justice

The Fabulous Fashion! The Falls! The Fornication!

Posted on March 5, 2018

It's after midnight, Firers, but we can't stop posting! There is SO much to break down from the events tonight. From the (perhaps tone-deaf) opulence of gazillions of crystals embedded into the stage to the unprecedented amount of unexpected wins and losses—aside from Ava-Lily Manderson, all the front runners went home empty (the Hollywood bookies must have made a killing this year); the resolution of Alma Astley's mysterious death; Janie Jones also falling down stairs, though thankfully not to her death, and Jonny Evans publicly making out backstage with his stylist Belinda Grant (while we hear on the grapevine, his wife Tabitha was occupied in the hotel upstairs!) WHAT A NIGHT!

Let's start with Jonny Evans since he's lit up all the airwaves with his electrifying performance (it's rumored the $100k Diamond cufflink that flew into the audience when he ripped open his shirt has yet to be found); his making out with the rapper Turell and his stylist mentioned above; plus his expletive-laden, JAW-dropping speech that has outraged the Christian right and already racked up 10 million views on YouTube. (Click here.) But we digress! Let's get to the important stuff: the fashion!

What is there to say, except that by perfectly fusing Hollywood glam and rock 'n' roll in two spectacular looks tonight, this Henri LeRoque ambassador killed it STONE DEAD. The electric blue metallic suit and matching shirt he wore for the performance was clearly meticulously planned. Beneath the Swarovski-designed arch, strobing bolts of matching blue light bounced off his phenomenally ripped body and created a Frozen-esque landscape so HAWT, it would surely reduce Elsa, like most of the ladies in our office, to a wet and warm puddle.

His red-carpet look was also a standout! The slim-fit, notch lapel, butter-soft black leather tux was worn closed and shirtless with white cap-toe Oxfords. The finishing touches were David Yurman jewels—a Mori Skull black diamond necklace and multiple stacked black titanium and pavé rings. It was so refreshing to have interest in what was an otherwise staid parade of famous men in virtually identical (*insert designer here*) suits. We won't insult you by pretending to debate the virtues of double-breasted

v. single or the 'daring' boldness of those who chose to be tie-less. (See tomorrow's round-up of all the male fashion!)

Closing this post before my eyes do, with the unexpected end-of-show announcement that Alma Astley's death was an accident. (Click here for our previous post about her excellent midlife style.) Belinda Grant and her new beau must be immensely relieved this evening.

What think you, Firers? Comment below with your favorite OSCAR moments!

(To review our community guidelines, please click here)

@daisyduking I LOVE HIM 🔥 🔥 🔥

@mynamewastaken666 snooze. An old druggie and a nobody fashion idiot. Why is this important

@bashingfash The patriarchy keeps men confined to boring suits. Both sexes are boxed in. Women can't be boring on the red carpet, and so-called manly men can't be interesting.

@jenelopyjazz There are so many people at the Oscars, and this post is just about Jonny Evans - someone has a crush.

@magicmike666669 his speech, and Ricky Gervais were the only respite from the insane amount of congratulations and pats on the back this industry gives itself.

@jonnyevansfanclubaberdeen @magicmike666669 and yet you watch them and comment on a fashion site... hmmm

@yesnope that man has been busted for drugs more times than I've had breakfast. How does he still get revered and get campaigns and shit?

@suitinglife @yesnope bc he sells shit, obv. Capitalism doesn't care about crime if you bring in the 💰

MONDAY 5ᵀᴴ MARCH 2018

"You will do foolish things, but do them with enthusiasm."
—Colette

Sticky Shame

BELINDA STIRRED, DISCOMBOBULATED, as her '*Work Bitch*' ringtone broke the morning silence. Reluctantly, she unsealed her bloodshot eyes, startled to see her white linen pillowcase covered in crimson streaks and pieces of jam-covered toast. She shook her head, releasing more crumbs, and searched for her phone under the chaos of scattered pillows next to her.

"Hi, Devon," she croaked quietly.

"Well, good morning, booze queen. I really hope I was the only one you were sending texts about—and I quote, 'your miserable, selfish, cunty clients.' There was also a voicemail at 3 am my time, with Jasper singing 'fuck the bitch up' backup to you yelling expletives. It's hilarious. I saved it."

"Oh, Christ. Ugh, I did? Fuck. Sorry, Devon." Shame and fear washed over her sticky body. She tried to sit up and promptly stopped as stale tequila-soaked brain matter sent fireworks exploding from her forehead to the base of her neck.

"Anyway, honey, I'm so sorry about Jonny, but he'll be divorced within the year, especially after that Instagram post. Dirty move, Bels. I'm impressed. And Ava-Lily, now that was unlucky. But come on, she'll get over the cat thing and be back—fame is the most addictive of drugs. And as for Chloe, well, I agree with Jasper and his c-word lyrics last night. I'll have words with Lacey today. It's bullshit and so unprofessional."

"Fuck, I can't believe I posted that Jonny pic. What was I thinking?"

"I can't answer that, but you are temporarily quite famous. Page Six is all over it."

"We weren't kissing on the mouth. It's just the angle."

"I know that! And even if I didn't, Getty has 100 more backstage images from an accurate angle. Back to the bad news, Cocotte emailed this morning that they are going to use their person in NYC. They dared to say, '*It's only a white t-shirt, after all.*' After *all* of those never-ending demands. I have managed to get you a small cancellation fee, which is miraculous because it's not within the strict 48 hours laid out in the deal memo. But I think they agreed because you have already started working on it. Someone in corporate has a heart. Who knew?"

"That's not much consolation, to be honest, Dev—"

He cut in, "But honey, let's be honest, isn't this good news? You wanted Lara gone; she's given you so much hell this last year. Well, all the years. You practically *manifested* this. And what a high to go out on. I mean, there's no doubt that you won the red carpet between her and the cat teenager yesterday. Have you looked at the press?"

"Devon, it's 7:30 am in LA. I've been in bed for five hours. When would I have seen the press?"

"Well, my office sent you some of what's out so far, so try not to worry about getting new clients. We will find others for you, no problem. You might want to avoid Eve today. She's on some warpath about Janie not getting the same attention as the others. It's bullshit because she looked absolutely stunning."

"Oh, you mean the others who were either nominated, presenting because they won last year, or performing? Jesus, that woman is on crack."

"Much like you last night, darling. Anyway, gotta run, but chin up. And you must call Instyle in 30."

"Okay," Belinda sighed, "talk later." Realizing he was already gone, she clicked on the link he'd sent during the call.

RUNWAY

TODAY'S STORIES

OSCARS BEST DRESSED

By Jacinta Von Butler

The Oscars are the main event of the fashion spectacle that overtook Hollywood this weekend, and before we get to the slew of after parties that usually bring out the more exuberant looks, let's start with the most audacious on THE red carpet of ALL red carpets.

Ava-Lily Manderson

Last night's Best Supporting Actress Oscar winner outshone and out dared all the ladies on the carpet in a simply stunning custom palazzo jumpsuit by Tom Ford. The cream halter four-ply silk creation was fitted to perfection, cut to reveal a daring slice of taut midriff, while the glimmering 10-foot train was nothing short of magnificent. It's custom lapis floral beading took the extraordinary Tom Ford team 200 hours to apply and—thankfully—was removable for the after parties. Ava-Lily rightfully chose to forgo other options and remained in this look for the whole night.

Lara White

Lara is a red-carpet queen and a perennial on best-dressed lists—especially for the Oscars. This year was no exception. Her vermilion bejeweled custom Cedric Tatou was tailored to perfection. The sweetheart neckline, voluminous tulle skirt, and tumbling crystals blended seamlessly, boldly accentuating her sublime figure—a true standout. Last year's best actress winner accessorized with Jimmy Choo shoes and perfectly placed Dazzle Diamonds jewels.

Lara also decided to remain in a single dress for every event on this fashion-drenched day, describing this choice as 'a nod to the overconsumption of a burning planet.' These A-List style icons are known for supporting the latest causes, and we sense a trend here.

Sophia Porter

Ms. Porter presented the Lifetime Achievement award last night. With a career that spans six award-winning decades, she has attended too many Oscar presentations to count. Through it all, she has embodied the exquisitely dressed essence of an A-list star. Today, she continued her sartorial reign—once again showing her masterful grasp of classic with a twist—in a slinky chain mail <u>Ralph Lauren</u> column gown, <u>Roger Vivier</u> shoes, her own (frequently worn) <u>Von Speers diamond cluster earrings</u>, and a dainty pavé encrusted <u>Omega watch</u>.

This inspirational trio—spanning multiple generations—encompasses everything a fashion lover could ever dream of. *Truly next level.*

Click *Here* for More Great Oscar Coverage from Runway

"Not all storms come to disrupt your life.
Some come to clear your path."
—Paulo Coelho

The Morning After

7:40 am

THE DOOR BURST OPEN and Jasper bounced in and plopped himself down on the bed pulling closed the short pink and black lace and silk robe he wore over his Gucci briefs.

"Holy *shit*, you scared me!" squawked Belinda. "Christ, I forgot you were here. Why are you wearing Rose's robe?"

"It's all I could find in her bedroom. Why does she have this slutty Victoria's Secret item anyway? Not so age-appropriate, babe?"

"She found it in the office. They must have sent it for someone. She didn't take it off for a month. We got weird looks at the supermarket, but now, thank god, she's much more tie-dye Sporty Spice."

"My hubby is *very* mad at us, in case you were wondering, Bels, and you shouldn't be because he called you last night and yelled at us for a full ten minutes, which is why I stayed over. Can you make me coffee please? I'm sooooo hungover."

"Oh yes. Sure. Maybe that will help my head." She threw back the white linen comforter as Jasper, watching her, burst out laughing. "Gurl, you're still fully dressed."

"Ugh, no wonder I was so hot last night," said Belinda, shaking her head and immediately regretting it as the pain thundered and a wave of nausea undulated violently through her body. "God, I feel so sick."

"Yeah, well, prepare for more. Did you read the email from Eve?" Jasper, in monogrammed Gucci socks, padded behind her into the kitchen. "Jesus!" He surveyed the landscape in front of him. "*What did we do?*" Their eyes followed the trail of tomato sauce splattered from the stove over the wall of white cabinets, trailing off lightly on the tiled ceiling. Sauce-drenched penne dotted the black and white tiled floor. The piece de resistance was two stone bowls full of marinara pasta sitting untouched in the middle of the island countertop.

"Well, it appears we made a delicious pasta dish from scratch, used it to Pollock the kitchen, and abandoned it before eating a whole loaf of toast with jam—which we also used to add texture to the fridge door, my bed, and our hair."

"Should we clean it up, Bels? Before Paola gets here?"

"We should, yeah. Ugh. But let's get it over with. Read me what Eve said while I make us coffee."

RE: Janie Jones/Yesterday's Red-Carpet Look

From: Eve Wright Eve@unentitledpr
To: Daria Hastings Daria@managementfourmillion
Cc: Belinda Grant Belinda@BGstyle.com
  Jasper DLC Jasper@BGstyle.com
Date: Mar 4, 2018 at 7:33 am
🔒 Standard encryption (TLS)
  Learn more

Dear Belinda,

Please see below reviews from publications/sites regarding Janie's look yesterday. I think we can all agree this is devastating. It is unclear to me and my team why, when you have such apparent success with other clients, you cannot fulfill easily achievable expectations for Janie.

Let's set up a call ASAP to discuss how you will rectify this, or I will be forced to advise Janie that moving on to a more *invested* stylist will be the best option for her.

Daria—we will check that the timing works for you
and patch you into the call.

Eve Wright

Executive CoFounder Unentitled PR

She/Her/Hers

*"Integrity is choosing your thoughts and actions
based on values rather than personal gain."
—Unknown.*

Sent with♥

Attachments Indiatimes.pdf
TheKansasexpress.pdf TMZ (Denmark).pdf
Jerseycollegeoffashion.pdf TheTVtimes(UK).pdf

Belinda handed Jasper an espresso. "I didn't know the TV Times did fashion reporting—and I'm English. A college blog? And what the fuck is the Kansas Local Evening Express?"

"Beats me, sweets. My Google alerts say she smashed it. Eve must have mined the depths to find these." Jasper looked down at the email. "Unentitled she/her/hers, to quote Yelena, *is such a beeeeetch.*"

FIRE THE STYLIST

Dishing Daily Doses of Fashion Justice.

And the Fashion Razzies go to...

Posted on March 5, 2018

Firers, we are mainlining coffee over here at #FTS. We've been up all night ranking the worst Oscar looks for your benefit! Let's get straight to it and name the disaster of the night, which everyone here at #FTS agrees was presenter Juliet Hunt (37). Allowing herself plenty of time to preen, Juliet showed up early to a red carpet that began a full three hours before the telecast. Why, we wonder? Was it to give us time to ponder if she was wearing her custom puce Bebe Klein gown backward? Yes, now we've pointed it out, you'll never be able to unsee it. The deep plunging neckline is not this girl's friend; the high back, however, might have been. And as for the jewelry—dripping in diamonds does not begin to cover this carat tsunami. We can only assume the Dazzle Diamonds jewelry deal was LIT. Coco must be rewriting her infamous quote from the grave.

It is unclear if Jonny Evans' wife, 'model' Tabitha Evans (25), understood which event she was attending yesterday. Her white Henri LeRoque men's tux with custom hot pants and crystal-embellished cream Doc Martins was giving first-day Coachella vibes. Disheveled hair, an untied bow tie slung casually around her neck, and a long, double-wrapped diamond chain did little to dispel this notion. Bizarrely, she mostly posed, sticking out her tongue and/or rubbing Jonny's chest salaciously. What can we say, except it looked less red-carpet-ready and more like Melrose Ave (the grubby end) was missing a regular.

Janie Jones (42'ish) wasn't all bad in an intricately crocheted Clara Jank cream gown. It was certainly refreshing to see her moving on from the tulle convections coveted by mermaids and brides everywhere. That said, there were some unforgivable lining malfunctions (click here for images of stylist Belinda Grant, (age unknown) crouched on the floor with her hands up Janie's skirt.) Firers, it is extraordinary that the dress was even lined at all—totally unlike her to be displaying this level of modesty but, with all the resources at their disposal for this, the red carpet of all red carpets, there is simply no excuse for the substandard finish of the underpinning. Fire that stylist!

As always, leave comments below!

(To review our community guidelines, please click here)

@chaneldreamz Stunning women. I think they all look lovely. What a dream to look like they do and wear such gorgeous works of art... And we keep dieting... sigh. (Sips green tea and munches chia seeds for lunch)

@inlovewithpaul they are all pretty forgettable mostly. We are bombarded with SO many dresses these days—even the bad ones don't stand out.

@bluntlyput those white DMs were giving 4th grade art class embellish-your-crocs-diamanté goodness. Sliving.

@rubygreenfingers community guideline? HA, what do they say, "Feel free to demolish women as you please?" What a f**ing joke.

@imogenrules I wanna be a stylist. What a cushy job. How hard can it be to be?

Jetting

Hi, darling Bels and Jasper!

Thank you SO much for yesterday.

The look was a smash!

And guess what? Pierre was so floored by me that

we got back together!

I'm just boarding his PJ to Dubai! Aren't you so thrilled for me!

I can't thank you enough for the dress and the excuse for him to keep putting his smooth hands up it to perfect my lining (if you catch my drift 🔥🍆)

Love you!

Ps Penicle campaign is off now. Pierre doesn't need the world thinking he can't get it up. I mean, what could be further from the truth? See you whenever. Pierre is going to buy me out of Mortal Queen 6 YAYYYYYYY.

> Who the fuck is Pierre?

I think he's that billionaire investor dude that she dated last year for a hot insane spending month.

He paid for the ice rink or the shag-a-thon yacht on the lake, I forget which ♂

"If you can't bite, don't show your teeth."
—Unknown

Orgies & Dreams

BELINDA THANKED THE UBER DRIVER as she climbed out carrying a garment bag. She walked to the entrance of Lara's house and stood for a minute, trying to still her shaking hands before pressing the buzzer. "Hi, it's Belinda. I've come to pick up the dress."

"Ohhh, um, hi," Kelly responded, surprised, "I didn't realize you would be coming *yourself*?"

"I'm going straight to Tatou this morning and since Lara doesn't allow messengers at the house, I offered," Belinda lied.

"Um, okay." Kelly, sounding unsure, buzzed her in.

Belinda hurried up the newly shorn pathway and was panting when she reached Kelly, already outside with the enormous Cedric Tatou garment bag. "Here you go." She rapidly handed it over. "I can't find the shoes or clutch, but the jewelry was picked up this morning at 9, which you probably already know since you guys organized it."

"Thank you, Kelly, and I appreciate you waiting out here for me, but could I have a quick word with Lara before I leave? It's important."

Kelly, one eye twitching, was visibly nervous. "Oh, I'm, um, not sure about that, Belinda. It was a late night, and she, she just got up—"

It's now or never, thought Belinda and, digging her heels in, interrupted: "Please, Kelly, it will only take a few minutes. Could you ask her?"

"Okay, sure. Let me check." Kelly looked sympathetic but couldn't quite meet her eye. "Come in." She skipped across the room and ran up the stairs, taking two at a time.

Belinda was triumphant that she'd gotten inside the house, knowing that Lara, with her self-proclaimed 'impeccable manners,' wouldn't risk throwing her out, though she felt guilty about Kelly, who, she guessed correctly, was being bollocked for admitting that Lara was home. As the minutes passed, she grew increasingly anxious. *Had she lost her mind? Maybe she was still drunk?* She was about to make a bolt for it when Lara appeared in yet another brown caftan, edged in handmade turquoise pom poms. She was makeup-free, blotchy, and tired.

"What is it, Belinda?"

"Can we talk in private?"

"It's really not the best time. I didn't get back from Madonna and Guy's (her manager *not* her ex-husband) party until 3 am. My husband is still sleeping—naughty boy was out until 5 with Lil Nas—and the children are overwrought. It's audacious of you to turn up without notice, and I hope this isn't about the Cocotte campaign. I'm aware that Marco has already spent a great deal of time explaining the intricacies of my situation to your agent. But I suppose I can allow you five minutes. We can go into my office."

"No, it's not about that. . . ." Belinda's voice tapered off as she followed her into the office, squinting up at the navy ceiling cut with long, narrow skylights streaming stripes of winter sun. Lara walked past a large bookshelf of unread titles organized by color to look like a rainbow and stood silently by her desk, staring at Belinda expectantly.

Shriveling under her piercing stare, Belinda's throat threatened paralysis, and terror thumped through her hungover veins. Searching for calm, she mentally chanted, *If not now, when? If not you, who?* Putting the garment bag down, she focused on the enormous candy-pink-striped chair beside her.

"Isn't it divine?" Lara pointed. "Do you see the spherical ottoman tied with a chain at the base?" Belinda nodded, still urgently searching for her voice. "The piece is a metaphor that recalls ancient statues of fertility goddesses. The ball and chain emphasize how women have been unwilling prisoners of themselves. It is *such* a significant feminist statement. Magnificent and *so* comfortable, like pockets in a couture dress. But I digress—"

"No, Lara, *it's not about Cocotte*," Belinda blurted out. She would never figure out if it was the painful superiority of Lara's tone, the beta blockers kicking in, or a combination of both that unwired her jaw. "It's about *these*."

Belinda removed three photographs from her Gucci bag, moved nervously to put them on Lara's desk, and tripped on the ottoman chain. She just managed to stay upright as her left foot demolished a towering pile of scripts, scattering them all over the floor. The photos fell from her hands and landed on the fertility chair.

"What are th—?" As her brain reconciled what her eyes were seeing, the blood drained from Lara's face, and she recoiled, knocking over her Oscar, which had been balanced on a pile of actors' biographies. "*I . . . I . . . don't understand. What? . . . But how? SHIT. What the . . . ?*" Lara's mouth continued moving but made no more sound as she unconsciously backed away from the images. "NO, this cannot be happening. No, this is not me." She added quietly, "*Not anymore.*"

She stood motionless for a few seconds, staring at Belinda with the eyes of a cornered animal. As her body slumped in defeat, she asked, "What do you want?" For the first time, her Midwestern accent was discernible, if faint.

"Well"—Belinda's heart was beating so hard she looked down to see if her chest was vibrating—"t . . . t . . . two things. First, the small thing." She paused, questioning if she could do this. Looking at her feet, she saw the fallen Oscar, and the gold statue triggered a flood of traumatic memories, igniting a spark of anger that lit up her courage. "You unceremoniously removed a chunk of my income without a second thought, or, more importantly, any notice, despite knowing I had absolutely nothing to do with Alma's death. Now I find myself in a tough financial situation in terms of Jasper—"

"I am not solely responsible for you, Belinda," Lara interrupted, "and to insist that I am is outrageous. I will not be paying you any money." She twitched, glancing in the direction of the chair. "You're trying to get your job back? Hmmm, I suppose I could tell Cocotte I've changed my mind." She stopped, noticing Belinda's incredulous expression. "OH. I see . . . um. Well, how much money do you want?"

"*Jesus*, Lara! I don't want your money, and I am aware you have no responsibility for me. I am a freelance Hollywood stylist and, as such, have no HR department, union, or safeguards—by which I mean no rich spouse or parents. So YES, every single day of my life, I am very fucking aware that I am the only person responsible for me." Belinda toyed with a box of Gucci Post-it notes.

"You fired me on a *whim* after four years of expecting service 24/7. You praise me to the world when you want to sound magnanimous while in private you act as if I'm lucky to have you to play with. Styling is not a skill to you. It's a hobby that's not really worthy of actual money. Do you think of us as human beings who need to buy food, pay mortgages, or, you know, *just basic necessities*? No, I don't think you do. To you, we are enlisted fairy godmothers, serfs that are expected to absorb constant beatings from your rampant insecurity until we need to take anti-anxiety meds just to be around you."

She paused, momentarily shocked at the boldness and truth of her words. Then staring straight at an ashen-faced Lara, she continued. "Back to Jasper, yes, his name is JASPER. His true love is design, and he is incredibly talented. He makes gorgeous pieces in his spare time but has never had the confidence or money to pursue it fully."

"But what does this have to do with—" Lara tried to interrupt.

"I am getting to that, Lara. I love his work and would like you—on social media at least—to love his work too. Post pictures of yourself in his line, at least once a month for—say—a year, for your 60 million followers to also love. Additionally, give me your word that you will throw in a premiere or some other significant red-carpet event."

"This is ridiculous, Belinda. You have lost your mind."

"Have I, though?" Belinda picked up a photo, shuddered, and dropped it again. "Oh, and you will also *pay* him for these clothes."

"Are you *blackmailing me*? I could call those detectives, you know, the ones you're so friendly with."

"Oh, you want to show them the photos?" Belinda inwardly cheered at her counter-attack and wondered if she knew herself at all.

"Okay, fine," said Lara, retrieving her Oscar from the floor and placing it back on Woody Allen's face. "Can I at least see them? The pieces? I suppose that's them?" Lara pointed at the garment bag. "Not that it makes any difference." She stroked her Oscar like a comfort toy. "So yes, I have to give you my word, don't I?" She looked Belinda up and down. "You are not at all the person I thought you were."

"No, Lara, you just don't know me at all. And let me show you how hard this will *not* be for you." Belinda unzipped the fabric garment bag she'd brought and pulled out the pieces. An embellished, deconstructed men's tuxedo sculpted to fit a woman—white and yellow crystals clustered on the cuffs of the jacket and the hem of the pants; a white dress shirt reimagined as a one-shouldered top, and a yellow satin cummerbund to cinch the waist.

Lara gasped. "Oh my god. Stunning!"

"Yeah, like I said, it's not the biggest ask."

"Truly superb, a melding of the masculine and feminine, so modern and fresh. How have you never shown me his pieces before, Belinda?"

"Oh, I have. I've slipped them on your racks. 'What is this Etsy attire?' I believe was one response. You broke his heart, not to mention cratered his already humble confidence." She shook her head and, retrieving the pictures, plopped down on the fertility ottoman.

"Which brings me to my second thing. Jasper knows nothing of these pictures. He knows nothing of this meeting, and I don't want him *ever* to know. We will let him think that I left pieces here for you to see, and once you eventually opened the garment bag, you felt compelled to share his *exquisite line* with the world. Playing it forward because you *discovered him* just as someone *discovered you*. Blah blah blah—you don't need me to tell you how to pontificate perfectly."

Belinda looked Lara in the eye. "Because here's the thing, Lara. I desperately wish I'd never seen those pictures, and I certainly don't wish them on anyone else. I couldn't give a shit that you had orgies or took drugs. So, you lived a different life when you were younger. So what, who the fuck didn't? And I'm guessing you didn't—or couldn't—consent to being photographed, which is so fucking disgusting it makes me want to scream. But *they out there* won't care, and you and I both know they will joyfully *crucify* you if this gets out."

Lara nodded in agreement, attempting to blink away the dread in her eyes as Belinda continued, "So the only thing I can see to do is . . . *to burn them.*"

Lara gawped at Belinda, wondering if she was serious. Eventually determining that she was, she exhaled, "Oh my god. *Oh my god.* Fuck. Thank god. *Wait,* you don't have copies?"

"Lara, this isn't a fucking movie. Of course, I don't have copies. I nearly died when I opened Alma's envelope. Seriously—*come on*—I can't even believe I came here to do this. I was just going to burn them and not tell anyone." She paused. "But then I thought of all the times Jasper and I watched you revel in your self-anointed superiority, not for one second recognizing, let alone acknowledging, your immense privilege." She stroked Lara's Hermes hand-stitched leather-covered stapler. "We watch you latch performatively onto this cause and that cause, outwardly speaking of equity, love, and responsibility, yet treating everyone around you like shit. Where's the equity between you and me, Lara? Or you and Kelly? Or you and the million hairdressers you have tortured along the way. The glam who do your numerous charity appearances for free? The designers whose clothes you lose or just decide to keep—*steal* . . ." She looked at a framed picture of Lara—standing in the middle of a refugee soccer team— holding the ball. "You dangle your power to nickel and dime everyone. And you don't get your own hands dirty—you use your team to do it for you. You pretend not to know, but you know—and *we all know you know.* Then, we have to go to work and sit in a luxury room you own, or that has been rented for you, and *ooh* and *ahh* as you tell us about your new painting, your husband's new Ferrari, the million-dollar interior design budget on your $10 million Del Mar weekend place . . . Anyway, whatever." Belinda stopped abruptly, exhausted. "I'm done. I'm just wasting my breath—"

"No, Belinda, you're not. I have been listening. I have always been open to constructive criticism and—"

"You know what," Belinda cut her off, "we can post on Instagram right now. Why don't we go up to one of your closets and find the *perfect* shoe for this tux? You will announce your plans to mentor Jasper in the caption. Then we can sit by that gorgeous hand-painted fire pit of yours and torch these fucking images. Since you will have given me and a gazillion fans your word, I trust you'll keep your promise on the rest of our arrangement."

"But I haven't had glam, Belinda! I look terrible!"

"Nothing Chloe sunglasses, a red lip, and a filter won't cover. I can put your hair in a French twist."

"Oh, that works. Why don't I know you can do hair?" Lara, cocking her head, stared at Belinda with renewed interest. "Are you *sure* you don't want your job back? Because you are very good—and mostly don't annoy me like the others. Plus, as I have learned here today, you are evidentially a true feminist. I should have trusted my original instincts. I am willing to admit I may have been a little hasty—"

"Are you fucking kidding? *No!*"

"Okay, okay, don't get irate. Would you like a mint?" Lara picked up a mini-Louis Vuitton bowl of Altoids. "You do smell a little like tequila. You are perhaps hungover today? I think you'll change your mind, but in the meantime, which stylist do you recommend for me? Someone excellent, of course. *Perhaps a gay man this time . . . I do like to support the community.*" Belinda, walking towards the stairs, ignored her.

In her closet, Lara hovered her hand over a few different heels before reaching for a pair of neon yellow Louboutins. "These?" Belinda nodded her approval as Lara continued, "Yes, I think they will perfectly enhance the exquisite detailing of the crystal." She placed them on the loveseat while she pulled on the pants. "Goodness, they fit me like a glove! Well, this is turning out to be very exciting! Pass me the shirt, Belinda. Now, thank god that she did, but why on earth *did* Alma give these pictures"— she shuddered—"*to you of all people?*"

"Fame was only thrilling until it became grueling. Money was fun only until you ran out of things to buy."
—Gloria Swanson

Alma's Gift

Friday 23rd February. 5:45 pm

ALMA STOOD BEHIND HER IMPOSING AND STARK DESK. Only a large Smythson envelope labeled Belinda Grant and the documents she had just set down on one corner indicated that any kind of business sullied this polished, flawlessly restored antique. She sighed and shook her head, looking over what was before her.

• A copy of the medical report of a woman's broken jaw and multiple pictures of bruising on her face and thighs. STD results from both the girl and Jason White. Positive for herpes. Another copy of an earlier STD result for Jason White from five years prior, positive for herpes.

• Rape accusation in writing and a copy of the rape kit.

• Stills of a recognizable Lara with a penis in her mouth and another in her ass. A picture of a woman snorting cocaine off Lara's very perky teenage breasts. A shot of a mass of sexually co-joined bodies, Lara, front and center, apparently orgasming.

• A contract with an SAT firm to arrange for a student to take the test in place of Sara Jones and a copy of the check paid to that firm.

"Nasty spoilt children, they never learn," she muttered as she swept the documents into a single pile and walked around to the front of her desk, quoting her favorite Shakespeare line, *"There's little choice between rotten apples."* Glancing at the photocopier, discreetly positioned and partially obscured by her lush jungle tree, she checked her watch: 5:45. Yes, she had plenty of time before her 6 pm.

Quietly humming as she began her task, she was startled by a weak knock and turned to see her door opening tentatively. *"YES?"* she called out sharply, grabbing the envelope and rapidly sliding the documents inside.

Behind the fractionally cracked door, a nervous voice answered, "Hi, Alma, it's Belinda Grant."

"Belinda. You are early," she replied sharply, returning the envelope to the desk and smoothing her impeccable hair. "I said 6 pm. Did you not get the message?"

"You own everything that happened to you. Tell your stories. If people wanted you to write warmly about them, they should have behaved better."
—Anne Lamott

Avoidance

VOICEMAIL FROM ALICE SHERMAN
Literary Agent, Flox Corp. 10:25 am

"HI, JASPER. THIS IS ALICE SHERMAN. I'm a senior agent at the literary division of Flox Corp. I've been trying to get hold of Belinda Grant all week. I understand you are her assistant, so I hope you can help me. We wanted to talk to her about possibly writing a book: fiction, non-fiction, her choice. There's much interest in her story and your business in general. What goes on behind the scenes on the red carpet is a fascinating mystery to most of us. Anyway, I'm rambling. I would much appreciate it if you could ask her to get in touch. My number is 310 679 3000 extension 730. Thank you. Bye for now."

Home-Wrecking is Out

Belinda! What was that snogging Instagram post? Were you drunk?

I didn't snog him. It was the angle, and I was drunk with anger, probably.

I know it was stupid.

I can't believe how much press it got.

I know you didn't snog him!

But take it from me and tabloid Emily (who's apparently fasting at a yoga retreat); it will blow over. Please do yourself a favor and post a picture of Jonny and that awful wife on the red carpet, a standard, gushing-over clients look post and follow it with one from the CORRECT angle of your backstage (NOT) kiss yesterday. Reference that in the caption. Take back the power, Belinda. You want to minimize the home wrecker shit. Trust me.

What would I do without you?

I'll do it now.

Promise?

Check your Instagram in 20.

MONDAY 12TH MARCH 2018

(1 WEEK LATER)

"Justice is too good for some people and not good enough for the rest."
—Norman Douglas

Gifting

"OKAY, SEND HER UP." Ortiz looked over at Cheryl and smiled seeing her crossed feet, encased in new black Air Jordans, on the desk. "Belinda Grant from the Astley case is on her way up."

"Yup, there she is." Cheryl waved her over to their desks and stood up.

"Hi, Belinda. Nice to see you again. I hope everything got better for you at work. You know, the rumors and all?"

"Well, yes and no . . ."

Not the best answer, Cheryl thought, but decided she nevertheless seemed much more relaxed—happy even. "Nice sneaks!" Belinda grinned, looking at Cheryl's feet.

"Yeah, Ortiz has been giving me style lessons." Belinda looked at Ortiz, flushing perceptibly, and then back at Cheryl, smiling broadly.

"Anyway," Cheryl coughed, suddenly sheepish, "what can we do for you?"

"Well, as a parting gift from a couple of my ex-clients, I had them sign some photos for your sister." She handed Cheryl an envelope. "I hope she likes them."

"Oh, that's so cool. She's gonna freak."

Ortiz pulled the photo of Lara out of Cheryl's hands. "Don't give that to your sis. We can sell that in here or barter it. Most cops are star fuckers, you know."

"Give that back, and no, we will not be doing that. Thanks, Belinda!" Cheryl grinned.

"My pleasure, now I really have to go. I have a meeting down the street with a literary agent. I might be writing a book, detectives!"

"No way! That's fucking way cool. Will we be in it?" Ortiz winked.

"Maybe! TBD! But it's fiction, so you'll never really know. She winked back. "And Detective Ortiz, don't think I forgot you." She pulled another envelope from her Celine tote and handed it to her. "I don't know if this is your area of policing, but maybe since you love this guy so much, you might be able to get something done about him. There's a possibility, which I cannot confirm or deny, that copies were anonymously sent to TMZ . . ."

Ortiz looked confused as Belinda continued, "The documents in there were in the envelope with my contract for Janie Jones for some reason—zero idea why. Anyway, I'd appreciate it if you could keep me out of it. I've had enough tabloid shit for a lifetime. But an update for a writer would be nice if you feel so inclined."

They high-fived goodbye, and Cheryl walked her to the elevator.

After watching the doors close, she turned to walk back to her desk. Seeing Ortiz waving at her urgently. "Hey, get back over here." Cheryl jogged to her and studied the documents on her desk. "Fucking hell!"

"No shit. We really should have checked that contract envelope."

"That freaking photocopier always bugged me."

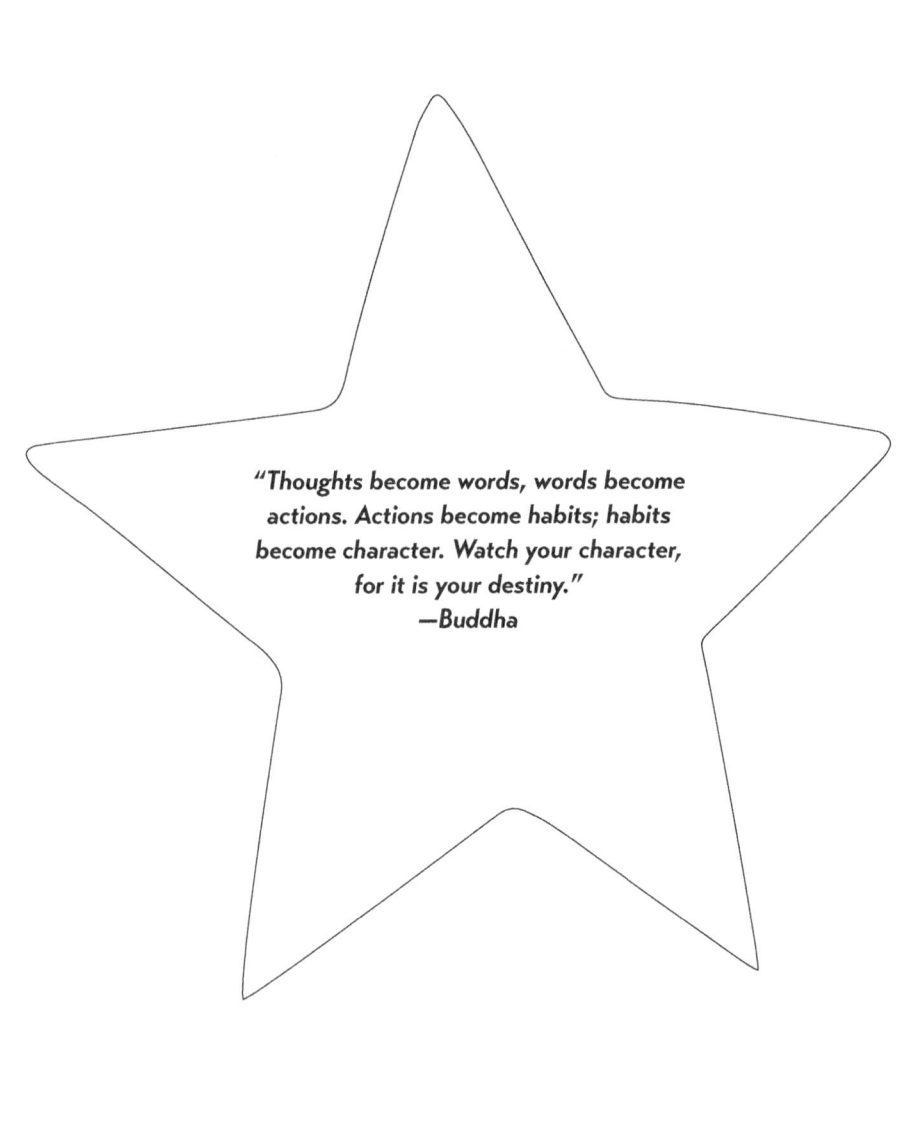

"Thoughts become words, words become actions. Actions become habits; habits become character. Watch your character, for it is your destiny."
—Buddha

Half-Dressed

Friday 23rd February. 5:54 pm

"WHAT IN THE ACTUAL FUCK, JAMIE? Why did you let them drive one of the fucking cars?" Alma switched her phone to speaker and positioned it on the slate counter, stepping out of her black YSL mini tunic. "Jesus, no. Of course, I know you wouldn't have let them. Sorry. They are out of control." She rubbed La Mer cleansing oil onto her face aggressively, scrubbing off any trace of makeup with a warm face cloth from her dual mini fridge/warmer.

"You're sure they're okay? Should we take them to Dr. Grove to double-check anyway? I could skip bowling?" Sitting on a black fur chair, she tugged off her thigh-high boots. "Okay, right, if you're sure. Well, thank fuck for all those swimming lessons. Private driving lessons should be next—plenty of room at the Colorado ranch. How's the car?" Unlocking one of her custom closets with a small key from her bag, she pulled out a pale pink polyester bowling shirt with *Anna* stitched in cursive above her left breast. Sliding it over her head, she asked, "How do we get it out of the pool?" She was tugging on pink bowling socks when she was disturbed by the faint sound of another phone ringing. "Hang on, Jamie." She crept out of the bathroom to the railing and looking down, saw Belinda, on tiptoes, running out of her office.

☆ *489*

Alma froze. Her desk was now empty, the envelope gone. She frantically ran the scenarios through her mind. What would be worse? To chase her now and risk being caught on camera in her bowling gear? Or to change and follow her to her house to retrieve the envelope? She sped back to the bathroom and stood immobile, deliberating for a few seconds. Shit, what if the stylist opened the envelope in the car? Decision made, she sped, in her socks, back along the highly polished concrete floor, losing control as she reached the stairs. Sliding as if on ice, she crashed into the railing and yelped in fear as she tried—and failed—to grab ahold of it. She bounced down the metal staircase like a rag doll, dislocating her femur before breaking her long porcelain neck.

And, as it turns out
when all is said and done,
grief is the price we pay for love."

Forever in Pink

DRESSED IN HER PINK BOWLING OUTFIT, June dragged a wood laminate table over a few feet until it was in front of the picture wall. She pulled a red tablecloth from an old cardboard box and draped it over the table and began placing tourist-style Oscar statues around the perimeter, taking time to perfect the positioning of each one. Ignoring the curious looks of early evening bowlers, she added a champagne bucket and ten glasses, polishing each one with a clean pink rag. "Ice," she said aloud, checking the time. She filled the pail behind the cafe counter, opening a fridge to remove organic apple juice and one of two bottles of Veuve Clicquot, trashing the post-it that read, "TOUCH THIS AND YOU ARE FIRED." She raced back to the table, arriving just in time to greet the first of her guests.

Jamie, awkwardly stood in the doorway, holding the hands of his tall, blonde daughters, who were dressed identically in black denim. His whole demeanor emanated sadness. The girls stared down at their sneaker-clad feet.

"You must be Jamie, Jemima, and Evie?" June asked. "I'm so glad to meet you finally. We loved your mom—and your wife." She nodded at

Jamie compassionately. "I'm so bad at knowing what to say, but I'm very sorry for your loss. She was a wonderful woman and teammate. Oh look, here are the other girls." The others, also in the best version of their team attire, walked up to the table and, one by one, hugged Jamie and each of his daughters, quietly offering up their condolences.

June turned down the music and clapped her hands gently, before passing around the glasses and handing the champagne bottle to Jamie. "Could I ask you to do the honors?" She poured apple juice for the girls and accepted a drink for herself from Jamie.

"Now, if everyone could gather round, please." She brushed away moisture in her eyes as the guests formed a semi-circle in front of the picture wall, partially covered by hanging red silk.

"Will you do the honors, Clare?" June said, turning to her lanky, twenty-something teammate.

"Of course." Clare crouched down and, holding the two bottom corners, dramatically ballooned the fabric to reveal a large, ornately framed picture of Alma in action. Beneath it, a spray-painted gold plinth displayed her favorite battered bowling ball.

"*TO ALMA! TO ANNA!*" They toasted, huddling together tearfully and clinking glasses. "Now, Jamie, Jemima, and Evie, I don't know if you feel up for this, but we have reserved our best lane tonight. We canceled our league game, and it would be our honor to play with you." June presented them with team jerseys embroidered with their names. "But, of course, no pressure. You can just take these home and be welcome back anytime."

"Oh . . . I . . . I don't know"—Jamie's voice cracked—"But this is so kind." He approached Alma's picture, reading the engraved plaque beneath it.

Anna 'Alma Astley' Applegate.
You had a perfect game.
Rest in power.

He stroked her bowling ball, then turned back and wrapped his arms around his children. "What do you think? Shall we play? I think Mom would like that."

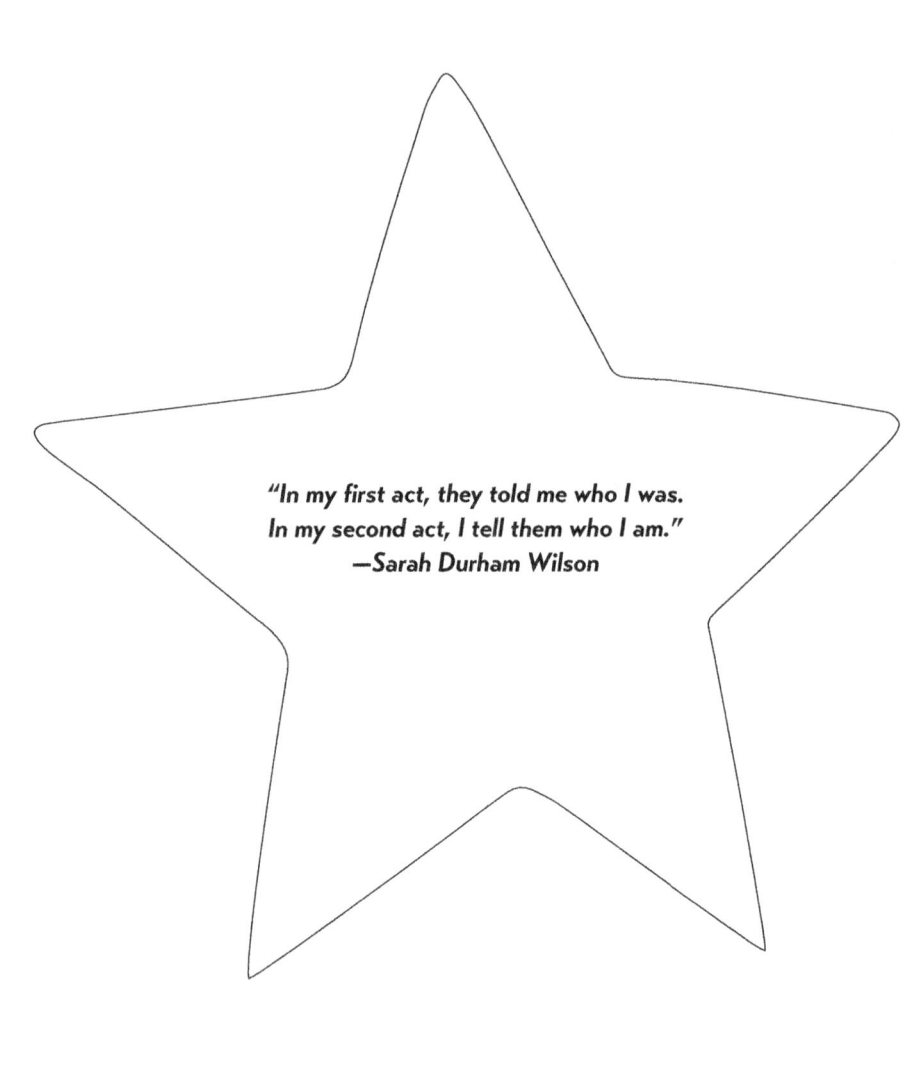

"In my first act, they told me who I was.
In my second act, I tell them who I am."
—Sarah Durham Wilson

Behind the Curtain

CALL FROM ALICE SHERMAN
Literary Agent, Flox Corp. 5:45 pm

"BELINDA! IT'S ALICE! HOW ARE YOU DOING? I just wanted to update you! So much interest in your story. I smell a bidding war! And we think, if done correctly, it will eventually make a great TV show. Have you had any more thoughts since our meeting? I have a shortlist of ghostwriters for you to meet if you want to go in that direction. Or perhaps try it yourself first? I reviewed the columns you wrote for FEMME, which are outstanding. With a little support, I think you'll discover you have a real writing talent."

"Oh, that's exciting! I keep pinching myself; it's all so unbelievable and *new*. I'm a little nervous, but I'd like to try writing it myself."

"That's great, Belinda. We will help you with this, we can get you an experienced editor. It's you and your experience we really need, your intimate knowledge. A look behind the curtain, so to speak. So don't use your energy to doubt; use your energy to believe! Now, tell me, even though we're veering towards a fictional novel, how much of the juicy stuff do you think you'll be able to disclose?"

"Well," Belinda shrugged, picking up the envelope containing the last of Alma's kompromat. Only the evidence of Janie's admissions conspiracy remained. She tossed it into the fireplace and wrapped her arm around Rose as she watched it burn. "I never did sign an NDA . . ."

THE END

EPILOGUE

"Never cut what you can untie."
—Joseph Joubert

THREE MONTHS LATER

FIRE THE STYLIST
Dishing Daily Doses of Fashion Justice

Rumors Update!

Posted on June 4th, 2018

FIRERS! There is some gossip today regarding the mysterious stylist that is (was?) Belinda Grant (age unknown). After an ICONIC career-making Oscars, she has all but vanished into the fashion wilderness. Aside from a couple of appearances by Emily de Vries, she has quietly backed away (for undisclosed reasons) from everyone she dressed on that triumphant day. To update:

Jonny Evans has seemingly been stylist-free and is just re-wearing Henri LeRoque pieces (bravo to him for repurposing). As an aside, he is also newly wife-free—see our post last week featuring Tabitha Evans, 25, leaving her divorce lawyers' office in a bikini and Biker jacket. Has Belinda been hiding in his bedroom? No word yet—but who would blame her?

After four weeks of 'retirement' at the cat sanctuary in India, Ava-Lily Manderson, 19, returned and—as no fashion follower could have missed— is now working with Orlando. The pair appear to be competing for most social media posts of the week (44 including stories. Yes, our intern counted.) Who is in any doubt that Orlando feels Ava-Lily is the most #iconic, #inspiring, and #magical of all the human beings?

Lara White, 33, has famously been glued to the side of Belinda's former assistant, Jasper De La Cruz, who, after scoring her as a muse, has risen in the last few months to become a highly coveted young designer. This week, rumors are flying about him having imminent CCLB backing. (The inseparable new besties were photographed in Paris on Tuesday at lunch with Group Chairman Andre Blanc and his bodacious wife Sasha LeBrock.)

Until *NOW*, no information regarding Belinda's disappearance has been forthcoming. Even the most informed and reliably loose-lipped Hollywood fashionistas have been frustratingly out of the loop.

HOWEVER! We can finally share the *breaking news* that Belinda Grant has reportedly just signed a SEVEN figure book deal with Venture House!

Will she dish all? Is the red carpet about to get devil wears Prada'd? OH MYYYYYYY, STAY TUNED, Firers. You know you'll hear it all here first!

As always, leave comments below!

(To review our community guidelines, please click here)

@voorhiesruth Ooooooh - I hope she spills ALL the tea! 📣 CAN'T WAIT!

@servinitpiping Lara, you in 7-figure danger, gurl!

@porkycheeks Imagine leaving that fantastic job. What a moron.

@haveyoumetme6 You shag a famous dude and then get to write a book for 💰 💰 💰 and I bet she calls herself a feminist.

@laraismywholelife What a muse. Jasper must pinch himself every day!

@darkAF Like, didn't she kill a woman? Wtf? Rich bitches always get off.

@milkandwhisky Jasper De La Cruz is SO talented. Belinda is probably nothing without him - everyone knows assistants do all the work. I can't wait to see his next collection! Lara and Jasper are perfection!

★ ★ ★

Hiiiiii ex-boss or should I say, 'bonjour chienne!' Congrats lady. You a rich author now! Wooo hooo. Writing always made you happier anyway. Miss you and your murderous rumors. I have almost forgiven you for saddling me with Lara for life. She'll make it a shorter one fo sho — and weeee driiink 🍷 🍷 🍷 🍷 🍷 🍷 🍷

GO TO SLEEP, JAS. It's 1 am there!

JE T'AIME POUR TOUJOURS ♥

Ps. I bet she remembers your name now...

Finally I cross from the ghost world into the light!

"If you want a happy ending, it depends, of course, on where you end the story."
—Orson Welles

Acknowledgements

So many excellent people made this previously unimaginable journey possible that I debated listing them alphabetically, but it seemed very clinical, so I'm going chronologically.

To Megan F for breezily assuming I could—and should—write a novel. To Mole, thank you for generously offering hundreds of hours of brainstorming on FaceTime during lockdown—your patience and creativity are on every page. To Paola, for your relentless faith and gentle nudges with your weekly requests to read more. To Adam B for hours of listening to my unedited prose and adding hilarity. To my chosen sister, Ruth, for partnering with me on the business side, unwavering support, and for making it all a magical reality. To the early readers who plowed through the terribly punctuated ramblings and gave thoughtful feedback: Kathy, Suzanne, Colleen, Megan D, Justine, EO, Marcelle, and Shana.

To my brother Adam for design and cover copy brainstorming. To Kimball for the brilliant cover art inspiration and network support. To Chris B and Megan M for inspired copy editing and a masterclass in grammar. To Laura for the formatting design of my dreams and to George for building a brilliant website.

To Charla, driving in cars with you was the best of times. To all the other real-life Jaspers and Chanelles who came into my world. Thank you, thank you, thank you. Being a stylist—then and now—would be unbearable and impossible without you. To Kent, my endlessly patient long time styling agent, for putting up with me.

And lastly, to Imogen, the love of my life, for unrelenting grace and patience when your Mum disappeared into her iPad to write 95,000 words (give or take). May you always joyfully create on the outside, knowing that your greatness lies within.

About the Author

Penny Lovell is a Brit who arrived at celebrity styling in Hollywood via a career in fashion in NYC and London. She has spent almost two decades dressing some of the world's most recognizable people. She lives, works, and now writes in Los Angeles with her daughter, their two small dogs, and far too many handbags.

Discover more information at pennyalovell.com

Instagram:
@pennylovellstylist
@IneversignedanNDA
@fire.the.stylist

Made in the USA
Las Vegas, NV
08 March 2024